Always Yours

USA *TODAY* BESTSELLING AUTHOR

KENNEDY FOX

"I don't hate you
No, I couldn't if I wanted to
I just hate all the hurt that you put me through
And that I blame myself for letting you"

"Wrong Direction"
-Hailee Steinfield

CHAPTER ONE

MADDIE

I SHOULD'VE KNOWN things were too good to be true.

Liam and I were living in a perfect bubble, just the two of us, and happy as hell. I knew Victoria was being her normal pain in the ass self, ordering Liam around, and had him by the balls. I trusted him, though. Trusted he'd fight this battle with me by his side.

I should've known better.

The moment Victoria shows up with Liam's dad, it's game over. She announces she's pregnant with twins and claims Liam's the father.

And then I notice the look on Liam's face when he realizes Victoria has revealed the secret he's kept from me.

Devastated.

Just like my heart.

After Victoria butters up Liam's dad and talks about Liam moving to Vegas, I fake politeness and get the fuck out of there. Liam knows nothing he can say will keep me from being pissed even though he begs me to hear him out. The pain is too fresh, but it doesn't matter because he can't change what's happening.

Once I'm in my room, I lock the door and focus on my breathing. Tears threaten to surface, but I hold them back. I won't break down while she's in this house. I refuse to give her that satisfaction. Or him.

I spend hours in my bed, waiting for the darkness to swallow me whole. My worst nightmare has come true, and I can't do a damn thing about it. Victoria's the puppet master, and Liam has no choice but to do what she says. Now that she's pregnant, nothing can go back to the way it was when we were sneaking around. There's no way she'll let him go if those babies are really his.

Liam blows up my phone with text messages, and it's not until he sucker punches me with our *promise* that I finally find the strength to respond.

Liam: You promised, Maddie. You promised no matter what, you were mine, and I was yours.

Maddie: That was before you knocked up your WIFE, asshole. Fuck off. Go to Vegas and stay there this time.

I don't mean it. I want him here with me, but I'm so damn hurt that I convince myself it would be for the best. He needs to leave so I can get over him once and for all. It's his final text that has me falling apart.

Liam: I am so sorry.

So much meaning in those four words.

Sorry for what he did, sorry this happened, sorry it has to be over.

Tears spill over, falling down my cheeks, and I don't even

have the strength to wipe them away. I gave him my heart, my *virginity*, and trusted him amongst all the Victoria drama. I'd fallen for him so effortlessly, and he lied so easily. Liam kept the truth from me and used me as a distraction to his reality. My body shakes as the tears come faster now, soaking my pillowcase. Curling up into a ball, I just pray for the ache in my chest to take me under.

It's sometime after midnight when I get up to use the bathroom and grab a banana from the kitchen. Everyone's passed out, and by morning, Liam and Victoria will be gone. None of this feels real.

Once I'm back in bed, I fall asleep with my heart shattered into a million pieces.

"Maddie, wake up," someone whispers while shaking my shoulder. "Wake up," she repeats. "Time's running out."

Huh?

"What?" I ask, blinking and holding up a hand to cover the bright light coming from my lamp. "Victoria? What time is it? Is Liam okay?"

She rolls her eyes as if me worrying about him annoys her. "It's after three, and you need to get your ass moving. Pack a bag. You're leaving."

That gets my attention enough to sit up and glare at her. "Excuse me?"

"You need to do exactly as I say, Madelyn," she roughly whispers.

I scoff, crossing my arms. "And why should I? In case you haven't realized, I hate you."

A slow, smug smile spreads across her gorgeous face. I hate how pretty she is. "Listen closely, little girl." She closes the gap between us, leaning down until our eyes meet, and jabs a finger into my chest. "I know you've been fucking my husband, and that stops *right now*. You're a distraction he

3

doesn't need. If he's going to keep up with his part of the deal, then I need you out of the picture."

I swallow. What the hell is she talking about? "I don't have anywhere else to go."

"I've got it covered," she states proudly. "And unless you want Liam to get killed for betraying me and my family, you'll do what I say. Trust me, it's for the best."

"For you, maybe," I mutter. "I'm in college, so I can't just vanish. Plus, my sisters and Liam would look for me."

"Don't worry, princess. You can defer for a semester, leave your sisters a note, and I'll keep Liam plenty *busy*." Victoria grabs one of Sophie's suitcases from the closet and throws it on the bed. "Hurry up, Maddie. It needs to look like you left of your own free will. Take what's important."

"Where's my phone?" I ask when I notice it's not on my nightstand.

"You won't be needing it."

"You can't just kidnap me and expect I'll go quietly..." I stand, wondering if I can make it to the door without her grabbing me first. If she's as crazy as Liam's said, she might be carrying a gun.

Victoria smiles as if I'm not a threat. "Oh, you'll go willingly. Trust me." She rubs a hand over her small belly bump. "Because if you don't, Liam will suffer the consequences."

My heart stops as my breath hitches. I have no doubt she would take it out on him, considering the bomb she dropped tonight. Her father's bodyguards have been following him for weeks and probably have all the evidence she'd need to prove his infidelity. Lord knows what they'd do to him once revealed.

"Tick tock." She taps her wrist where a watch would sit. "Take what you want, or I'll do it for you. And trust me, it

4

won't be those sports bras and booty shorts you wear around my husband and do yoga in." She clicks her tongue. "And those car rides." She dramatically rolls her eyes. "It's like you two weren't even trying to hide it."

"You're the one who had us followed," I say aloud when I realize the truth. Liam's relentlessly asked for her to get her father to stop watching him, but it was Victoria all along.

"And you've underestimated what I'll do to get what I want. I saved Liam's life, and he *owes* me. So unless you want my family to know what my husband's been doing behind closed doors, you'll do what I say and walk out of here. Got it?"

I grind my teeth, knowing I have no choice. She doesn't love Liam like I do—even if she pretends she does—so she won't think twice about jeopardizing his life. All she cares about is getting her trust fund money and doesn't care what happens to him in the process.

"Fine," I say begrudgingly. Grabbing my necessities, I watch her closely as she types on her phone. "Do I at least get to know where I'm going?"

"On a plane," she says dryly, not taking her eyes off the screen.

"For how long?" I ask, digging through my closet.

"As long as it takes." She finally looks at me. "That's all you need to know."

As long as what takes? This is sounding worse by the second.

I glare at her, though she's not fazed. "How am I supposed to know what to bring?"

"There'll be a washer and dryer. Whatever fits in your bag should be enough," she says with amusement. "The bathroom will be stocked with whatever you need," she adds. "You'll have a warm bed and food, so don't worry. In fact, it's going to be like a luxury vacation compared to being in this dump." She snickers and sticks her nose up as if this place is filth, which pisses me off. I'd rather sleep in a cardboard box than go where she tells me.

After grabbing a few things from my closet, I dig around in my dresser for leggings and underwear.

"Don't forget to take your school shit or whatever it is you do. It has to look like you brought your essentials."

"I'm a dancer," I tell her, reaching for my backpack that already has some of my notebooks, books, and practice clothing.

"Well, whatever. Make it look like you left to go live with a friend, so they don't question it."

I snarl but keep my lips tight as I move around the room, making it look like I left of my own free will. "They'll never buy it," I whisper to myself.

"Liam's life depends on it," she reminds me before locking her gaze with mine. "By the look on your face tonight, he didn't tell you we were expecting. But you care about him, so I know you'll do whatever you can to keep him safe." The amusement in her tone has me digging my nails into my palms. I want to rip out her throat.

"If they're even his babies…" I mutter.

"They are, trust me. We've had *a lot* of sex. Unprotected."

My blood boils, nearly causing my entire body to overheat. According to Liam, they were together once since they got hitched, and he used a condom. I so badly want to trust his word, but after this shitstorm, I don't know what to believe.

"Either way, DNA doesn't matter because we're married. It'll be enough for Daddy. His first grandchildren and adding heirs into the family legacy are all he cares about."

"You'd deceive your family and your own children?

That's the kind of mother you're going to be?" I arch a brow, zipping my bag closed.

Victoria stalks toward me, her eyes narrowed as she scowls. "Mind your own damn business. Liam's life isn't the only one on the line."

"No? Gonna kill me too?" I deadpan, not letting her words get to me. I hope she burns in hell for all the hurt she's caused.

"If necessary," she says dryly. "Liam's father, Sophie, Mason. Don't forget who my family is, Maddie. My father's a powerful man, and no one in their right mind messes with him or me, including the authorities. So listen to what I say, and no one will get hurt." Then she plasters on a saccharine smile. "Time to write your note."

I grab a piece of paper from my notebook and choke back the emotions swirling inside me. Victoria tells me to keep it short and simple.

Sophie,
I had to leave and get away from all the memories of Liam here. I'm sorry, but please don't come looking for me. I'll come back when I'm ready.
Love you,
Mads

"Good enough?"

"It'll do." She shrugs, then holds out her hand. "I'll place it in the kitchen so she finds it right away."

Part of me wants to argue that there's no way Sophie will believe I left in the middle of the night with nowhere to go, but it's no use. Victoria has already orchestrated this and won't reason with logic. My sisters know I don't have money to go anywhere and will automatically think I went to Utah.

"They're gonna call and text me," I tell her.

"I'm taking care of that." She winks, then looks at her phone. "Your ride is here. Give me your keys. Time to go."

"My keys?"

"Yes, my bodyguards are driving you to the airport in the Suburban. I'll handle your car so it looks like you left."

I have so many questions I know she won't answer, so I don't even bother. Fishing my keys out of my backpack, I hand them over. If anything happens to it, considering Liam's the one who bought it for me, I'll be so pissed. "Anything else?"

Victoria flashes a grin, and I can tell she's used to getting what she wants. It's as if she's never heard the word *no* in her entire life. She's a mobster princess and spoiled brat. I bet she'd put Veruca Salt to shame.

As the memory of watching *Willy Wonka and the Chocolate Factory* as a kid emerges, I grab my bag and suitcase and quietly follow Victoria out of the house. I refuse to show any emotion around her, so I straighten my spine and tighten my lips.

Two men are standing next the black Suburban parked out front. "She's ready," Victoria tells them. One of them opens the back door while the other loads my things into the back. Before I hop in, Victoria grabs my elbow, digging her fingers into my skin. "Remember what and *who's* on the line here. Play by my rules and nothing bad happens. I'll be in contact with you soon." Then she releases me and walks toward the house, the very home I'm not sure I'll ever return to.

After I'm forced to wear a blindfold the entire flight, we finally land. I lost track of time, but a couple of hours had to have passed, though I can't be sure. The guards talked softly, and I could hear them moving around, but other than that, I sat and waited.

Waited for what? Who the hell knows?

"Can you stand?" one of them asks after unbuckling me. I push myself off the armrests, and he grabs my elbow. "This way."

"This would be a lot easier if I could see," I tell him.

He grunts. "Not yet."

I can sense the other guy behind me, his steps following mine.

"There's a railing on your other side you can grab while we go down the steps," he directs and holds me tightly. I don't know if it's because he thinks I'm gonna bail or if his orders are to keep me alive, meaning don't let me get hurt. Either way, I grip it tightly as I take each stair.

"Your ride is here," he informs me as we walk.

"I'll take it from here, Oliver," another man says. This voice is much softer and kinder. Oliver releases me as the other one grabs my arm.

"I'll let her know she's arrived," Oliver says, and then he's gone.

"Okay, this way." The new guy leads me, and then I hear

a door opening. "It's a big step in," he tells me. I don't know why, but he feels safe, which is probably fucking crazy. They're all must be criminally insane if they work for the O'Learys.

Once I'm buckled in, the door is shut. Then I hear two more doors open and close.

"How many of you are here?" I ask softly as the truck takes off.

"Two, miss. I'm Ty, and this is Eric."

Well, he sure doesn't sound like a murderer, but then again, they never do.

"Where are you taking me?" I ask, hopeful he'll actually give me answers.

"To a cabin. You'll be safe there," Ty responds.

Safe? There's nothing safe about this. Hell, this sounds like some twisted witness protection except the person I need protecting from is the one keeping me hostage.

The drive is long, and just as I start to doze off, we slow down and then park. My heartbeat races as the fear of the unknown takes over. I tried to be strong earlier and not let my guard down, almost not believing this was really happening. Though now that the shock is wearing off, my adrenaline is taking over.

I can't be here.

My sisters and Liam are going to freak the hell out. There's no way they'll believe I left.

But if what Victoria said is true, then this will allow Liam to stay focused on doing what she asks. If her father finds out their marriage is a sham and that Liam's been unfaithful, I don't even want to think about what Johnny O'Leary would do to him. In some weird, fucked-up way, I think maybe she's right. I am the reason he's lost focus in playing along in their messed-up marriage arrangement. He wants out, I know that, but until Victoria releases him, he has to follow her orders and make their relationship believable.

"Ready?" Ty asks after he opens the door. I reach out, and he assists me to my feet.

"Thanks," I murmur awkwardly.

"You can take off the blindfold as soon as we're inside," he informs me as if he knows how frustrated I am.

I hear Eric at the back, grabbing my things, and then the three of us walk some more. A door opens and Ty ushers me in.

"Alright, I'm going to remove your blindfold, but before I do...let's go over the rules."

Rules? How about rule number one: don't kill me.

"There are cameras in every room of the house except the bathrooms. Victoria can see live footage, so I wouldn't try anything. Eric and I each have a room next to yours. The house will be on lockdown, so even if you stupidly tried to run, you won't be able to get out without sounding the alarms."

"And we're both carrying," Eric adds roughly. His hoarse voice sends a shiver down my spine and not in a pleasant way.

I swallow hard. "Got it." I have no idea what they know about me or if they even know why I'm here, but I'm smart enough not to play games around people who could easily end me with one bullet.

Ty steps closer, and his fingers brush my neck before he lifts the cloth over my head. I blink, studying my surroundings.

Well, it's not the worst place to be held hostage. Victoria was right; this is luxury living. Looks like something she'd own too, which she probably does. This is no small cabin in the woods; this is a *mansion* in the woods.

My eyes finally land on Ty, and he narrows his gaze, studying my face as if he's wondering what the hell I'm doing here too.

"You must be Ty," I say stupidly to break the awkward silence. If I had to guess, he's probably a few years older than Liam.

He gives me a curt nod.

"I'm Maddie." Though he probably already knows that.

His lips part, and his throat moves, but he doesn't say anything else. Almost as if he's not allowed to.

Eric huffs and walks past us with my backpack and suitcase. "C'mon. I'll show you to your room."

As I follow him, I immediately notice how extravagant the place really is when I see large flat-screen TVs, an oversized gas fireplace, a modern kitchen with high tech appliances, and countless fancy chandeliers.

Why would Victoria send me here?

This looks too good to be true.

Then again, Victoria is the *queen* of mind games.

CHAPTER TWO

LIAM

MY HEART IS LODGED in my throat as the anxiety of Maddie being gone violently creeps in. Victoria's behind this, or she wouldn't have said what she did.

"I warned you to behave, hubby. But you didn't listen." Her words echo in my head, over and over, and the only thing that forces me back to reality is Sophie following us into the living room. All I hear are threats to call the police. Her hand is unsteady as she clenches the note in her fist.

"They can't do anything if she left willingly," Victoria states confidently from beside me. Sophie takes two steps forward, looking her up and down. Mason comes in and pulls her away, creating much-needed space between the two, but Victoria isn't fazed in the least. I'm sure she's had her fair share of fights, but she's always won because she plays dirty.

"I'll get to the bottom of this," Sophie threatens between clenched teeth before she turns to me, seething. "This is your fucking fault."

"Soph," Mason says. I'm sure she would've clocked me right in the face if he hadn't stepped between us. Mason

13

manages to temporarily calm her as Victoria announces we need to get going in her sugary-sweet tone that nearly sends me into a rage. My world is spiraling out of control, and all I can do is sit back and watch the clusterfuck unfold before my eyes. I should've been more careful. I should've pushed Maddie away to keep her safe, but I didn't. I *couldn't*.

"Can't be late, sweetie." Victoria grabs my hand and squeezes, but I pull away from her.

"I'll be right up," I force out before she raises up on her tiptoes and kisses my cheek. I can't even smile this time. Once Victoria is out of sight, Sophie walks over and pushes me with all her strength. I barely lose my footing because I tower over her, but her frustration and anger aren't lost on me. It's more than warranted.

"She's gone, and considering she name-dropped you in this note, I have no choice but to blame *you*."

"Soph," I say softly. "I'm so sorry. I'll find her."

She glares at me with disgust before walking away, but Mason stands tall with his arms crossed, studying me. "We can all agree that this isn't like Maddie, and I have a feeling there's more to this than what that damn letter said."

Guilt washes over me, and I nod, agreeing with him. "It's not in her character. And I'm concerned too, but I promise you, Mason, I will track her down."

"I know if anyone can find her, it'll be you," he tells me. "I hope you weren't stringing her along somehow because if so, that's utterly fucked up, Liam, even for you."

I wish I could spill all my truths to Mason, but I know I can't. Sophie has accused Maddie of messing around with me already, and she's overly suspicious, so I can read between the lines. Instead of explaining, I accept his disappointment, which makes me feel like a bigger piece of shit.

Mason gives me one last look before going upstairs to

comfort Sophie. I run my fingers through my hair and take a few deep breaths as Victoria sashays into the living room with her designer suitcase behind her.

"Ready to go, *hubby*?" She grins. I'm two seconds from telling her to go fuck herself, but I fully understand she holds all the cards right now. So instead of setting her off, I go to my room, change clothes, and then grab my bag. Before I meet Victoria downstairs, I knock on Mason's door, but they don't answer.

"I'm sorry," I say again, hoping they hear me, then walk away.

Victoria's sitting on the couch with her legs crossed, and I can't help but notice how pregnant she looks. The change in her appearance is so drastic from the last time we were together. It's almost as if it happened overnight.

"Our ride is outside," she tells me after glancing at her phone.

"I can drive," I say.

"No," she snaps, then stands. I begrudgingly follow her as she goes to the door, and we climb into a limo with windows so dark it'd be impossible to see in from the outside.

On the way to the airport, we don't exchange a word. I'm too lost inside my head, trying to figure out what the fuck happened. I mentally try to put the pieces together as if I'm tracking a fugitive. The note was in Maddie's handwriting. Some of her shit was gone, along with her car. She left hastily, though, as if her departure was unplanned, and if she was driving, she couldn't have gone far. I'm sure Sophie's already checking with her parents and Lennon. There are only so many places she could go because it's not like she has a ton of money. Another reason I believe Victoria orchestrated the entire thing because she's the ultimate puppet master and gets off on having control.

I just want confirmation Maddie's okay, and I want her to know how fucking sorry I am about this whole ordeal, but I don't expect her to forgive me. Not this time. I should've fucking told her, but I was scared as hell that'd be her final straw, and I didn't want to ruin the happiness we'd fought so hard for. If I can prove those babies aren't mine—and I will, somehow—maybe she'll give us another chance.

The car slows, and the door opens, and soon, we're boarding the private jet with our bags. As the plane travels down the runway and takes off, Victoria smirks as she interlocks her fingers with mine. We're being watched by her bodyguards sitting in the back, so once again, I'm forced to play the part of the loving husband.

I lean over and whisper in her ear. "I need proof that Maddie isn't hurt."

Laughter escapes her as she releases my hand and playfully pats my leg. "I bet you do."

My jaw clenches as I growl. "What the fuck have you done?"

Slowly, she turns her head and looks me in my eyes but lowers her voice. "What have *you* done? Fucking her behind my back after I've warned you to be careful wasn't a logical decision. The last thing you need is any more distractions, considering you're about to be a father to twins. Your problem is you don't know how to listen, Liam. This isn't a fucking game, but you acted as if it was. Instead of being smart and thinking with your head while your life and all your friends' lives are on the line, you've allowed your dick to call the shots. That all ends now."

Her words are like poison running through my veins.

"So you know where she is?"

The maniacal smile on her lips is frightening. "Maddie and I had a chat before she left."

I narrow my eyes. "You lay a finger on her, and you'll be sorry."

"Threaten me again, and you'll be the one who's sorry. And let me remind you that you have zero power here. You'll get more information about her when you've earned the privilege. As of right now, I owe you nothing, and you owe me *everything*. You'll have the chance to prove yourself when we're with my family this afternoon, but so far, you've done nothing but compromise everything like a fucking idiot. I really thought you were smarter than that, Liam. You're a true disappointment."

I pull away from her and nearly bite off my tongue I'm so infuriated, but it was the confirmation I needed. While I suspected Victoria, because it's typical of her, I also understood how angry Maddie was. There was always the slight chance she had left on her own.

"Where did you send her?" I finally ask, not giving up.

She chuckles. "You'll never find her, Liam. Never. Not even your bounty hunter skills will help you track her down. But know she's in a better place than that dump of a house you all live in. And maybe I'll eventually let her go...or not. Your actions will determine how this ends. She might not make it out alive, but that's up to you."

"You're a bitch," I say loud enough for only her to hear.

She laughs. "I know."

I nearly grind my teeth flat by the time the plane lands. Our bags are loaded into a large SUV, and we climb inside. Vegas used to be a city that brought me joy and hope, and maybe a little relief from the everyday grind of tracking people, but now, it's my own personal hell on earth. When this marriage is over, I don't think I'll ever return to Sin City. It's been tainted by the O'Learys and too many bad memories for me to ever enjoy it again.

17

The truck slows, then stops. After I grab our shit, we take the elevator up to her penthouse. It's squeaky clean, as always, mainly because her maid does a great job. Victoria doesn't lift a pinky; instead, she uses her daddy's money for tasks that are below her.

She sits on the couch and pats the seat next to her.

"We need to discuss what's going to happen in a few hours," she says, showing off her pearly whites.

I remain standing. "Go on."

"My father has decided he wants the family together tonight for dinner. Everyone will be there. Well, those of importance. I'd like to make the official announcement about the babies then."

"Figured as much," I state dryly.

"But I need you to step up your excitement about being a father because you've failed to convince me so far."

"And you need to confirm Maddie is okay, but you refuse."

A roar of a groan echoes through the living room. "Are you going to play along, or do I need to use force? I know your girl is a dancer. A broken ankle might do her some good and prove to you I'm not fucking around."

Holding out my hands, I surrender. She knows Maddie is my weakness, and she'll use her against me every chance she can. "Fine. I'll do whatever you want," I finally say. My heart beats erratically at the thought of what she's capable of doing.

"Very good."

I want to slap the smug grin right off her face.

"I'd like you to wear your Armani suit. I bought you a green shirt to match my dress. I've also hired a photographer to be there because I told Daddy I wanted family photos. However, my mother won't be available because she had a fundraiser to attend in the morning in New York. It was a who's who type of affair."

All I do is nod, and she looks over my shoulder at the crystal clock on the wall. "Looks like we have a few hours before we need to get ready. You should shave beforehand. Try not to look like a caveman."

The digs are starting to wear on me, but I take them because what I want to say will give her more leverage to hurt Maddie. "Anything else?"

"I think that's it."

As I turn to walk to the room I stay in when I'm visiting, she says my name. I stop for a moment. "I'm sorry I had to do this, but you tied my hands, and I had no other choice."

Instead of responding, I continue forward. As soon as I'm alone, I ball my hands into fists needing to release my anger. The frustration I'm experiencing is like nothing I've ever endured before. It's a prison of emotions, tucked deep inside, and I have to play along. I'm not convinced Maddie is fine, and I'm unsure of her currently situation. Victoria grew up watching her father be merciless, and I know the same cold blood flows through her veins. The woman wouldn't know empathy if it slapped her in the fucking face.

Kicking off my shoes, I lie on the bed and stare at the ceiling until my vision blurs. My head pounds as I think about my life. I could've never predicted any of this. Knowing my father is now a target along with Maddie being taken brings this all to the next level, and I'm not sure how I'm going to get us out of this.

Though hours have passed, time feels as if it's standing still. Considering we'll be leaving soon, I jump in the shower, then shave my face as Victoria requested. *Her wish is my command*—a mantra I'm sure I'll repeat a dozen times before the night is over. When I walk into the living room, the shirt she bought for me is lying on the back of the sofa. I grab it along with my bag and get dressed. Three knocks on my door tell me it's time to put on the performance of a lifetime.

"Ready, hubby?" Victoria coos.

I nod, and we leave. The ride to meet her family is full of mental anguish. I try to remember the last time we had sex along with how far along she is. The math adds up correctly if she's being honest, which could account for the size of her belly with twins. However, I can't be sure if I'm the only guy she's been with since we hooked up. The first night we met, Victoria admitted she wasn't a one-man type of person, but she's also been watching her back because of our marriage. The babies only complicate this scenario further.

She admitted she wanted out of the mob life once before. The reason she needed her trust fund early was so she could be free from it all. Having a baby meant getting more money in the end, so I can only imagine what the monetary value is for two. She seems overly thrilled by it, though—the dollar signs, that is. Before, she mentioned she'd have so much cash she'd just hire a full-time nanny to raise the kids, with no intention of changing her jet-setting lifestyle. The thought alone makes me sick. I never imagined having children, but I'd never abandoned them either. They'll be her pawns that'll allow her to get more of what she wants.

The car eventually slows in front of an Italian restaurant. When we get out, I wrap my arm around Victoria, and she leans into me. Her skin against mine feels as if it's leaving third degree burns.

"Make me proud, and I may reward you later."

She's now resorted to treating me like a dog.

I swallow hard as we walk through the restaurant to the private area reserved for the O'Learys. Once we enter, everyone rushes to give us hugs and side cheek kisses. Wine glasses are passed around, and Victoria refuses one, but I don't. Might as well get sloshed to take away some of the pain I'm feeling.

Victoria's grandma comes over and squeezes me tight. If the circumstances were different, I'd actually enjoy being around the woman because she's nice, and I truly believe she sees the best in people. Though it's possible she's wearing a disguise and is as cold-hearted as the rest of them.

Johnny comes over and gives me a firm handshake, and I meet his grip with the same pressure. "Been treating my daughter right?" he asks with a grin, eventually letting go of my hand.

"Yes sir, like the queen she is. Isn't that right, sweetheart?" I turn to Victoria, placing a soft kiss on her plump lips.

"Mm-hmm. We've been doing great, Daddy."

He hugs Victoria and kisses her. "That's what I like to hear."

The staff enters carrying trays of food and sets up an area that acts as a buffet. There are no less than thirty people in the room. Victoria reintroduces me to cousins, aunts, uncles, and after I realize how many people are here, I get nervous. Of course I've met them before, but I can't remember half of their names because her family is so large. Considering the magnitude of this dinner, I understand how much everything will change once she announces the pregnancy.

The smile I wear is as fake as Victoria's tits, but I play the role of doting husband so well her cousins are jealous of our relationship. I want to scream out that it's not real, it's pretend, and explain how much I actually despise the woman standing next to me. While I owe her my life, I feel as if I'm repaying her with it. Free will isn't something I'm privy to anymore because I have zero decision-making power. At this rate, I'm better off dead.

After everyone has filled their plates with food and the tables are full of her family, Victoria stands and reaches for me. I grab her hand and stand.

"I just wanted to take this opportunity to let you all know we're expecting!" Victoria beams excitedly.

The room bursts into cheers and congratulations, and her grandmother cries. I kiss Victoria and hold her in my arms as she smiles. "Tell them the rest of the news, sweetie," she adds.

"We're having twins!" I force out as cheerfully as I can as the photographer snaps an ungodly number of pictures.

"Twins?" Her father gasps. "What a blessing!"

The words that come out of his mouth are full of hypocrisy. He can celebrate his daughter's pregnancy with such ease yet doesn't think twice about stealing life from others. Pretty sure he's the actual devil.

Hours pass in a blur, and after we've eaten and Victoria has shared all the information about the babies, it's time to go. The entire family is overly ecstatic about the news, and I'm exhausted from listening to their plans and guesses about the genders. At this rate, she'll have no less than five baby showers and diaper parties, along with exclusive baby clothes made by her designer aunt. We say our goodbyes, and by the time we make it home, I have a full-blown migraine.

We take the elevator up, and once we're alone, the act is quickly dropped.

"You seem pleased." I loosen my tie and remove my suit jacket.

"I am." She grabs my hand. "I was thinking you should consider moving here, maybe for the next year or so, to help with the babies and prove to my family that we tried to make this work."

"No." I rip my hand from hers, fully aware of the manipulative tactics she's trying to use. "It wasn't part of the agreement."

"Me getting pregnant wasn't either but look what happened." She shrugs with a half-smile.

I suck in a sharp breath. "I need proof they're mine."

"And when you have that, then what will you do?"

"I'm done talking about this," I state firmly, and she grins. "Are you going to tell me where Maddie is now?"

"No. She's fine, but if you keep it up, she won't be. Just keep pressing me. Understand?" She bats her eyelashes, loving the control she has over me.

"Heard you loud and clear," I say before turning and going to my room, not having the strength to argue with her after tonight, hoping that Maddie really is okay. I could try to steal Victoria's phone and scour through her messages, but she doesn't allow it to leave her palm. Without a doubt, the information I need is on that device.

The day replays in my head, and it's hard to believe how much has happened in twenty-four hours. Her family now knows the secret. It won't be long until the whole city does, considering how proud Johnny was about becoming a grandfather. The thought of it makes me sick because just when I think things can't get any worse, the universe laughs and shows me otherwise.

CHAPTER THREE

MADDIE

I'VE BEEN a *hostage* for two days. Hostage might be a stretch, considering they aren't torturing me, and I'm allowed to eat and basically do whatever I want—as long as I don't try to escape.

Ty is nice so far, but Eric acts like he has a permanent stick up his ass. I've learned that they work for and report directly to Victoria, not her dad. Neither of them knew what their mission was before coming here and were told shortly before my arrival. I'm good at asking the right questions even if they hadn't meant to tell me that information. Eric scowls at Ty anytime he talks to me, but I'm bored as fuck. If I don't talk to *someone*, I'll go insane.

The cameras freak me out a little, but after a day, I stopped looking up at them. I know she can see me, which means I have to play along in her game and behave until I can leave. I hate not knowing what's going on and how long I'll be here, but she won't tell me anyway so I don't bother asking.

I miss Liam even though I'm pissed at him.

I miss the way we teased each other.

I miss his touch. His lips. His large hands.

I miss the way he'd look at me as if he couldn't help but stare. Like he wanted to devour me.

But he lied or, rather, kept the truth from me. And that's what keeps a fire lit under my pain. After everything we've been through, he didn't even have the courtesy to tell me Victoria was pregnant.

It's almost eleven, and after sleeping all night and half the morning, I'm energized and ready to do something. There's a hot tub outside, but I didn't pack my swimsuit. I could wear shorts and a sports bra, but I have a feeling that'd be frowned upon.

Instead of letting myself go crazy, I decide to change into some leggings and a leotard. If I can't go to class, I might as well practice. First, I'll do some stretches and meditation and then work on some dance techniques.

I pull my hair up into a ballerina bun and saunter into the living room, which is honestly as big as Liam and Mason's entire house. The sectional sofa takes up one side and expensive looking chairs are on the other. If I wasn't a ball of nerves, I might actually enjoy the space and binge-watch TV shows.

Scrolling through the channels, I can only find a yoga class for beginners and decide it's better than nothing. Eric's in the corner watching my every move, an annoying shadow that never goes away, but the moment I hear Ty clear his throat, I nearly lose my tree pose balance. I haven't seen him all morning, and he just shows up out of nowhere.

"I've got it from here," Ty tells Eric. "You can go on break."

"I don't need a break," Eric argues, keeping his stance firm.

"Too bad. Boss wants you to call her," Ty retorts, his eyes burning into Eric's.

They stare at each other, neither moving nor speaking.

What the fuck?

"Or you could both leave because I'm a big fucking girl and don't need a babysitter," I blurt out, then smirk when they turn and glare at me. "I'm not going anywhere, geesh. I don't even know where I am, and I'm not dumb enough to start running in a random direction outside in the middle of nowhere. I've watched plenty of horror movies and know that never ends well. So if you two need to have a lover's spat in private, I'll be right here doing yoga when you return." I tilt my head and smile sweetly.

Eric looks as if he wants to strangle me, his dark eyes turning to slits as he scowls.

Ty has the faintest smirk on his lips that he tries to hide with a fake cough.

"I'll be back in twenty." Eric breaks the silence, then stomps out of the room like a man-child. My eyes follow him until he's out of sight.

"I think your best friend hates me," I tease before turning back to the TV and moving into the same position as the teacher.

Ty stands on the opposite wall with his hands folded in front of him. He's not buff like Liam, but tall and lean like a swimmer. His biceps bulge from his shirt, and it's hard not to notice his muscles. Ty looks like he's a fast runner, which means even if I did *try* to run, he'd catch up to me in half a second.

"Would you mind grabbing me a bottle of water?" I ask as I switch into downward dog.

"I'm here to watch you, not wait on you."

"And you'll be performing CPR when I lose my breath and pass out," I retort. Stretching, I move my body until my eyes are on the ceiling. "Hope you've been trained for that."

I risk a glance at him and see the corner of his lips tilt up just the tiniest bit. He's amused, but he tries to hide it.

"You remind me of my boyfriend," I tell him when I stand and exhale. "Well, probably ex-boyfriend now that he hid the truth from me, and I ended up here with you." I flash him a sarcastic smile. Not to mention he's married to another woman. Legit or not, he's still legally bound to her. "He was all quiet and reserved around me too, but I eventually broke him down." Lifting my arms above my head, I shift from side to side and stretch my muscles. "Took me a bit, but now that I'm well-practiced, I'll be much faster at breaking through next time."

Ty shifts uncomfortably as if he's trying to keep a straight face since there are cameras. He's more easygoing than Eric, and if I have any chance of getting out of here, Ty's my ticket.

"Maddie." Ty and I turn to face Eric who's standing behind us. "You need to respond to a text so your phone will stop blowing up."

I walk eagerly toward him with Ty on my heels. I hadn't known where my cell was until now, but it makes sense that Victoria would have them keep it. If I don't respond to my sisters after a couple of days, it'll send a million red flags, and after Sophie's kidnapping last year, they won't think twice about reporting me missing.

"There are rules…" Eric warns harshly. "You can use it with supervision only. Type out your message, then one of us will read it and give you permission to send. Failure to cooperate will result in consequences." He repositions himself so I can see the two guns in his shoulder holster. "Text your sisters only."

Nodding, I look at the screen and see twenty-five unread messages with ten from Liam. The others are from Sophie and Lennon. Along with over a dozen missed calls and voicemails.

> **Liam: I know you didn't leave willingly. If by any chance you get this, give me some kind of clue to where you are. I'm going crazy.**

> **Liam: I won't let her do anything to you. I swear, Mads. I miss you and will do whatever it takes to get you back.**

> **Liam: When this is over, please let me explain. I know you're mad at me right now, and you have every right to be, but what we have is stronger than this. Please.**

I clench my jaw, unable to keep reading his messages. I'm so pissed at him, even if my heart aches for his touch. I miss the way he'd whisper my name as our bodies unraveled together, the way he'd hold me, and the way he'd suffer through hours of mindless TV and movies because he knew it made me happy.

But that doesn't excuse what he did. I was blindsided by Victoria's news. *Their* news.

"Hurry," Eric demands.

I glare at him, keeping my angry thoughts to myself. I look at my sisters' messages and see they started a group text.

Sophie: Where the hell are you?

Lennon: You can stay here if you need space. We'll make room.

Sophie: Are you safe?

Sophie: Who are you staying with?

Lennon: Please answer so Sophie can stop freaking out.

I scan the rest of their messages with the most recent one being from Sophie ten minutes ago.

Sophie: I'm about to call the fucking National Guard if you don't answer me. You know Mason's job has connections, and I won't stop at anything to find you. So you either respond with a selfie so I know you're alive or I'm having Mason's friend track your phone.

Shit.

"She wants a selfie," I say.

"I know," Eric replies. "The location has been disabled on your phone, but do what she wants so she stops freaking out." Sophie won't stop until I'm back at home, but I don't tell him that.

Swallowing hard, I nod and walk around to find a good spot for a picture. I'm sweaty from yoga and look like a hot mess, but maybe that'd actually convince her I'm alive and well. I find a blank wall and then position myself. I stick out my tongue, hold up a peace sign, and give her my best Miley Cyrus impression before snapping a pic. Then I attach it to the group message.

Maddie: I'm fine, was just doing yoga actually. See?

I show Eric and wait for his nod of approval before hitting send.

Sophie: Madelyn Grace! Where the hell have you been?

Lennon: You look sweaty like you've been having lots of hot sex. If you ran away with a sexy billionaire, just tell us.

Maddie: Yes. His name is BOB. He's the grandson of a dildo inventor, and he swept me away to the Alaskan mountains where we're hot-tubbing naked and drinking five-thousand-dollar bottles of wine.

I type out my response, then show Eric who looks less than amused.

"Trust me, if I'm not my normal sarcastic self, they'll know something's up," I explain.

"Fine, but you have a minute, and then I'm taking your phone back."

I hit send and wait for their responses.

Lennon: Told ya she was out getting dicked. You owe me 20 bucks, Soph.

Sophie: You two are the most annoying sisters
ever! I hate you both.

Maddie: I'm fine! I'm not a child and can take care
of myself for a week or two, okay? I just needed
some space, and I can't have that being in the same
house as him.

I hit send before showing Eric, needing to wrap up this
conversation.

Sophie: You really sure you're okay?

Maddie: I promise. I'll reach out when I'm ready.

Lennon: We're here if you need anything, Mads.

Sophie: Please don't stay gone too long. I miss you.

Maddie: I know. I miss and love you both.

Then I show Eric and give him back the phone.
"Well done." He tucks it into his pocket.
Lying to them when they're so damn worried makes me
feel sick to my stomach. I have to do what's necessary, but it
doesn't make it any easier to swallow.
"I'm going to shower and take a nap," I say. Walking past
him to the kitchen, I grab a bottle of water from the fridge.
Before heading to my room, I turn and watch as Ty shoots
daggers at Eric and wonder why the hell Victoria would send
two people who obviously have a beef with each other to an
isolated location.
Maybe that's a bonus punishment for me. Stick me with

31

two macho men who want to kill each other and probably me in the process.

Once I'm in my room, I strip out of my sweaty clothes and get into the shower. For the past two days, I've stayed strong, and perhaps in a state of shock, but reading Sophie and Lennon's text messages and seeing how worried they've been has me breaking down. My tears mix with the water stream, and the reality of my situation hits hard.

I have no idea how long I'll be here, if I'll see Liam again, or if I'll get to go back to my old, boring life.

Oh how I'd kill for hectic class schedules and rehearsing until my toes bleed.

After I'm clean and cried out, I change into something comfortable and lie in bed. I end up falling asleep and wake up to the smell of food. Making my way down the hallway, I spot Ty in front of the stovetop in the kitchen.

"You cook?" I ask him. He doesn't even startle as if he'd somehow heard my soft footsteps.

"Of course."

"Interesting. Another thing to add to the 'things I know about Ty' notebook," I tease, walking over and looking inside the skillet. I wrinkle my nose at the weird dish. "What is it?"

"Cajun sausage skillet pasta."

"Sausage what? I've never heard of it." I watch as he stirs it, the scent of garlic hitting my nose.

"It's a Southern dish," he responds as I take a seat at the breakfast bar.

"Wait." I smile when he looks at me over his shoulder. "Are you Southern? Where's your accent? Say y'all…"

He turns back around. "Yes. I don't have one. And no."

"Who taught you to cook then?"

"My grandmother."

"And where is she?"

"You ask too many questions." I watch as he turns the burner down and covers the skillet.

"What else am I supposed to do?" I cross my arms when he faces me.

"Eat, behave, sleep," he repeats robotically though that same half-smirk from earlier surfaces.

"I'm bored as hell. The least you could do is entertain me." I pout.

Something glimmers in his eyes, and then as fast as I recognize it, it's gone. His throat moves, and he stiffens as if he remembers I'm his mission to keep safe and quiet. He's not supposed to be friendly, and we're not supposed to be friends.

"I'm from Utah," I blurt out. "My father's a pastor actually. My mother was a stay-at-home mom and helped him with church duties."

"Oh." He busies himself, digging through the drawers and cabinets for plates and forks.

"I have two older sisters, one niece, one nephew, and where did you say you grew up?"

"Alabama," he says, then immediately stops and faces me with narrowed eyes. "How'd you do that?"

Looking sheepishly at him, I smile and fake innocence. "What?"

"You're sneaky."

"Not the first time I've been called that," I say proudly.

Ty serves up his dish on two plates, and I notice Eric isn't around tonight.

"So where's my other shadow?"

"Working out," he replies dryly.

"I was thinking of trying the gym out tomorrow. Maybe I'll get buff and be able to take you two," I taunt.

"Good luck with that." He bows his head, but I see his

smile. "What do you want to drink?" he asks, opening the fridge.

"I thought you weren't here to wait on me," I throw back his words from earlier.

"The lines are a little blurry actually."

"How so?"

"Not wanting to resuscitate you if you start choking on the spicy sausage and simultaneously not wanting you to get any ideas that I'm your servant."

"Hmm...valid points. But don't worry. I'm very capable of swallowing down spicy sausage." I poke a piece of meat with my fork, then shove it into my mouth. My eyes start watering, and I spit it out. "What the hell? Are you trying to kill me?" I pant and stick out my tongue.

Ty's laughing—actually laughing—and not hiding it. I like the sound of it, too. "You want that drink now?"

"Yes!" I reach out for the water in his hand. "Gimme, dammit!"

Taking the bottle, I suck down half of it before stopping.

"That was fucking cruel." I scowl. "My eyes are still watering!"

Ty leans against the counter with his arms crossed and shrugs. "Thought you could handle your sausage."

"Let me eat a box of Red Hot candies and suck you off and see how you feel afterward." The second my words spew out, Eric stomps into the kitchen, glaring at both of us. I swallow hard as if Ty and I are two kids in school being scolded by the principal. "That'd be the equivalent to it, is what I meant to say."

"Boss is on the line for you," Eric tells Ty.

"Let her know I'm eating dinner and will call her once I'm done," Ty states firmly.

"She says it's urgent," Eric argues. "Sounds pissed so you better answer."

Ty shifts uncomfortably, then nods. "Alright." He pushes off the counter and takes a step before stopping and facing me. "You have to stir it before eating. All the seasoning sits at the top and that's why it was so spicy." Then he *winks* and walks down the hallway.

CHAPTER FOUR

LIAM

IT'S BEEN seven days since I arrived in Vegas to play the part of doting husband and father-to-be. It's been the worst week of my life. Stress and guilt are my new constants along with playing by Victoria's rules. Considering she's essentially kidnapped Maddie and has formed this strange new bond with my dad, I'm afraid this is only the beginning of the end. There's no way she'll allow me to walk away after our six-month agreement, especially now that she's carrying twins. I should've known better than to make deals with JJ, but when it came to Victoria, I had no choice. She may have saved my life, but now I'm wondering if I was better off dead.

Tonight Johnny is hosting a dinner for Victoria, one of many that'll be happening until the babies are born. He's over the moon excited to be a grandfather, and each time it's brought up, it makes my stomach coil because I know what kind of monster he is.

After I'm dressed, I go into the kitchen and pour a double of bourbon. It's better for me to be inebriated than to be around everyone sober. Alcohol soothes the anger and pain, even if it's only temporary. I've drunk myself stupid several nights this week, hoping to get some sleep, but fail each time.

Victoria saunters by, grabbing a bottle of water from the fridge. "Please tell me you're not wearing that."

Words form in my mouth, but I swallow them down. I probably shouldn't tell her to fuck off when I've accomplished walking on thin ice all week. I'm hoping my good behavior will allow me to get more intel. Maybe I can beat her at her own game, though I have a feeling she's already a mile ahead of me. If anything, the O'Learys are strategic as hell. Well except for JJ, he's the family dumbass.

She clears her throat, grabbing my attention again after I shoot down the alcohol and pour another double. I glance over at her as I take it with a big gulp. "Can I help you?"

"The last thing you need to do is show up to this party drunk. It's disrespectful to my father."

"Sweetheart, it's gonna take a lot more than a few shots, trust me." I glare at her, put the bottle to my lips, and drink. Placing it on the counter, I walk to my room and fall onto my bed, closing my eyes. I feel nothing. After a moment, Victoria barges inside, fury written on her face.

"Goddammit, Liam." She crosses her arms and scowls. "You better be on your best behavior tonight."

"Planned on it," I snap, annoyed. I've been a *good* boy all fucking week.

"We leave in an hour," she tells me before slamming the door behind her. I check the time on my phone and end up scrolling through the last text messages I sent Maddie, a shitty reminder of how things were left between us. Tendrils of turmoil suffocate me and I sit up, rubbing my hands over my face, trying to gain what little composure I have left. My sweet, innocent Maddie could be hurt right now, and the only person I can blame is myself. I miss her so fucking much that it hurts. I'd do anything to talk to her, but Victoria would never allow it, so I don't bother pushing the subject.

Knowing I'll need to impress the O'Learys tonight, I put on my costume of a suit and tie. It doesn't take long before Victoria is screaming like the witch she is that it's time to go. The drive over is a blur and so is the dinner as she talks about all our plans to her family. Her father and grandmother sit around the table, along with a few cousins and her brother. I nod and smile like I'm supposed to, randomly leaning over to give her kisses while keeping my arm placed firmly around her petite body. To anyone looking in, we're the perfect couple just starting a new life together. The reality is much more dreary than that because I'm nothing more than her prisoner. When she says jump, I'm required to ask how high.

"Two babies are a miracle, Victoria," her grandmother says. She's been talking about the pregnancy nonstop, which only vindicates Victoria further.

"Oh, it won't be the last great-grandchildren you get. I want a big family," she says, interlocking her fingers with mine. Smiling, I take a sip of wine to wash down the bile creeping up my throat. I glance at Victoria and notice she's pale.

"You okay?" I whisper.

For a moment, she seems like a normal human being. "I feel sick. I don't think the food agreed with me."

"I have a big surprise for everyone," her father announces, grabbing our attention. "I rented out the pub a few blocks down and sent out invites. I wanted a proper way to announce the pregnancy to our friends."

Before Victoria can say a word, she begins dry heaving. Quickly, she stands and rushes to the bathroom, and I do as I'm supposed to and follow her. I grab the doorknob, but she locked it, so I press my ear against the door and listen to her emptying her stomach.

"Victoria, you alright?" I ask.

But she continues to puke. After five minutes of waiting, she opens the door with a cold rag pressed to her head. "I need to go home."

"Okay, not a problem," I tell her, and we walk back to the formal dining area.

"Sorry, Daddy. What were you saying?" she asks, taking a small sip of water.

"I rented the pub on the corner to celebrate, but you don't look as if you're up to it, princess." He leans forward and kisses her cheek.

"No, Daddy. But I'll send Liam to stand in, if that's okay. Something I ate isn't settling well, and I think I need to sleep it off."

Concern is written across his face, but he concedes and tells her to lie down in his room instead of leaving. Victoria agrees, and I follow her down the hallway. The room is fit for royalty with a California king bed, gold fixtures, and carpet so plush it feels like I'm walking on clouds.

Victoria climbs on the mattress and settles under the comforter, placing the cool rag over her forehead and closing her eyes.

"Don't embarrass me at that party," she mutters.

"Is this a setup, or are you really sick?" I heard her throw up, but I still don't trust her. She's used shady ass tactics before.

Victoria grunts. "Fuck you, Liam. I feel like shit."

I hold up my hands. "Okay, I'm sorry."

"Don't keep everyone waiting," she snarls, then rolls over on her side, dismissing me. I turn on the lamp next to the bed and turn off the main light, then walk out. At least if I want to leave the party, I'll have an excuse, so that's a plus. Maybe being alone with her family will be a good thing. I won't have her beady eyes watching everything I do or listening to every word I say.

Johnny tells Victoria goodbye, and we head to the pub. On the way over, he passes out Cuban cigars and pats me on the back with his strong, bone-breaking hand. "I'm glad I didn't kill ya, Liam," he tells me as we enter the building that's full of people.

"That makes two of us," I say. Johnny introduces me to his longtime friends, and I can't help but wonder how each of them is connected to his business. Regardless, they all look like they're the types who have guns and money.

After I make my way around the room, introducing myself to those who don't know me and answer where Victoria is at least fifty times, I go to the bar and order a drink. I need it more than anyone can understand because all this acting is fucking exhausting. As I sit on a stool, drinking scotch, Johnny plops down next to me. My nerves are on edge because I know every word I say is being analyzed.

"When do you plan on moving to Vegas permanently?" he asks, not segueing into the conversation whatsoever, but that's who he is, sharp and rough around the edges.

"We're still trying to work out the details, but I'll be here for all appointments." I hope my answer is good enough, but when he narrows his eyes, I have a feeling it's not.

He scowls, then orders Irish whiskey. "You need to be here for your wife. My daughter shouldn't be second place in your life." His voice is gruff and commanding.

"She's my number one," I say, but I think about Maddie when the words leave my mouth. A small smile touches my lips when I remember the good times we've shared over the past few months. So much has changed. The thought of her brings the strength I need to talk with Johnny. Then I get an idea that might give me answers that Victoria won't share.

"I do have one favor to ask," I say, finding my courage. Victoria thrives on control, which means Maddie is somewhere she's familiar with and can access anytime she wants. No doubt it's someplace she or her family owns. "I'd like to take Victoria somewhere secluded, away from all the hustle and bustle. A babymoon, I guess they call it, and since we didn't have a honeymoon, it could count for both. Maybe help take her mind off everything and relax a bit, but I'm not sure where to take her. Do you have any suggestions?"

He eyes me curiously. "I have a few properties you could go."

"Really?" I want to ask where, but I impatiently wait for him to continue.

"Got a condo in New York and Colorado, a cabin in Montana, a lake house in Tahoe, beachfront property in Florida, and a few other places," he brags proudly. "Victoria really loves the mountains, but I'm sure you know that already."

"Of course," I say immediately, faking pride in my voice.

"Montana's always held a special place in her heart. Probably because the house is so big and luxurious. Completely secluded and miles away from town. Beautiful scenery this time of year too. If you want to take her there, let me know, and I'll make sure the plane is reserved."

I give him a smile. "Absolutely. Thank you."

"You're family now. We take care of each other," he states, which sends shivers down my spine. I don't want any part of this damn family.

I nod, agreeing, and shoot down my drink as JJ sits on the other side of his father. This is as close as I've been to him since Victoria and I got married. My glass is refilled, and

I can't help but think about all the different places Maddie could be. If I know Victoria as well as I think I do, she more than likely brought her to one of the family properties.

Johnny turns and narrows in on JJ who's going on about someone he saw recently.

"And the bastard looked at me like he saw a goddamn ghost." JJ laughs. "Mickey isn't anything other than DeFranco scum."

The room stills and conversations move to hushed whispers as everyone turns to JJ. Johnny snaps at him and shakes his head, as if telling him to shut the hell up. I swallow, wanting to know more, but know I shouldn't push my luck. But I am a part of the family now.

"Who are they? The DeFrancos? Mickey?" I ask, keeping my voice low.

Johnny glances at me over the rim of his cup. "Dead, if they come near us."

I nod, repeating the words Victoria has said to me in the past. "Any enemy of yours is an enemy of mine."

He slightly raises his glass and chugs the rest of the amber-gold liquid.

Victoria texts me and says she's going home because she's feeling a tad better, and I send her a thumbs-up emoji. Johnny is still annoyed about the mention of the DeFrancos and looks as if he's chewing rocks as he takes several shots. His hair is a mess, and he looks completely unhinged. Leave it to JJ to ruin a semi-normal night. I mean, hanging out with mobsters is never normal, but no one spoke of killing anyone until he opened his big mouth. If Victoria were here, she'd be pissed and would've already slapped that grin right off his dopey face.

After another hour, I tell everyone goodbye and schedule an Uber to take me back to Victoria's. When I walk in, she's sitting on the couch watching TV with her feet propped up in fuzzy slippers as she drinks water from a straw. I sit on the loveseat and look at her. She almost looks normal with her hair piled on top of her head while wearing comfy clothes. Pregnancy sickness has made her the nicest I've ever seen.

"So how was the party?"

"Fine. Well until JJ brought up the DeFrancos. Then it got weird."

Victoria stills, then sits up and narrows her eyes. "Why the fuck would he bring them up?"

I shrug. "He ran into some Mickey guy and was bragging about wanting to kill him."

Her entire mood shifts, and she groans with an eye roll. "What an idiot. Sometimes I wish someone would cut out his tongue and do us all a favor."

The visual her words create is almost too much, but she seems serious. She'd have no problem getting rid of her own brother, which proves what kind of monster she truly is.

"We need to talk," I say, abruptly changing the subject but keeping my tone level.

"Agreed," she quickly replies but then speaks before I can. "You need to stay for the next two weeks. I need you here, or my father will get suspicious and assume you don't care about me and the babies."

My face contorts, and while I want to disagree, I decide to negotiate. "Yes, he did make a comment about me living here, but I assured him I'd make it to all your baby appointments. Also, you said a week would be enough time, and it's been seven days. I'm supposed to leave tomorrow. I need to get back to work."

Placing her hand on her growing belly, she speaks, "And things changed."

"I'm leaving tomorrow," I snap, standing.

"No!" She's growing more upset. "You can't."

"I can, and I will," I say as I walk toward my room, undoing my tie.

She says my name, stopping me in my tracks. "Liam. Let's play let's make a deal, shall we?"

The coldness in her voice sends a chill up my spine, but she has my attention and knows it. I go back to her, cross my arms, and wait. Of course she smiles like the devil she is.

"Why don't you sit?"

I don't.

"You stay as long as I need, and I'll show you proof your precious little home-wrecker is safe." She cocks an eyebrow and smirks because she knows she has me by the balls.

Swallowing down the lump in my throat, I nod, wanting to put a time limit on how long I'll be here but understanding this opportunity to see Maddie may come only once. "I want proof before I agree to anything."

Leaning over, she swipes her iPad off the glass coffee table and unlocks it. "So, that's a yes if she's okay?"

"Yes." Among everything, I need the peace of mind, for it to be driven home that she's being taken care of. While Victoria has given me her word, there is zero trust between us.

Grinning, she swipes through pages, logs into an app, and pats the seat next to her. My heart races knowing I'm about to see Maddie and see what condition she's actually in. After everything that happened with Sophie last year, I'm not sure I'll be able to handle it if Maddie's in any distress.

I move next to Victoria, and she refreshes the app so I know it's in real time.

"There she is…" she gloats, knowing she owns my ass even more now.

Maddie. Fuck, she's beautiful. I miss her so goddamn

much. She's sitting at a breakfast bar, talking to a guy who's standing in front of her, but I can only see his back. Heat rushes through my body when she smiles at him. Quickly, I study the white walls but can't see much of anything, considering it's dark outside. My mind begins to reel as I replay all the places Johnny said the family owned.

"See? She's being well taken care of, living it up in a luxury cabin, so you have absolutely nothing to worry about." Victoria's pleased with herself as she watches me. "Until you stop playing by my rules, of course," she adds arrogantly.

Cabin. Confirmed. Maddie's in Montana. But where? I'm not sure I'll have another opportunity to get Johnny alone for the address without him wanting to schedule a private jet to take us there. It'd be disastrous, and Victoria would never fall for it, not in a million years. Now I'm wondering if he knows what Victoria has done and is aware she's using their property to hold someone hostage. Or is she doing this all behind his back?

I can't stop staring at the screen, and I'm somewhat annoyed there's no sound, but I'm sure she has it muted to keep my mind spinning. The guy stands up and walks to the fridge, and when I see his face, my heart stops. What the actual fuck is *he* doing there with Maddie?

I try to keep my composure so she doesn't notice my reaction, but inside, I'm confused as hell.

Tyler, one of my closest friends, is laughing and talking with the one girl I want more than anything to be with right now. How the hell did this happen?

"They seem to be getting along perfectly fine, don't they?" Victoria asks, digging the knife in a little deeper, noticing my expression when I saw Tyler. She probably thinks I'm jealous and is hoping for it. Put Maddie in a position to flirt with another guy and watch me squirm, knowing I can't do shit about it. But what she doesn't know is that Tyler is on *my* side. We're as thick as thieves, which will most definitely hamper her plan, whatever it is.

Maddie watches him, smiling, and I try to act unfazed. Tyler hands her a bottle of water, and Maddie says something to him. Some smart-ass remark, I'm sure. Another guy comes into the picture, and he looks like a total asshole with hard lines and a scowl on his face. He says something to the two of them, and Tyler nods, but Maddie shakes her head. The guy continues for a few more seconds before storming away.

Maddie eventually bursts into laughter. How I wish I could hear that sweet sound. The things I'd do to go back to that time when life was easy. Before Victoria and before any of this ridiculousness.

"That's enough," Victoria says, yanking the iPad from my hands and locking the screen. "You got what you wanted. She's completely safe and more than preoccupied with Ty and Eric."

I look straight into her green eyes. She called him Ty, and I hold back a smirk. No one calls him that, which means he's acting and playing a part. He told me he was planning something but wouldn't tell me what it was. He said it was for my own good not to know until it was the right time. He infiltrated the O'Learys, and I wonder if Victoria has any idea there's a chink in her armor. As long as Tyler's around, he won't allow anything bad to happen to Maddie, and that brings me a huge whoosh of relief.

My girl is safe, for now. I just wonder how the fuck Tyler's going to get them out of this situation or how I'm going to help without blowing his cover.

CHAPTER FIVE

MADDIE

I'm STARTING to understand why inmates go crazy in a cell.

Day after day, the same routine, the same walls, same *everything*.

At least the well-behaved ones get to go outside for some fresh air. I don't even get that. I do yoga, practice my dance techniques and old routines, work out, take baths, and observe Ty cook while trying to get more personal details out of him. I've watched reruns of *Glee*, *The Big Bang Theory*, and started the first season of *Game of Thrones*.

I'm bored as fuck.

I've been here for ten days, and I miss Liam more than ever. Part of me hates that I do while the other just wants to make sure he's okay. And to let him know I'm alive. I doubt Victoria told him much about what she's doing with me and is probably using it to her advantage to get him to do her bidding.

Unless we all play nicely, none of us will get out unscathed.

"Where ya going, Beanstalk?" I ask Ty when I see him grab car keys and slip on his jacket. I also gave him an appropriate nickname on day five because he's a freaking giant with long-ass arms and legs. He told me he wouldn't respond to it if I called him that, but eventually, he caved, and now I think he likes it.

Eric, on the other hand, doesn't like his nickname — Captain Asshole. I even shortened it to Captain, but he still scowled at me.

At least Ty is nice enough where I don't think he'll kill me in my sleep. However, Capt A-hole looks like he wants to smother me with a pillow dipped in chloroform. I can't help it that I'm annoying and obnoxious after being stuck inside for a week and a half. I literally have cabin fever. If Liam were here, he could attest to my actions. Locking me up without letting me out of the house is a one-way street to hearing me talk nonstop.

"I have to run into town and get some supplies and food," he replies. It's the first time he's left since we've been here.

"Do I get to go if I promise to behave?" I ask, hopeful though I know better.

"No," Eric responds for him. He's always creeping up on us like a goddamn sniper. After the second day when Victoria called for Ty, he went back to being more reserved and distant. I have no doubt she saw us on her fucking cameras and didn't like how he was getting comfortable with me. It took a few more days after that to soften Ty up again, and now our conversations are effortless until Eric ruins it, which happens often.

"I need things," I turn and tell Eric. "*Womanly* things."

He shoves a hand in his suit coat and then slaps a notepad down on the counter. Grabbing a pen, he places it next to it. "Write it down. He'll get whatever you need."

I arch a brow at Ty who looks less than thrilled to shop for girly shit.

"Okay, if you insist." I smirk and start jotting down a list. Then I hand it to Ty.

"Is this a joke?" he asks, cocking an eyebrow. "Tampons, pads, Midol, Dove dark chocolate, three bottles of red wine. *Condoms*."

I shrug, holding back a smile. "You never know when an opportunity will arise."

Eric's eyes are ice cold, and it's obvious he's had enough of me, but it's comical to see how far I can push him. He was clearly born without a sense of humor.

"What size would you say, Captain? Magnum's extra-large?"

The douche doesn't even flinch at my obvious compliment to his dick size. "Ty, go."

Ty gives me a slight nod, then turns toward the door. "And some red nail polish!" I call out. "If I'm getting laid, I need to give myself a pedi."

I hear Ty snort as he opens the door, then shuts it behind him. Eric glowers, crossing his arms over his broad chest as if he's been waiting all day to scream at me.

"You have quite the mouth on you. Victoria doesn't like it," he states. "If you don't leave Ty alone, you'll get both of you killed. Enough is enough."

Narrowing my gaze at him, I wonder how hard it'd be to grab one of his guns and shoot him before Ty returns.

"Don't even think about it, little girl," he says as if he read my mind. "Victoria would have the perimeter swarming to find and drag you back by your hair."

It's the most Eric has spoken to me at one time.

"Yeah? Maybe you should ask her why she's so threatened by me…" I keep my eyes on him, then stalk away. My heart thrashes hard against my chest as I walk to my room and lock the door behind me.

49

I decide to change into different clothes and work out my frustrations while I wait for Ty to return with my goodies. There's no doubt he'll get everything on my list minus the Magnums.

There's a kickass stereo system in the gym, so I crank some Demi Lovato and stretch before I hop on the bike. After thirty minutes, I'm sweating and take a water break before I run on the treadmill. I haven't worked out this much in weeks, but it feels amazing to blow off steam.

"Maddie." Eric's booming voice scares the shit out of me, and I nearly trip over myself.

"Jesus. You need a bell around your neck." Turning off the treadmill, I step off and face him. "What?"

"Boss has a message for you." He holds out my phone, and I blink up at him, unsure if I want to read it. "Take it," he orders.

Swallowing hard, I step closer and grab it from his grip.

Victoria: Liam can see you. I'd be careful if I were you.

What the fuck does that mean? Is she trying to threaten me?

Instinctively, I look up at the cameras and wonder if he's watching right now. Either way, she most definitely is, though, and is hoping for a reaction. Instead, my lips form into a smug smirk as I type out a response.

Maddie: Isn't that what you want? For him to see me flirting with your guards so he'll crawl to you?

Victoria: You're so naive, sweetheart. Liam's in my

bed every night. You're no longer my problem, but if you don't behave, Liam pays. Remember that.

If Victoria wants Liam as a husband and a father to their children, she won't hurt him. Keeping me away ensures she'll get what she wants, but I don't buy her empty threats. It's a way for her to keep control and scare everyone in the process. However, she has the ability to destroy me and my family if I don't cooperate, so I'll do as she demands.

Maddie: You got it, Boss lady.

I hit send, then slap my cell back in Eric's palm. With one more look at the camera, I scowl, then turn to Eric. "She's a bitch, and you're a bastard for working for her. When I get out of here—and I *will*—I'm reporting her for abduction and blackmail. She won't think twice about throwing you under the bus, so I'd run after I'm gone."

I know my threat bounces off him like a rubber ball, but I'm so pissed and annoyed my words spew out before I think twice. He doesn't even balk at me and is probably laughing at me in his head, but I don't care. I hope her entire empire burns to the fucking ground.

Eric walks out, and I'm more fired up than before, so I get back on the treadmill and run as fast as I can. With my heart beating out of my chest and sweat burning my eyes, I can no longer feel my legs. At the sound of a light knock, I hop off and nearly fall to the ground panting.

"Hell, Maddie." Ty walks over and stands above me.

Blinking, I try catching my breath as my arms and legs spread out on the cool mat. "Hey."

"Uh…I got everything on your list except the condoms.

They were out," he teases, lifting the bag in one hand. "I'll just put it on your bed."

He turns, and I quickly speak up. "Wait." Ty spins around and cocks a brow. "Can you help me up? I think I overdid it. My body feels like jelly."

Ty smirks and nods. Leaning down, he grabs my hand and slowly pulls me up. Once I'm back on my feet, he releases me and grins. "Heard the Boss got a hold of you."

"Oh, you mean Crazy Bitch? Yeah, we had a good chat." I exhale roughly and remember he's on her payroll. He might be nice to me, but that doesn't mean I can trust him. She probably planned for me to feel safe with him, so when I least expect it, he'll whack me with a crowbar and bury my body in the middle of the woods.

He holds out my items, and I take them. We stand awkwardly, both aware Victoria can see us.

"I told Eric I'd cook dinner tonight. Any requests?" he asks, breaking the silence.

"Well...I'd kill for some Chinese food. General Tso's Chicken and an eggroll. Mmm," I moan, then smile when he furrows his brows. "Okay, so not an option?"

"No."

I inhale sharply and shift my neck from side to side to release some of the tension. "You should let me cook. I make some badass breakfast dishes." The thought reminds me of Liam and when I lost our bet the very first weekend I came to live with him after my apartment caught on fire.

"Not a good idea." He shoves his hands in his pockets. "Think about it and let me know."

Ty leaves before I can say another word.

The next morning, I can barely get out of bed. My entire body is stiff and sore, and I'm cursing myself for working out as hard as I did. Last night, Ty made Southern-style chili, and it was as delicious as everything else he's prepared. The three of us eat at the kitchen table, and it's more awkward than going to prom with your first cousin. At least during the day I can eat at the breakfast bar and chat with Ty while Eric does other shit.

Instead of my typical routine of asking him a million questions he doesn't always answer while he cooks, I start a hot bath. I twist my hair into a high bun and slip out of my clothes before I get into the massive tub. Victoria might be the biggest bitch of the century, but her taste is admirable. The jets soothe and release the tightness in my muscles.

I add some bubble bath and actually relax, forgetting for a moment that I'm being held here against my will. Most days, it's easy to push it to the back of my mind, but as time passes, I lose a sense of reality and the outside world.

Once my body feels good and loose, I drain the water, and that's when I realize I forgot to grab a stupid towel. It wouldn't be such a big deal if the linen closet wasn't on the other side of the gigantic bathroom. The chill of the air hits me the second I get out and tiptoe across the floor. As soon as I grab a towel, I immediately start drying off. Once I'm dry, I'll wrap myself in one of Victoria's plush robes.

"Maddie."

At the sound of my name, I quickly spin around and drop my towel in the process. When I see Ty in the doorway, I shriek.

What the hell is he doing in here?

"Fuck, sorry." He turns around, but only after I catch his gaze on my nipple rings.

Swiftly grabbing my towel off the floor, I wrap it tightly around my body. "What are you doing?" I ask nervously.

"I knocked on the bedroom door and called your name, but you didn't answer, so I let myself in," he explains. "I'm really sorry. I thought something was wrong."

"Why would something be wrong?" Not like the windows aren't locked and deadbolted. Or the two cameras in my room aren't spying on my every move.

"You didn't show up for breakfast, so I came to check on you, and then you didn't answer, so…"

"You thought I escaped," I finish for him.

"It was one thing that crossed my mind," he admits.

"And there was another?" I prompt, walking toward him.

Ty slowly glances over his shoulder as if to make sure I'm no longer naked. When he realizes I'm not, he fully turns and looks at me. "Honestly, I thought maybe you'd harmed yourself or something."

There are no cameras in here, but unless the door is shut, the ones from my room can see inside. I've never seen Ty this vulnerable before, and it makes my heart race at the thought of him being worried about me. At times, I get the feeling he's putting on an act for his job's sake. Still, I can't be too careful because anyone in Victoria's world is shady and deceptive, just like her.

"No, I just worked myself too hard yesterday and needed to soak in hot water."

He blinks as if he's fighting to keep his eyes on mine. "If you want some tips, I'm pretty knowledgeable about how to work out without hurting yourself. A close friend of mine owns a gym I used to work at, and I've been lifting and boxing for years. I know all about feeding and fueling your body properly."

"Really?" I ask with excitement, and he nods. "You sure you're *allowed* to?"

Ty tilts his head and flashes a small grin. "You let me worry about that." He winks, then steps back. "I'll let you get dressed now. Sorry again for barging in. Breakfast is ready whenever you are."

A genuine smile splits my face. "Okay, thank you."

That afternoon, I skip the gym and decide I'll take Ty up on his offer tomorrow when I'm not so sore. Instead, I find a meditation class on TV and work on de-stressing before I have a panic attack from being locked in here. If I'm going to stay sane, I need to keep levelheaded. Stretching and breathing techniques help keep my core strong and ready to tackle whatever is thrown my way.

"You ready?" Ty asks me the following morning. "Made you a pre-workout chocolate shake."

"Where's breakfast?" I frown, looking around the empty counter. Though I typically eat light in the morning before classes, I've gotten used to Ty's cooking.

"In that cup." He jerks his chin toward it.

Grabbing it, I look at the thick liquid and glower. "It doesn't look like eggs and hash browns."

Ty snorts and shakes his head. "No, but it'll help give you energy so you don't burn out after one rep."

"Oh, God," I groan. "I'm gonna regret this, aren't I?"

"Nah." He shakes his head. "You're a dancer, so you should be drinking this anyway."

"Agree to disagree." I sniff it first, then take a drink. "It's no crispy bacon." I gulp the rest of it down and make a sour face. "Chocolate takes offense to that being called *chocolate*. More like chalky vomit."

He scoffs, shaking his head at me. "It's not that bad."

"Next time, just feed me a cup of dirt." I snatch a bottle of water and take a long sip.

He pops a brow, then leads me down the hall to the gym. "Anyone ever tell you how dramatic you are?"

"Only since birth." I chuckle, thinking of my sisters who'd wholeheartedly agree.

After Ty spends twenty minutes explaining the proper way to lift weights without straining my muscles, I sit and take a break to rehydrate.

"So, tell me about this boyfriend of yours," he says after I catch my breath. "Or, *ex*—as you said."

I arch an eyebrow, curious if he really wants to know or if he's just gathering information for Victoria. Though, she already knows Liam and I were together behind her back, which is why I'm here in the first place.

"You want to know about Liam?" I ask, cautiously watching his expression.

When he barely flinches and keeps his eyes on me, I decide he's being genuine.

"Whatever you want to share." He shrugs, then continues, "How long were you together?"

"Uh...well." I chew on my lip, thinking about how to answer that. "That's a difficult question."

Ty chuckles. "That's supposed to be an easy one."

"Technically, we first met my senior year of high school four years ago. I lied about my age, he scolded me for almost getting him into legal trouble, and then I moved to

Sacramento a year later. We were reunited when my sister invited me to a party, and it was Liam's house."

"I bet that was a shock."

"Oh, it was. Then he basically ignored me for three years. Well…he tried to anyway." I swallow down another gulp of water. "We were around each other a lot because his best friends are dating my older sisters."

"Really? Mason's dating your sister?"

I narrow my eyes at him, studying his expression as he swallows hard. Almost as if he hadn't meant to say that.

"Yeah, but how'd you know his name was Mason?" I ask, tilting my head.

"You told me the other day," he quickly responds.

I know for a fact I didn't. There'd be no reason for me to mention anyone's name until this conversation. However, I'm not about to challenge him or give him any reason to hurt, kill, or throw me out to the wolves.

"Oh, uh, right." I palm my forehead. "Liam's roommate."

"So you started seeing Liam not long ago?"

"Yeah, it's recent. So recent, in fact, it's like it never happened." I pinch my lips together and stand. "Okay, break's over. I need to hit something."

"That I can definitely help you with." Ty smirks and nods his head toward the punching bag in the opposite corner.

An hour flies by, and I'm drenched in sweat. I haven't worked out this hard in months, but it felt great to relieve some stress.

"Come, I'll make you an after-workout drink. You need to stay hydrated," Ty says as I follow him into the kitchen.

I groan, leaning against the counter. "Ugh, when do I get to have real food again?"

"Don't worry, you'll get plenty of protein for lunch." The

corner of his lips tilts slightly as he digs into the fridge. For some reason, his sentence comes off dirty, and I chuckle.

"Why does this all of a sudden feel like boot camp?" I tease.

"This is nothing like a *real* boot camp. Trust me, you're living in paradise compared to that."

"You were in the Army?" I ask, standing taller.

He grabs a handful of veggies and fruit, then places them on the counter. "I'll put these in your smoothie, and you'll barely taste the protein powder."

The way he ignored my question doesn't go unnoticed. I want to pry, but I know there have to be boundaries while we have eyes and ears on us. It'd make sense, though, considering how meticulous and strategic he seems. How the hell did he go from being a soldier to working for the mob?

"Well?" Ty asks after I take my first sip of the drink he made me.

"Better than the first one," I tell him and wrinkle my nose. "But still, it's no steaming hot breakfast."

"I'll make pancakes and bacon tomorrow. Don't worry," he tells me with a grin. Of course, Eric saunters in and ruins the nice moment we were having with his loud and commanding demeanor.

"We need to talk," he states, staring at Ty.

"Sure. What's up, Captain?" I say, though I know he's not addressing me.

Eric's eyes snap to mine. "Enough!" he barks, and I jump. "Go to your room until told otherwise."

I risk a glance at Ty who looks like his jaw might snap.

"We can talk in the office," Ty tells Eric, shuffling to put the items back into the fridge.

"No, now. Maddie can leave," Eric states harshly.

"Maddie's leaving," I say, mimicking his tone. He doesn't

approve of Ty treating me like a human being, that much is obvious, but why does he have to be such a dick?

I set my drink down and awkwardly leave the kitchen. The air is still and silent, and after I walk a few steps, I freeze at the sound of Eric's voice.

"Victoria's getting impatient with your behavior. She's sending a replacement in a couple of days and wants you to start packing for your departure," Eric tells him.

What? *No!*

"I haven't done anything wrong," Ty argues. "Just because I'm not an asshole to her doesn't mean I'm not obeying orders."

"You're getting too close," Eric says roughly. "Which means you'll think twice about taking care of the situation, if needed."

What the fuck does that mean?

My skin goes ice cold.

Is Victoria ever going to let me out of here? I'm afraid to even think about the answer to that because deep down in my gut, I know there's only two possibly ways I'm leaving this place— in a body bag or running like hell and escaping.

CHAPTER SIX

LIAM

I've slept better now knowing Tyler is with Maddie. Though I'm still stuck in this fucking hellhole with Victoria, her threats bounce off me a lot easier. It's been two weeks since everything imploded in my face and I lost Maddie, but I'm gonna do whatever it takes to get her back. To prove my love and loyalty.

Victoria, on the other hand, is on my last fucking nerve, and I'm using all the willpower I can to keep from telling her off and risking everything. I don't know what Tyler's plan is, so I can't act until he does. I contemplate texting him, but I have a feeling he's not allowed to use his personal phone, or if he is, it's probably being watched. Either way, I'm in limbo waiting for his next move.

"Good morning, hubby," Victoria singsongs as she walks into the kitchen wearing lingerie. I roll my eyes when she grabs food and juice from the fridge. "I was thinking we should do some shopping today. We need to register for the babies and get some stuff for their nursery. Daddy wants to buy their cribs, and Nana wants to buy a double stroller, but we'll need a lot more than that. Plus, I want some new bras."

I clench my jaw, swallowing down the words I really want to say. "Isn't it a little early for all of that?"

Victoria spins around and glares at me. "It takes time to get everything together, Liam," she snaps. "I want to repaint and have new carpet installed. Then there's research for the right equipment—baby monitors, bottles, bassinets, pacifiers, changing tables. We need to make sure we get the right brands."

Narrowing my eyes at her over my coffee cup, I take a sip and scowl. She knows damn well there's no "we" in this situation, but she pushes it every chance she gets.

"I've been here long enough. I need to get back to work," I tell her after I set down my mug.

"You *need* to be here with your pregnant wife," she retorts, pouring herself a glass of apple juice.

"Your grandmother went back to New York, and your dad is plenty convinced. What more do you need?"

"I need you to move here."

"That wasn't the deal," I remind her, and I'm starting to sound like a broken record. "I want a paternity test."

"And I want to know why you were asking my dad about what family properties we own," she abruptly changes the subject. How the hell does she even know that?

I groan as the memory of JJ being at the bar surfaces, and there's no doubt he overheard the conversation and told her. I dream of the day I'll get to kick his fucking ass.

"What's wrong with talking to your father? Isn't that what you want anyway? We get close, and he believes our marriage is legit?" I ask, shrugging off her suspicions.

She inches closer, leaning her elbows on the countertop and showing off her breasts. "I'm not a goddamn idiot, Liam. I know what you were fishing for, and you better stop before you regret it."

I smirk, knowing Maddie will be fine as long as Victoria isn't near her. "I've done everything you've asked, now let me go home. I have a life I need to get back to."

Victoria pats my head as if I'm a small child. "Shopping first." Then she takes my cup and pours the rest of my coffee down the sink. *Bitch*. "Go get dressed. We leave in thirty."

After I'm showered and ready for what's surely going to be an awful day, I wait in the living room. I'm tempted to take my shit and leave right now, but knowing she's able to make my life a living hell, I stick around. Playing this fucking game is getting old, and I really do need to get back to work, but Maddie's safety is my top priority. If that means parading around the city as Victoria's husband and buying baby shit, then I'll do it all day long.

But I don't have to be happy about it.

"You look nice," Victoria singsongs, pressing a palm to my chest and sliding it down to my belt buckle. "Very handsome in fact." She starts undoing my jeans, and I see red.

Squeezing her wrists, I push her away. "Not a chance in fucking hell," I hiss, growling as I step back.

"You expect me to stay celibate?" She scowls, crossing her arms.

"I don't fucking care what you do, but it won't be with me," I warn, walking around her toward the door.

"You really think she's going to take you back?" she says from behind me. "She's cozying up to one of my men as we speak. She's forgotten all about you, Liam. It's time you realize you belong here, with *me*."

I swallow hard, resisting the urge to snap at her. Looking over my shoulder, I say, "I wouldn't let you touch me if you were the last person on earth."

Victoria actually looks hurt, but what did she expect?

She's trying to blackmail me into having sex with her, and there's nothing she can say or do to make me change my mind. I'd let her father kill me before I ever make that mistake again.

She swallows and straightens her shoulders, then walks to me. "I don't give a shit what our arrangement was, so it's best you forget it. The moment you violated the terms and screwed her while we were supposed to be proving to everyone that we were happily married is when you threw it all away. Now, you'll do whatever I say because you have no other choice. Got it?"

That's what she fucking thinks, but I hold back the smug grin I want to flash at her. Instead, I force out a smile. "Sure, wifey. Ready to go now?"

The corner of her lips tilt up in victory, and I can't wait to see the shock on her face when she discovers holding Maddie hostage didn't work. I have faith in Tyler and whatever he's planning.

The morning is filled with Victoria bossing me around as her driver takes us from store to store. The number of things a baby needs is absolutely ridiculous, and she's shopping for two, which makes it worse. We register at five different places, which is insane, considering Victoria's loaded and could buy it all herself. But not the O'Learys. They need big, glamorous parties to show off, and I have no doubt that if she gets her way, she's already planning for me to be at all of them.

At each shop, she looks through baby clothes and purchases more than I think any baby could actually wear without changing them twenty times a day. By the last one, there are ten large bags in the car, and I know because I've carried each of them.

"Are we done now? I need to eat something," I say when we get into the back of the car.

"Yes, let's stop for a late lunch. It'll be good to be seen eating out together," Victoria says, then directs Hector where to go. "Which means—"

"Cherish the ground you walk on, hold your hand, show affection. Yes, I know," I grumble. The same shit I've been doing all morning since we've been in public.

"Good." She smiles as if she's successfully trained me like a dog.

Hector makes a stop at the light, and we're roughly jolted forward as the sound of metal on metal rings out. Victoria smacks her head against the window, and the seat belts tighten around us, locking us in place. She squeals, and I curse when the belt digs into me. *Fuck.*

I turn around to see a large truck has slammed into the back of the SUV. Small fender benders like this are common, but Victoria isn't having it.

The next half hour passes in a chaotic blur as Hector nearly knocks the guy's teeth out and I call 911. Victoria cries in fear about the babies and tells the police officers she wants the driver who hit us unnecessarily arrested.

It's a fucking shitstorm.

They take her in an ambulance, and I'm forced to ride along as her worried husband. I play my damn part, but I'm slightly eager to talk to a doctor not on her family's payroll. I want to see an ultrasound in real time and find out how far along she truly is, considering how big she looks.

"Thanks for staying by my side," Victoria whispers as she lies on the bed, waiting for the ultrasound tech.

"Of course," I mutter.

The tech introduces herself as Talia and explains she's

going to take some measurements and pictures for the doctor to make sure everything is fine. Though the impact was minimal, Victoria was determined to get checked out.

Victoria raises her shirt up to her bra, and for the first time, I see her bare round belly. Even lying down, I can tell she's bigger than she should be for this far along. I've been suspicious since the moment she announced she was pregnant and started reading up on it, and even with twins, she looks twice the size of the pictures I saw online.

Talia reassures us that both babies look great. The heartbeats are strong, and they're moving around without any distress. Victoria exhales in relief, but I study the size of them. She claims she got pregnant over the Fourth of July week when she came to California, which would make her about two and a half months. I'm not buying it.

But I'm about to find out the truth.

"Can we get some pictures?" I ask like an excited father-to-be. "With the number of weeks on there?" I ask, then smile wide. "For the babies' scrapbook."

"I already have some from a couple of weeks ago," Victoria blurts out, but Talia is already printing them out.

"Absolutely! They change so much at this stage, so it's nice to have more!" She hands them to me, and Victoria looks like she's ready to rip off Talia's head. "Everything looks really good, but the doctor will still want to review it all. Once he does, he'll be in to discharge you."

I thank her, and the moment she's gone, I stare at the images and read the small print at the top.

O'Leary-Evans, Victoria
GA=18w4d

I learned from researching that GA means gestational age, which is how pregnancy weeks from the woman's last menstrual cycle are counted. This means the babies were conceived about sixteen weeks ago and that was right around the time Johnny was about to kill me.

"You wanna tell me how it's the middle of September and this is saying you're over eighteen weeks along? Pretty sure the first week of July was only ten weeks ago." I squeeze the pictures tight in my hand, rage building in my blood at the audacity this bitch has to lie to me over and over. "There's no fucking way they're mine."

"We've been married for four months, so it's very believable we got pregnant right away and that they're yours," she states matter-of-factly.

"But we both know they're not." I'm fuming and can barely control myself. "You were already pregnant when your father was about to shoot me, weren't you?"

I don't need her confirmation to know she was. She would've been super early, but it's possible she could've known at that point. What other motive did she have for saving me? She needed someone to marry her and claim the babies.

But why?

"What's it matter? We're married, and you'll be the father to them," she says sternly.

"You *bitch*," I whisper-hiss. "This was never about getting your trust fund and out of the family business, was it? You needed a father for them. Who's the real one?"

"Shut. Up," she snaps. "This conversation is over."

The fuck it is.

"What exactly were you going to say when you went into labor two months early?" I push.

"Twins come early all the time." She brushes it off like

66

I'm a goddamn idiot. "I'm giving birth in a private suite, and it'll be kept quiet until it's time to announce their births."

"You're seriously delusional." I shake my head in disbelief. "The moment your father finds out you got pregnant by another man, he'll understand why I divorced your ass." And hopefully let me leave without putting a bullet in my head.

Victoria scoffs with a smug grin. "Well, good luck proving it."

I fucking will and won't need luck, princess.

Once the doctor tells her to take it easy for a few days and sends us on our way, we finally make it back to her place with all the bags. She demands I unload them and set everything out on the dining room table. I do as she says to keep the peace, but my mind is still reeling from the information I just learned.

I know her family is religious, and she wouldn't want to be pregnant out of wedlock, but I can't figure out is why she didn't just marry the real father instead of someone she barely knew. That part doesn't quite add up, but if I know anything about Victoria, she does what will benefit her the most.

A paternity test would easily prove it, but it won't be easy to get one done if she fights it. However, her being farther along means this pregnancy will be over a lot sooner and she won't be able to hide her secret for long. Now that I know the truth, I have a little more weight in this deal.

Hours pass and when I don't see or hear from Victoria, I assume she passed out for the night.

Thank God.

I make myself dinner, then head to my room to watch meaningless TV and try to keep my mind off Maddie, which of course never works.

Just as I'm dozing off, my phone beeps with a message.

Unknown number: It's Tyler. I'm getting Maddie out of there and have the proof you need to get your freedom. I'll call you as soon as I can. Gimme a few days. Until then, sit tight.

CHAPTER SEVEN

MADDIE

TY'S STILL HERE.

Thank God.

It's been two days since I overheard Eric tell Ty he's leaving, and I'm scared like hell that his replacement is going to somehow be worse than Eric. Ty is my only saving grace while being stuck here.

Even after that happened, Ty never acted like anything was wrong. He helped me in the gym yesterday and this morning as if things weren't about to change. I want to ask him about it, but I'm worried I'll set him off or something since Victoria can hear us on the cameras.

What happens after he goes? Is he put on another mission? Fired? *Killed?*

I can't even stomach the thought of Ty not being here because he gives me some hope that things will be okay. And he keeps me company since he's the only one who doesn't seem to want to murder me.

"Ty, I have a question," I ask him as I finish my cool-down on the treadmill.

"What is it?"

"Do you think I could text my sisters today? Just give them a little 'I'm alive' update?"

His eyes finally meet mine, his lips in a firm line before he speaks, "That should be fine. I'll need to supervise you, though."

"Of course," I say, knowing the rules. I'm just glad I'll get to talk to them for a couple of minutes.

"Go clean up, and I'll get Eric on board. Meet in the kitchen when you're done. I'll have your phone then."

"Okay," I say softly. "Thank you."

He replies with a curt nod before walking away. Once I'm done stretching, I go to my bathroom and take a quick shower. I'm anxious as hell to communicate with them. I know they're worried to death because ignoring their texts isn't normal for me. They're going to know something's up even though I chatted with them when I arrived and told them I was fine.

"Here you go." Ty hands me my phone as soon as I step into the kitchen. "I'll read over your shoulder so you don't have to hand it to me every time you send a message."

I smile wide at his generosity, and I'm surprised Eric isn't here to supervise. "Thanks!"

But my lips turn into a frown at the numerous missed calls and unread messages. *Shit.*

Sophie: I talked to Joel, and he says you're missing classes?? You don't ever skip dance rehearsal, even when you're dying sick. What's going on, Mads?

Great, she's talking to Joel. No doubt he's worried about me now, too. But she's right. I love it too much to miss it.

Lennon: I know you're in hiding, but let me know

if I can do anything for you. I know a thing or two about unbearable heartache.

My throat goes dry as I think about what Lennon went through when she lost Brandon. She was a mess and luckily had Hunter to pick up the pieces, but who's going to help them all when I'm gone for good?

The morbid thoughts hit me at my lowest points.

No messages from Liam. According to Victoria, he knows I'm here and could see me on the cameras. Does that mean he's stopped caring? Is he not worried?

Did I really mean as much to him as he said?

Questions swarm my mind as my chest tightens with what she's making him do for her. Imagining them together makes me sick.

I decide to respond to them in our sister group chat. Lying about my phone being dead or having to replace it feels cheap, especially because they'd know better. There are too many ways to stay in contact for them to believe I was unable to through social media or email. I have no other choice but to play the broken heart card.

Maddie: Sorry, I haven't been in the mood to check my cell in a few days. I'm not skipping classes, I told my professors. Don't worry about me. I told you before, I'm fine, and I just need some time and space.

Sophie: It's about damn time, oh my God. Maddie! This is irresponsible and childish. Come back home! Liam isn't even here!

Lennon: Soph, she's not a kid. Let her cope on her own terms.

Sophie: She can do that here where I can watch her and help her through this!

Maddie: Guys! Stop fighting. I want to wallow alone, okay? I already told my professors I'd be out a few days and will make it up before the end of the semester.

Sophie: Mads, I love you. Just tell me where you are, please.

"Wrap it up," Ty tells me softly. "I had to fight for you to have this chance."

I nod, thankful he managed to even get me this time to give my sisters some kind of closure so they'd stop freaking out.

Maddie: I'm sorry, but I have to go. I'll text you guys in a few days, okay? Love you both.

I hand Ty the phone and hold back my emotions that threaten to spill out. Lying to them sucks.

"Thank you again," I say before numbly walking away and going to my room.

I collapse on my bed, and the tears fall.

They fall for the life I miss—school, my friends and sisters, normalcy.

They fall for Liam—terrified of what he's going through and scared like hell I'll lose him for good this time.

They fall because I feel so damn alone.

I don't know how much time passes by the time I wake up and realize I've fallen asleep. When I make my way to the kitchen and check the clock, I see it's three in the afternoon. My eyes are puffy and red, and I'm starting to feel at my breaking point.

"You missed lunch. I put a plate in the fridge for you," Ty says from behind me. I quickly turn around and look at him cautiously and see concern written all over his face. I can't ask him what's wrong because I've already gotten him into trouble by getting too close. The fear of what's going to happen once he leaves already haunts me. What will Victoria do to him? Me?

All of us?

"Thank you." I smile sheepishly. "What'd you make?"

The corner of his lips tilts up slightly in amusement. "BLTs and fruit salad." He takes the items out of the fridge and sets them on the counter.

"You know..." I linger, thinking twice about my words but say fuck it and continue anyway. "I've never been fed so well before. All these balanced meals, working out, and protein shakes. It's like I'm being trained for some kind of fight club."

Ty chuckles softly. "She knows what to do to get what she wants and not keeping you safe nor well-cared for would only backfire on her," he explains, and while he doesn't say her name, it's obvious he's talking about Victoria. I want to ask him what he knows and how kidnapping me adds to her overall goal of keeping Liam as hers.

Things could definitely be worse, but I'm isolated, and for someone who thrives on being around others, it's torture.

"Here." He slides the plate toward me with a glass of something. I don't even bother asking what it is and take a seat. "You probably won't be hungry in a couple of hours, so I'll make a late dinner. Any requests?"

I take a large bite of my sandwich and chew. "Actually..." I swallow hard. "I'm craving Hawaiian pizza like a mo-fo. Any chance we get delivery out here in Bumfuck, Nowhere?"

Ty tenses and stands straighter, looking around me. I feel his presence before I even have to look, but glancing over my shoulder, I see Eric walk into the kitchen with his usual pissed-off expression. He looks as if he's always constipated.

"No delivery," Eric barks. "And if you can't eat with us at normal times, you don't eat until the next meal."

Ty sucks in a sharp breath, but I keep my gaze locked on Eric.

Did he just say what I think he said?

"What is this?" I stand and cross my arms. "A *Beauty and the Beast* plot? Am I forbidden from the west wing too?"

"It's called structure and following rules," he states firmly. God, I want to take a fork to his neck. "And if you can't..."

"You'll put me in the dungeon?" I retort. "Don't you know the candlestick and clock will come alive and save me?"

Eric steps closer, but I hold my ground. I don't give two shits who he is or what he's capable of doing. I'm sick and tired of his attitude toward me when I don't even want to fucking be here. He treats me like it's my fault he has to babysit me.

"Don't tempt me, Madelyn."

"Eric, that's enough." Ty's booming voice comes closer. Grabbing my arm, he pulls me back and steps between Eric and me. "Get the fuck away from her."

"Watch it. You're already in hot water," Eric warns.

"Fuck off." Ty's taller than him, but Eric looks like he

wouldn't think twice about killing him. He's probably fucking Victoria on the side and will literally do anything she asks.

The two of them have a silent stare down as my heart thrashes in my chest, beating faster with every passing second. I don't want Ty to get hurt because of me and my smart-ass mouth, but I also really loathe Eric.

So I do the only thing I know in awkward situations and make jokes.

"If you two murder each other, I'll be able to escape so you might want to pull back your testosterone and relax. In fact..." I clap eagerly. "We should all do some yoga and cleanse our minds and bodies." I smile wide when they both glare at me. "What? It's good for the soul."

Eric huffs before stepping back and finally walks out of the kitchen. Ty scowls at me as if he didn't appreciate my vocal interruption, but hey it got Eric out of here so I'm not even sorry.

"What?" I ask innocently. Shrugging, I take another bite of my BLT and smile.

"Go back to your room when you're done eating. Stay out of his way." Ty's voice is anything but friendly, which is a contrast to how he was being before Eric interrupted us. He steps around me, and before he walks into the hallway, he stops and adds, "And mine."

This day has been fucking weird. After I eat, I do as Ty asks and go to my room. A throbbing headache keeps me planted in bed for most of the evening, and when Eric announces I need to come and eat dinner, I tell him to eat shit. However, he doesn't like that answer and barges into my room.

"What are you doing?" I shout when he grabs my arm and yanks me up. "Don't touch me!"

"You eat when it's time," he responds coldly. What the hell is it with this man and *time*? Like we have anything else to do all damn day and need to be on a strict schedule.

"I can walk by myself. Get your perverted hands off me," I hiss through my teeth.

He responds by squeezing my arm tighter and jerking me down the hallway until we reach the kitchen. I immediately notice only two plates are set at the table.

"Where's Ty?" I ask, walking to one of the chairs.

"Don't worry about him. He's been taken care of."

My stomach drops and nausea surfaces as the contents of my lunch threaten to come up.

What the fuck does *taken care of* mean? I'm afraid to even ask, but I do anyway.

"What's that mean? Is he gone?"

Eric sits in the chair across from me, not looking in my direction.

"Eat. Then I want you back in your room."

"I thought I was allowed to go anywhere," I say, having no appetite. I can tell Eric cooked tonight and though it doesn't look bad, it's nothing compared to Ty's Southern recipes.

"The rules have changed."

It's after nine p.m., and as I pace my bedroom, I can't

stop thinking about Ty and what they did to him. It's all my fault; I should've left him alone and stopped trying to get too close. Being trapped here with nothing to do and no one to talk to is fucking lonely, and when Ty gave me an opening for some kind of friendship, I took it and demanded more.

Now he could be dead because of me.

My head's still pounding, and I can't sleep, so I tiptoe to the kitchen to find some medicine. When I finally do, I swallow down two pills with some water and reluctantly go back to my room. Deciding a hot bath might help, I grab some comfy clothes and one of the plush robes I hung up on my door, then head to the bathroom.

Just as I start to undress, a hard body presses against my back as an arm tightly wraps around my waist and a hand covers my mouth. I immediately try to scream and twist around in his grip, but he's too strong and squeezes me into his chest. Eric's probably twice as strong as I am, but I'm not about to go down without a fight.

"Maddie, quiet," a whispered voice says in my ear, one that I recognize. "It's Ty. I need you not to scream, you hear me?"

Ty? What the hell is going on?

I wiggle against him, trying to look over my shoulder to see for myself. When I'm met with his intense brown eyes and feel his facial hair scratch against my cheek, my body relaxes in his hold.

"I'm not here to hurt you," he reassures, slowly removing his hand. When he's confident I won't yell, he turns me to face him. "I have a plan, but I need you to trust me. We're getting you out of here tonight."

His soft non-threatening voice is different from his normal commanding tone, but I like it. When I trail down his body, I notice he's dressed differently too, similar to what

Liam wears when he's out on a job. Bullet-proof vest and a duty belt around his waist.

"Are you an undercover cop?" I ask quietly.

Ty slowly reveals a grin. "Not exactly, but I was undercover. You need to trust me, okay? Stay in your room and start packing your stuff. I'll be back for you shortly."

My heart rate quickens. "What does that mean? If you're not a cop, then…"

"I'm a friend of Liam's," he tells me. "Tyler Blackwood. I know all about you, Mads."

At the sound of my nickname, my eyes widen in shock. "Oh my God." Blinking, I try to piece this information together. What? How? When? He must've been working for Victoria long before I was kidnapped.

"Is Liam okay? Does he know what's going on?" I ask.

"He's fine as far as I know. I texted him a couple of days ago to let him know I was getting you out, but that's it." He inhales sharply, then looks at his watch. "I reset the cameras, and in a minute, they'll restart so I need to go. You'll hear some noises, and then all the lights are going to go off."

"Wait, what?" I panic.

"Stay here until I come back for you, got it? I need to take care of Eric and then handle Victoria so she doesn't send backup."

This is too much at once, and I feel like I'm going to let him down.

Ty opens the bathroom door, then turns. "Pack your stuff. We have five minutes or less."

Then he walks out.

Frantically, I grab the suitcase and backpack I arrived with, then shove my clothes and books in them. In the midst of it, I hear shouting down the hallway and crashing as if they're fighting. My nerves are shot, and I'm terrified of how this plan will affect Liam, but what other choice do I have? I put on my shoes and a sweatshirt, then impatiently wait for him to return.

Abruptly, everything goes quiet, and then moments later, the power goes off.

I see brightness as my bedroom door opens and blow out a relieved breath when I see Ty with a flashlight.

"Ready? We gotta move."

Gulping, I put on my backpack, and Ty takes my suitcase. "The truck is out back. Let's go."

Ty leads us through the house, and my erratic breathing and the hard pounding of my heart are all that can be heard. What did he do to Eric? Where are we going? What happens if we get caught?

He throws my bags inside, then opens the passenger door. "Buckle up. We're about to race the fuck outta here." Ty winks, then rushes around to the driver's side.

"I see your mind's spinning," Ty says after five minutes. "I know this is a lot to take in, but since Victoria was about to send a replacement for me, I had to execute my plan a little earlier than anticipated."

"And what was your plan exactly?" I ask nervously.

"Well, basically this, but I had hoped to get Eric on board. However, since the bastard's head was so far up Victoria's ass, I realized there was no way it would happen. So, I took matters into my own hands."

I'm too afraid to ask him what he did exactly, so I don't. The less I know, the better in case this doesn't work out. All I need to know is how we're getting out of this.

"How do you know Liam?"

"I actually met him through Mason. I was his boxing trainer in Sacramento before I moved to Vegas and met Liam at the gym one day," he explains, then something clicks in my head.

"I knew I never told you Mason's name!" I point at him. "You slipped!"

We both laugh, but I feel better knowing I wasn't going as crazy as I thought I was being stuck there.

"So, how'd you become one of Victoria's guards anyway?"

He looks over and smirks. "Now that's a story for another day. Right now, we need to get into a different car since this one has a GPS tracker."

I nod, understanding. "Can you at least tell me why then?"

"I knew Liam was in trouble with the O'Learys, and when I offered to help, he told me to stay out of it."

"Which clearly you didn't."

"Nah, not my style. I told him I'd figure out a way to help him but didn't tell him what I was planning in the event they found out. That way he wouldn't be forced to give up any information on me. I knew what Victoria wanted from him and how she was playing him. I fuckin' hate them all, so I was ready to go undercover to get information that'd help Liam out of his fucked-up deal."

"And did you?" I ask eagerly, staring at him in hope. "Get info that'll help him?"

"Oh, I sure fucking did." A wide grin splits his face. "I hadn't expected this little detour assignment to Montana, and I sure as shit wasn't expecting you."

"You knew who I was then?"

"As soon as I heard your name was Maddie, I did. Playing hard ass while wanting to protect you wasn't a walk in the park, and hell, you didn't make it easy either, but I don't regret it."

"Wow…" I say in amazement, my heart softening for this man who's so damn selfless. He risked his own life to help save not only Liam's but also mine. "I don't know how to thank you, Ty. I wish I'd known so I didn't get you into trouble."

"I'm not fucking concerned about Victoria, so don't worry. She'll be handled accordingly," he reassures me. Ty's a fucking badass, and I have so much respect for him that I don't even know how to express it properly.

Twenty minutes later, we're in a little town and switching into a different vehicle outside a brick building. It's pitch black outside, and I can't see a thing, but I trust Ty wholeheartedly.

After an hour passes, his phone rings, and we both see Victoria's name flash on the screen. He previously mentioned he needed to deal with her, but I wasn't sure what that meant.

"Don't say a word," he warns, then answers the call on speakerphone.

"Blackwood," he says in a deep commanding voice.

"What's going on with the generators? Eric isn't answering his phone."

Ty handed me Eric's phone earlier before we switched cars and instructed me to throw it out the window.

"The generator's out of fuel. I'm heading into town to fill up some gas tanks," he answers. "Eric's with Maddie, but if he's not answering, I assume his phone died, and he can't charge it until the power is back on."

"I could've sworn Eric took care of that recently…" she mutters as if speaking to herself. "I want those cameras back up and running immediately!" she barks.

"Yes ma'am. As soon as we get power, they should reboot."

"It's late, and I don't have time to worry about this, so I expect you to handle it."

"Absolutely. I'll text you as soon as it's taken care of," Ty says.

"Good," Victoria says and then hangs up.

I blow out a relieved breath. "What a bitch."

Ty chuckles. "You have no idea." Then he turns off his phone and hands it to me. "Throw this one out too. It has a tracker on it, and I bought a burner phone when I went shopping the other day."

I roll down my window and chuck it. "Now what?"

"I'll text Liam when we're closer to Oregon."

My heart drops into my stomach.

"Wait. We're not going to Sacramento?"

"Not yet. I'm taking you somewhere safe for now. You gotta trust me, okay?"

I do, *mostly*. But that was when I thought he was taking me to California. Now I'm being moved from one secret location to another.

"Okay," I whisper. "How long until I can go home?"

Ty doesn't respond right away, which means it's not going to be an answer I like.

"It depends."

"On?" I prompt. "Tell me."

I don't want to be handled with kid gloves. I want to know all the possibilities of how this could backfire and keep me away from everyone I love.

"On when Victoria releases him," he finally says. "I have enough shit on her to give Liam leverage for a divorce, but it doesn't mean she's gonna let him go without a fight."

"Of fucking course not," I grumble.

"Don't worry." He reaches over and squeezes my hand.

"You have me on your side, and I'll stop at nothing to help Liam. Or you."

Resting against the seat, I try to relax. I'm still comprehending this whole fucking day, but it's hard to wrap my mind around it. Memories of every encounter I've had with Ty over the past two weeks flash in my head. Why he was so invested in me, why he'd be hot one moment and cold the next, why he *cared* more than Eric did—these questions are finally answered.

"Can I ask you something personal?" I ask after more time passes.

"Sure."

"Are you married?

"No."

"Girlfriend?"

"Nope."

"Hmm." I pinch my lips and move them side to side.

"Why are you asking?"

"Why are you single?"

Ty laughs. "This sounds like a dating interview."

"I'm just shocked you aren't taken. It makes me believe there's something wrong with you because it's certainly not your good looks or heart of gold. Do you have a weird third nipple or something? Chicks can be so vain sometimes. And you have that Southern thing going for you, which most girls like, so that's a point in your favor. From what I noticed, you're fit and you're also tall, which women also love. So honestly, what is it? What's wrong with you?"

Ty's silent before he looks at me and cracks a smile. "I've learned you're a rambler, especially when you're nervous or bored, so I'm going to take what you just said with a grain of salt."

I laugh and throw back my head because dammit he's

right. I'm totally a rambler. "Sorry. You're correct. I talk a lot when I feel like I have no control, and right now I'm driving myself crazy with overthinking."

"I told you to trust me, Maddie," he states confidently. "I didn't let Eric near you, nor did you go hungry, and I even bought you tampons you probably didn't need."

I cackle at his words. "You're only proving my point further. The perfect guy. So what's wrong with you? You wanna keep my mind occupied, talk to me about you."

He shrugs, but I catch the corner of his lips as it tilts up. "Alright, I guess I can handle that. We'll be driving all night anyway."

"Good."

"For starters, you can call me Tyler. Ty was what I told everyone, so it'd help me stay in character when I heard it. I'm single because, like Liam, I didn't have the best upbringing. I don't trust myself in a relationship due to past experiences, and now I don't date women long enough to know if I can trust them."

"Well, that certainly sounds like Liam." I half-laugh, half-frown.

Tyler continues to entertain me by telling me a little about growing up in Lawton Ridge and how he got into boxing and became a trainer. It's fascinating.

I end up drifting off, and when Tyler wakes me, I realize we're stopped.

"What's going on?" I ask, looking around and noticing we're at a truck stop in the middle of nowhere.

"I texted Liam to let me know when he was alone and could talk. He just responded. It's time."

CHAPTER EIGHT

LIAM

VICTORIA HAS BEEN sicker than usual, and while I'm somewhat concerned and try to help, she blows me off. I'm not a complete dickhead when someone isn't feeling well, but she's shown her true colors this past week when the truth came out. Sympathy is the last thing she deserves from me. However, I'm damned if I do and damned if I don't. Between the morning sickness and her body recovering from the fender bender, she's extra whiny.

Standing in the kitchen, I make myself a sandwich because it's a safe bet. The other day when I warmed food in the microwave, Victoria nearly castrated me when the smell made her nauseous, so I've resorted to ham and cheese.

As I spread mayo on a piece of bread, my nerves get the best of me. How much longer is this going to go on? I've been so unhinged since I received that text from Tyler. I've been anxiously awaiting an update and have grown more concerned by the silence. No news isn't always good news when dealing with the O'Learys, especially because two people I care about are in a remote location. If anything goes wrong, it could take days for me to find out from Victoria, if she even mentions it.

Pulling my phone from my pocket, I check it in case I missed any calls or text, but there's nothing. After I eat, I change into some workout clothes and go for a run in the gym Victoria has setup in her penthouse, though she never uses it. I'm convinced it was something for her to spend extra money on.

I run until my heart feels as if it will beat straight out of my chest. My shirt is soaked, and I stand with my hands over my head, trying to breathe. Unfortunately, my mind is still on Maddie and Tyler, and I stupidly hoped wearing myself out would force me to think about something else. The stress of all of this is almost too much.

Victoria's game is to make Maddie fall for someone else—like Tyler—and hope I'll stay being her husband and father to her babies. She knows losing Maddie would hurt worse than any physical thing her father could do to me, which is why she did it.

The rest of the day, I try to stay busy and am overly nice to Victoria. It pleases her, but I know it's short-lived. We eat dinner, a pasta dish she ordered from one of her favorite restaurants, and when we're done, we go our separate ways. It's impossible for me to be around her for long periods without wanting to strangle her, so I go to my room and watch TV, wishing I could fall asleep. Not sure why, though, because tomorrow will be the same, and every day will be until I hear that Maddie is safe and out of Victoria's reach.

Just as my eyes begin to feel heavy, my phone vibrates with a text message from the number Tyler contacted me from before. Adrenaline bursts through my veins as I open it, but all it says is to call when I'm alone. Considering it's so late, I'm convinced that Victoria is in bed asleep, but instead of risking it, I get up and check on her.

Most of the lights are off in the house except for a single

lamp in the living room. I cross the space and go to her bedroom where the door is cracked. Carefully, I open it and see she's in bed, snoring with an eye mask over her face. I let out a steady breath and walk back to my room, where I nervously call the number. Immediately, Tyler answers with a chuckle, and relief washes over me because I know at that moment, everything's going to be okay.

"You're alone?" he finally asks, and I can tell I'm on speakerphone.

"Yes, tell me what's going on," I say eagerly. After Tyler explains how he infiltrated the O'Learys, I feel so fucking honored he's on my side. The fact that Victoria asked him to protect Maddie is a miracle, and I'm shocked by how perfectly everything worked out. It's almost as if the universe is on Maddie's and my side.

While chatting with Tyler, I keep my voice low though I want to scream from the rooftops how happy I am. I try not to celebrate too soon because I know this is just the beginning of a bad situation once Victoria finds out they escaped.

"Before I was put on this assignment, I got intel on Victoria that you'll need to get you out of this big fuckin' mess," he says, and I can feel the shift in his mood. "I took a page from your bounty hunter book. I followed her for about a month while you were back in California. I have photographs and even have audio recordings because I bugged her car."

My eyes go wide. "What the hell. How'd you manage that?"

"She needed an oil change on the Mercedes she drives when she's doing shady ass shit. It literally took me an hour to get everything installed, and she has zero idea. Honestly, after being on this side of things, I'm convinced all the O'Leary kids are a bunch of dumbasses."

A smile touches my lips. "I've noticed. So, you followed her. What did you get photos of exactly?" I question, knowing she's sly and can make up lies about anything.

"The DeFrancos," he says so nonchalantly.

I feel as if he's going to drop a huge ass bomb, one that Victoria won't even suspect. "Does the name Mickey ring a bell to you?" Tyler asks.

Pausing for a moment, I replay the conversations we've had in the past when they've been brought up. I know for a fact they're mortal enemies of the O'Learys, and even Johnny has made off-colored remarks about murder anytime they're mentioned. Closing my eyes, I think back to the convo in the bar, and the couple of times JJ has gone off about them, then distinctly remember hearing Mickey's name. "Yeah, actually it does."

"Victoria has been fucking him. I have photos. I have audio. Her father might kill her when he finds out. That is, *if* he finds out. They've been secretly seeing each other for years, knowing their families would never approve. The pregnancy was a surprise for them both, and you just so happened to be in the wrong place at the right time," Tyler explains. "But I think it's enough to make her back off and to free you. From what I've seen and heard these past several weeks, I think Victoria would rather have a divorce on her record than to be known for betraying the family."

"Wow," is all I can say. "A few days ago, we got into a fender bender, and she went to the ER. They did an ultrasound, and that's when I found out she's farther along than she claimed. It was confirmed then the babies weren't mine. She knew all along but doesn't give a shit and said it doesn't matter since we're technically married. Now it all makes fucking sense. She needed a father since she couldn't tell the truth that she was sleeping with the family's sworn enemy," I explain. I replay everything, learning about the correct due date and how smug Victoria acted about it. She knew they were Mickey's babies and needed a scapegoat, and I've been wrapped up in her deceptive web ever since. The marriage was only the first step that led to the pregnancy. It makes me sick knowing how much she had planned beforehand. Considering the magnitude of hate her father has for the DeFrancos, I imagine she could've married anyone, but the position I was in made me easy prey.

Tyler lets out a breath. "Dude. She's a psycho, and it doesn't surprise me at all that she used you. They were sneaking around so much that I'm honestly surprised no one found out. If Johnny did, he'd disown her. At this point, she has more to lose than you do. What do they call that in poker?" he mocks.

"Shut the hell up," I say. "But thank you so much. Knowing the truth and actually having proof might actually take her down. For the first time, in a long-ass time, I think I might actually be in shock."

"You owe me, man."

"I do. I owe you everything. My life, actually. I don't know how I'm going to repay you," I admit, feeling so fucking thankful.

By the sound of his voice, I can tell he's smiling. "I'll think of something, I'm sure."

"I'd much rather pay my debt to you than Victoria, but I'm not going to pretend to be married to you," I jokingly warn. "Seriously, thank you."

"I know, I know. But I am a catch," he jokes, and for the first time in weeks, I genuinely smile.

"So Maddie, how is she? Where are you? Where are you going?"

"Hold on, Tonto. Not so fast. She's right here, and she's fine, but first, we need to activate the next step in my brilliant plan. You need to get all of the proof I have as soon as possible. Once Victoria discovers we're gone, no one's safe until you have your evidence."

"Got it," I say. "Tell me what to do."

"You're gonna need to go to my apartment and get everything as soon as you can break away. Make sure you're not followed because I don't want her to be tipped off when Eric manages to get into contact with her. Once the live feed on the cameras doesn't return, and I don't answer her calls, she'll grow more concerned and send someone out here. You're a bounty hunter, so you know how to be strategic, but right now it's going to be so fucking important."

"I understand," I tell him, my heart pounding hard. I can't afford to screw this up.

"I'll text you the passcode to get into my apartment when we hang up. You'll need to go into my bedroom and under my bed is a laptop. It has files of photos and audio recordings of her with Mickey. It's all labeled, so it shouldn't be hard to find. Once you have that, go through everything and print out the pictures, then send the audios to your phone so you can present it all to her. I have everything uploaded to my iCloud so even if she destroys what you show her, I have backups. If any of that just so happened to make it to Johnny, Victoria would lose everything and be out of the business just as she said she wanted but without her trust fund. I don't think the mafia princess could handle being in the real world. Most people can't." There's more in his statement than he leads on, considering his past, but I don't comment. "I'll keep

Maddie safe until all is clear. You need to secure your freedom, so until she signs the divorce papers, none of us can go home."

I soak in everything he's just said, my mind spinning as I try to absorb it all. This bitch is about to have the shock of her life once I get my hands on the proof I need. "Thank you so damn much." I can't say it enough.

"Now on to your other questions. We're out of Montana, but honestly, I think it's best if I don't tell you where we're heading just yet. If you don't know, then she can't torture it out of you or something. You'll be the first person she confronts, but I can assure you, Maddie will be more than safe with me."

My heart races just thinking about her. I haven't seen her in two weeks, and I miss her so much. "Now don't go fallin' in love with my girl."

"I don't know. She's pretty charming."

Maddie chuckles in the background, which confirms she's heard the whole conversation.

I groan. "If you weren't saving my ass, I'd be kickin' yours."

"You have nothing to worry about, man," he reassures me, though I know Tyler would never betray me.

"Can I talk to her?" I ask eagerly.

Tyler laughs. "I'm surprised it took you this long to ask. Just one second."

It seems as if time stands still as I wait for him to take me off speakerphone and hand it over to her.

"Hi."

I nearly fall to my knees at the sweet sound.

It takes so much for me not to bombard her with questions. "Mads, are you okay? I've been worried sick about you."

She snorts with a low laugh. "Never been better. Your friend has been taking good care of me."

"Hopefully not *too* good," I tease, causing her to laugh, and it's music to my ears. "God, I've missed you so damn much. You have no idea, Mads."

A second passes before she speaks. "I've missed you too, but I'm still pissed at you for keeping secrets from me."

"I don't blame you, and I more than deserve it after this fucking shitstorm I got us in. I'm content with spending the rest of my life trying to prove to you how damn sorry I really am," I tell her earnestly.

"It might take that long," she jokes. "Honestly, I've been concerned about you too, hoping you were okay with the Wicked Witch of the West."

Knowing she was thinking about me makes me smile. "We're gonna get out of this, baby. I'm just so goddamn happy you're out of there and with Tyler," I say. "He'll keep you safe. You can trust him."

"Yeah, considering he bought me tampons and chocolate, he seems like a good guy." She chuckles, and then I hear him laugh as if it's an inside joke between them. I'm jealous she's been with him and not me, and while I shouldn't feel that way, I'm envious of anyone who gets to spend time with her.

"He didn't," I deadpan.

"Yep, he did, but he's the chump who fell for it," she admits, laughing softly.

"Tell him what else you asked for…" I hear Tyler prompt in the background, but Maddie laughs and tells him to stop eavesdropping. Considering they're in the same car, I chuckle.

"Do I even want to know?" I ask.

"Probably not. It was when I was trying to get under their skin because I was bored as hell," she says. "Don't worry, Eric got the brunt of my sarcasm and annoying remarks."

Memories flash of when Victoria let me see Maddie on camera for the first time, and she and Tyler looked like they were having a great time. I'm glad he was able to ease her fear of being there and let loose a little, but the regret I have fills me deeply. She shouldn't have been there in the first place.

"Good. Guy looked like a douchebag."

"Even more than Hunter when I first met him." Maddie cackles, and I do too.

It feels so easy chatting with her almost as if nothing has changed between us, but I know better. We're not out of this yet. "Maddie, I'm really fucking sorry about this, for lying to you and ultimately getting you involved when I knew the risks. I never wanted any of this to happen, but I couldn't stay away from you. I don't think I can apologize enough—"

"Liam," she interrupts. "I don't blame you for this. I was upset and hurt at first, but after I've had time to process everything, I understood why you didn't tell me. If the positions were reversed, I think I would've done the same thing to protect you and our relationship. I trust you, Liam. You've always had my best interests at heart, always tried to keep me safe and protected as if I'm going to break. I can't fault you for any of that. I do hate the way things ended between us the last time, though."

My emotions get the best of me, but I tuck them away as usual. "Me too. I've only always wanted the best for you, and there are times when I felt like I wasn't, that I'd never be good enough regardless of how much you pushed. Doesn't help your sisters are scary as hell," I say with a grin.

"You're right. Trust me when I say they already want to castrate you," she slyly mentions. "Especially Sophie."

"I know. I can't wait to tell them everything and clear the air. They deserve to know the truth. I'm sick of lying to them, and I hate the way they looked at me, as if I'm a monster."

Maddie snickers. "You're not the monster. You're just married to one."

I sigh. "That much is true," I agree.

"You're breaking up a little bit," she says, and I can hear Tyler in the background mention they'll lose service soon. Considering they're more than likely traveling down remote mountain roads, it doesn't surprise me in the least. While I want to talk to her all night long, I know I can't, and our time is coming to an end.

"Alright. I'll let you go then," I tell her.

"Okay, please take care of yourself. As long as you're in Vegas around that psycho, you're not safe."

A grin touches my lips, and I find it adorable she's concerned about me. "I can handle her especially since Tyler got me a Get Out of Jail Free card. Be careful, and listen to him, as hard as it is."

She snorts. "Whatever you say."

I grin at her sassy tone. Classic Maddie.

"And Mads?"

"Yeah?"

I hesitate for a moment, imagining a different way for how I'd tell her this for the first time, but if I've learned anything this past year, it's not to take a second for granted. I can't hold it in anymore. "I love you," I tell her. "I love you so fucking much."

The other end goes silent, and for a moment, I'm scared she didn't hear me because we lost connection, but then I hear her sniffles. Emotion briefly takes over before she speaks. "Says the man who thought he was incapable of love," she says softly, then continues, "I love you too. I always have."

I feel as if I'm dreaming, and if I am, I don't want to wake up. Hearing her say those words back means more than she'll ever realize. It means everything.

"Good night, sweetheart. We'll talk soon."

"Good night, Hulk."

I press end and sit on the edge of my bed, my body buzzing. Every text message and call from that number is deleted before I place my phone on the charger. There's no way I'm leaving any sort of evidence behind for Victoria to find. I'm filled with shock and awe, and I'm so damn grateful for Tyler. The man is honorable and loyal, and without him, I'm not sure how I would've gotten us out of this mess.

After a while, I lie on my bed, adrenaline pumping through my veins as I figure out what to do next. Somehow, I have to break away from Victoria's hold and go to Tyler's to get his laptop. The only problem is time because it's running out fast, and she'll want to retaliate any way she can once she discovers Maddie is gone. Eventually, I'll have all the cards in my hand, and she'll have nothing. It's about damn time.

CHAPTER NINE

MADDIE

WE'VE BEEN DRIVING for hours, and my back is killing me from sitting for so long, but I'd sit for days if it meant escaping Victoria's wrath. The only thing I really regret is not being able to see her reaction when she learns what Tyler did and that she no longer has a hold on us. Thinking about it brings an evil smile to my face, but I'm sure Liam will fill me in on her reaction when we're reunited. I just hope he's careful because he's about to be in an extremely risky situation. Hopefully, Victoria doesn't blame him for this because he didn't have anything to do with it, but I'm happy he's aware of it now so he doesn't think the worst happened to me. Undoubtedly, Victoria would use me missing to her advantage as she played puppet master in the background and taunted him that she disposed of me. She'd say anything to him to get what she wants and has proven as much.

Liam.

Just the thought of his name causes my breath to hitch and my body to tingle. Even though we're miles apart, he still somehow has that effect on me. Liam told me he loved me, and I knew with every fiber of my being that he meant it.

Heat rushed through me, and his confession left me briefly speechless, which doesn't happen very often. The words burrowed deep into my soul, implanting themselves on my heart. Repeating the words back felt so natural, because the truth is, I *do* love him. I've always loved him and there's no denying how I've felt for years, but being in love with him is an indescribable feeling. It's always been more than a stupid little crush, and I knew the first time we met there was a connection that neither of us could explain. I refused to give up on us regardless of how much he wished I could. Being relentless paid off, but now we're in a world of a mess, and I'm not sure how we're going to get out of it.

I wish I could talk to him again although his words are on replay in my mind. Not being able to speak with Liam or know if he was okay was more difficult than I ever imagined it would be. The unknown of what was going on in the outside world cut through me like a knife, especially after Victoria used Liam as bait to force me to leave. She knew he was my weakness and understands I'm his, so of course she manipulated the situation to her advantage and played us against each other, and it worked. She's devious and cunning, and has all the key qualities of a truly evil person.

Liam's voice was both soft and gruff, and I could hear the worry coating his tone, but I hope I was able to ease his mind, even if it was only slightly. I trust Tyler and so does Liam. I'm safe now or at least I feel that way, but it doesn't mean I won't constantly look over my shoulder to make sure we're not being followed. I've been through too much to walk around blindly, and I'm not sure I'll ever be able to again.

That's the worst part about this whole thing. Even if Tyler's plan works and Liam's free and we're able to go home, I'll never truly feel like this is really over. I'll still jump at dark shadows and wonder if any of the O'Learys will come and finish the job for her instead. I know what Victoria is capable of, but I imagine her father is much worse. Even with the evidence Liam is going to present to her, no one knows how she'll react. She could shoot him right there, and then I'd be on the run for the rest of my life.

The dark thoughts cause a nervous shiver down my spine.

This will work, I reassure myself. *It has to.*

As I watch the headlights of the car reveal the narrow road ahead, I become more lost in my head. I wish I could predict the future and knew how this will all play out. There are too many bad scenarios, but I have to have faith. I'll be happy when this is nothing more than a faded nightmare of a memory.

I lean my head back on the seat. As my eyes flutter closed, I listen to the quiet music as we travel down the road. Events from the past two weeks flash by in a blink from Victoria showing up announcing the pregnancy to her threatening me to leave. Then there's Tyler, who has risked so fucking much to help Liam and me. I'm not sure I'll ever be able to properly repay him for his selflessness, but I'll never stop trying.

Eventually the car slows and we roll into a large, secluded parking lot. I must've drifted off because when I look at the clock, I see it's after seven in the morning, and the sun is beginning to rise. Sitting up, I rub my hand across my face and look around. My back and neck hurt for being in the car for so long, but I suck it up. I have no right to complain about any of this.

"Oh, look. Sleeping Beauty is awake," Tyler teases. Glancing over at him, I notice how exhausted he looks. I feel bad that he drove while I slept on and off.

"Where are we?" I finally ask because nothing looks familiar.

"Portland."

"Already?" I look back at the clock. He told me where we were going when we first got on the road, and it seems we've made good time, though we've been driving for nearly nine hours. We only stopped for gas, and Tyler made it very clear there'd be no emergency bathroom breaks. Not as if there were tons of places to go anyway, considering how remote the areas were. I'd much prefer a gas station bathroom than squatting in the dark woods. Regardless, it seemed like time passed in a blink.

"Told you I wasn't stopping until we got here unless absolutely necessary." He grins, and I roll my eyes at his stubbornness. "I have some friends who live here. I trust them with my life, so I thought it'd be the safest bet for us." Tyler pulls his phone from his pocket and sends a text, then reclines his seat back before he closes his eyes. I'm sure he's tired from driving, so I don't give him shit about it even if I really want to. At one point, I offered to take over just to give him a break, but he refused to let me and was overly adamant that he had it under control. Since I don't drive at night that much, I didn't argue.

Although I slept for a few hours, I'm still beat, and my muscles feel sore and stiff. When I open the car door, I get out and stretch. Tyler rolls down the window and barks at me. "What are you doing? Get back inside."

"Geez, I just need a minute. My limbs feel like jelly." I stand tall and raise my hands above my head allowing each vertebra to pop before bending over and touching my toes. Quickly, I do a few arm reaches, then get back in the car. Tyler looks at me when I rebuckle. "We can't be too safe right now. I don't know all of Victoria's connections, considering who her father is, or when she'll put a search out for the both of us. Perhaps she has already. The fewer people we come across, the better, because she has the money to have us found."

I look around, not seeing a soul in sight. Not even a freaking bird in the sky. "There's literally no one around us, but okay, I get it. Victoria kinda gave me PTSD too, especially after I found out she had me followed."

"It makes me even more happy that she'll be getting a taste of her own medicine soon. The problem with the O'Learys is no one really questions or tests them. They play by their own rules and laws and aren't used to anyone retaliating, other than the DeFrancos, which is why they don't like each other. Everything's gonna work out, Maddie, but we have to be smart and not make it too easy for her. I promise, she has the money to have the entire underworld searching for us by the time the sun sets again." Before Tyler can say anything else, his phone buzzes with a text. He opens it and grins. "Finally."

"What is it?" I study him.

He yawns. "We've got a condo setup on the other side of town for as long as we need."

"How do you know all these people who are so willing to help?"

With a lifted eyebrow, Tyler smirks. "It's probably best if you don't know the answer to that question."

I open my mouth, then close it, knowing even if I push him, he won't crack. Tyler has given me enough information to feel as if I know him, but he's still reserved and keeps a lot to himself. He's more like Liam than he even realizes. The two of them are like vaults, keeping their secrets tucked away.

Readjusting his seat back to normal, he pulls us onto the

main road, and we travel through downtown. I can't help looking at the tall buildings as we pass. Any other time, I'd want to explore it all and do the touristy type things in the city, but it's not safe for us to be seen. I really hate Victoria.

Eventually, we arrive at a complex, and Tyler drives around to the back, then parks. He turns off the car and sighs before looking at me. "Ready to see your new home for a bit?" he asks with a hint of amusement.

"As long as you continue to cook for me," I tease with a bright smile.

"We'll see."

I follow his lead once he gets out, grabbing our bags from the back seat. After a minute, I ask if he wants help, but he shakes his head. We walk down the sidewalk, and when Tyler punches a code into the door, it unlocks. Once inside, I'm shocked by how big and nice it is. This condo is equally as fancy as Victoria's mansion, but not as large. It's an open concept with hardwood floors, a giant ass TV, sectional sofa, and a loft that oversees the living room.

"Whose place is this? Damn," I say with my mouth open, knowing whoever lent this home to Tyler has a lot of money.

He chuckles. "Yeah, not answering that question either."

"You are literally no fun."

Tyler sets my bag on the floor, and I explore the kitchen and bathroom. The fridge is completely stocked with food, and I notice several types of herbal teas in the pantry. I'd be lying if I said I wasn't excited about the cast iron tub that's connected to the only bedroom. The master with a king-size bed has a patio with a small flower garden attached to it. This place is gorgeous, and a selfish part of me wouldn't mind staying here a while.

"You can have the bedroom if you want," I tell Tyler when I meet him back in the living room.

"Nah, I'm gonna sleep on the couch. I am a Southern gentleman, after all," he says with a forced drawl, then adds, "And Liam would kick my ass if I made you sleep on the sofa." Tyler laughs, kicking off his boots. He sits and yawns just as his phone goes off.

"Fuck yes!" He's grinning wide as if his favorite football team just won the Super Bowl.

"What?" I search his face as he replies to the text.

"Liam did it." Tyler's ecstatic, finding a burst of energy, and no longer looks like he's about to pass out. "He has the laptop with the pictures and audio."

My eyes go wide, and I start laughing. "Already? That's incredible!"

"It's not over yet, though. Now we have to be patient and wait for him to put everything into motion. He has what he needs to take that bitch down a few pegs or completely destroy her. It's Victoria's choice. I'd personally destroy her and send it all anonymously to her father without giving her a chance, but I'm letting Liam take the lead on this one."

I sit next to Tyler on the couch, knowing we can't celebrate too soon because this is just the beginning. "What do you think she'll do? Like, you don't think Victoria will hurt him, right?" Every scenario sprints through my mind, and that's when the worry begins to take over. It starts in the pit of my stomach and forcefully rushes through me. I don't think I could handle it if something terrible happened to Liam, not when we're so close to having it all. As if Tyler reads my thoughts, he tilts his head and pats my hand.

"Hey. Liam is one of the most resourceful people I know. Victoria needs Liam more than he needs her, and the evidence will drive that home. She'll be undoubtedly blindsided when she finds out we escaped, and I'd be lying if I said there won't be issues regarding that. Based on what I know about Victoria, she's going to lose her shit, but she'll play it off like nothing happened. I'm sure she'll even tell Liam she got rid of you to look like she planned it all because she's a manipulator. If worse comes to worse, I'll send the shit to her dad myself. I was tempted more than once, but I'd rather give Liam the opportunity to bargain with her first. The two of them might be able to find common ground where everyone wins here."

"Is it possible to ever walk away from the O'Learys, though?" I challenge, arching a brow.

Tyler sucks in a deep breath and exhales it slowly. "That I don't know. She's a spoiled bitch and is unpredictable, but she's been sleeping with the son of her father's mortal enemy and is pregnant with DeFranco DNA. It's disrespectful to the family name and a stab in the back to her father. It's an unforgivable offense, so she really has no other option but to do what Liam says. While I was being trained, I'd overheard that Johnny shot his own brother for doing some shady shit, and he put a bullet in both his arms and thighs as a warning. Then he left him to bleed until someone finally took him to the hospital. He needed surgery and was hospitalized for months. His own fuckin' brother. One of the other guards said Johnny only went to visit him to remind him where his loyalty better stay or next time the bullet will be in his head. He's a goddamn monster, so tell me, what makes his daughter safe from his wrath on something as bad as sleeping with the enemy and getting pregnant? She isn't. Relatives will want blood and will want an example made out of her, pregnant or not. The fact that Victoria's children will be half of them and half DeFranco means she better fucking run to avoid her father's retaliation. He's cold and merciless. If she wants to protect herself, the babies, and Mickey, she'd be smart to do anything Liam says."

The thought makes bile rise up my throat. While I despise Victoria, she is pregnant, and it's disgusting to think someone would hurt a woman carrying not one but two babies. Then again, the O'Learys are despicable people. It doesn't surprise me, though it should. This isn't a life I know, and I've been thrust into it without warning. I close my eyes and say a silent prayer, hoping Liam is careful and that it all works out in our favor.

Tyler yawns again, and I stand, allowing him to fully stretch out on the couch. "You should get some sleep, Beanstalk."

Leaning back, he adjusts a throw pillow and grabs a small blanket that doesn't fully cover his body. "I'm just gonna nap for a few hours."

"Sounds good. I think I'm going to do some yoga and meditate. I'm overly anxious and won't be able to rest anyway."

He nods, closing his eyes. "Just don't go outside or get into any trouble. If my phone rings and it's Liam, answer it. He's going to check in later if he can."

"Don't worry, I'll be a good girl," I tease, then turn serious. "Tyler?"

"Yeah?"

I fall to my knees and wrap my arms around him the best I can in his lying down position. His body stiffens as I take him off guard, but then he relaxes and wraps his free arm around my back. "Thank you for risking everything for us." I smile against his chest, hoping he understands how much his sacrifice means to me.

"Liam would do the same for me without hesitation," he states matter-of-factly, and I wonder about what they've been through already.

"I would too," I admit, pulling back and grinning. "Good

night, get some sleep. Those dark bags under your eyes aren't a good look for you." Then I grab my stuff, turn off the light, and leave him be.

As soon as I walk into the bedroom, I sit on the mattress and pull off my shoes. Then I fall back, closing my eyes and taking in several calm breaths. I won't be able to think straight until Liam checks in and tells us what happened.

Does Victoria have a gun? A knife? Will she try to silence Liam before he can beat her at her own game? Obviously if I'm thinking about these things, Liam already has. Being a bounty hunter has allowed him to always be two steps ahead of his opponent, but when it comes to the goddamn mob, he needs to be *miles* ahead. I wish I could do something more, but this situation is out of my control, and it makes me feel helpless. I hate this.

Right now, all I want to do is call my sisters. I wish I could talk to Sophie and Lennon and tell them everything that's happened so they'll stop worrying. I want her to know I'm with Tyler, Mason's old trainer, and that I'm safe. There's a lot of explaining to do, but I don't even know where to start. They need to know who Victoria really is and how this affects all of them. The magnitude of it hits me like a ton of bricks because it doesn't seem real. So much has happened in so little time.

CHAPTER TEN

LIAM

RELIEF DOESN'T EVEN PROPERLY EXPLAIN what I feel when I get Tyler's laptop and see all his files. The pictures and the audio—the evidence of her lies and betrayal to her family—give me everything I need to demand a divorce. Her hands are going to be tied to do whatever the fuck I say when I shove it all in her face because with one click, I'll email everything over to her father, and I'll be damned sure she knows that, too.

After ending the call last night, I checked on Victoria, and she was sound asleep. She hasn't been feeling well, so there's no way of knowing when she'll be up again puking her guts out or asking for something from me. I need to act fast if I'm going to sneak out of her penthouse.

Deciding to wait a few hours, I slept until five and then left a note saying I was leaving to get her something to eat and drink. The smoothie shop across town is her favorite and opens early for the gym rats, so it was believable. I went over to Tyler's first and found what I needed to finish this shitstorm.

Since I'm a nice guy and all, I did go and get her stupid

strawberry-banana-flavored drink after I picked up the prints of the digital photos I ordered. I'm making sure my presentation is clearly laid out, giving her two options.

One: File for divorce and sign the papers, letting me and everyone I love go for good.

Two: Tell her daddy the truth and let him decide her punishment.

If she's smart and wants to live, she'll pick the former.

"Where the fuck have you been?" she shouts the second I walk into her room. She's leaning against the headboard, raging pissed.

I'm fully confident she'll be changing her attitude in less than five minutes.

"Didn't you read my note?" I ask nicely, setting her smoothie down on the table next to her bed.

"You left almost two hours ago." She holds up her phone. "I get a notification every time someone opens the front door."

I restrain from rolling my eyes. Of course she fucking does.

"Well, my dear wife, I had some errands to run," I say in an overly sweet tone, which immediately makes her suspicious as she eyes me carefully. This is the first time I've left for more than an hour, knowing if I didn't return, she'd give Maddie my punishment.

Not this time.

Victoria throws the covers off her body and pushes herself off the bed. "You better watch your tone, Liam."

"Or what?" I ask, crossing my hands in front of me with a large manilla envelope between my fingers.

Her eyes lower, and she finally notices I have something. "What is that?"

I bring it to my chest and slowly open it, pulling out the

first eight-by-ten photo of her and Mickey fucking in his car. "I'm so glad you asked. Let me show you."

The moment she lays eyes on it, her evil grin drops. Her shoulders straighten as she swallows hard. "Am I supposed to know what this is?"

The photo is dark, and you can't one hundred percent see who the people inside are, but unlucky for her, Tyler took multiple shots of the car, the license plate, and even used night vision settings to get clear shots of their faces.

"Maybe these will help jumpstart your memory…" I set one after another on the bed, letting her see each one of her and Mickey.

Them sneaking into a bathroom.

Them in a dark-lit bar in a corner, her lips attached to his cock.

Them in his bed, completely naked.

I'm not even gonna ask Tyler how he got that one.

A shiver runs through my body at the lengths he went to get these. Grateful doesn't even begin to describe how I feel.

"Where the fuck did you get these?" she finally hisses after examining each picture, knowing she can't argue her way out of it. It's crystal clear who the people are in them.

"What's it matter, princess?" I dip my head down and speak low, "You're not the only one with friends in low places." Then I take out my phone and play one of the audio files I sent to myself. Tyler managed to record them talking, and it's when Victoria calls him Mickey Baby and he calls her Sweet Tits. She waves a hand in the air, and I turn it off.

"Big deal," she scoffs, crossing her arms. "You won't do anything with them." Her confidence is laughable, considering her bottom lip is trembling.

"On the contrary, I think Daddy dearest wouldn't be so happy to see his only daughter with the family's nemesis.

Didn't the DeFrancos betray your family? Mickey's grandfather stole millions and tainted the O'Leary name for generations, causing a forty-year brawl between them. Amazing what you can find when you know the right people." I smirk, then continue while her jaw hits the floor. "Not to mention what Johnny will do once he finds out Mickey's the one who knocked you up and is the real father. I doubt Daddy's going to welcome Mickey into your family with open arms. I'm guessing more like a bullet between the eyes. Wow…" I shake my head in amusement. "Imagine the horror on his face when he learns of your betrayal. You said it yourself. You wouldn't put it past your father to kill you if you stepped out of line. Those poor babies. Gonna be orphans. Or dead too."

She inches closer, reaching out before clamping her fingers around my arm. "You won't do that, Liam."

"And why's that?"

Victoria retreats and places her hands on her hips. "I have Maddie."

"Hmm…that's right." I put a finger on my chin, pretending to be concerned. "You give me a divorce, and I won't send these to your father."

She scoffs. "You send those to my father, and Maddie pays."

I tsk. "I'm pretty sure you and Mickey will be the ones paying."

Victoria walks around me and grabs her iPad from her nightstand. "I'll tell my men to kill her." She returns, standing in front of me. "Unless you hand everything over. Duplicates, copies. Everything." Victoria looks me dead in the eyes, and in about five seconds, she'll realize Maddie's gone.

I lean down and whisper softly, "Then do it."

Her eyes widen in shock. "Liam, I'm serious. If I give the order to shoot her, they won't think twice about it."

"And your father will know the truth." I shrug. Victoria swallows hard. "Oh wait…" I snap my fingers, smiling. "I don't need to bargain with you because you have nothing I want, and I have *everything* you want."

"What does that mean? You'd never let Maddie get hurt."

"Correcto." I point my finger at her. "Why don't you show me how she's doing on your little surveillance cam?"

Immediately, she signs into her iPad and opens the app, then logs on. I watch as she swipes, looking from room to room in the cabin with no one in sight.

"This is impossible," she mutters.

Walking behind Victoria, I look over her shoulder. "Hmm…interesting. Looks like it's empty."

"What the fuck did you do?" she shouts, tossing her iPad on the bed. "Where are my guards?"

"Like I said, princess. You're not the only one who has connections."

She grinds her teeth, contemplating her next move. Before she can walk around me, I grab her wrist and pull her back into my chest. With my lips to her ear, I speak low. "Don't think so. You're not the only one with a gun, and as much as I'd really hate to use it, especially on a pregnant woman, I will if I have to defend myself."

I managed to get a gun from Tyler's place since I knew Victoria kept one in her bedroom. Shooting me was her only option to get out of this, but I'm not about to let her do that. "You have two options," I whisper in her ear. "Give me a divorce and this all ends for good. Confess I'm not the father so your dad doesn't come after me, and we both walk away without pissing him off. Or he gets all the evidence of your betrayal. If he doesn't kill you for it, he'll for sure wipe you of your little trust fund, and you'll be out on your ass. In fact, he'd probably keep you alive and feed you to the wolves instead. Plenty of people would love to get their hands on a mafia princess." I hum, knowing it'll piss her off. "You could shoot me now, but just know if I don't come home in one piece, the photos will be sent to him from someone else. Either way, baby, you lose if you don't obey *my* orders this time."

"Let me go," she growls.

Slowly, I remove my arms, and she jumps away. "Just stay married to me for a year, after the twins are born, then I'll grant you the divorce. I'll tell my family it's my fault, and no one has to know the whole story."

Oh, hello bargaining. I expected you.

She's desperate. Neither options are favorable to her, but I gotta say, the truth not being revealed should be an obvious choice.

"No," I say firmly, then twist my ring off and flick it into the air. She watches with horror as it flies across the room. I've been wearing that dreaded thing since we announced the marriage in July. To keep up the act around my friends, I wore it at all times. Feels good to finally get rid of the damn thing. "I want papers drawn up today. We both sign and then await a court date. You let me walk away and leave us alone, for good."

She shakes her head. "Being a pregnant divorcee would be as bad as the truth. I can't."

I shrug nonchalantly. "Okay then." I take my phone and start swiping.

"Wait! Wait, please!" She reaches for my cell, but I retreat so she can't grab it. Victoria stays silent as if she's trying to buy time, but my patience is wearing thin. It looks like she needs a reminder of what she's done.

Shoving my phone in my front pocket, I steeple my fingers. "Let's go down memory lane, shall we? You start fucking Mickey DeFranco. Damn, he must be good because you kept going back for more. Even though you told me months ago you don't do relationships, I'm thinking you have real feelings for him. You know it's wrong to be with him, so of course it has to be a secret. No one can ever find out. But...oopsies. You fall pregnant. Now what? You're Catholic, so abortion is out of the question. However, getting hitched without a big church ceremony would be more forgivable, but who's gonna be the lucky bastard to walk down the aisle with you?" I snap my fingers. "JJ's gambling buddy. He owes the family a shit ton of money, so saving my life and my debt being forgiven meant I now owe you big time. I'm desperate and thankful to be alive, so I take your six-month agreement and become your husband. If only that was the actual deal you stuck to. You knew the only way for me to believe you're pregnant is for us to have sex so you coerce me into it, knowing my hands are tied due to your threats of hurting my friends or telling your father. If he found out our marriage was a sham, he'd kill me instantly, so I had no choice. So that brings me to the moment you arrive at my house two weeks ago with my father and announce you're having twins!" I flash a crooked smile at her. "You have me followed, ruin the only relationship I've ever wanted, and then you fucking kidnap the woman I love. So please, Victoria, tell me how I should have any fucking sympathy for *you*..."

"You won't hurt me," she states oddly. "You're a lot of things, but you're not a monster who'd hurt a pregnant woman."

I see red at her challenge, as if I'm weak and should buy into her pity party. She's trying to use reverse psychology on me, and it's not gonna work. I stalk toward her until her back presses against the glass balcony doors, then I lower my face to hers. "You're absolutely fuckin' right. I'm not like you or your family, but that doesn't mean I can't have you thrown off this balcony. I'll make sure it looks like a goddamn suicide. After all, you did betray your family and you'd rather die than face your father. Right, honey?" I mock in a snarky tone. "You wanna play this fucking game with me?"

Victoria swallows hard, and it's the first time since we've met that I see real fear in her eyes. The last thing I want to do is hurt her, but scaring her into releasing me is the only option I have left. She has to believe I'll really send the evidence to her father, and since it's my only weapon, I'm using it to my maximum potential.

"Fine," she says softly.

I tilt my head. "What was that?"

She groans, narrowing her eyes at me. "I said *fine*!"

Slowly, I reveal a satisfied grin. "Good. I'm glad you finally came to your senses. I really didn't want to have to go to plan B." I shoot her a wink, which makes her glare at me harder.

"What was plan B?" she boldly asks.

I'm so fired up with adrenaline rushing through my blood, I don't think twice about grabbing the gun out of my waistband, taking the silencer out of my back pocket, and twisting it to the barrel. Then in one swift movement, I point it at her head and undo the safety.

She inhales sharply with a gasp, shock and horror written all over her face.

"As I said, I'm really happy we came to an agreement."

"You *are* a monster," she says.

I shrug. "Guess I learned it from the best." Then I lower my weapon, clicking on the safety, and shove it back into my jeans. "And, Victoria, if you do try anything, I know where your little boy toy lives."

"You're cruel," she spits after I walk toward the bed. "Maddie was never in danger. She was at a luxurious cabin with cable, food, a gym, and a hot tub. I didn't hurt a hair on her."

"You did the second you blackmailed her into leaving me," I retort. "And I'm gonna be watching you until the second our divorce is finalized. In fact, you better look over your shoulder for the rest of your life because trust me, I have no problem giving your father that info. He might be able to accept his grandchildren are half DeFrancos, but he'll never forgive you, and he won't spare Mickey's life," I remind her. "So from this moment on, you stay in line. You mess with me or anyone I love, and he'll find out. I'm not the only one who has copies either. You have one week to get our divorce papers drawn up and signed. Got it?"

CHAPTER ELEVEN

MADDIE

EVER SINCE LIAM confirmed he got the computer, I've barely breathed as we wait for the news that he's confronted her. Not knowing what's being said or how Victoria's reacting drives me insane. I know Liam can take care of himself, but that bitch is a fucking psycho. What if she lets him leave and then retaliates ten times harder? She has an abundance of resources and money and could end all of us with a snap of her fingers.

From the phone conversation with Liam and what Tyler has told me, there's enough evidence of her affair that would shun her from the family. But will it be enough for her to let Liam go and give him a divorce? I can't help but feel like no matter what he does or says, it'll never be over.

After an hour of pacing in the bedroom and doing some yoga, I decide to try out the bathtub and hopefully ease my mind. I'm too worked up to sleep even though my body is tired. I won't be able to fully rest until Liam is here, and I can feel his heartbeat against me.

"Maddie?" My eyes bolt open at the sound of Tyler's voice on the other side of the door.

"Yeah?"

"Doing okay?"

"Yes, I'll be out in a moment," I call out and realize how cold the water around me feels. Shit, I must've dozed off.

Once I'm dry, I change into my last pair of clean leggings and an off-the-shoulder sweater, then make my way into the living room. If we're going to be here a while, I'll need some supplies and a washer and dryer. Victoria's bathroom was stocked full of beauty products, and I was able to do my laundry there every few days. Considering I couldn't bring a lot of things with me, I've been limited on my wardrobe.

"Tyler?" I ask when I don't see him sitting on the couch.

"Kitchen," he shouts.

"Are you making me your delicious eggs and bacon?" I chuckle though it's closer to lunch. My nap in the tub was over two hours long and my skin is all pruney now. "Though, I'm kinda in the mood for—"

I stop dead in my tracks when I turn the corner and see Liam leaning against the counter. His ankles are crossed with his arms over his chest, looking sexy and confident as hell. Dark bags are under his eyes and his hair is a hot mess, but I love it when it looks like that.

Swallowing hard, I blink a few times to make sure I'm not imagining things.

"Liam?"

"Get your ass over here, woman," he demands with a boyish smile.

I rush over and leap into his arms. He easily catches me as I wrap my legs around his waist and cling to his neck. Liam holds me tight as I inhale his scent and hold back tears at how happy I am to see him.

Alive.

"How are you here right now?" I ask, pulling back, and

he sets me down on my feet. My hands remain on his chest as he holds me close. "I didn't expect you to come so soon."

He tilts his head and grins. "I couldn't stay away another fucking day, Mads." Then he cups my face and brushes his mouth over mine, soft at first, but when I part my lips, he slides his tongue between and dances with mine.

"Third wheel over here." Tyler groans, and I burst out laughing, breaking the kiss. Tyler turns and looks at Liam. "Can't tell you how relieved I was to know Maddie was actually real after hearing you go on and on about her for weeks. I thought maybe you made her up or she was a figment of your imagination."

"Dude," Liam says. "Bro code?"

"You gushed about me, huh?" I tease, smiling so wide I can't control it.

"How do you think I knew who you were right away? He painted a very clear visual of what you looked like, how you talked, the way you shake your ass when you walk."

"Oh my God!" I screech, playfully swatting Liam's chest.

Tyler's chuckling as Liam shoots him a death glare, then meets my eyes. "He's messing with you. And me."

I turn and scowl at Tyler who's grinning. He shrugs. "It's too easy."

"Real cool, Beanstalk. Now I don't feel bad you're sleeping on the sofa."

Liam's head falls back with uncontrollable laughter. "Go figure, you know him for two weeks and have already given him a freaking nickname."

I throw my hand toward Tyler who's mixing pancake batter in a bowl. "Look at him, he's a giant! It's a proper one at least."

"Yeah, *Hulk*," Tyler singsongs.

"If I didn't owe you my life, I'd deck you right now," Liam taunts, keeping his arm around me.

"Which means I have lifetime privileges to tease the ever-living shit out of you," Tyler retorts.

Liam smirks, then scoops me up. "You're right, man. Now excuse me while I *properly* reunite with my girlfriend."

Tyler groans. "Seriously?"

"Don't worry, we'll keep it down." Liam chuckles, then carries me to the bedroom.

I'd feel bad for leaving Tyler all by himself, but I need time alone with Liam right now.

"Tell me what happened," I say as he walks into the bedroom, then kicks the door shut. "I've been anxious just thinking about how it went down."

He sets me on my feet, then gently cups my face. "I will, but we need to talk about us first."

I nod. We have a lot to discuss, considering everything that's happened since the last time we were together.

Liam cradles my face, bringing our foreheads together. He sucks in a breath. "I was so distraught when you left," he says softly.

"Imagine how I felt when I heard Victoria was pregnant," I remark even though he knows I had no choice.

Liam leans back slightly and his face drops. "Mads, I know, and I'm so goddamn sorry."

I look at his pained expression. "I left for you," I tell him. "She would've punished you even more if I hadn't *willingly* gone that night. It was the only way to save you from her wrath, because I knew she was capable of hurting us all if she didn't get her way."

Liam shakes his head, cupping my cheeks. "I don't deserve you. I hate myself so much for lying to you and fucking things up between us. You deserved to hear it from me, but—"

"Your heart was in the right place," I finish for him, resting my palm on his chest. "Now knowing the truth, that they aren't yours and how she used you to facilitate this whole picture-perfect family, I understand you were just trying to protect my feelings."

"I never want to hurt you." His hand wraps around my neck, and he pulls me against his chest before pressing a single kiss to the top of my head. "These past two weeks were the worst ones in my life. You're all I could think about, and it was the thought of finding you that got me through every miserable day. I hated that you were blackmailed into leaving, but once I knew Tyler was with you, I was more determined than ever to get back to you." Liam's voice is sincere, and I hate how we were both thrust into this madness. I have to hope it'll only make us stronger, though. "Please let me make this right. Tell me we can get through this. I can't lose you."

"You have some groveling to do," I tease, but when he pulls back and we lock gazes, I see the heavy emotion in his eyes. Liam is rarely vulnerable and remains strong on the outside, but this Liam looks more broken than I've ever seen him.

Then he surprises the shit out of me when he falls to his knees in front of me and grips my hips with his strong hands. "I'll do anything. I meant what I said on the phone. You know I've never done a relationship before and have definitely never told a woman those words before."

My eyes water, and I know I can't stay mad at him. He told me the truth when I found the photo of the target over my face, and although I was blindsided by Victoria, I know he'd never intentionally hurt me. Liam is all I've ever wanted. He's not perfect, and both of us will screw things up sometimes, but it takes a real man to admit and apologize when he does. "We'll get through this," I assure him, leaning down to softly brush my lips against his. "She can't break us."

Liam grabs the back of my head and pulls me toward him and deepens the kiss. "Thank God. She's ruined so much. I don't know what I'd do if she tore us apart after I finally got you."

His sincere words hit me straight in the gut. For years, I fought for Liam, but here he is, fighting like hell, so I'll give him another chance.

He stands and holds me. It feels so good to be back in his arms. I momentarily close my eyes as I soak in his touch that I'd been so desperate to have again.

"Before I knew Victoria had something to do with you leaving, I thought you'd left me," he confesses. "I was going out of my mind, thinking that I'd fucked everything up for good. I'll make all of this up to you." He brings his forehead to mine, and I hear him inhale a sharp breath. "I love you, Mads."

"Say it again," I encourage.

The corner of his lips twitches as he leans back slightly and locks eyes with me. With one palm on my cheek, he says, "I'm in love with you, baby. I love you so much that my chest physically aches when I think about how much you mean to me and what losing you would do to me." He licks his lips. "Being apart put a lot into perspective, like how much time I wasted avoiding how I felt, or thinking you were better off with someone else. Though I will always believe you're too good for me, I know there's no one who could ever love me the way you do. I'm one lucky son of a bitch who gets to have you."

The tears I was holding back fall at his heartfelt confession—one I wasn't sure I'd ever get from him—but now that I have, my entire world feels complete. Who knew this macho, relationship-phobic man had a heart as big as this? Though I had always hoped.

Reaching up, I grab his face and bring his lips to mine. I kiss him hard and quick. "Feels like I've waited four years for that." I grin. "I love you, too. More than I can comprehend, which scares me sometimes, but it's you. It's *always* been you."

"I can't tell you how goddamn sorry I am for..." He pauses briefly as if it pains him to talk about how much he hurt me. "God, *everything*. Should've never kept secrets from you, and I promise I never will again. I told you I'd inevitably screw things up, but with you, I want to do better. You deserve the very best version of me, and that's exactly what you're going to get."

"You made a mistake, Liam," I reassure him. "But the important thing is learning from it and leaning on each other. We'll stay strong together." I try to comfort him.

"You're truly amazing, Mads." Liam dips his head and kisses me, our arms and bodies tangling together as he walks us toward the bed.

"Just tell me one thing..." I push against his chest slightly so our eyes lock. "Is it almost over?"

He doesn't have to ask what I'm referring to because he knows. My expression tells him exactly what I'm talking about.

"Almost, baby. Then the only ring I'll be wearing is the one you put on my finger." He winks, and heat rushes between my legs. That's either the hottest thing I've ever heard or the scariest. Either way, I'm all for it.

"Where's the guy who told me only a few months ago he wasn't capable of loving someone?"

"You wore him down until he had no choice but to admit his true feelings." He flashes an amused smirk, causing me to laugh. "Just like you always said you would."

I shrug playfully, wrapping my arms around his neck tighter, and make a show of checking him out. "Can you blame me?"

"Can you get naked?" he mocks.

Snorting, I nod. We take turns undressing each other, slowly and torturously, then I admire every inch of his muscular body and gorgeous tattoos. Liam throws me in the middle of the bed, and I laugh at how he does it so effortlessly. He crawls over me, dipping his head low as he feathers kisses between my legs.

As I arch my back, Liam makes his way up my stomach and chest, then swirls his tongue around my nipple ring. My fingers thread through his hair, craving more, wanting to have all of him.

"Okay, get inside me now. I'm dying," I tell him.

He lifts his head with a sexy smirk, then after a beat, it turns into a frown. "Ah, shit."

"Uh…" I furrow my brows as he lays next to me and cups my cheek. "What's wrong?"

"I don't have any protection."

I suck in a breath and groan. "Dammit. I knew I should've made Tyler buy some."

One brow perks up, curious. "Excuse me?"

I dramatically lie back and pout. "It was on my list of supplies, and he didn't get them for me. Totally lied and said 'they were out.'"

He leans up on his elbow and stares at me. "And why did you ask for condoms?"

Liam's face is tense, and I love messing with him, so I play dumb. "So I don't get pregnant, duh."

"Maddie, I swear to God..." He rolls over me and takes my wrists, then pins them above me. "Don't make me get all possessive of you more than I already am."

"Why not? It's pretty damn hot..." I waggle my brows, and he growls.

"Alright, you asked for it."

Liam tortures me by sucking on my clit as he fingers me. He pushes me closer to the ledge, then slows down, over and over until I'm begging him to let me come.

"Please..." I plead, feeling like I'm going to die if he pulls away again. Liam thrusts two fingers inside and flicks my clit with his tongue until I'm seeing stars and falling faster. "Oh my God."

Panting, I try to catch my breath as Liam rises above me with a shit-eating smirk. "I missed the taste of your pussy."

His bluntness causes me to chuckle. "Think we can get one-day shipping on condoms?"

"I almost forgot how sex-craved you are," he teases.

"I can't help it! Look at you." I gaze down his chest and then to his very thick and hard cock rubbing against me. "You should let me take care of that."

"I think if we're gone much longer, Tyler might get suspicious."

Rolling my eyes, I lean forward and force him to lie on the bed, then straddle him. "Pretty sure he's well aware we're not *napping* in here."

Then I kneel between his legs and wrap my fingers around his shaft. The guttural moan he releases has me smiling wide. When I circle his tip with my tongue, he moans louder. I watch as Liam's head falls back, then his hands ball into fists as his body stiffens.

So damn hot.

As I suck and stroke him, working his body faster and harder, Liam sits up and grabs a fistful of my hair. Pulling my head back, he thumbs my chin and brings our mouths together in a white-hot kiss.

"Do you have any idea how fucking sexy it is to watch you get me off?" His voice is low and deep, lighting up everything inside me again.

"Mmm..." I lick my lips. "I can taste how much you like it."

I can tell he's close when his cock throbs against my palm. "I don't want to get it all over you, baby."

"Don't worry, you won't." I wink, then lower myself again so I can finish him off properly.

Moments later, he moans loudly as he comes inside my mouth. I make sure it doesn't get on the bed or on us and smirk as I take all of him.

"Next time..." I straddle his waist and hover over him. "I'm holding it in, then spitting it into your mouth."

The look he gives me has me bursting out laughing. Like I'm fucking crazy. "You kiss me after you go down on me, so how's it any different?"

Liam narrows his eyes at me, shaking his head. "What the hell is wrong with you? Your bedroom talk is about as good as your sexting." He sits up with me in his lap, then reaches around and slaps my bare ass. "You've been watching porn, haven't you?"

I shrug. "It was a long and boring two weeks."

We finally manage to leave the bedroom and both start laughing when we see Tyler in the kitchen with headphones on. He's digging around the pantry, so I sneak up on him.

"Boo!" I push against his back, but he doesn't even flinch.

Slowly, he turns around and takes them off, eyeing me with a deadpan expression. "I have extensive training on not getting attacked. Sorry, princess."

"Not fair." I pretend to pout. "Where'd you find those anyway?"

"My friend's gaming headphones. Noise-canceling." He smirks.

Liam grunts. "Way to be dramatic."

"Way to *not* keep it down."

I giggle at their banter. "Okay, I'm hungry now. Whatcha gonna make me, Beanstalk?"

The three of us spend the rest of the day hanging out and making a plan for what's next. Liam described Victoria's reaction and explained how he handled her. I'm impressed and proud of how he stood up to her, though I'm still worried she'll find a way to retaliate, but I've never felt safer than I do with Liam and Tyler.

I'm not sure what happened to Eric, and I'm too scared to know the truth, so I don't ask. The question comes up if Tyler is going back home, but Liam wants us here until Victoria signs the divorce papers. Until that happens, she could find us and do God knows what. I'm not convinced she'll be able to get it done in only a week, but she's an O'Leary, so if anyone can make it happen, she can. There's no telling who she has on her payroll. Wouldn't surprise me if she throws thousands of dollars at her attorney to rush it just to avoid those pictures being leaked. I can only hope, though, because I'm dying to go back to Sacramento.

"Will it be safe for Tyler to go home even then?" I ask while we're watching TV.

They both shrug, but then Liam speaks up. "Actually, you should probably come with us to California," he states. "If Eric told her what you did, she'll know you were the mole and come after you. At least until the divorce is finalized in a couple of months. Then hopefully everything will be cleared, and you'll be safe to leave."

"Probably for the best," he agrees. "Though if she wants to play that card, I have plenty of other shit on her I can use. I followed her for weeks."

A bad feeling surfaces up my spine, and I hate that Tyler could be in danger because of me.

"Aww, Beanstalk. We'll be roomies again!" I gush, knowing it'll annoy him.

"On second thought, I'm willing to risk Victoria finding me."

"Haha." I lean over and punch his arm. "You love me."

"This might be a good time to call Sophie," Liam states, and I swear my heart stops.

"Really? We can call her?"

He grabs his phone from his pocket and hands it over. "Yeah, let's put her out of her misery."

I'm giddy as hell when Sophie picks up on the second ring. "Liam?"

"It's Maddie," I tell her. "I'm with Liam."

"Oh my God!" she screams. "Where the hell are you?"

I swallow hard. "I can't say right now, but I can tell you we're both safe."

"What do you mean? What's going on?" She's panicking, and I hate that we've had to lie and keep so much from her.

"Soph," Liam intervenes. "We'll tell you everything once we're home, but for now, we just wanted to let you know I had Maddie and we're in a safe place."

"Meaning what? She wasn't before?" she scolds.

Shit.

"We'll explain when we can, okay?" I say. "I miss you guys."

"When are you coming home?" she asks. "I've been going out of my mind."

"I know, and we're both sorry about that," I tell her.

"If all goes according to plan, we'll be back in a week," Liam says.

I smile at him, then grip his hand. "Has everything been okay over there?" I ask cautiously.

"Besides me going nuts? Oh, yeah, sure." She breathes out harshly. "Can I know this, did you really write that note and willingly leave?"

"No," I confirm. "That was Victoria's doing, which is why we can't come home yet. So if she shows up, don't let her in and call the police."

"Is she really pregnant with twins?"

"Yeah."

"Damn, so no kicking her ass."

I snicker. "No."

"Are they Liam's?" she hesitantly asks.

"No," Liam answers without explaining more.

I put the call on mute and tilt my head at Liam. "Let's tell her about *us* at least."

He waves his hand toward me. "Do the honors, baby."

Smiling wide, I unmute the call and clear my throat. "Soph, there's something else I gotta tell you."

"What is it?" she asks wearily. "Should I be sitting?"

I snort at her dramatics. "No, well…maybe." I laugh. "Liam and Victoria's marriage was an arrangement, and we've been secretly seeing each other for the past two months."

"I knew it! Oh my God, I so knew it!" she shouts. "Are you fuckin' kidding me? Oh my God."

"Stop freaking out!" I chuckle.

"I knew there was no way he'd marry that bitch. I hope

127

you knew the truth when you two were…"

"Soph! Of course, I did."

"Wait…" She pauses. "Did Liam touch you? Like…all the way?"

Liam and Tyler groan as I burst out laughing. Sophie would ask that.

"I can answer that for them…" Tyler interjects. "Yes."

"Uh…who is that?"

"His name is Tyler. He's a friend of ours." Nervously, I ask, "How would you feel about another housemate when we return?"

"Where the hell would he sleep?"

"He can stay in my room," Liam confirms.

"It's a long story, and we promise he's a good guy," I assure her. "He needs a place to stay until Victoria and Liam's divorce is finalized."

"I better get a full explanation!" she warns. "Be home in a week, you said?"

"Yep. Text me on Liam's phone, though, because mine is gone." Which reminds me, I should cancel my service if Eric still has it and get a new one.

Sophie sighs. "Okay. I'm very confused, but I trust you'll take care of my sister. Right, Liam?" Her voice grows louder with each word.

"Absolutely," he says immediately. "I'll protect her with my life, Soph."

"Good." She blows out a breath. "And for what it's worth, I'm glad you finally came to your senses, Liam. But if you hurt her, I won't think twice about kicking your ass, then throwing you to the wolves to let them eat you alive."

"If I do that, I give you permission," Liam says confidently. "Trust me, though, it's the last thing I want to do again. I love her."

"Aww...wow," Sophie singsongs. "Never thought I'd hear that come from your mouth, Liam Evans."

"Yeah, yeah." He grunts at her playful teasing.

"I'll text or call tomorrow, okay? We're gonna get ready for bed," I tell her.

After a few moments, we end the call, and I beam at Liam. "Well, she didn't cuss you out, so that's a plus." I shrug.

"That was only one sister..." he says, breathing in through his nose as if he's expecting the worse from Lennon. "Then I have to deal with the wrath of Mason and Hunter."

I pat his hand like a child's. "Don't forget my parents too, eventually."

Liam pales with a groan.

Tyler laughs. "I don't envy you, man."

"You ever bring a chick home to meet the parents?" I ask him.

Tyler's lips immediately turn into a frown, and I fear I've hit a sensitive topic. "Hell no."

"He has a hot sister, though," Liam taunts, and I scowl at him. "Or so I've heard."

I roll my eyes. "Yeah, nice save." Then I look at Tyler. "You didn't tell me you had a sister. What's her name? Where does she live?"

Tyler pushes his hands on his knees and stands. "And that's exactly why I didn't."

"Oh come on!" I pout. "If we're going to be roomies, I need some personal info."

He contemplates it for a moment. "Six feet five, a hundred seventy-five pounds, brown hair, and brown eyes. Favorite color is orange, and I like spicy foods," he rambles off, then gives me a shit-eating grin.

"That's not what I meant!" I groan. "Wait. Your favorite

color is orange?" I chuckle. "That's cute."

"Can I go now?"

I groan, narrowing my eyes. "At least give me your sister's name!"

"Fine. Her name is Everleigh." He gives in, and I grin victoriously.

"Maybe I'll get to meet her someday." I smile hopeful, but he doesn't take the bait to give me more information.

He nods firmly at me with tight lips, and I know he gets uncomfortable talking about himself. That part was genuine while at the cabin. When he avoided telling me anything personal, it wasn't just an act. "Alright, lovebirds. I'm gonna shower, then go to sleep."

"I think that's code for get off the couch," Liam says, grabbing my hand and pulling me up.

Tyler walks toward the bathroom, then turns and smirks. "Well, I'm definitely not sleeping in that bed. I'll be wearing the headphones, though."

The past six days have all been long and repetitive. It's felt like Groundhogs Day except Liam's been too paranoid to let any of us out of the condo, so we have food delivered, and Tyler's friend who owns the place dropped off some other supplies for us. Condoms included this time.

I can tell Liam's been on edge the past couple of days as

he waits for Victoria to make the next move. I also know he hates sitting around and is probably eager as hell to get back to work. Sophie and I text every day, and I even called Lennon to give her the same updates. Once we're home, we plan on sitting with everyone and telling them the whole story. Now that Victoria isn't playing puppet master, they need to know everything in case anyone in Victoria's world tries to talk to them.

Then Liam has to talk to his father and give him a brief summary of why he's no longer staying married to her and how the babies aren't his. I know he's super stressed about the fallout of having an arranged marriage and now having to apologize to everyone for lying.

There's a lot on his plate, so I try not to push him to talk about it because there's nothing that can be done until Victoria sends the papers. Until then, we're living in limbo.

"What are you hungry for?" Tyler asks as I sit at the breakfast table.

"A triple berry smoothie from Frenchie's Cafe," I smart off. "They have the best muffins too. Mmm." I release a dreamy sigh as I think about being back in Sacramento.

"Alllllright, well…" he ponders. "I can make you a fruit and yogurt smoothie, and there's some blueberry muffin mix in the pantry. How's that?"

"Deal."

"Good, then you can do my laundry while I cook."

"Oh my God. You too? Liam does the same shit to me." I groan.

"What do I do?" Liam comes behind me and wraps his arms around my waist, then presses a kiss to my neck.

"Sneak your laundry in mine so I'll do it," I tell him, then elbow him in the stomach. "Now Tyler is trying to be sneaky and barter for his cooking."

Liam walks around me and goes toward the fridge. "Smart man. He works his strengths in his favor."

"I'm good for more than just cleaning." I groan.

"Like what?" Tyler pries. "Because all I've seen you do is watch Netflix, do yoga, and dance around the living room for the past three weeks."

Liam whips his head around and faces me. "You were doing yoga and dancing in front of him?"

"I. Was. Bored!" I say for the hundredth time this week. "He's the one who watched..." I hold out my hand, putting the attention on Tyler instead.

Tyler snickers, shaking his head. "It was my *job* to watch you. Remember?"

"You better be keeping your beady little eyes off her now," Liam warns, and I can't tell if he's being serious or not. His voice is firm, and he flashes Tyler a murderous glare. Liam looks like he's ready for a fight.

"Liam, relax," I tell him, walking over and rubbing my hand over his arm.

"Yeah, Liam, relax," Tyler mimics in my same tone. "Plus, I only saw her naked *one* time. Nice nipple rings."

I knew he looked, the bastard!

Tyler shrugs, and within two seconds, Liam's charging for him.

"Dude, not fuckin' cool!" Liam has Tyler's shirt fisted in his hands as he pushes him up against the wall.

"Liam!" I scream. I've seen Liam pissed off before, but never like this. He's worked up and taking it out on the wrong person.

"Maddie, stay back. It's fine," Tyler says, then looks back at Liam, not even defending himself. "Go ahead, punch me. Get your anger out."

Tyler's voice is calm and calculated, which means he knows what he's doing, and that Liam won't actually hit him.

Liam pulls back, dropping his arms. "Shit." He glances at me, looking fucked up, then goes back to Tyler. "I'm sorry, man." Liam shakes his head, then lowers it. "Being stuck inside and not being able to work out and not hearing from Victoria…" He pauses and inhales a deep breath.

"It's okay, really." Tyler puts his hand on Liam's shoulder. "I get it. You're used to an outlet, and you're not getting one."

"It's no excuse. I should never lose my temper like that, especially to lay a hand on *you*." Liam sounds distraught, and I've never seen him like this before.

"Liam, it's fine." Tyler rests both of his hands on his shoulders and pushes him back slightly so he'll look in his eyes. "You're at your breaking point. We all have one. Perhaps you need to do a yoga workout video." He smirks, causing Liam to relax and blow out a breath.

"Maddie told you, didn't she?"

"What can I say…" I chime in. "I'm a rambler when I'm bored." I shrug when he eyes me.

Liam steps toward Tyler and wraps his arms around him in a big, manly hug. I smile wide at the gesture, knowing Liam isn't close to many people. There's his small inner circle of Mason, Hunter, and my sisters, but now Tyler is one of us. He's our family now, too.

"Sorry again." Liam slaps his back before pulling away.

"We're cool, man. Don't worry about it."

The rest of the day passes, and by ten, we're ready to pass out. This routine is getting old, and I can't wait until I can go back to my dance classes—assuming I haven't been dropped from them.

I'm woken up the next morning by Liam's booming voice

echoing in the distance. I blink, then look over and see he's not in bed with me. Right after I throw off the covers and set my feet on the floor, the door whips open. Liam charges toward me with a wide smile.

"What's going on?" I ask, confused. It can't be any later than nine.

"Victoria just texted me. She has the papers and signed them."

My brows rise. "She did?" I throw my arms around him, and he lifts me up, my legs wrapping around his waist.

"Yep." He kisses me before setting me down. "She's sending them to the house, but I had her send me pictures of the docs for proof. We were only married for four months, so it's very basic. Her assets are hers, mine are mine, and we never had anything joint or shared, so I'll sign and send back for her to file. Then depending on the court's schedule, hopefully in six to eight weeks, we'll go in front of a judge."

"Then what?"

"Then it'll be final."

My heart races when I think about Liam finally being a free man. "I'm so relieved."

"Me too, baby. So fucking relieved." He cups my face, and I pull him closer as he brushes his lips against mine. After the incident in the kitchen last night, Liam was so pissed at himself. I know he'd never intentionally hurt anyone he loved, especially not Tyler. He apologized over and over for showing that side of himself, but I want it all. The good, bad, and ugly parts of him. Neither of us is perfect, but together we're stronger and much happier. Fortunately, Tyler handled it all well and knew how to deal with the situation.

Liam smiles. "Let's go home, sweetheart."

CHAPTER TWELVE

LIAM

MADDIE and I were so happy to finally be home after spending seven days in Oregon. I was anxious as hell waiting for Victoria to file the papers, but once she finally did, I felt like I could breathe a little easier. Once we were back, we could finally be open about our relationship, and it's been what dreams are made of. I've never had this feeling before, but everything I've gone through to get Maddie in my arms every night is worth it.

Being apart from her, I was so damn worried about her safety that I'd nearly forgotten to take care of myself. Sleep was ever fleeting, and I had no appetite. Though once I knew she was safe with Tyler, I felt relieved, but there was always that chance that something terrible could have happened. I would've never been able to live with myself if she had been hurt.

Though we're trying to find our normal, we're both well aware that it won't be happening until the divorce is final and the weight of Victoria's threats is lifted. I also have a lot of making up to do because I hurt Maddie in ways I wish I hadn't. I should've told her about the pregnancy, and it's something I regret not doing. The hurt on her face the night she found out nearly destroyed me, and it's something I won't forget for as long as I live. While she says she's forgiven me and understands, I'm going to do whatever it takes to rebuild that trust between us.

Maddie spoke with her advisor the day after we returned. She had to get permission from her professors since they can kick her out for missing so much, but after speaking to the dean and giving an explanation, they're allowing her to return this week. Considering the car I bought her is still yet to return to the house, it's probably for the best since I'm still working on how to get it from Victoria. At least then Maddie can find her own personal normal without having to depend on anyone to drive her. It bothers the hell out of her because she wanted to be independent.

"What do you want to watch?" Maddie asks me as we sit on the couch. I was lost in my thoughts again, not paying attention. It's happened more times than not since we've been home.

"Uh, I don't care," I mutter. It's Sunday evening, and Lennon and Hunter are on their way over to visit. Maddie's been wanting to see Aaron and Allie, and there are a lot of things I need to tell the two of them. Sophie and Mason said they'd grab pizza, and we'd have a small get-together like old times. If anything, I'm grateful for my friends and how forgiving and understanding they are for this shitshow I've brought to them.

Maddie flips through the channels and stops on Lifetime. It's like Hallmark, but with sex and cursing, and she's all about the cowboy romance movie she's watching. It literally took two minutes before she was sucked into the plot. Go figure, cowboy boots and a Southern accent are all it took to have her swooning. I wrap my arm around her and pull her a little closer, happy we can have this time together, because weeks ago, I wished for moments like this with her. As best as I can, I'm going to enjoy this time because it's been relentlessly proven to me how fast things can change.

Once the couple makes out and their intimate moment fades to black, Tyler comes downstairs.

"What the hell are y'all watching?" he asks, plopping in the recliner.

"Don't you recognize a cheesy Southern flick when you see one?" Maddie taunts. "They talk like you."

"Har har. I don't talk like that," he remarks. Tyler's quickly made himself at home, and I'm gonna miss him when he leaves in a month. He's so easily fit in with everyone, and it almost feels like he's always been one of our roommates. It helps that he and Mason already have a good relationship, though, from when he was Mason's trainer.

Lennon and Hunter eventually arrive, wearing grins when they walk through the door. Maddie is over the moon excited to see the kids. I watch her with Aaron and see how her face lights up as she talks to him and how Allie smiles and laughs at Maddie's words. They love her so much, and one day, I know she'll make an amazing mom. Sophie arrives with six pizza boxes, and Mason walks in not long after with two six-packs of beer. It's D-Day, the day I sit down and explain to everyone what happened from the top. It's something I've wanted to do for so long, and the time is finally here. I'd be lying if I said I wasn't nervous about it, but I'm glad Tyler and Maddie are here to help tell the whole story.

As we eat, Maddie looks at me, smiling and encouraging me to start.

"So, I have a lot of explaining to do...but first I owe every single one of you an apology." I speak up, finding confidence within myself. "I'm so fu–freaking sorry." I look at Allie playing on the floor with a doll and decide not to teach her curse words.

I start from the very beginning and explain my gambling addiction, and then the big stakes poker game I lost. Sophie's eyes are wide when I tell her how JJ harassed and blackmailed me.

"And they threatened to hurt me," Maddie adds. "Sent him a photo with a target over my head. They followed me around campus too, knowing I was Liam's weakness."

Mason stops eating. "Why didn't you say something to us? I could've helped."

Shaking my head, I meet his eyes. "It was too risky. I didn't want to get anyone else involved especially after I'd risked so much by having Tyler help me, and they were already targeting Maddie. I thought I had control of the situation, but clearly I didn't, especially once Victoria dropped the pregnancy bomb on me."

"You would've done it for me," Tyler states confidently. "It was the least I could do."

"Man, we're here for you," Hunter adds. "You're our brother. We fight together. We do all this *together* and have since the very beginning."

"I know," I offer, pissed at myself, realizing how ridiculous it all sounds. "It's something I'll always regret, but I really thought I was protecting you guys."

"Wow," is all Lennon says, watching me with wide eyes when I tell them about Johnny nearly shooting me and Victoria saving my ass at the last second but with an ulterior motive. By this part, everyone has stopped eating, and they're watching me intently. Maddie interlocks her fingers with mine and inspires me to keep going.

I put it all out there—the marriage arrangement, her being pregnant before this all started, the threats to obey, and learning Victoria was sleeping with the enemy. By the time I'm done, it feels as if a million pounds are lifted from my shoulders. They're all in shock, and their jaws are on the floor.

"I don't even know what to say. I want to be pissed at you, but I understand why you did what you did," Sophie offers. "None of it seems real."

"Right? It's like a messed-up gangster movie," Maddie tells her, and they all nod in agreement.

I smile. "As long as there's a happy ending with you in it, I don't care."

"There will be, baby," Maddie says, then giddily explains when we started our relationship and why we had to hide it. She's not a bit shy when it comes to us or anything sexual, and I have to stop her from giving too many details when the guys start to openly cringe.

"Spare Hunter and Mason, please," I interrupt with a laugh.

"And me too," Tyler interjects with a grunt. "I heard enough in Oregon."

"Thank you!" Hunter grins. "I don't wanna hear about my friend's dick."

Mason nods. "What he said."

"Why not? It's a very nice one." Maddie grins, knowing it'll make them uncomfortable.

"You hurt my sister, and you'll think Victoria was nice compared to me," Lennon warns, effortlessly changing the topic off my cock.

"Shit." Hunter chuckles. "You're scary, sweetheart."

Sophie clears her throat and grins. "It's okay. Let's plan a spa day, and you can tell us all the details then." And of course, Sophie would bring it back.

Maddie claps her hands in excitement. "Sign me up."

"Should I be okay with this?" I ask, narrowing my eyes. "Why do chicks talk so much?"

"When you date one Corrigan, you volunteer to have your penis talked about." Maddie pats my leg. "I know all about Hunter's and Mason's. Well done, boys."

We all burst into laughter, and it feels great to have them accept our relationship. My friends are my family, and they love me unconditionally even through this. Says a lot about their character and who they are. I wouldn't want anyone else on my side. After we clean up and have a few drinks, we say our goodbyes to Lennon, Hunter, and the kids.

"I'm glad you're both okay," Sophie says before heading upstairs.

"Me too," Mason says. "And glad you're finally together too. It's good for both of you."

"Thank you," I offer before leaning over and placing my lips softly on Maddie's. She sighs against my mouth.

"Guess there will be a lot of that." Sophie giggles.

"If you hear any moans in the kitchen, don't enter," Maddie warns with a wink.

"Oh God," Sophie playfully groans. "We're supposed to be the soon-to-be newlyweds who can't get enough of each other." She smirks at Mason.

"Trust me, we witnessed plenty of your make-out sessions," I tease.

Sophie smirks. "Good night, you two."

"Night!" Maddie calls out.

I look at her. "Let's go to bed, baby."

She yawns. "Yeah, I'm tired."

Loving that I can easily carry her, I pick her up in my

arms and walk us to her room. I place her on the bed, and she grins.

"You should just carry me around everywhere from now on." She stands and removes her clothes, changing into something more comfortable. I strip down to my boxers and crawl into bed, then she snuggles up against me, and it's never felt more natural to have Maddie in my arms.

"Love you, Liam," she says in a sleepy tone.

"Love you too. Good night." I kiss her forehead, and we fall asleep within minutes.

I open my eyes, wondering what time it is because I feel as if I just drifted off. Slightly turning my head, I see Maddie sleeping so peacefully next to me, and I can't help but drink her in. I'll never take this woman for granted, not the way her soft skin feels pressed against mine or how her hair smells like a mixture of honey and flowers. The way she laughs brings joy to my core but so do her smart-ass remarks. I can't get enough of her, and I don't ever want to. Ever since we've been home, I've lived in the moment, enjoying every second I get to spend with her. I've basically moved into her room since Tyler is sleeping in mine, but it took zero convincing on my part. I would've been in her bed every night anyway.

The sun has barely risen, and a warm glow splashes through her bedroom window. I suck in a deep breath and let out a relieved one. I could die a happy man right now being with her like this. Maddie snuggles closer to me, letting out a small moan, and it causes me to smile. She's looped her leg over mine, and we're tangled together like a pretzel. That is, until she moves a little too swiftly and knees me in the junk.

A loud groan escapes me, and she pops up in bed like a groundhog. "What is it?"

"My…dick," I hiss, holding my groin and hoping the pain passes quickly. "Good morning," I somehow force out, my voice a whole octave higher.

"Oh my gosh." Maddie leans over and kisses my face as she runs her fingers through my hair. "I'm so sorry, babe. I didn't mean to." The sincerity in her tone has my heart swelling.

"I know." I close my eyes and try to think of something else but totally take advantage of all the kisses. Once I'm able to breathe again, I wrap my arms around her. "Okay, I think I'm good now. You're adorable in the morning—when you keep your knees to yourself that is." I laugh at her typical Maddie eye roll. "I don't want to go to work today."

"And I've kinda gotten used to staying home with you all day." She smirks. "But I've missed too much school and have to go."

"Good point. Guess I won't be a bad influence and beg you to stay," I say. "Though it's really tempting when you're lying next to me, looking cute as hell."

She giggles. "Don't worry, you already are."

Just as her lips paint across mine, her alarm buzzes at a level-ten volume. She reaches for it, but it falls off the side table onto the floor, blaring through the room.

"Dammit." Maddie crawls over me, making sure to roll her hips as she straddles me before trying to escape. I groan, and she laughs before sliding away and turning it off. It was almost as if I didn't hear the annoying buzzing when her legs were wrapped around my waist. She has the ability to make everything around me disappear. After setting her phone down, Maddie returns to her position on top of me, then dips down and slides her tongue between my lips. Moaning against her, I run my fingers through her long brown hair.

"Don't tease me," I warn when she plucks my bottom lip

into her mouth and sucks. I'm hard as a fucking rock, needing her more than I need air.

"Tease you? I only *please* you, Liam." Slowly, she removes the tiny shirt she was sleeping in, putting her perfect tits on full display. The nipple rings glint in the early morning sunlight, and I desperately want to place them both in my mouth, then worship her body all damn day. It doesn't take long before I'm inside her, and we're making love. It's more than just sex. Always has been with Maddie.

Though we both have to leave soon, neither of us rush, taking our time, not wasting a single second of being together. Maddie rides me, flipped her messy morning hair over her shoulder, and before she comes, she dips her head down and kisses the fuck out of me. Before long, I'm losing myself inside her, and the only noise that fills the room is our satisfied pants.

"I'm calling in sick," I taunt after we clean up. Being a bounty hunter means I make my own hours, but I have weeks to make up for my loss of income. "You should too."

"I wish." She slaps my chest. "If I want to pass my classes, I have to go."

I'm aware of how much stress she's been under for missing a few weeks of school. It pisses me off that Victoria involved Maddie to the extent she did, but we're trying to move on with our lives and put this all behind us. We're slipping into our old habits but without all the hiding and secrets.

Placing my hands behind my head, I watch her with a smirk as she gets dressed. "Plus side is I only have three classes today."

She shimmies into a pair of pants that look like they're painted on and grins as she puts on a T-shirt. "I should make you breakfast. I have a few minutes, I think."

"It's my turn!" I say, hurrying to slip on some jogging pants. We've been eating breakfast together each morning before going our separate ways. She follows me to the kitchen, giggling, and as she makes the coffee, I grab the egg carton and bacon from the fridge. While I scramble eggs, Maddie makes herself a cup of tea, allowing me to steal a few kisses before filling my mug full of coffee.

"Get a room," I hear Sophie say from behind.

"We've got one." Maddie shoots her a wink before giving me a sexy grin. "You need coffee, Miss Grumpy?" Maddie pours some for Sophie and slides it to her.

Sophie lets out a yawn. "We're practicing for our Christmas performances, and I'm already over it. We're barely into October."

I laugh. "Oh, so you're just being a Scrooge."

"Basically." Then she leans over and watches me cook. "Hey, I hope you made enough for me," she says.

"And me," Mason enters and gives Sophie a kiss on the cheek before sitting.

"I didn't realize I was cooking for the whole family," I murmur, giving Sophie and Mason the food I cooked for us, and put more in the skillet. I honestly don't mind and am okay with it, considering we've had our rough patches the past few months. Sophie and Mason have somewhat forgiven me, but Sophie has warned me several times that if I break her sister's heart, she'll still chop off my balls and feed them to me. At one point, she threatened me with a butcher knife in her hand if I ever hurt Maddie. Sophie's scary at times, but passionate about her sister's well-being. I get it. I am too.

There's something to be jealous of when it comes to the Corrigan sisters and their undying love for one another. Makes me sad that I don't have siblings of my own, but at the end of the day, I suppose it's better. Fewer people for my mother to ruin with her abandonment. After the second helping of eggs and bacon is nearly finished, Maddie pops some bread in the toaster, then spreads avocado over it. By this time, Tyler is entering the kitchen.

"Well fuck," I say, laughing. "Sorry dude, you're gonna have to cook for yourself."

He gives me a big grin and a middle finger, but then goes straight for the caffeine as Maddie and I try to quickly eat. We have about thirty minutes before we both have to leave, but it's hard not to want to stay in the house all day and hang out with everyone. Before they really knew what was going on, I felt so alone and desperate for them to learn the truth, but not wanting anything to happen. Now that the curtain has been removed, I at least sleep better at night.

Once my plate is cleared, I snag a piece of bacon from Maddie's, and she glares at me, making me laugh. Sophie and Mason thank us for breakfast, and Tyler announces he's going to the gym. "Mason, you got time for a few rounds?"

Mason cracks his knuckles. "I've been a little rusty lately. I'd love to but gotta be an adult and go to work. Can I take a rain check? Maybe tonight? It'd be nice to get back in the ring."

"You're just trying to avoid getting your ass kicked, aren't ya?" Tyler taunts.

"Ass kicked?" Mason scoffs, putting up his arms and punching Tyler's shoulder. "I recall kicking the shit out of you several times."

"If you did, it's because I felt sorry for ya and allowed it." Tyler blocks his second hit, then swings and smacks Mason. Getting out as much aggression as possible helped Mason in those early days he was grieving his girlfriend who passed away years earlier. It's one of the reasons I've always respected Tyler. He helped my best friend when he was depressed, and here he is, helping me too.

I finish my coffee as Maddie walks through their fake boxing match toward me, and I think about my life and where everything is. Sucking in a deep breath, I can't help but be grateful. I know we're not in the clear yet, but I can see a glimmer of light shining through the darkness. It's something I wasn't sure I'd ever see again.

"You should get dressed," she tells me, then wraps her arms around my stomach, pressing her tits against my back before feathering kisses along my skin. I turn around, not wanting to waste her lips being against mine.

"I thought I'd go like this," I beam, giving her shit.

Looking me up and down, she raises her eyebrows. "Must be following a woman then, because no guy is going to want a Hulk of a man showing up looking like this. Shirtless and..." She glances down at my cock, which is steadily growing hard for her.

I give her a boyish grin and a shrug. "You never know."

Playfully, she slaps me. "If you don't put on some clothes, I'm going to be late for school unless I need to find a different ride." She pretends to pout, sticking out her bottom lip. I bend down and pluck it between my teeth before smacking a quick kiss on her mouth.

"No, no. Give me five minutes." I rush to the bedroom, put on some jeans and a black T-shirt, grab my utility belt, and meet her back in the kitchen. She takes my hand and I lead us to my truck, but we both glance around before climbing in. I don't know how long it's going to take for us to stop looking over our shoulders, but at this point, after everything we've been through, I may never. Victoria has ruined me more than tracking fugitives ever could. I've always been cautious, but this is a whole different level of paranoia, and rightfully so.

Once I see the street is clear of black Suburbans, I let out a sigh of relief and so does Maddie. As I pull out of the driveway, I glance at the G-Wagon that's still here and make a mental note to tell Victoria to come pick it up. I don't want her handouts. I don't want anything from her, but to be left alone.

On the way to the university, Maddie talks about her classes, how long she'll be in rehearsal, and when we pull in front of the dance hall, she asks if I'll be picking her up afterward.

"Of course, why wouldn't I?"

"Well, if you get caught up today with work. I just want to make sure."

I lift her chin, forcing her to look at me. She's been worried about me ever since we returned home, and it breaks my heart. The only time either of us is okay is when we're together. Too much can happen when we're apart.

"I'll keep you updated on where I am. The job I'm doing today is local. I'm not even leaving the city. I'll be here. I'm gonna be okay, sweetheart," I say as she searches my face with concern.

"I just..."

"Worry, I know. We have to be careful, but we can't keep living in fear. I'm always a text away. I don't care what I'm doing, I'll text you back as soon as I can if you ever feel anxious or concerned about me, okay? I promise. But that means I'm going to be blowing up your phone while you're in class because it goes both ways."

"Annie already told me if my phone goes off one more time, she's locking it in her office until after practice." She snickers. "You're gonna get me in trouble."

"Apparently, I'm good at that," I say, giving her a wink.

She leans over and presses her mouth to mine, and I fist her hair in my fingers.

Reluctantly, I pull away before things get too heated. "Have a good day. I love you."

"I love you more," she insists, and before I can tell her how wrong she is, Maddie hops out of the truck, blows me a kiss, then walks away. Of course I watch how her hips sway when she walks and it causes a smile to fill my face as she shakes her ass.

She's mine and always will be.

CHAPTER THIRTEEN

MADDIE

WHEN I WAS STUCK in the middle of nowhere, I dreamed about my monotonous life of going to school every day. I'm thankful to somewhat have my old life back and don't have much to complain about these days. In my regular classes, it seems like no one noticed I was gone for over three weeks other than my professors, but that all changed as soon as I went to dance. I'm bombarded with questions regarding where I've been and what happened. Thankfully Joel walks up, wraps his arms around me, and shoos everyone away. We've got ten minutes before we start, so I take the opportunity to stretch.

"Thanks for saving me," I finally tell him, dropping to the floor and reaching for my toes.

Joel lowers his voice. "You're not getting out of it that easy." He gives me a boyish grin and continues, "I was worried. You ever gonna tell me where you were? I spoke to your sister, remember. I know something's up."

I give him a small smile, hating that I'm still lying to people I care about because of Victoria. They say the more you lie, the easier it gets, but I call bullshit. Each time I do it,

149

I die a little inside, but I can't tell him the truth. Most people wouldn't believe me anyway.

I dodged the question as soon as I came back, but it's now the third time he's asked so I can't keep putting it off. "There was a family emergency so I flew home to Utah."

His face contorts, full of worry, and it seems like he's going to push me on the issue. I know Sophie called him and asked him if he'd seen me, which kinda puts a hole in my story, but I'm going to roll with it. Before he can continue with more questions, I add wanting to talk about anything else, "Everything's okay now."

The day after we returned home, I went and got a new phone and called my parents. I had to confess I missed the first three weeks of class, and yet again, I had to lie. I made up a story about needing space because I wasn't sure that this was the right career path for me, and after some deep soul searching, I decided to keep pursuing it and returned to school. I'm not sure if they've been calling or not, but my mother sounded panicked, so I'm guessing Sophie and Lennon were hearing the wrath of her worrying as well.

Joel smiles, almost as if he's relieved, and drops it. That's one thing I really like about him, he knows when to pry and when to leave things alone. He's my favorite dance partner for a reason.

Annie walks into the room wearing dance flats and leggings. She glances at me with a small smile as if she's surprised and relieved I returned, then starts the class. I'm not exactly sure what my teachers were told once I explained I had an "emergency" to my advisor and the dean of the college, but I'm just happy I wasn't kicked out. Thankfully, they gave me another chance.

Joel and I get into place after we warm up and start working on choreography. I didn't realize how behind I was until now. The whole routine is complete, and I'm frustrated as hell that I'm twirling around mindlessly, not knowing my next step. Feeling like a newbie doesn't happen often for me, but right now, I'm out of place. When we're given a ten-minute water break, Joel comes over to calm me down.

"Don't be so hard on yourself," he tells me sincerely, noticing my aggravation. He doesn't realize it stems from being frustrated with myself, the situation, and even Victoria. Her name is like poison on my tongue, but I swallow down the venom I have for her and force a smile.

"I know. I'm just annoyed. I don't like not knowing what's going on and feeling like a transfer student." I chug half my bottle of water, determined to recount every step, dip, and jump. Joel tried to lead me as best he could, but I should've just watched from the side, like the kid who didn't get picked for a school sport.

"Mads. You've been gone for over three weeks. You can't expect to hop into the middle of a routine and predict the next move. That's just insanity."

I let out a huff the suck in air through my nose, trying to calm down. "You're right."

"We can stay after class and go over it a few times if you want. You'll have it by next time. I know how meticulous you are." He places a hand on my shoulder and squeezes before we're called back to the floor. I didn't realize how stressed I still am from being gone, even though we've been home for a little while. Is it possible that the whole experience changed me? That thought alone has me cursing under my breath.

The next time we go through the routine, I'm not as lost. Joel grabs my waist and gives me a supported cartwheel before I land into a perfect split. The toe work will take some time, but for the most part, I think I have the basics.

Thankfully I'm a quick learner because I might walk out of here in tears otherwise.

I want to be the best at everything I do. The best dancer, sister, and even girlfriend. It's why I try to give my whole heart to Liam every chance I get and why I agreed to leave in the first place. I might've recently given away my V-card, but when Liam and I are together, it's special. What we have is more than just sex or the meaningless motions of two people being together. It's always been more than that.

After everyone leaves, Joel and I stay behind, and I'm grateful for the extra thirty minutes he gives me of his time. We start slow at the beginning, then go faster, and I even recorded us on my phone so I could watch it again at home. It's something I learned in high school so I wouldn't forget the details my teacher gave. Once we change out of our practice clothes, relief washes over me that I made it through another day. Things aren't back to normal yet, but maybe I'll find it soon.

"Thanks, Joel," I tell him as we go our separate ways down the sidewalk.

"For what?" he asks, though I think he knows exactly why I'm thanking him.

"For not calling me a sucky ass partner and requesting someone new to dance with while I was gone."

He shakes his head, his lips turning up. "Pfft. You're the best dancer at this school, even on your worst days, Mads. You're stuck with me until we graduate."

I laugh and shoot him a wink before heading to calculus.

A month has passed since Liam and I got back to Sacramento, and so far, the bottom hasn't fallen out. Not that I expected it to but when Victoria is involved, you never know.

I wrap a towel around my body and towel-dry my hair before getting dressed. Today, I have a date with my sisters, a much-needed one at that. Though, I'm not sure how long we'll be together because we're doing our last fitting for our dresses for Mason and Sophie's wedding. She's been overly particular about colors and flowers. It could either be quick or painstakingly long. The plan is to just go with the flow because it's her day, and I don't care what we wear. I know Liam will want to tear it off afterward anyway.

After I'm ready, I go downstairs where Sophie is eagerly waiting for me as she types away on her phone, probably to Lennon.

"That took forever!" she exclaims with a big cheesy grin on her face. She's been waiting for this for weeks. Liam left before the sun rose to track a fugitive up north and Mason went to the office to help oversee some big investigation he's working on at the moment. It's going to be us girls only, and I couldn't be more excited. When I was cooped up in Montana, I dreamed about being able to speak with Sophie and Lennon. It nearly killed me not being able to or, even worse, missing something as important as this.

"Lennon's meeting us there after she drops off the kids with Mrs. Locke. She said something about mimosas and massages."

"And that's why she's my favorite sister," I throw in, just because we have this running joke between us, but honestly, I could never choose. I love them both for different reasons and some of the same ones too. It's almost unfair to everyone else that I got two of the best people in the world as my siblings.

"Come on, turd," Sophie says, grabbing her purse and swinging it over her shoulder.

Laughter tumbles out of my mouth. "Turd? We're going G-rated with the name-calling these days?"

"Would you prefer shithead?" Sophie giggles and unlocks the car once we're outside.

"You've been hanging around Hunter too long. I think you've got dad jokes now," I tell her as we climb inside and buckle.

"You know I can drive us," I tell her, looking at my car. I'm so damn happy I got it back and don't have to bum rides, though I enjoyed getting to spend more time with Liam. I glance over and see the G-Wagon on the street and look back toward Sophie, wishing every piece of Victoria would disappear from our lives. If Sophie notices my change in mood, she doesn't mention it, which I'm grateful for because I don't want to keep talking about it.

"Are you getting more excited about the wedding now that it's only a couple of months away?" I ask her, knowing she loves to chat about it. Mason and she are getting married the first week of December, and it's almost go-time. Sophie's meticulous about everything, nearly as much as Lennon and me—a Corrigan trait— so she hasn't left a stone unturned when it comes to planning. Hell, the two of them have been thumbing through wedding magazines every weekend at breakfast for months.

I watch as she sucks in a deep breath and lets out a dreamy sigh and a smile. "Yes. I seriously can't wait to marry the man of my dreams. I'm going to be Mrs. Sophie Holt. Mason and Sophie Holt. Mr. and Mrs. Mason Holt." I crack up at the way she's trying her soon-to-be last name. "Do you think it sounds weird?"

"Not any weirder than Lennon Manning," I snicker, and Sophie swats at me. "Be nice."

"It's just all the n's. Makes me want to sing the *Batman* tune."

Her eyes go wide. "I'm telling her you said that."

"I already have! She thought it was adorable in the way Lennon thinks everything is adorable these days. I think it's the mom in her," I suggest.

Sophie parks the car and we see Lennon waiting in the front. Even after all these years, she's still punctual as hell. As soon as we make it to her she gives us hugs. "You're five minutes late."

"Blame that one." Sophie points at me.

"I had to shower! Unless you want me sweaty and dirty," I exclaim.

"Is that a sex joke, Maddie?" Lennon asks and I nod, completely claiming it. Nothing about having sex with Liam embarrasses me. I want the whole world to know he's *all* mine. I've only been waiting since I was seventeen. The thought causes a blush to hit my cheeks.

"Lord. I can't take either of you anywhere." Sophie grins and shoos us inside.

As soon as we're at the counter, one of the workers walks up and introduces herself as Mel. She smiles as she types on a keyboard, then tells us she'll grab our items. Mel walks us into a private area with mirrors and dressing rooms, then asks Sophie if she'd like help putting on her wedding gown. Sophie's adamant she can do it herself so Mel hands us our garments and it takes no time for me and Lennon to slip into ours before Sophie begs for help.

"If it's hard getting into it, don't you think it's going to be even more difficult to take off?" I ask with a cheeky grin as we step in and notice she's frazzled, trying to reach the beautiful buttons that go up the back.

"Mason will find a way, trust me." Sophie drops her arms, giving them a rest. "It's almost worse than putting on a sports bra after taking a shower and being damp."

"Let me help," Lennon gently tells her, using her calming mom voice.

"The only thing worse than putting on a sports bra is taking it off after dancing for three hours. It literally rolls up my back and—"

"Almost done," Lennon interrupts, changing the subject as she clasps each button.

Sophie looks at us with tears in her eyes. "I just noticed your dresses. They're beautiful. You both look so good."

I place a hand on my hip and give her a wink. "Because we take after you."

"The red is perfect," Lennon states, and I confirm with a nod.

"It's going to be a Hallmark wedding, for sure!" I clap my hands, excited to celebrate Christmas soon. It brings back so many good memories from last year after I first moved into the house. Sophie and I would bake cookies and have all night watch-a-thons together. Eventually, after she and Mason get married, I know they'll move, and I'm going to miss that special bonding time we had together.

"What?" Sophie notices my change in mood.

I shake my head. "Nothing. I'm just going to really miss you at home."

"Don't you dare start that. I'm already getting emotional." Sophie fans her face as if that's ever helped stop the tears.

"You two better stop," Lennon chimes in. "Look at you, Soph. You're gorgeous."

We stare at her in awe. The cream-colored dress has a crystal beaded waistband, illusion sleeves, and a plunging neckline showing just enough skin to be sexy but not scandalous. "You look like a Disney princess," I whisper.

"Because I am." Sophie snickers, then looks back and forth between Lennon and me. "I wish Mom were here."

"She would've come." Lennon moves Sophie's long brown her off her shoulder, really showing off the sheer sleeves.

"I know, it just seemed ridiculous to have her travel here for a wedding dress try-on and all that. Plus, I have you two."

I'm smiling so big it nearly hurts. "You'll always have us, Soph. Always. Now, let's FaceTime Mom so she can see us all." We move out of the dressing room where there are more space and mirrors, and I grab Sophie's phone to call our parents. There are too many pictures to be taken with mine. After we say our hellos and I flip the camera around so they can see Sophie in her beautiful wedding gown, I hand the phone to Lennon and pull out mine. It's such an important memory to capture, and I make sure to snag all the best angles. I swear any time my sisters have big life events, I become the family photographer, but I don't mind. If for some reason dancing doesn't work out, I may have found an alternative career.

"I want to see all three of you together," Mom says and

Mel comes over and takes the phone and holds it so all of us are in the frame.

"Wow, my girls. I'm so proud," she says, and I can tell she's choking up.

"You're going to make the most beautiful bride, Soph. We can't wait," Dad adds with a big toothy grin. My heart is so warm as I look at my sisters laughing and chatting. Moving to Sacramento to be with them is still one of the best decisions I've ever made in my life. It sits right next to being relentless with Liam.

After final checks are made on measurements and everything seems to fit perfectly, we're all given the talk to maintain our weight before the wedding. "Last minute alterations cause for unnecessary stress," Mel reminds us as we sign our paperwork and the gowns are released to us.

"So that means no getting knocked up, Lennon," I tease.

"Me?" she screeches. "You're one to talk. Are you even on birth control?"

"Oh my God," Sophie groans, shaking her head. "Can we just agree everyone waits until after the wedding to get pregnant?"

"I'm waiting like ten years, so fine by me," I say. I love my niece and nephew, but I'm way too young to be thinking about having kids. Though I really want the marriage and babies life with Liam, we have plenty of time and don't need to rush for that.

On the way out, the three of us are nothing but smiles.

"Mimosas and massage time?" Lennon asks, looping one arm in mine and the other in Sophie's.

"Aren't you still breastfeeding?" I ask incredulously.

"I have enough milk in the fridge to last a few days, so we're golden. I booked us an appointment at the spa for one o'clock, which means we still have an hour."

I clasp my hands together. "Does that mean we can eat first? Pretty please?"

Sophie nods. "Yeah, there's a sandwich place right around the corner. Shouldn't take us too long."

My mouth starts watering thinking about it. I decided to sleep in and skip breakfast since Liam left the house around five. My stomach is angry growling, and I need food before I turn into a hangry monster. Lennon decides to leave her car in the parking lot and rides with us. By the time we go inside the shop, I'm ready to order one of everything off the menu. After we pay, we sit at a table close to the windows and wait for our food.

Just as I'm taking a big sip of water, my phone buzzes in my pocket, and I pull it out with a huge grin.

"It's Liam, isn't it?" Sophie asks, already knowing.

"I bet she doesn't react that way when I text her," Lennon says with a smirk.

Liam: I miss you so much.

Sophie and Lennon's eyes are glued to me, but I try to ignore them as best as I can.

Maddie: I miss you more.

Liam: Really? Prove it. Tit pics.

I snort, then look up at my sisters and tuck my lips inside my mouth.

Maddie: I really doubt Sophie and Lennon would appreciate that but hold please.

Quickly, I do a Google search and find the first picture of a tit that comes up. I was scared of what would pop up, but to my surprise the images are completely harmless. The cutest little photo of a neon green and bluebird is on my screen and I try not to burst into laughter as I send it over to him with the caption, 'cute little tit.' I can only imagine the look on his face right now.

Liam: Uhh. What the hell is this?

Maddie: That sir is a New Zealand Tit ;)

Liam: Next time I'll specify a nipple-pierced Maddie tit. But I do miss you, sweetheart.

While reading that last text I take a gulp of water. It probably wasn't the smartest idea and it takes everything I have not to spit it all over my sisters who are watching me incredulously.

Maddie: You're in big trouble. My sisters are glaring at me.

Liam: Tonight, you're all mine. I have something special planned for us.

Maddie: Something special, huh? You trying to get laid or something?

Liam: Well, since I had to leave early and miss out on our morning sex routine, figured I'd mix things up a bit. Plus, now I'm imagining you sitting on my face and am rock hard.

Maddie: Proof?

Liam: I'll prove it plenty when my cock is in your mouth later.

My cheeks heat because I start imagining it too.

Maddie: You're getting me all flustered.

Liam: Good, that means you'll be wet and ready for me ;) Have fun with your sisters. I'm almost done here and should be home in an hour. I love you!

Maddie: Love you too. See you soon!

"Oh God, it always ends in that expression when she's texting with him. I can only imagine what he said," Sophie says.

Lennon gives me a cheesy look. "She's got the love bug. Look at her."

"Learned it from you two," I playfully throw back at them. "Anyway, enough of that."

"Mads," Lennon says, then glances at Sophie nervously before focusing her attention on me. She lowers her voice. "So tell me, are you on birth control or not?"

I was actually wondering when they'd give me the talk. "No."

"No? You need to be unless you want to get pregnant." Lennon gives me a stern look.

I shrug. "I just haven't gotten around to it yet."

They're both shocked.

"And you're not pregnant right now?" Lennon just comes out and asks.

"No!" I whisper-hiss. "Jesus. I want kids eventually, but most definitely not for a long time."

"Does Liam want kids?" Sophie asks.

I shrug. "He doesn't mind practicing to make them, but we haven't had the conversation yet. We just started dating."

"Well, maybe you two should talk about it so you're on the same page. I love my babies, but it's better to be prepared for it. It's a life-changing experience and once you're a mother, it's up to you to make sure a baby human is taken care of. Mads, you need to be responsible and make an appointment."

Thankfully our food arrives and interrupts the conversation, but only temporarily.

"Mads," Sophie says, grabbing my attention from the wrap I was devouring. "I'll go with you. I mean, if you want to. It's better to be safe."

"Thanks, Soph. And I know. I just haven't had time with everything going on lately. But yeah, I will set something up and go see a doctor." I take a huge bite of my wrap to end the subject.

Thankfully, Lennon starts talking more about the wedding and the venue that Sophie chose. We've only seen photographs, but I know it's going to be absolutely beautiful with the large windows that overlook the lake. Considering it'll be December, she's hoping snow will lightly dust the surroundings to make it even more magical. I love the way Sophie lights up when she talks about marrying Mason. I can tell it comes from a real place in her heart and it's genuine.

Once we're finished eating, we leave a tip for our waitress, then head toward the spa. After we each have a mimosa, we get one-hour hot stone massages. The whole afternoon is complete bliss as the masseuse works out all the tension and stress from my muscles. By the time we walk out of the building, we all feel like jelly.

"We need to start doing that at least once a month," Lennon says with creases on her forehead from the massage table.

"Oh, definitely." Nodding in agreement, I realize how great a deep tissue massage would be when I'm overly sore from dancing.

Sophie hasn't stopped grinning since we walked out. "I feel like smoosh."

I burst out laughing. "Smoosh? What does that even mean?"

Lennon snorts and it causes me to lose it to the point of tears rolling down my cheeks.

"I'm going to pick up Aaron from Mrs. Locke, but she begged to keep Alison tonight. Hunter is at your house hanging out with the guys, so I'll meet you there for some afternoon coffee." After we exchange hugs and thank Lennon for treating us both, Sophie and I head home.

"Sorry you were put on the spot at lunch," Sophie says.

"Pfft. I'm used to it with you two, but I'm not disagreeing. I want to graduate first and actually enjoy kissing a man who isn't married before we jump to the next step. I've been waiting for years, and I don't want to rush."

Sophie tucks a piece of hair behind her ear. "Yeah, because we all know I didn't approve of your relationship when I thought he had a wife, but it seemed to all work out even though you lied to me."

I scrunch my nose at her because we've already talked about it several times, but she's not going to let me live it down. "I had to, Soph. For your protection."

"Mm-hmm," she tells me.

Last weekend, Liam went back to Vegas to finalize the

divorce with Victoria. I was hoping this day would come though I was somewhat weary it never would. My trust when it comes to her is zero. Liam made sure to text and call me as much as possible while he was there because my nerves were wrecked when he left. He was confident everything would be okay, and it was, but I couldn't help but worry it was a trap. Thankfully, it wasn't.

Now that mostly everything has settled down, Tyler decided to go back too. We asked him if he wanted to stay longer, but he insisted on going home so he could get back to work and sleep in his own bed again. Considering he lives in the same city as the mob does business, it has me concerned, but he knows what he's doing. Tyler has connections with all sorts of people, and sometimes gets caught up with some shady shit, but he's used to taking care of himself, so I didn't push it. I did force him to keep in touch with me no matter what because I care about him and he promised he would. We were all starting to get used to Tyler being around too. While I was sad to see him leave, because he quickly became a friend to me and was there to help when I desperately needed it.

A smile fills my face when I think about Liam. It's a relief knowing he's not legally married anymore and can be open about how we feel. We don't have to worry about wandering eyes and hiding from guards. Something I've desperately wanted for so long. Liam's taken every opportunity to take me out in public, hold my hand, and kiss me with no fucks of who's watching. It's all I've ever wanted. Now that he's no longer Victoria's bitch, we can have the life we've always dreamed of, one I almost thought we'd never have.

We pull up to the house, and I'm so excited to see Liam. I've been thinking about him all day. We walk inside where the guys are drinking beer and hanging out in the living room. Liam's eyes meet mine, and I feel as if I could get lost in them. Rushing to him, I happily hop on his lap, and press my lips to his.

"Well, good to see you too," he says, nuzzling his nose against mine.

"Aww." Hunter chuckles and Liam smacks him on the arm with his free hand. I hear a car door close and know it's Lennon so I get up to meet her. Sophie follows behind me and we watch as she gracefully takes Aaron from his car seat and places him on her hip. I reach out to grab him, giving him all the love as we walk back inside the house.

"There's my boy," Hunter says, stealing him from me, but I can't deny how adorable Aaron is when he sees his daddy.

"Did you have fun today? Oh look at what Mommy dressed you in, a Green Bay Packers shirt."

"Eww!" I say, knowing it rubs Hunter the wrong way because he's in love with Aaron Rogers. "Green Bay. Barf."

"Better than, oh wait, Utah doesn't even have an NFL team," he teases.

"Who cares. Football isn't my thing anyway, I just enjoy messing with you." I shrug, and he knows his insults are wasted.

"Go figure since football is actually hard and ballet is easy," he throws out, and I know he's purposely pushing my buttons, but it's what he does best. Hunter has taken his big brother role seriously since marrying Lennon.

My eyes go wide, and Liam pretends to hold me back when I lunge for Hunter. Before long, Sophie gets up and makes a pot of coffee and even gets me a cup of tea as the boys continue sipping their beers and talking shit to each other. Looking around, I'm in complete bliss. Being here with my sisters and the man I love is the perfect and simple life I've always dreamed about.

"Oh, I got you something the other day," Liam tells me, grinning and standing with me. "It's in the G-Wagon. Wanna go see?"

I narrow my eyes at him wondering if he's up to something, but I follow outside anyway, not wanting to be away from him.

"Are you just trying to get me alone? Perhaps some back seat sex for old times' sake?" I waggle my brows at him seductively.

"Maybe." He removes the space between us and moments later my back is pressed against the front door, and I can feel his hardness against my stomach.

"Mmm, I'd be okay with that," I whisper, fisting the bottom hem of his shirt, wanting him to be closer, though our bodies are pressed together.

"Fuck, I need you so goddamn bad." He nibbles on my ear before placing his lips against my neck and paints kisses across my skin.

When we break away, I laugh. "So you didn't get me anything?"

"I really did," he says, placing a kiss on my forehead. He digs in his pockets and realizes they're empty. "I was so excited to kiss the hell outta ya, I left my keys inside. Let me go grab them."

"Just tell me what it is!" I exclaim.

"You're impatient, just wait." He twists the knob and goes inside the house, then returns with his keyless pad, holding them up for me to see. Instead of waiting, I follow behind toward the G-Wagon as he unlocks it.

It happens so fast I can't even process it—a loud explosion and a burst of flames erupt—then complete darkness.

CHAPTER FOURTEEN

LIAM

I WALK OUTSIDE with the key and Maddie starts following before I press unlock. Then it all happens way too fast. As soon as I hear the double beeps of the G-Wagon unlocking, it explodes in front of us, and I fall to the ground. As I look toward Maddie, I see a piece of metal flying off the vehicle, and it strikes her. It's in flames, burning, hissing, cracking. Smoke invades the air, and the heat nearly burns my skin because I'm so close, but I stand and rush to Maddie, picking her up and carrying her away from the debris. She's limp in my arms, and there's blood dripping down her face. Sophie opens the front door and hysterically screams at the sight in front of her before everyone rushes out. She dials 911 and frantically speaks fast. I'm in shock, trying to wake up Maddie, noticing she has a large gash on her head.

"No, no," I whisper, adding pressure to the wound with my hands. Mason takes off his shirt, then hands it to me, and I try to contain the bleeding. My brain is scattered, and I know how dangerous it is for us to be standing close to the burning vehicle and inhaling the smoke, but I can't think straight.

"Who would do this?" Lennon cries, and Sophie begs Maddie to open her eyes.

"Where is the fucking ambulance?" I ask, feeling helpless, and need them to come faster.

Mason is bent over, checking her pulse. "She's breathing, but her heartbeat is weak. I think she might have gotten knocked out from the blunt force, but there could be internal bleeding in her brain."

I look at him with worry in my eyes as adrenaline pumps through my veins. I'm in so much shock, I barely notice the sirens in the distance or the police car pulling up. Moments later, there's a firetruck and the EMTs bring out a stretcher, and I move back slightly so they can examine her.

"What's the patient's name and age?" one of them asks me, but I can't move my lips. I'm stunned into silence.

"Maddie, she's twenty-one," Sophie answers.

"Any allergies?" the other asks as he places a brace around her neck.

"No. I don't think so," Sophie responds again, looking as worried as me. Mason holds her close while Lennon stays close to the house with Hunter and Aaron.

The EMTs talk to each other and count to three, then lift her up onto the stretcher. "She'll need a scan of her head and probably some stitches," one of them informs us as I stand. "We'll take good care of her, don't worry." I watch as they stroll her to the back of the ambulance, and that's when I finally snap out of it. Maddie needs me, and I can't be lost in my thoughts right now. Whoever did this will fucking pay. I don't give two shits about that G-Wagon, but the fact that Maddie's unconscious has me seeing red.

"You all need to back up. It's too dangerous until we get this fire contained," one of the firemen come over and warn us.

"I have some questions first." I hear a familiar voice, turning to see Blake and his partner walking toward me. Of fucking course.

Narrowing my eyes at the asshole, I grunt. "I don't have time for this right now." I follow behind Maddie as they load her inside, adding an oxygen mask to her face and checking her blood pressure.

"We need your statements and to write up a report considering your car exploded," Blake says sternly. "You think you're getting out of this that easy?" He steps closer, lowering his voice so no one else hears. "I know this shit is your fault."

I flex my jaw. "Still pissed you didn't get that second date, huh? Go fuck yourself," I whisper-hiss loud before stepping into the ambulance.

The EMTs look at me.

"I'm riding with her," I demand before the back doors close, and they drive off. I take Maddie's hand and rub my thumb across her knuckles, hoping she can feel me comforting her. I grit my teeth thinking about what happened. One button is all I pushed, and a goddamn bomb went off. The vehicle has keyless-go too, so as long as my keys are on me, all I have to do is touch the handle and it unlocks. So whoever did it probably hoped I'd be next to the vehicle when it exploded so that I'd blow up with it. Two days ago, I moved the G-Wagon into the street to get to my truck and left it there since I don't drive it anymore, so this had to be planted between then and now.

What the actual fuck? None of it makes sense.

Someone was watching me and planned this recently.

I've sent some bad guys back to prison over the last year, ones that weren't happy I caught them, but for some reason, this has Victoria's name written all over it. However, she bought the G-Wagon and when our deal ended, she wanted it back. If it was her, I don't understand her motives, but then again, I never have, not until it's too late. Unless her plan was to kill me and get the ultimate revenge so I couldn't use those pictures against her ever again.

We finalized the divorce last weekend, and she seemed fine in court that it was over. It's not like we ever loved each other, and the marriage was strictly business. She said she'd pick it up when she could. So if it wasn't her, I'm gonna have to explain what the hell happened, and at this point, I have no idea. My mind goes crazy with theories, but I need to focus on Maddie right now.

Leaning over, I whisper in Maddie's ear, telling her everything is going to be okay and that I love her. Nothing will ever make me leave her, not even Blake and his insinuations. Her being unconscious and her having the possibility of internal bleeding from the hit concerns me the most. The piece that smacked her flew over so fast, there was no way she could've seen it in time to move out of the way. Guys on my college football team used to get concussions all the time but were never out for this long. Granted, they were much bigger than Maddie.

The ambulance slows and pulls into the bay outside of the emergency room. They unload the stretcher, but I don't let her out of my sight as they rush Maddie inside and take her into a room. I hear one of the EMTs giving the nurses a brief summary of what happened and her injuries. I watch in panic as chaos ensues, a nurse hooks her up to an IV of fluids, another puts a blood pressure cuff around her arm, and another inspects the wound on her head. They talk to each other, listing what tests need to be done, and what they're looking for.

"Her O2 is a little low, putting an oxygen mask on," a

female nurse instructs to the other who's typing on a portable computer desk.

"What? Why's her oxygen low?"

"It's not uncommon, especially if she inhaled any smoke." She gives me a soft smile. "It's mostly precautionary."

I can't inhale deep enough to fill my lungs so I'm nearly gasping for air. Maddie lays on the bed, looking so fragile and battered, and I feel helpless as hell. Standing here, all I can do is hold her hand and beg her to wake up.

"Wow, this one is deep," one of the nurses says as she inspects her head wound.

"Is she going to be okay?" I ask nervously.

She glances up at me. "Are you her husband?"

I swallow hard. "I'm her boyfriend and was with her when this happened," I explain, looking down at my shirt, noticing blood on it. Maddie's blood. All this time, I've been worried about her getting hurt being around me; however, I never imagined something like this could happen.

Once the wound is cleaned, a male doctor enters and introduces himself to me. Next, the nurse reads out pertinent information, and he looks at her cut. After a moment, the doctor explains he'll suture the cut to hopefully avoid infections and to stop the bleeding. Afterward they'll take her for a CT scan to check for any fractures or internal bleeding. All I can think about is how confused she's going to be about all of this. She'll have a lot of questions, but unfortunately, I don't have many answers.

Whoever did this will fucking pay, it's the last thought that comes into my mind as my phone buzzes with a group text message from Lennon, Sophie, Hunter, and Mason.

Sophie: We're all on our way there right now.

Lennon: I'm so worried. Please update us, Liam.

Hunter: Yeah, let us know how she's doing. Also, I talked to the cops. They said a detective may meet you at the hospital.

Mason: What the fuck happened?

I read them all, already overwhelmed.

Liam: She's stable. They just stitched the cut on her head, and they're taking her to get a scan soon. Finding out as much as I can, but it's gonna be a while. Don't know what happened. I pressed unlock to the G-Wagon and it exploded. That's all I know.

They each send a thank you. There has only been a handful of times in my life where I've felt so defeated, and this is one of them. I stare at Maddie as they continue to work on her, then wheel her off for a CT scan. She's gone for almost an hour, and I can barely concentrate. Everyone's in the waiting room since they'll only allow one person in here, and I told them I'd take turns if they wanted to see her. I pace, reading all the medical signs posted on the wall, and just when I sit down in the chair, she's brought back in.

I stand over her, gently brushing my fingers against her arm, overly anxious.

With a raspy voice, she looks at me. "Liam?"

Relief and joy flood through me, and I kneel so I can be closer to her face. "Mads. Baby."

"What happened?" Wincing, she reaches for her head,

but I grab her hand and place kisses along her knuckles. "My head hurts so bad. The room feels like it's spinning."

"I know, baby. There was an accident. Someone planted a bomb in the G-Wagon, and when it exploded, a piece of metal flew off and struck you. It gave you a pretty big gash and bruises but they stitched it up. You probably have a concussion, but they did a CT scan to check for bleeding or fractures. They should be back with the results soon."

"Wow." She blinks. "I don't remember any of that," she says, closing her eyes tight, and I can't imagine how much pain she's in. "Feels like a hammer is pounding against my skull, though."

"I'm so sorry, Maddie. God, I'm so sorry," I repeat over and over, choking on each word.

"You didn't do this," she says, even in a state like this. Sweet, compassionate Maddie won't allow me to blame myself.

I shake my head. "It's all my fault. I was targeted and you got hurt. This is my worst nightmare," I admit, hating the discomfort that's written all over her face.

"I'm okay. It'll be okay." I fucking hope so. But I know she's a fighter.

"Your sisters are here. Do you want to see them? We'll have to take turns, but I'll force myself to leave and let them in."

Her eyes are sad, but she nods. "Yes, please."

I smile and give her a soft kiss before standing.

"I love you, Liam," she tells me before I walk out of the room.

"I love you too. Always."

I go into the waiting room, and Sophie and Lennon both jump up when they see me.

"Well?" Sophie asks.

"Just waiting on the results of the CT scan, but she's finally awake," I explain.

"Oh, thank God," Lennon breathes out and places her hand over her heart. Hunter is holding baby Aaron in his lap, but he's listening intently to everything we say.

"She wants to see you two." I look at Lennon and Sophie. "I told her you were here."

The two of them argue about who's going first, but Sophie plays the oldest sister card and wins. "I won't be too long," Sophie tells her, then gets a visitor's badge and is escorted to the back. Before I can sit down with the others, a detective walks up. Mason stands and shakes his hand, and I'm sure they know each other because of their professions and who Mason's father is.

"Hi, Liam Evans?" He's older, but it looks like he could take any of us in a fight.

"Yeah," I say. "That's me."

"I'm Detective Knight." He turns his head and looks around. "Do you have a moment to chat in private about what happened?"

I glance at Mason and Hunter. Mason gives me a head nod, and by his reaction, I know I can actually trust this guy. The two of us walk into a long hallway with no one else around us other than the random person going from the vending machines back to the waiting room. The detective pulls a small notepad from his pocket and begins with his questions.

"So the car is registered to Victoria O'Leary. Did you not change it over into your name?"

"That's my ex-wife," I explain. "She was coming to pick it up soon." I blow out a breath. "I actually have to call her and tell her about this because she's not aware."

"Oh, alright, makes sense. Can you tell me what you were doing before the explosion?" he asks.

I go through the afternoon, about how I went to work and explained what I do for a living. Then I tell him we had a few beers and the girls came back from being together, and how I remembered I had bought something for Maddie. I recall every step from kissing her, to going inside, to unlocking the vehicle.

"So it blew up after you hit unlock?" he asks.

I nod. "Within seconds."

He studies me carefully. "Do you know anyone who would have some sort of vendetta against you? Someone who'd want to hurt or kill you?"

"Considering my profession, I'd say there are a lot of people who don't really care for me."

"Enough to want you dead?" he asks.

My mouth goes dry as I go through the list of people I've brought to jail this year. "Most of them have issues. They all seemed pretty upset, but I couldn't name any one who would go to this extreme."

"No one?" he presses.

I think about Victoria again, but the last thing I want to do is name-drop her and bring more attention to the mob than necessary. It'd just open more drama, and she'd somehow spin it to make me look insane, but it *could* be her.

"No one," I say matter-of-factly.

"Well, here's my card. If you think of anything or anyone, please give me a call. We'll be doing a full investigation due to the nature of the explosion. Stay safe, Liam. This is a dangerous situation until we figure out who did this."

"Thanks, Detective." We exchange a firm handshake, and before I go back to the waiting area, I pull out my phone, look around, then call Victoria.

Having to reach out to her fucking sucks, but I need to confront her, though I'm not sure she'd admit it anyway. Surprisingly, she answers the phone on the third ring.

"What do you want?" she asks in her typical bored tone.

Not the nicest way to answer, but not completely unexpected either.

I let out a long sigh and keep my voice low. "What the fuck are you trying to do?"

"Excuse me?"

"Listen. I know you tried to fucking kill me, Victoria. You planted something in the goddamn Mercedes so it would blow the hell up when I unlocked it. That's really messed up, even for *you*."

"What are you talking about? I didn't try to kill you because honestly, I don't give two shits about you anymore. And what do you mean, blow up? I already scheduled to have it picked up next week."

I pause for a moment, trying to comprehend what she said. "What?"

Between gritted teeth, she speaks. "I had already found a buyer for that vehicle. Now I'm fucking livid. Is this a fucking joke?"

I pinch the bridge of my nose. "No! But it's destroyed. A piece flew and struck Maddie in the head," I grit, still fuming. "You sure this isn't just another one of your childish games?"

"How dare you! Why would I destroy something I spent nearly a quarter of a million dollars on? Are you an idiot?" Her voice raises in octave until she's nearly screaming. The sound is like nails on a chalkboard. "Wait, never mind. That was a stupid question."

It's not healthy for her to be so upset while pregnant, and even though I don't give two shits about her, I'm not going to let her use this to blame me for her going into preterm labor or anything, so I try to be civil and end the conversation. "I apologize for accusing you and sorry about all this. I have no idea who did it."

"Thankfully, I have insurance on it," she throws back without any compassion that Maddie got hurt. "Guess it's not a complete loss."

I roll my eyes. "The detectives are going to do a full investigation, so I'll let you know if I hear anything."

"Alright, great. Well, I gotta go. You've wasted enough of my time already," Victoria tells me before ending the call.

Frustrated, I shove my phone in my pocket, then walk back to the waiting room and see Sophie has returned. As soon as she sees me, she gives me a hug. I can tell she's upset.

"They're going to move her into another room soon to observe her overnight. I'm so glad you're okay. You could've died, Liam." Sophie searches my face, and I place my hand on her shoulder.

"Soph, I'm fine. A little shaken up and anxious about Maddie, but I'm okay. And she's going to be okay too." I try to console her and it seems to work because she sits down and places her head on Mason's shoulder, who wraps his arms around her.

"What did Logan say?"

"Logan?" I question. "Oh, Detective Knight. He told me to be careful and to call him if I think of anything that may help them find who did this."

"It's obvious this was done intentionally to kill you," Hunter speaks up, Aaron asleep in his arms.

"Yeah, and that's the scary part. Whoever it is knows where I live. Knows what I drive. I don't think this is going to be over anytime soon, and I need to get to the bottom of it so no one else gets hurt." I can't even bring myself to make

177

eye contact with them. It's not only me who's in danger, but my friends too.

A nurse explains they're moving Maddie to the sixth floor of the hospital and gives us the room number. All of us make our way to the elevator, and I once Lennon is back, I hear her tell Sophie they'll need to go soon because Aaron is getting cranky. We say our goodbyes, then Mason, Sophie, and I step inside. We're quiet as the elevator climbs, and I'm still trying to understand everything.

Before we walk inside the room, Sophie stops me. "Do you think Victoria is behind this?"

Mason stares at me.

"Not anymore. I called her, and she was actually pissed off because she had already sold it."

"That's frightening, Liam," she says. "The enemy you know is always better than the one you don't."

"I know." I let out a ragged breath and contemplate putting cameras outside the house. Perhaps one of those camera motion-sensor doorbells would be smart so if whoever did this returns, I'll be able to see who it is.

Maddie's bed is adjusted higher than before, and she grins when she sees us.

"How are you feeling?" I ask, brushing my fingers gently against her cheek.

"Like shit." A small smile follows her words, and I offer to help adjust her pillow until she's comfortable.

Sophie chats with Maddie, asking her what she remembers from today. It takes her a minute to recall walking outside with me. After a second, she turns to me. "Wait, weren't you going to give me something? I imagine it wasn't a cut to the head and a concussion," she jokes with a weak chuckle.

I try to laugh but can't even force it. "I got you a T-shirt with a ballerina on it. Thought it'd look cute on you."

She sticks out her bottom lip. "That's sad. Do you think it's ruined?"

Mason chuckles. "There's nothing left but the tires and frame."

I remember the file folders of research I had moved in there too. It's going to take me weeks to compile all that again, but right now, I can't worry about it. The only thing I'm concerned about is Maddie because she's the most important. The Mercedes, the paperwork, the shirt—all of it can be replaced. Maddie can't.

Mason stands and stretches as Sophie yawns.

"You all should go. I'm pretty tired," Maddie says.

"Are you sure?" Sophie asks. "We'll stay here with you for a little while longer."

"No, I'm good. I've had a long day," she insists. "Plus hospitals suck. I know those chairs can't be cozy."

Sophie shrugs. "Okay, if you're sure that's what you want."

"I am. Go. I'll be fine as long as they keep pumping me with the good stuff." She closes her eyes tight, and I know it's her head. I had a concussion a few times, and it was terrible. I was unable to focus, and felt disoriented and exhausted all at the same time.

Sophie leans over and hugs Maddie. "I'm so glad you're okay."

The doctor walks in with a folder and looks around the room before going to Maddie. "I wanted to go over your CT scan results with you. Is it okay if they're in the room?"

"Yes, they're family," she says, and the doctor nods.

"There are no signs of swelling or bleeding, which is kind of a miracle considering how hard you were hit. So we'll just keep an eye on your vitals, and if everything looks fine throughout the night, you'll be released tomorrow." He pats Maddie's hand with a small smile. "Sounds like you took a pretty hard fall, so enjoy the meds while you can."

"I feel like I got beat up." She musters a laugh.

"Do you have any questions for me?" He glances at Maddie, then at the rest of us.

We all shake our heads.

"I'm good, I think," Maddie speaks up. "Just tired."

"You might feel like that for a few days," he warns. "It's normal. If you need anything or start feeling worse, let us know, okay?"

"I will," Maddie says.

Sophie and Mason say their goodbyes after the doctor leaves, and then it's just Maddie and me.

"Are you going too?" she asks.

"Absolutely not." I pull the chair closer so I can sit next to the bed and still hold her hand. "I'm staying here with you until you're released. It's the least I can do so the guilt doesn't eat me alive."

"Guilt?" She looks confused.

I kiss her knuckles. She slides her hand across my cheek and smiles.

Bowing my head, I say, "You wouldn't be here if it weren't for me."

"I already told you this wasn't your fault, Liam." The fact that she's consoling me has me feeling bad because I'm supposed to be the strong one for her.

"Well, I feel responsible as fuck. Someone's after me, and you got hurt in the crossfire. I'm going to find out who did this and make them pay," I promise.

She furrows her brows and shakes her head. "No. Two wrongs don't make a right."

The room grows quiet before she turns her head and flips through the channels, then stops on *Dirty Dancing*. "Remember this movie?"

"How could I forget it?" Our eyes meet again.

"You ever had sex in a hospital room?"

I glare at her. "You literally have a concussion and were knocked unconscious a few hours ago."

She shrugs and lifts her eyebrows. "Well, my lower region feels just fine."

"You are so bad." I smirk and wonder if she's playing with me or not. "We could get caught."

Laughter escapes her. "That hasn't stopped you before. But I guess you're right, but also so tempting."

Arching a brow, I smirk at her playful banter, thankful she's able to somewhat be herself. "I might need to call the doctor back in here and make him double-check that you don't have brain damage or something," I tease.

She takes my hand again and interlocks our fingers. "I love you. Have I told you that today?"

"You have, but I never get sick of hearing it. Love you too, baby."

We continue watching *Dirty Dancing*, and Maddie whispers every line, which causes me to smile. Concussion and still has it all memorized. I lay my head on the bed, and she runs her fingers through my hair, calming me when I should be calming her. I could've lost Maddie today, and the thought alone nearly destroys me.

It's been two weeks since Maddie was released from the hospital. She recovered fine and the cut on her head is barely visible now. Two days afterward, she was able to go back to school but was told to take it easy for a week, which meant limited dancing. I've apologized so many times that she's started slapping my chest to stop me from feeling guilty.

The anxiety I had when Victoria was following our every move has returned. I'm not sure this feeling will go away anytime soon, not until I find out who's responsible for this. Though there's an investigation, the detectives and police have zero leads. I'm sure this won't ever be solved because whoever did it knew exactly what they were doing not to leave any evidence behind. So until I give them names for people who may want me dead, they have no idea where to start. The problem is, I'm on too many people's shit list.

Once Maddie gets out of the shower, I have my final tux fitting for Sophie and Mason's wedding that's in two weeks. Maddie said she'd join me, and we're making an afternoon out of it. Honestly, I can't believe the big day is almost here. I feel as if I'm losing track of time. Maybe it's because so much shit has happened in the past year that my head is still spinning from it all.

Soon, Maddie comes downstairs smelling like honey. I want to eat her up, but considering we got naked and sweaty before she went upstairs and my appointment is in thirty minutes, there's no way.

"What?" She laughs, drying her long hair with a towel.

I stand and cross the room until I'm in front of her. Without saying a word, I dip down and place a chaste kiss on her lips, and she melts into me, releasing a long sigh. "You taste good," she whispers across my lips.

"You do too." I want her again.

"You're insatiable, you know that?"

I lift an eyebrow at her. "You're not complaining, are you?"

"Of course not!" She pulls me close to her. "But we don't have much time."

"All I need is fifteen minutes," I purr against her ear. "Ten if you scream my name really loud."

She throws her head back and laughs before grabbing my hand, then leads me to the bedroom. In a snap, we undress and are on the bed, fucking like our lives depend on it. Considering we're home alone, Maddie moans loud enough for the entire neighborhood to hear. It doesn't take long before we're both unraveling and losing ourselves with each other again. She topples on my chest and smiles, trying to catch her breath. "Damn."

"Same." I smile, wrapping my arms around her body.

"Can we skip the fitting and just stay here all day?"

I chuckle hard. "Sophie will murder us both. You want that?"

She pouts. "No. You're right. Better get going."

We clean up and put on our clothes, then we're out the door. On the drive over, Maddie talks about the wedding and how excited she is for Sophie and Mason.

"So, I wanted to talk to you about something," I say. "I

know you mentioned you'd stay with your parents in Tahoe City, but I was thinking you'd stay with me instead."

Her eyes go wide. "My parents will know I'm with you. They'd so not approve."

"Do your parents make all your decisions for you?" I challenge, knowing the answer as she looks down at the butterfly tattoo on her wrist.

"Well…" She pauses. "No, but it's best if they don't know about our sleeping arrangement."

I park the truck and turn toward her. "Okay then, never mind."

"No, no. I'd love to stay with you, but I need to figure out what to tell them."

Leaning over, I slide my lips across hers. "Tell them you'd rather fuck your boyfriend all weekend."

She rears back and playfully slaps my arm. "Pretty sure my dad would kill you. Nope, he definitely would."

"Then I guess he can get in line." I smack my lips against hers real quick before we get out of the truck and walk inside the shop smiling.

Once we're through the doors, one of the sales reps named Thomas grabs my tux and guides me into a dressing room. He gives me shoes and a red tie to complete the look. It all gives me reminders of Victoria and how she forced me to get fitted for expensive suits. I push the thoughts away as quickly as they come and adjust my tie before stepping out and showing Maddie.

Her mouth falls open as she studies me from head to toe. "Uhh."

I smooth my hands down my chest. "Do I look okay?"

Maddie swallows hard. "No words." She walks toward me and wraps her arms around my waist. "You look like a hot CEO or something."

"You've been watching way too much TV."

"Mmm," she says as a throat clears behind us and interrupts our moment. Thomas flashes a smile, then asks to take a look. He checks the hems and inseam of my pants, then the length of the arms. "Looks like it's a good fit. Do you see anything you'd like changed?"

I shake my head, moving slightly. "No, feels great."

"No complaints from me," Maddie adds, interlocking her fingers with mine. I love that we can be like this publicly after hiding for so long.

"Awesome, I'll just get you to sign some paperwork to finalize everything. Then you can pick it up three days before the event."

"Perfect," I say.

Thomas walks away, and I sneak a kiss from Maddie before going to change.

She's all smiles when I walk away. As I'm putting on my jeans and T-shirt, I think about spending the weekend with her in a small little cabin I rented by the lake. It's got the best view I could find. I plan to make all her gushy romantic dreams come true with an unlimited amount of chocolate-covered strawberries, champagne, and a crackling fireplace as the snow falls outside. Hallmark won't have shit on me, but we may not leave the bed for days.

CHAPTER FIFTEEN

MADDIE

My winter recital went off without a hitch. Liam was there watching me along with my sisters, Mason, and Hunter. I worked hard all semester, and now I just have to study for finals before Christmas break.

Today is finally Sophie and Mason's wedding day, and I'm overjoyed by all the excitement. I love weddings more than any of my sisters and can't believe it's actually here. It's been a year since Mason proposed, and four months ago they picked a date. Since then, Sophie has busted her ass to get everything together to make sure the ceremony and reception are flawless.

Sophie made us meet in the dressing quarters early so we could start drinking champagne beforehand. Though my mother scolded us because she doesn't approve of drinking, Sophie didn't care, and I don't blame her. This is her special day, and she should be allowed to do whatever the hell she wants, even if that means a slight buzz.

So we could all be picture-perfect, Sophie hired a hairdresser and makeup artist to pamper us. We've been sitting around goofing off and have nearly emptied the whole bottle of bubbly between the three of us, but she brought a backup.

"Are you nervous?" I ask Sophie as she looks out the window with her fluffy bride robe wrapped around her body.

"Hell no," she says. "I've been dreaming of marrying Mason for way too long. I'm more than ready."

Mom keeps coming in and out of the room, chatting with our family that arrived early, then returning to check on us. She's running around like a chicken with her head cut off, but she lives for moments like this. We're her baby girls, and she likes to feel needed. I'll be the last one who's not married, and while I'm not upset about it because I don't want to rush anything, I hope I'm not waiting a decade for a proposal. Though it took Liam four years to admit he even liked me, I know he's the only one I want to be with for the rest of my life.

Sophie wanted the wedding to be small and intimate and only invited close friends and family. Mom and Dad wanted to give an open invitation to the entire church, but Sophie put her foot down and refused. They had no choice but to agree.

An hour before the wedding starts, I decide to go out and see who's all here. I slip on my dress and leave Lennon and Sophie as a few of our aunts and cousins walk in. The first person I want to find is Liam, but I'm stopped by Serena and the baby. I pull Marcus into my arms and want to capture the most adorable little boy in the world. "Oh my goodness, Serena. He's getting so big, and he's such a cutie."

"Thank you." She beams. "I'm so happy to be able to be here for Mason and Sophie. This place is beautiful."

"Isn't it?" I look up at the high ceilings that remind me of a cathedral. The space is what wedding dreams are made of.

Marcus grows fussy so I hand him back to Serena before he starts crying. He's only five months and probably wants to eat or be changed, and I can't help with either of those.

"You make mom life look easy," I tell her, when he suddenly calms down in her arms.

She playfully rolls her eyes and laughs. "I kinda had to figure it all out, didn't I?" Serena shrugs, but honestly, she's an inspiration. Before she got pregnant, she was working a million hours a week as a lawyer, and even though that's still her job, she now balances it with being a single mom.

"You're doing a great job. Marcus looks healthy and happy." I rub the pad of my finger along his chubby cheek as he sucks his fingers.

Serena looks like she's going to cry as I give her a reassuring smile. She thanks me, then goes to the gigantic room where the ceremony will be held while pulling a bottle out of her shoulder bag. Knowing where the guys' dressing area is, I walk down the hallway, and before I can knock, my hand is being grabbed, and I'm being tugged away. I turn to see Liam who plants a wet kiss on my lips. Funny enough, he tastes like whiskey and mints.

"Have you been drinking?" I giggle.

"Have you?" Liam grins wide. "You taste like champagne. And you look fucking gorgeous. Damn, how did I get so lucky?" He wraps my hands around his waist and pulls me in closer.

I lean forward. "That's a very good question, and you just might get *lucky* later. Keep the tux on when we get back to the cabin so I can rip it off with my teeth."

"It's a rental, so no ripping." He chuckles and narrows his eyes. "What did you tell your parents?"

"What you told me to tell them a few weeks ago. That I'd be fucking my boyfriend all weekend and staying with him."

For a second, he stills and his mouth falls open. "You did not."

I shrug and pretend to walk away, but he gently loops his arm around my waist and stops me.

"Mads, I haven't seen your dad yet. He'll strangle me with his bare hands, send me to hell, and then I won't be able to be Mason's best man."

Grinning, I stand on my tiptoes and kiss his scruffy jaw. "I told them I was staying with one of Sophie's friends this weekend. Which technically, you are, so I didn't even have to lie."

"And they didn't ask you which one?" He furrows his brows as if he doesn't believe it's this easy to get away with this.

"No. They know not to press me because I'll tell them to mind their own business and stay out of mine. Plus, my sisters have done so many worse things, at this point, they wouldn't be shocked by anything. I've basically got a Get Out of Jail Free card from the sister who got pregnant before she was married and the other who lived with her boyfriend before marriage. So I pretty much can do no evil."

"You're terrible," he quips.

"Because you made me that way," I tell him innocently.

Shaking his head, he chuckles. "Oh hell naw. You were like this from the moment I met you. I did zero corruption. In fact, you corrupted me."

"Mm-hmm." I smirk. "You sure about that?"

He lifts his hand and shows an inch with his fingers. "Okay, I might be slightly guilty."

"Liam," I hear my father say from behind. Liam's eyes go wide, and he stiffens.

Liam spins around and straightens his shoulders. "Mr.

Corrigan, hello." He holds out his hand, then shakes my father's. "How are you, sir?"

"Fantastic." Dad lets go of Liam, then gives me a hug. "Madelyn, darling. You look great." For a second, I think I see him tear up. "My girls are becoming so grown. Now I feel old."

"Old? You don't look a day over forty, Daddy," I say, and he grins.

"Thanks, sweetie. Must be all those essential oils your mother makes me use," he says, and before long, we're being interrupted by Lennon and Hunter, so Liam and I excuse ourselves.

"Do they know we're dating?" Liam finally asks as he leads me down a private hallway that has a window with the perfect view of the lake.

I bite my lip and shake my head. "I haven't broken the news to them yet. After the whole wife announcement at Lennon's house this past summer, and all the things my mother said about how in love you two looked, it seemed awkward to bring up. Plus, they know we all live together. Sophie already mentioned that. Funny enough though, they think Sophie and I share a room, like we're kids again."

There's something in Liam's expression that I can't quite place, and it seems as if I hurt his feelings. I don't want my parents to judge him based on his past because Liam is the love of my life. I want them to accept him as easily as they accepted Hunter or Mason. "Are you okay?"

"Yeah, I just don't know how I should act if they don't know." He lets out a breath and forces a smile.

"Fine, I'll tell them right now if that's what you want. I think we should wait, you know, so they can't corner you and ask you a million questions."

Grabbing my hand, Liam pulls me back. "No, that's not

what I want. I understand timing is everything. But I don't care what they or anyone says, you're mine."

"I'm always yours, baby," I tell him, stealing a kiss.

"What time is it?" he asks, and I realize I need to go back to the dressing room.

"I need to get back to Soph," I say.

"You should. Love you." We kiss again, and I pour myself into him.

"Love you too." I give him a wink before walking away.

By the time I get back to the room, Sophie's slipping on her dress and Mom and Lennon are helping with the buttons in the back. The photographer is busy taking photos, and once Sophie's all dressed, I stand in front of her, and we exchange a big hug.

"You look so gorgeous!" I beam. "Mason's gonna pass out in shock," I tease, wiping the corners of my eyes.

"Don't you dare cry," she says. "If you start, then I'll start, and we don't want to ruin our makeup."

"I know. I'm just so happy for you guys."

Lennon pats Sophie on the shoulder and my mother and her step to the side, grinning proudly. "You're all ready to go," Lennon announces.

"Okay, can we get the four of you together," the photographer asks, and we happily pose. The camera clicks a few times, and when she's done, she shows us some of the shots she's gotten so far. Already they look so good, and I can't wait to see them all.

"Sophie, I have my partner bringing Mason so we can get a few 'before the wedding' shots, but I'll make sure he doesn't actually see you yet."

"Oh my God, I love pictures like that!" I exclaim. "There are so many creative ones on Pinterest."

"Then you're gonna adore what we have planned," she replies, and Sophie follows the photographer.

"Guess we should start getting lined up then?" Lennon asks as soon as our father walks in. My heart is racing thinking about the ceremony, and I can only imagine how Sophie feels right now. The photographer positions Sophie against the door and tells her to wrap her hand around the door, and when Mason gets closer, she directs him to the other side of the door so he can't see Sophie. It's such a cute pose, and I can't wait to see the shots. Once they're done, I tell the soon-to-be-married couple we'll see them at the altar before we make our way to the back of the church.

As soon as Hunter sees Lennon, he greets her with a kiss, and Liam is hesitant, but I kiss him anyway. I might be more brave because I know my Dad is with Sophie and my mom isn't around yet. My parents will find out sooner or later, and while I don't want to explain everything right away, I'd rather not hide the way I feel about Liam either. We did that for way too long already. We're laughing and goofing off when Mason arrives with my bouquet I forgot in the bridal suite.

"Ooh, thank you. You're a lifesaver."

Mason laughs. "No problem."

"You nervous?" I ask.

"Nah. I'm ready." He grins.

The music starts, and when Alison comes around the corner, I get all emotional again. She's the cutest flower girl in the world as she walks down with Bentley, one of our cousin's sons. Liam places his arm around me, and I lean into him, feeling his warmth.

"I'll see you soon," he tells me, kissing me sweetly before he and Mason walk to the side door. They wait to enter the front of the room.

Mason didn't invite his father because there's still too much bad blood between them. His mother is here, though, and she walked out with his stepdad after all of our grandparents. Mom is ushered down next, and I know when she takes her seat, the big show is about to start. Once the assistant pastor from my parents' church comes into view, so do Liam and Mason. Lennon is the matron of honor and glides down the aisle alone with her beautiful bouquet of red roses. I take a deep breath and look behind me when I see Sophie and my dad. I wave at her, then turn around and start walking.

My eyes land on Liam as I make my way down, and he's already staring at me. My body heats, and though fifty people are staring at me, the only person who matters to me is Liam. The smile never fades as I make it to Lennon, who wraps her arm around me and squeezes. My face already hurts from grinning so much, and the events have just started.

Alison moves forward throwing the flower petals on beat, and Bentley holds the cutest little sign that says "Here Comes the Bride." My heart melts. Lennon stands so proud as Alison continues forward, then goes and sits by Mrs. Locke. For being only two, she did a great job. When "Canon in D" starts and Sophie and our father appear, that's when the tears I was holding back begin to fall.

Sophie glides toward us, and while we stare at her, her eyes lock on her man. I catch a glimpse of Mason's face, and he's in complete and utter awe of his bride. When she greets him, he whispers something in her ear, and Sophie blushes. I glance at Liam, and our gazes lock, electricity streaming between us. I want to tell him how much I love him and how I want to spend forever with him, but I think he already knows. Something flickers in his eyes, and I can't stop thinking about how handsome he is. And that he's mine.

The ceremony runs smoothly, and everything about their love is admirable. Sophie and Mason say their I Do's, and soon they're sealing their love with a passionate kiss. Thank God for waterproof mascara and the tissues Lennon gives me because I'm overcome with emotions. They're finally starting the life they always dreamed of having together.

After the photographer takes more pictures, the reception begins, and I look out the window to see a layer of powdery snow covering everything. Sophie got her dream wedding. The party is quaint and doesn't last as long as most receptions, and I imagine it's because the married couple is ready to bang each other's brains out. I'm laughing at the thought of it as we all say our goodbyes. I wait for my parents to leave before Liam and I do so they don't get suspicious, and I won't have to answer any personal questions. The last thing I need is to be added to the prayer list or be given "the talk."

Liam opens the truck door for me, and I climb inside. He holds my hand and kisses my knuckles before we drive the short distance to the small cabin he rented that overlooks the lake. We had the rehearsal and dinner last night but were too tired afterward to enjoy the space, but now we're both buzzing from the wedding and can't keep our hands off one another.

As soon as I walk inside the cabin, I look around and gasp. Music plays softly, and wood crackles in the fireplace as the flames dance. Chocolate-covered strawberries and a bottle of champagne sit on the small coffee table in front of the couch. I glance back at Liam, who's watching me intently with a smirk on his lips.

"How did you pull this off? I never saw you leave." I

saunter to him and place my arms around his neck, pulling his mouth to mine.

"I know people," he whispers and grabs a handful of my ass. "You're so goddamn beautiful, you know that?"

Butterflies dance in the pit of my stomach as Liam leads me to the couch and pours us both a glass of champagne.

"What's the special occasion?" I ask with an eyebrow popped as I take a sip.

"You," he quips, setting down his glass on the table before we sit on the couch, laughing as we kick off our shoes. I snag a chocolate-covered strawberry and moan when I take a bite. It's so delicious.

Liam lets out a hearty laugh, watching me.

"This is amazing, babe. Be careful, I just might get used to this type of treatment."

Leaning over, he kisses me on my shoulder and trails his lips up to my mouth.

"Mmm," he hums.

"Can you taste the strawberry?" I whisper.

"No, but I can taste you." The husk in his voice has goose bumps trailing up and down my arms. Before I can reply, his lips are against mine, and I struggle to unbutton his suit jacket. Eventually, it comes off, and I yank his tie, forcing him closer as he leans into me.

"I have an idea for this." I wrap the red silk around my hand and watch something swirl behind Liam's eyes. He doesn't say a word as he removes it from around his neck and places it over the back of the couch. Standing, he gives me his hand and lifts me. With one swift movement, I'm in his arms, then he grabs the tie. I want him, all of him, and I don't know how much longer I can wait.

The only man on my mind is Liam. He's teasing and taking his time with me, driving me wild. He sets me down on the plush floor in the bedroom. Double-paned windows give an incredible view of the lake. Honestly, there's not a bad spot in this entire little cabin.

Carefully, he slides his fingers behind my back and unzips my dress until it falls to the ground in a puddle around my feet. My breath quickens when he unsnaps my bra.

"A red thong," he murmurs. "I'm gonna have to keep this."

I grin. "It was for you anyway."

Looping his fingers over the thin material that holds the panties to my hips, he tugs and snaps them off my body, causing me to gasp. His hands move down my side, then between my legs until he's circling my clit. I hang on to him, ready to crumple beneath his touch as he slides a finger inside me. A throaty moan escapes me as he pulls away, and I immediately frown at the loss of his touch.

"Fuck, Mads. You're soaking wet," he says, then places his finger between his lips. "You taste better than strawberries."

Liam grabs the tie and carefully places it over my eyes and wraps it around my head so I can't see a thing. My breathing is erratic as I feel him drop to his knees. Seconds later, he hooks one of my legs over his shoulder and starts devouring me. His tongue flicks and twirls against my clit, and at any moment, I'll lose my balance because I feel as if I'm floating. Then, just like that, he pulls away and stops. He pushes me slightly until the back of my legs hit the mattress, and I fall against the mattress. After a moment, he grabs my ass and shifts me closer to the edge of the bed.

"This is much better," he whispers against my skin, placing light kisses along my inner thighs before he returns to his place of solitude. With my hands in fists, I grab the comforter, knowing the orgasm is building fast and hard. It's obvious Liam knows it too because when my back arches, he increases his pace, waging war on my pussy with his mouth.

"Yes, yes, yes…Liam," I breathe out, my entire body seizing as I fall deeper.

"Come on my tongue, baby," Liam demands. "I can tell you're close."

Deep groans release from me as the orgasm nearly catapults me into a different dimension. I feel as if I'm floating before I fall back to reality. My eyes flutter open, exhilaration courses through my veins, and I pull off the makeshift blindfold and peer at him with an insatiable amount of want and need. He stands, then leans over my body, guiding his hand to my breast and playing with my nipple ring. Resting against the mattress as he devours my lips, I can taste my arousal on him.

Straightening up, Liam starts to undress, but I stand to help him, wobbly on my feet. I unclasp and unzip his pants before pushing them down with his boxers. Within moments, he's completely naked and hard in my palm. Sitting on the edge of the bed, I take his length into my mouth, paying extra close attention to the tip as I gently massage his balls. His head rolls back as he lets out animalistic grunts. My goal is to pleasure him like he's mother fucking royalty, not leaving an inch of his cock unworshipped.

Liam runs his fingers through my hair, and I push away to look up at him.

"I need to feel you more than I need to breathe," he growls, tracing my jaw with his thumb. Before he can command me, I move up the bed, giving him space to come to me. Slowly, he enters me, and I adjust my body to take all of him. I finally went and saw my doctor after Sophie and Lennon scolded me about it, which I knew was the smart thing to do. Getting on birth control means we don't have to frantically find a condom. His width and length nearly break me in two as he takes it slow and steady, making love to me, not fucking me like a weekend pleasure. Though, we've shared several of those moments. But right now, it's different. It's personal and intense, the pure emotion releasing from my breathless pants. I scratch my fingernails down his back as he pounds into me, giving me everything he has, and though I've got all of him, I want more. I *need* more of him.

"Liam, more," I whisper. Another orgasm begs to take hold, building, ready to spill over, and then I lose all control, which only encourages him to continue. I'm nearly blinded by passion, by love, by *him*. It's so strong, I can barely breathe, but my feelings for Liam have always felt overpowering. With an arched back, I ride the wave, never wanting to lose the high he brings me to.

"I love you," he says against my neck, and I feel it in his body. He's close.

"I love you too," I repeat. The words come straight from the heart, forged from deep within my soul. I dig my heels into his ass, encouraging him to break me in half. It's as if he momentarily finds his second wind before he sucks in a deep breath and completely unravels inside me. I lift and kiss his jaw, and we both let out a satisfied sigh, like drug addicts who got their fix. We both know it's only temporary, though.

After we take a shower together, washing each other's bodies from head to toe, Liam and I crawl into bed. My heart has finally slowed to a steady pace, and I feel myself drift off to sleep.

The next morning, I'm woken to the sound of eggs frying. The little cabin was stocked with food for the weekend, but I didn't think Liam would make me breakfast. I should've, though, because it's one of our things at home. Hurrying, I slip on one of his T-shirts and walk into the kitchen where he's cooking with a cup of coffee in one hand and a spatula in the other.

"Sleeping Beauty is awake," he teases with a grin.

"I feel sex drunk." I laugh, trying to smooth down my hair. I do the best I can, then decide to just go with it. Liam's seen the good, the bad, and the ugly when it comes to me, and somehow, he hasn't run away yet. It's official. He's a keeper.

I sit at the small bar, and he hands me a cup of English Breakfast tea. "Fancy," I murmur before taking a sip. The cracking sounds of the fireplace pop in the background, and I turn around and look at the huge window. Snow is covering everything now, and it's no longer a light dusting. A smile touches my lips because I know this was Sophie's wedding wish. Hallmark really ruined her, but hell, it ruined me too because I wouldn't mind this one bit for mine.

"So…" I look at Liam. "Got the wedding bug yet?"

He turns around and grins, pointing the utensil at me before going back to the stove. "The real question is, do you?"

"I've been planning my wedding since I was five years old," I admit, but back then, it was more of a Disney dream with me being the princess and finding my Prince Charming. "But," I add, "I don't want to get married until I graduate. Just one more year."

Liam plates the eggs and toast and sets them in front of us. He looks at me incredulously. "Is that a hint?"

I quickly shove food in my mouth and shrug.

"Marriage is a big deal," he says. "I've already been divorced once. You sure you want that baggage?"

His phone buzzes on the bar, and I see it's his dad calling. "Are you going to answer that?" I ask, knowing his dad doesn't call him very often but has more now since Victoria came into the picture. Liam broke the news to him about the divorce but left out all the dirty details.

Liam silences it. "I'll call him back later. I'm having breakfast with my girl."

I take a sip of tea and look at him. Studying his face, I take in the scruff on his chin, the way his bottom lip has an indent, and the way the corners of his mouth naturally turn up. "That divorce wasn't your fault. That was a business arrangement."

"So you're saying I still have a chance for a happily ever after?" He's joking with me, the mood staying light and playful.

"Maybe a ten percent chance," I throw out.

"Ten? That's insanity. I think it's more at ninety."

I giggle. "You quite confident, aren't you? So tell me this…do you want kids?"

Liam stills, and it feels as if all the air has been sucked out of the room. He looks at me, then back at his plate. After a minute, I interrupt his thoughts.

"You don't have to answer that. Forget I asked." I reach forward and grab his hand.

"Kids are a big step. I always thought a family wasn't something I wanted or deserved. After what my mother did to my father and me, I vowed I wouldn't. I didn't want to bring a child into this fucked-up world to have their heart broken like mine was. But, when I look at you, for the first time, I can see a future. I imagine the wedding, the house, the dog, the kids. All of it."

I swallow hard at his confession. It warms my heart to hear him say those things. The room suddenly feels hot, and my skin prickles with goose bumps.

"I don't want to lose you because I know there's a future

for us, which scares the shit out of me. I've never, ever felt this way about anyone in my life. Only you, Maddie."

Tears swell in my eyes, and when I blink, they trail down my cheeks. "Liam…"

"But that's not the answer you were looking for." He clears his throat. "Yes, I'd have kids with you, Mads. They'd be smart-asses like you and hardheaded like me, and all know how to dance or play football."

I move onto his lap, nearly straddling him in the barstool.

"There's no rushing forever," I say, pressing my forehead against his as the emotion takes over. I'm a sopping mess as I kiss him, wishing I could express how much he's always meant to me, but it's like my words won't come out. Once again, he's left me utterly speechless. His strong arms hold me close to him, and he slides his lips across mine when his cell phone goes off again and silences it. It pings with a voicemail afterward, pulling us both away.

Liam grabs his phone, and he looks confused.

"Who is it?" I ask.

He turns it around and shows me it's his dad again. "I guess I should see what's going on. He never calls me like this."

I nod, and he helps me place both of my feet on the ground. As he listens to his voicemail, I watch Liam's face contort. He stands with wide eyes, and I know immediately something isn't right.

"Listen to this." Liam places the phone on speaker and replays the message.

I cover my mouth with my hands as Liam's dad speaks frantically. "Liam. There was a house fire, and we lost everything. Your stepmom and I weren't home when it happened, thankfully, but there's nothing left." His dad chokes up, and it nearly destroys me. "I'm okay, but I wanted to let you know what's going on before you find out some other way. I don't know what happened. We're staying at Aunt Ruthie's house until we can figure out what to do next. Call me when you can."

He clutches the phone in his palm and begins pacing. "Fuck. Do you think this could be a coincidence? After the Mercedes blew up, I'm not so sure. I don't trust anything anymore, not since Victoria tracked down my dad."

"I don't know. You really think she'd do something that extreme to get back at you for divorcing her?" I go to him, grabbing his hand. "You need to call him back so he knows you're aware, and we should probably go home. He needs you."

Liam nods, and I can see the wheels spinning in his head.

"I'm going to pack our stuff. Call your dad," I tell him, walking toward the bedroom. We had to check out in two hours anyway. My thoughts are scattered as I grab our wedding clothes and toiletries. I change into something warmer before finishing up. Accidents happen all the time and just because the O'Learys are known for shit like this doesn't mean they're responsible this time. At least, I hope they're not.

I can hear Liam talking to his dad, consoling him, explaining everything is replaceable, but he isn't. It's exactly what I would've said if it happened to my parents, but it doesn't make it any easier. After Liam ends the call, he comes to me and is slightly distraught. "What if they would've been home?"

"You can't live in the what-ifs, Liam. That's how you drive yourself crazy."

He nuzzles my neck. "What would I do without you?"

"Be single forever?" I quip and feel him smile against me. I lean back. "Let's go home. Seeing him will make you feel better at least." I grab my phone to text Sophie, then remember they left for their honeymoon already and are more than likely on a plane. They planned it this way so they'd be back before for Christmas. It will be Liam's and my first Christmas together too, and I can't wait to spend it with him and start making our own little traditions.

Liam picks up our suitcases and brings them out to his truck, then we make one final sweep before we leave to drop off the keys at the main office. Before we shut the door, I take it in one last time, encapsulating the memories we shared in my heart. When we walk back outside, there's a tall, lanky man standing by Liam's truck, which causes him to tense. I glance over at Liam who steps forward in front of me to protect me. My heart races, and I'm not sure what to do.

"What the fuck are you doing here?" Liam barks.

The guy throws a wicked smile. "I want the money you owe me."

"What are you talking about?"

"Don't act stupid. You know damn well what money you owe me. The money your sorry ass lost. I had to pay every cent back to my father and just because he 'forgave' your debt doesn't mean I did. So now, you owe *me*."

"Did Victoria send you, JJ?" Liam asks.

JJ. My heart stills because this is Victoria's brother, the one who got Liam into this mess in the first place. I can't comprehend what's happening. I want to protect Liam, tell this guy to stop ruining our lives, but he looks crazier than Victoria.

Maniacal laughter releases from him. "This is between you and me. You two split, but I want my fucking money back."

Liam glares at him, unamused, but cautious nonetheless.

"Or what?" He crosses his muscular arms over his chest, not backing down.

"You tell me. Terrible things have happened recently, haven't they?" He cocks a brow. "And they'll continue to happen if you don't give me what I want. You'll never expect what's coming your way. And perhaps next time, I'll make sure the house isn't empty if you catch my drift."

In a blink, Liam charges toward JJ, then wraps his hand around his neck as he pushes JJ against the truck, squeezing so hard, JJ can't even begin to defend himself. "If you hurt anyone I love, I won't think twice about fucking killing you. Come near me again, and I will," Liam threatens, sending a cold shiver down my spine.

Instead of trying to push Liam away, JJ smiles as if he finds humor in all of this, and if I don't do something, Liam will crush his windpipe. I hurry forward, grabbing Liam's opposite arm to pull him away. "Liam, stop." He tightens his grip and narrows his eyes at JJ. I start to panic and squeeze my fingers around Liam's bicep tighter. "Hulk." I emphasize his nickname through gritted teeth. "He's not worth it. Drop your hands."

I finally break through Liam's anger, and he releases him, pushing away from JJ. Liam takes my hand and creates distance.

JJ clears his throat and grabs his neck, then forces out words. "Better save your energy. You'll need that rage to fight."

"What the hell did you say?" Liam spins around, seething.

"You want to pay me back? You want me to disappear?" JJ asks in a taunting tone but doesn't wait for Liam's answer before he continues. "One fight in an underground ring. You win, and you'll be debt free."

Liam glares at him. "Have you lost your goddamn mind? I'm not fighting for you."

"Then expect more shit to blow up," he deadpans. "I'll make sure there's more than a cut on your precious girl's head next time."

Liam's jaw clenches, and I squeeze his hand to keep him from charging JJ again. He's trying to rile up Liam, and it's working.

"How can I trust you? How do I know this will really be over then?"

With a shrug, JJ stuffs his hands into his pockets. "You have no other choice than to trust me. The fight is on New Year's Eve. Be ready because you'll be fighting for your life. *Literally.* The guys who get inside the ring fight for blood. And if you don't do it or try to run again...well, you'll see. You'll lose things that can't so easily be replaced." JJ looks straight at me, and his steel blue eyes feel as if they're cutting through my flesh. The insinuation is obvious; I'm his next target.

JJ doesn't wait for an answer from Liam before he walks away. Then over his shoulder, he calls out, "Start training. I'll be in touch soon."

Liam watches him and then once the black BMW peels away, he tells me to stand back as he cranks his truck. We all have PTSD from the G-Wagon exploding. After it's started, he opens the door for me, and I climb inside, my hands and legs shaking. I'm confused, and I'm riddled with anxiety over all this.

"You can't do this, Liam."

He backs out of the driveway, and we go to the main office to turn in the keys to the cabin. "I don't think I have a choice, baby."

I shake my head, not wanting any of this to be

happening. "No. You could get hurt or…" I can't even bring myself to say it.

Parking the truck in front of the building, Liam turns to me, anger taking over. "He burned down my parents' house. He's obviously the one who blew up the G-Wagon. JJ is responsible for it all. If he's already done that, then what's he capable of next? I can't keep living my life in fear, Maddie, or risk more people in my life getting hurt. I can't worry that every day I leave you, something terrible will happen while I'm gone. You're my everything, and I want to protect you. I'll train for this stupid fight if it means keeping you safe, and I'll be fine."

"You don't know that." A ragged sob escapes me as I cover my mouth, trying to swallow down my fears. He's trying to reassure me he'll be okay, but I'm not so sure this time. His life was spared last time, but what if he's not so lucky next time?

CHAPTER SIXTEEN

LIAM

I TRY to change the subject on our way home, but my mind is reeling. I'm so livid, I'm grasping the steering wheel so tightly, my fingers are going numb. Too many puzzle pieces snap together as I replay everything that's happened since the divorce. Stupidly, I thought I wouldn't be connected with the O'Learys, but all bets are off. Victoria wasn't lying when she said she didn't blow up the G-Wagon, and I'm half-tempted to call her and let her know it was her idiot brother, but what use would it be? She hates me just as much and would probably only encourage JJ's behavior to hurt me and the people I love. Maddie was hospitalized because of the explosion, and he probably wouldn't care if it'd been worse. The rage I felt when I saw him outside of our cabin reappears, and Maddie notices.

"Liam, you're doing that thing you do when you're about to lose your shit," she says, concern evident in her tone. I glance over at her and try to take deep breaths to calm down. She's the only person on this planet who can bring me back to reality and settle my nerves.

I arch a brow. "What thing?"

"Your shoulders tense, your eyes narrow, and your lips twitch. You look as if the Hulk is going to break out and start smashing people." I give her a look. "Please tell me you've watched *The Avengers*."

This causes me to chuckle. "I've seen bits and pieces of it but never sat through all of them."

Her mouth falls open. "What? Okay, add all the Avengers to our movie list."

For a moment, it's easy to ignore the fact that JJ stained our amazing weekend together. We shared so much in that little cabin overlooking the lake, and I'll keep those memories in my heart for the rest of my life.

Once we finally make it home and I unload our bags, the two of us decide to conserve water and take a shower together. We're both quiet the entire time as we touch and kiss, and I feel as if there are so many unspoken words drifting between us. After we're dressed and downstairs cozied up on the couch, I decide to call Tyler.

"'Bout time you made it home," he tells me before I go into the kitchen and grab a beer.

"Where's mine?" Maddie asks with a smirk, though beer really isn't her thing. I hand her mine after taking a sip, but she laughs, rejecting the offer.

Maddie gets up to make some tea, and I lower my voice. "We need to talk."

"Everything okay?" he asks.

"JJ was outside of our cabin this morning."

Tyler groans, and I can imagine him clenching his teeth. "Why was he there?"

"He said I still owed him. He was responsible for the G-Wagon, and he…" I pause for a second, trying to gain my composure because I feel as if I'm losing control. "He burned my father's house down last night."

"What the fuck?" I can hear the change in his voice, but I continue.

I run my fingers through my hair. "He told me we'd be even if I participated in an underground fight. What do you know about that?"

"You can't. It's too dangerous."

"I have to end this once and for all. I don't want to constantly be looking over my shoulder, waiting for the O'Learys to strike. I don't want to worry about Maddie when I'm not home. I don't need you acting as our bodyguard for the rest of your life either. Seriously, I don't want to live like this anymore. It's the only way. I fight, and I win. There are no other options. Either you'll help me or not."

The line is silent for a while. "You're a hardheaded motherfucker. You know that, don't you?"

"Isn't that a given?"

"When's the fight?" he asks as if he's actually contemplating it.

"New Year's Eve."

He lets out a controlled breath. "That's three and a half weeks to train. You understand how this works, Liam? When you walk into that ring with your opponent, there's a chance one of you won't walk out. They fight to kill or be killed, and they don't play by any set rules. It's underground street fighting. If you want my help, I'll help you, but you'll need to spend every day on this. I'll get in touch with a friend who trains here in Vegas closer to time. We'll start the day after tomorrow, so it gives me enough time to book a flight and rent a truck."

"Thank you. I owe you," I say. "I'll see you in two days."

The call ends, and I sit there numb.

Maddie returns with a cup of tea and a plate of cookies. I

snag one, and she playfully slaps my hand. Noticing a change in the mood, she looks at me. "What you two talk about? Having a lovers' quarrel?"

I laugh, finishing my beer, but Maddie waits for me to explain.

"Tyler's going to train me. He's a pro," I explain but am gutted when I see her expression drop.

"Liam, please," she begs. "I can't lose you."

Wrapping my arms around her, I pull her as close to me as I can, until our faces are mere inches apart. "I have to do this so then we *can* have a future together. They will never let me go otherwise. I know that."

A single tear drips down her cheek, and I swipe it away with my thumb. After a minute of holding her, she pulls away and looks into my eyes. "I was so hoping once the divorce was finalized, it would all be over."

"I know, baby. I had hoped that too. Trust me, I hate this. I hate what it's done to you and us. But I swear, if there were any other options, I'd take them, but I'm not running this time."

"Are you absolutely sure about this? You could get really hurt, even if you win. The guy could break your face or bones or something." I hear the worry in her voice, and it kills me. Our weekend was so special, and now we have another obstacle trying to tear us apart.

"Freedom is what I want, what we need. So yes, I'm sure that I have to do this. I know what's at stake, and there are no options other than winning. Tyler's well experienced on the ins and outs of fighting, even in illegal shit like this. I start training as soon as he gets here."

Maddie sniffs, but nods. "I hate that you have to do this, but I also hope Tyler knows what he's doing to get you properly ready."

"Don't worry, he is. He's been training at gyms for years and knows all about what goes into underground fighting. If I don't do this, JJ will come after you and *hurt* you. It was obvious what he was implying, and I don't want him anywhere near you again. It's not just my freedom I'm fighting for; it's yours too."

"I know," she croaks, and I hate that I've put her in this situation. She grabs the remote and turns on the TV, but I can't seem to pay attention to anything on the screen. My mind is in a different place but with reason. So much depends on me winning—my entire life and Maddie's too.

After our conversation, we watch TV until our eyes are heavy, then we go to bed. I hold Maddie in my arms as we fall asleep, listening to her soft breathing, and allowing her to calm my racing mind until I drift off.

It's been less than forty-eight hours since JJ reappeared in my life and shook it up like a snow globe. It's day one of training, and when my alarm goes off at four-thirty in the morning, I force myself to roll out of bed. I place a soft kiss on Maddie's forehead before getting dressed and grabbing a protein bar. Tyler arrived late yesterday afternoon and got settled into my room. It was almost like old times with him being here again, but I hate that it's under these circumstances. I check outside and see his rental truck is already gone because he's punctual as fuck, so I head to the gym to meet him. Once I'm parked and inside, I see Tyler in the kickboxing area eagerly awaiting me.

"We could've ridden together," I say as soon as I'm near him.

"Good morning to you too," he tells me. I notice he's dripping with sweat and can't imagine how long he's been here. He would've had to got here at least an hour ago to get a workout in before I arrived. "Are you ready?"

"I guess." I blow out an insecure breath.

Tyler forces me to run a mile and do several different stretches to warm my muscles. After I'm fully awake, he hands me a pair of gloves and puts some on, then moves toward me. He stands eye to eye with me, and I don't even flinch when he pretends to go for the gut. It's nothing more than a distraction. "They might not even give you gloves during the fight. If they're doing street rules, you'll get some tape on your knuckles, and that's about it. I'd suggest you get a piece of wood and start punching the hell out of it at home so you can build up your knuckle strength." He turns his back on me, and a second later, his fist slams straight into my gut. "*Always* watch your opponent."

"Not fair, I wasn't ready." I clench my fist in my glove and blow out a breath.

Tyler smirks. "That's the point. You need to be *ready* every second you're in the ring." He lifts his leg and tries to take me down, but I block him.

"What the hell?" I scowl.

"Street fighting isn't just hits and punches, Liam. You'll need to watch out for legs too," Tyler explains.

"So basically it's MMA rules on steroids?" I ask, taking a swing at him, feeling my bodyweight bounce on the practice mats.

"Pretty much. Mafia underground fighting has only one rule and one goal. No guns in the ring and kill you before you kill them." His leg quickly comes up, hitting me behind my knee, and I immediately lose my balance. When his glove meets my face, my anger level rises, and I block his hits until I get to my feet. I go to Tyler, throwing calculated punches, but he redirects every swing I make. I finally connect; however, he's two steps ahead of me and brings me down once again with another hit to the face. My heart rapidly beats, and my chest rises and falls as my adrenaline spikes.

"Do you wanna die?" he shouts, connecting his fist with my jaw, and that's when I see red and lose control. "Time to get your shit together. Focus, Liam." The anger takes over, and I'm fighting Tyler with all the strength I have, but he's quick on his feet, and I barely make contact with him. It doesn't surprise me, though. He's a professional and has been doing this for years.

"Better," he tells me, then sucker punches me right in the stomach. Taking a few steps back, Tyler calls a time-out, and we're both heaving. "You need to hydrate." We pull off our gloves, then walk over to his bag where he grabs a couple of bottles of water, then hands me one.

"You're out of practice," he scolds as I inhale my drink. "But I think we'll be able to get you where you need to be, but it's going to take a lot of work. You'll be working out harder than you ever have in your life."

I nod, trying to let my endorphins settle. I'm so goddamn worked up right now. "I can't lose this fight. There's too much weighing on it." I finish the bottle and throw it in the trash.

"I agree. They play dirty. You'll have to tune out everyone outside of the ring and focus on your opponent's moves. I'm guessing there'll be at least half a million dollars' worth in bets, so if you lose and live, JJ will make sure you don't walk away." I grit my teeth as Tyler continues. "I made a few phone calls to some friends who are involved in that circle. I'm trying to find out more about the guy you're fighting so we at least know what you're up against."

"Thanks. I appreciate it, man." I wipe the sweat from my brow and look at the clock behind Tyler. We've been here for over an hour, but we're just getting started. Once Tyler finishes his water, he slips his gloves back on, and so do I.

"Let's work on technique. Since legs and feet aren't illegal to use, anything pretty much goes. So, head, elbows, knees, and any other body part you can cause damage with is fair game." Tyler moves his body around showing different maneuvers against one of the dummies, then asks me to do the same. Keeping my body tight, I stay light on my feet as Tyler calls out what to do. I use all the strength in my quads to kick forward, and the dummy falls to the floor with a thud.

"Damn, that was good," Tyler says, picking it up and setting it in place. After I work on that for a while, he instructs me to take off my gloves and pulls the tape from his bag, then helps me wrap my hands the proper way to protect my knuckles. Once I'm set, he puts on some leather boxing punching mitts. "Now, let's focus on speed and output instead of power. Basic punches right in the center."

He flips the mitts around, and I see two white circles where I need to hit. "Keep your hands high, and after each set, you'll do a squat and increase two more punches until you're swinging twenty times in a row. It's a basic boxing drill to help with fast, consistent hand speed and endurance. We'll go for two minutes, counting your reps, break for five, then start at the top. We'll do this for the next hour."

I chuckle. "You're gonna wear me out before eight o'clock."

"You better believe it," he throws back. "It's gonna be exhausting, but you need to get your momentum up before we get to the hard stuff. Don't let your hands fall, and make sure you're supporting your weight on your hips. The squat helps re-center yourself. Ready?"

I nod and step up, taking a deep breath. As I start, Tyler calls out how many throws I need to do. At first, I'm fast, and it feels easy, but when I have twenty seconds left, I'm ready to give up. However, I keep going even though it feels like my hands and arms will fall off.

"Faster," Tyler calls out when there are only ten seconds to go. I find my second wind when he lets his mitts fall. "Good job."

I place my hands over my head and try to breathe for a few minutes, sweat dripping down my face. "Fuck, that's harder than I thought."

"Right? Two minutes seems easy until you get going. How are your knuckles?"

Flipping my hands over, I show him. Fingers are red, but there's no busted skin. I've made sure to keep my fingers in the correct position so I don't break them before the fight.

"They say Bruce Lee used to punch metal to strengthen his knuckles," Tyler tells me as I grab another bottle of water.

"Oh yeah? Is that tomorrow's drill?" I mock.

Tyler snickers. "Don't tempt me. When I was in the military, I used brick walls to condition my hands for fighting. That's going to be your homework. Also, break's over. Let's go again."

I let out a laugh before Tyler starts the timer, and then I begin again. We keep doing reps with breaks between. For

215

the next hour, we continue techniques, but he doesn't let me rest for long. Next, he has me working on more drills, leg kicks, and blocking. After three hours of working, I'm ready to pass the fuck out and beg for an oxygen line. My arms and legs feel like jelly, and I can already tell I'm going to be sore as hell tomorrow. Groaning, I lean against the wall with my palms on my knees, panting. Tyler laughs, looking like he hardly broke a damn sweat, and I stand, rolling my eyes at him.

"I went easy on you today," he tells me as he stuffs the mitts back into his bag.

"Easy, my ass," I say, my heart still racing.

He slaps me on the back. "It's just going to get harder from here, so you need to stay focused and highly motivated. You don't have time to slack off. I need you on your A game if I'm going to properly train you."

Moving my head from side to side, I crack my neck. Every part of me literally feels stiff. "And how would you suggest I do that?"

"My first suggestion: staying celibate."

I glance at him and chuckle, but his expression doesn't change. "Wait, you're serious," I deadpan.

He nods. "I am. No sex means you'll have pent-up aggression, and it'll motivate you even more to win. You're fighting so you and Maddie can have a life together. It's a mental technique, but it works. Famous boxers and UFC fighters stay celibate before a big fight to keep themselves focused."

My mouth falls open. "I'll murder someone." Or Maddie might murder me.

"And that's exactly the point," he quips, smirking. "Maddie will understand once she knows why."

"No, she's going to tell both of us to fuck off," I argue.

"What else is new?" He grins. "Hey, don't forget to ice your hands when you get home so they don't swell. Take a painkiller or anti-inflammatory, too."

"Okay, Mom," I tease, though I know he knows what he's talking about. I need to take care of my body while training for the fight of my life.

For the most part, I thought of myself as pretty fit and in shape, but Tyler proved me wrong. There's a lot of work for me to do, and it starts with eating right, getting enough sleep, and conditioning my body to be a fighting machine. At least, I can use my strength when wrangling criminals who want to fight back. Typically my size scares them, and I'm strong and fast enough to capture them, but when Tyler is done with me, I have a feeling my entire body composition will go back to how it was when I was an athlete.

Before I go home, I stop and get a protein shake to replenish my muscles. By the time I pull into the driveway, Tyler is already home, but Maddie's left for class.

"Doing alright?" Tyler chuckles when he sees me walking slowly into the kitchen.

"Kiss my ass." I grab a couple of ice packs from the freezer, then go to lie on the sofa.

Tyler follows. "Your body is used to cardio and lifting weights, but it'll adjust in a few days. Same time tomorrow morning?" He flashes a shit-eating smirk as he sits in the recliner.

I grunt, putting one pack on my shoulder and the other on my hand. "If I can even walk."

"Take a hot shower after you ice and drink lots of water. You should know the drill from football," he states.

"I graduated four years ago," I remind him. "Pretty sure I felt better my first day of freshman year when I nearly twisted my ankle and broke a rib."

"Well, good thing you won't have to worry about straining a muscle during sex."

"Pretty sure I wouldn't be able to even if I could," I say bluntly. "Maddie's going to freak out when she sees me. Pretty sure you bruised my entire body."

"And somehow, I doubt this is the worst she's witnessed." He flashes a wicked grin, knowing damn well what the O'Learys had done to my face.

"True, but I'd guard your nuts if I were you. She won't think twice about coming after you for punching me."

"*Training* you," he corrects. "And I can handle Maddie. I did for two weeks and saved her life, so if anything, she owes me."

I chuckle, though it hurts. "She won't see it that way."

Tyler stands, then purposely slaps my shoulder hard. "Quit being a pussy. Being in love has made you weak," he taunts.

"Asshole," I bite out. "I'm gonna get you back for that tomorrow."

"I sure hope so." He laughs. "Then I might actually break a sweat."

Once I'm able to get off the couch, I go upstairs for a hot shower and take it easy for the rest of the day. I still have to work, but the most I can do right now is research or pick up some local jobs. I need to make money, but this fight is my top priority at the moment.

When Maddie walks through the door, I'm on the couch with my laptop. I close it, then set it on the coffee table. Immediately, she drops her backpack and walks toward me. Seconds later, she's straddling me with her lips pressed against mine.

"Mads," I whisper, placing my hands under her ass. My self-control is already waning. I need to tell her about Tyler's no-sex rule even though I already know she's not going to be happy about it. "I'm really sore, baby."

She leans back and lifts off me. "Oh shit, sorry."

"Tyler kicked my ass training me today," I tell her. "It's gonna be a rough few weeks."

Maddie sits next to me and turns. "I know, but you'll get through it. I know you will."

"Well…" I pause briefly. "That's not the only reason it's going to be rough."

"What is it?" She looks at me cautiously, and I know she's worried. I need to just spit it out.

"Tyler suggested no sex until after the fight."

Her head falls back on her shoulders, and she laughs hard. "What? That's the most ridiculous thing I've ever heard. This is a joke, right?"

"I thought it sounded stupid at first too, but I think he's right. I looked it up, and it's a real thing. Plus, Tyler's been training people for a long-ass time. I trust his judgment, and if it will make me a stronger fighter, that's what I have to do…for us."

She searches my face. "So, no sex. Does that mean everything else is off-limits too? Like you can't touch me at all?"

I suck in a deep breath and nod. "It might be for the best. Otherwise, the temptation will be too hard to resist."

She sticks out her lower lip and adorably pouts. "Okay, I understand, even if I'm going to have sex withdrawals," she playfully whines.

"Me too, baby," I admit, already hating that I can't lay her down and kiss her the way I want to, but when I win this fight, we'll finally have it all.

It's been a week since I started training with Tyler, and while I'd like to think it's getting easier, it's not. Tyler has pushed me to the limit every single day and continues to do so. Practices are unpredictable, and I'm beat down until my muscles are weak and tired, but today I wake up ready to fight. I can already feel how much stronger I am and even started lifting weights a few times this week to break down the muscle further.

Yesterday, Tyler told me we were meeting at a gym known for boxing. Apparently, it has fighting mats and a ring, and it's better suited than my gym. When I show up at our regular time, I immediately notice Tyler chatting with someone.

As soon as I walk up, Tyler introduces us. "This is Rampage."

I shake his hand. "I'm Liam, nice to meet you."

The guy has tattoos trailing up his arms and legs. It's mid-December, and the gym doesn't have heat, but he's wearing shorts and a T-shirt with the arms cut out.

"Thought I'd give you a challenge today," Tyler says, grinning wide. "Rampage is one of the best in the area and has won a few underground fights. He'll be your opponent."

I feel a tad blindsided and intimidated, but I'm okay with it. Actually, going up against someone who I'm unfamiliar with will probably be more helpful and feel like the real thing. Considering the no-sex rule still stands, it might be nice to kick someone else's ass. I go to pick up the knuckle tape, and Tyler shakes his head.

"We'll use gloves today. Don't want you getting the shit kicked out of you *yet*. We'll save that for when you're training in Vegas."

Rampage laughs. "I dunno, Tyler. Liam's a big dude."

Tyler glances at him. "I know how you are. How about you not Tyson him like you did that other guy?"

Laugher escapes Rampage, and he looks pleased with himself. "Got it. No biting off ears."

"You did that to someone?" I try to keep my reaction flat as I tighten my laces.

He grins before stepping into the ring. "I'd do it again, too. The bastard deserved it, and there was a lot of money riding on that fight."

What the fuck did Tyler get me into? Or rather, who?

I follow him and stand on the opposite side of the ring. Tyler tells me he booked the space for an hour and will probably use up the entire time. After he sets the clock and talks about the rules—three to four rounds, three minutes each—we begin. The time counts down, and I size Rampage up, noticing how he doesn't take his eyes off me. It's as if someone flips a switch because, in a flash, he rushes toward me. His hands cover his face before laying into me with so much fucking power, I almost lose my breath. After a few seconds of taking a beating, I snap.

The maneuvers Tyler and I have been practicing every day come to me in full force, and a second later, I kick my leg out and take Rampage down, but he's relentless and snaps his fist behind my knee, and soon, I'm falling too. This happens over and over again through every round, and soon, I catch on to his moves and reactions, then allow my adrenaline to lead me. During the final round, we're both tired as hell but continue kicking each other's asses. About a minute in, he swings, and I duck, giving me the opportunity to put power into an uppercut using all the strength I have in my legs. As soon as my fist connects with his jaw, Rampage takes two steps back, then falls down.

Tyler jumps over the ring and goes to him, waiting for him to come to. My lip is busted, and my body hurts from being beat the fuck up, but I feel good. Tired, but good and confident. Rampage spits out blood, then Tyler helps him stand. He takes off his gloves and gives me a handshake.

"Great fuckin' job, man. You're a natural."

I almost laugh, considering what the past week has been like for me. "Nah."

"I'd bet on you," he says.

Tyler beams proudly. "That's just one week of intense training. Sending him to Dice in Vegas next week," he explains. "He'll be sweating his body weight by the time he returns."

That statement has my stomach roiling. I've been working out nonstop for seven days, and though I need a day off, there isn't time to rest or get lazy. Whoever this Dice guy is will make sure I'm prepared as much as possible.

I untie my gloves and get out of the space. There's a group of guys waiting to get in, and I can see how excited they are for their turn. For the first time, I understand why Mason used boxing to get out his frustrations. It really is a great outlet, and if I didn't have to do this because of a stupid situation I got myself in, I'd actually enjoy it. After we hydrate, the three of us stand to the side for a little while longer. Tyler goes over my strengths and weaknesses he observed, and Rampage gives me a few more pointers as well. I have a little over two weeks to make sure I'm prepared, and after today, I feel better.

As we're heading out, Tyler walks with me to my truck. "He didn't go easy on you today."

"I didn't expect him to. My muscles are sore as fuck." I rub a hand over my shoulder and squeeze.

Tyler grins. "It's progress, Liam. I'm proud of you."

"Thanks to you, man. Now I just need to win this fight and forget any of this ever happened." I sigh, feeling anxious as hell as the closer New Year's Eve comes.

We go our separate ways, and I text Maddie to meet her for lunch. She typically has a break between classes, and I miss her like crazy. By the time she gets home from school and her extra rehearsals for her upcoming senior recital, we're both exhausted. Things have been tense between us. The no-sex rule is driving us both insane, but we're making the best of it. As I'm arriving at the house, I get a text from her and smile because she's agreed to lunch.

Maddie: It better be something good. I need carbs before I kill someone.

She has a way of making me laugh.

Liam: Carbs are guaranteed. I'll pick you up at 11.

I shower and do some work on my laptop, then head across town to pick up Maddie. She's waiting for me in our old spot, and it brings back memories of when she first moved into the house. So much has changed since then, but she's been one of the best things that's ever happened to me. Maddie keeps me grounded when I feel as if my world is crumbling around me.

She climbs inside the truck and leans over, giving me a sweet peck on the lips. "Hey, handsome."

"Hello, beautiful. Missed you," I tell her, wishing we could spend the day together like we did during summer, and she was home a lot more.

"I've missed you, too. Have fun today so far?" she asks as I pull out and drive.

Just being around her calms me and is just a reminder of why I'm doing all this in the first place. "Fun?" I half-chuckle. "I fought some guy this morning with a lot more experience than me, but I managed to take him down. Tyler was proud."

"You kicked the guy's ass?" Maddie's grinning, looking so damn pretty in her sweater.

"I sure did, but I'm gonna be feeling it later."

She holds out her hand for a high five. While keeping my eyes on the road, I snicker and slap her hand.

"Good to know the no-sex thing is working." She laughs, and I roll my eyes. "Though I've had to bring BOB back into the shower with me."

Glancing over, I glare at her. "You didn't?"

"A girl has needs." She smirks, but I'm ninety percent positive she's joking. Well, maybe eighty.

"Yeah, well blue balls are a bitch." I pull into a small Italian restaurant and take Maddie's hand, then kiss her knuckles. "But they're worth it to know I'll be able to do whatever I want to you after the fight."

"I expect A-plus treatment," she teases. "Kinky, rough, hours long sex."

Groaning, I feel myself getting hard at her words. I adjust my crotch and clear my throat. "Alright, time to get out of here before I change my mind and jump you."

Maddie laughs, grabbing the door handle. "Good idea. Also, I was so going to suggest this place. I'm starving."

We get out of the truck and go inside. The place is crowded because it's not very big, but we're seated fairly quickly. As soon as the waitress greets us, we order our food and drinks since Maddie only has an hour before she has to be back at school.

"How are classes going?" I ask, genuinely wanting to know.

"Imagine choreographing a dance recital while studying for finals and not having an outlet." She flashes a snarky grin at me because I know exactly what she's referring to.

"Sounds like you have some pent-up frustration." I chuckle.

Maddie scowls. "It's been hell and exhausting. I can't wait until Friday when all this shit is over, and I can just lounge around in my undies until January." She pops an eyebrow, and I smirk.

"So, only a few more days until I lose my mind and have to start sleeping on the couch."

She giggles, then moves to sit next to me in the booth. "I mean, I won't tell if you won't."

"You actually are the devil, aren't you? Temptation and all." I wrap my arm around her, and she looks up at me with pleading eyes. I plant a soft kiss on her lips, and she moans into my mouth. I'm pretty sure after the fight, we're going to lock ourselves in her room for a month.

"I might be." She waggles her brows, and before I can say anything, our spaghetti and meatballs are being placed in front of us. Maddie stays next to me, and I place my palm on her leg, needing to touch her. I've been eating healthy all week, and after the fight this morning, I knew I needed to replenish my body. The two of us eat like we've haven't had a bite in a week, and there's not a morsel left on either of our plates by the time we're done.

Maddie leans back and places a hand on her stomach. "I don't know how I'm going to walk with this spaghetti baby."

Her words cause me to nearly spit out my water. That's one thing about her; she always keeps me laughing.

After I pay the bill and drive her toward campus, we chat about the weather and Christmas and everything in between.

"Hallmark movie marathon this weekend," she demands. "You kinda owe me."

Scrunching up my nose, I try to get out of it, but I know it's a losing battle. "Fine. But you're baking those amazing cookies you made last year."

"If we're giving demands..." She waggles her brows and bites her lip.

I park in front of the dance hall and lean over, then take her cheeks in my palms. She leans forward, our lips brushing together, and I don't want her to go. I want to be stingy and take her home. Before I leave for Vegas, I've been trying to spend as much time with her as I can. The clock's ticking. We both know the fight is coming, but for the most part, we don't talk about the what-ifs. There are too many.

What if I lose? What if I die? What if I'm badly hurt? What if JJ doesn't keep his word?

It's made things tense and awkward, so we try not to bring it up, and we've been overly careful in public, watching our backs at all times. I know she's worried, and I am too, but we're making the best out of it.

"I love you so fucking much," I tell her as we break apart, my heart racing as I want more of her.

"I love you, too." She throws me a wink before climbing out. "Thanks for lunch, Hulk. It was delicious." Before shutting the door, she adds, "The food wasn't bad either."

Shaking my head, I laugh. "Anytime, baby. See you in a few hours." I watch Maddie until she's completely out of sight. It almost feels like we're back to that point in time when she was a virgin, and I was denying her at every corner, but now I'm fully denying myself too.

When I walk inside the house, Tyler is laid out on the couch watching TV. He sits up and grins as if he knows how much pain I'm in. I plop down on the opposite end and see he's watching some movie with mobsters, and I nearly groan. The ones I've met really do act like these idiots.

"How are you feeling about this morning?" he finally asks, sitting up.

"Good, actually. My body is sore, but I think it's been in a perpetual state of that for the past week. It was different actually fighting someone I didn't know. There was a point where I was uber focused and had so much adrenaline rushing through me that I was worried I'd lose control on him."

"That's great. Just think about where you'll be in two weeks. I think you have a really good chance, Liam. If you didn't, I'd tell you so we could find an alternative."

Too bad there isn't an alternative. Not when JJ's put my girlfriend as his personal target if I don't cooperate.

"Did you ever find out anything about who I was fighting?" I ask.

"I've heard a few things but haven't gotten a name yet to research him. The guy is known for breaking necks, and has gone undefeated the last three fights he's been in. Killed two guys and one was put in the hospital. Lived but barely. He fights dirty, but apparently his goal is to get you on the ground. As long as you can stay standing and try to knock him out, you'll be okay."

I stare at Tyler. Blinking, I clear my throat, wondering

how he can talk so casually about this. "He's killed two people?"

He nods, and I wipe my sweaty palms on my jeans. The reality of all of this suddenly hits me hard. Whoever this guy is has tons of experience, and I'm coming in as a rookie. What the fuck am I gonna do?

"Listen." Tyler speaks up when I'm unable to say anything. "I've heard you're the same size as this guy. You have the same strength, and you're levelheaded other than the anger you harbor. You'll be more than ready, and you know what to avoid, giving you the upper hand. They know nothing about you, or the way you fight, or anything. This is a good thing."

Unless that means he'll just be prepared for anything...

"You're right," I tell him, yawning, though I'm not sure I believe my own words. "Think I'm gonna take a nap till Maddie gets home."

"Good idea because tomorrow morning is going to be intense," he says with a chuckle. "Even more than today."

"Of course it is," I deadpan, shaking my head.

Once I'm in Maddie's bed, I seem to instantly fall asleep. Hours later, I'm being woken to the sound of Maddie laughing in the living room. I get up and walk in to hear her giving Tyler shit.

"Speaking of the devil," she teases. "Sleep well?"

I stretch and suck in a deep breath. "Yep, but would've slept better with you beside me."

Tyler stands, goes to the kitchen, then returns with a beer before settling down on the couch.

"I'm gonna make some tea. Want some?" she asks me, dropping her backpack on the ground.

"Nah," I tell her and take a seat in the recliner. "But I'll take a water, please."

"What time do you fly out again?" Tyler asks.

"Sunday at ten a.m. Dice wants me to meet him as soon as I land. So that's gonna be fun," I say dryly. "Hey, when I'm gone, you're gonna stay here and keep an eye on Maddie, right? I don't trust JJ not to pull some shit before the fight."

As if she was summoned, she returns with my bottle of water. "I didn't need a bodyguard before, and I won't need one again." She crosses her arms.

"But you have to admit, Mads, I'm pretty damn good at it." Tyler smirks, gloating.

Maddie narrows her eyes. "Honestly, I barely noticed you were there."

"Damn! I'm pretty sure you just got burned," I tease, and Tyler scoffs.

"I would've killed for you, Maddie. Just know that," he tells her seriously.

I don't doubt him for a second, especially after everything he's risked. Tyler would do anything for us.

Maddie shrugs, but there's a smile playing on her lips. "Meh. I think I've had better."

"Really?" Tyler asks, grinning. "Who?"

"Liam," Maddie tells him matter-of-factly. "You know how much cock he's blocked over the years? Tons!"

"Baby, I live to guard your body," I say.

The teapot is squealing, and she runs off but not before giving me attitude. "Hardy har har har."

"I'll make sure she's okay. Won't let her out of my sight," Tyler tells me. "Wouldn't let you down, especially now that you'll be a better fighter than me."

I smile. "Thanks, man. I appreciate all you've done for us."

"Over the years, I've learned that we may not be able to choose our family, but we can choose our friends who become our family. I don't have a brother, but I've found a brother in you," he admits.

"Means a lot, Tyler. Really I don't know how I'm ever going to repay you for all that you've done."

Maddie comes back in the room, blowing on her tea, and sits on my lap. "What are we talking about now?"

Wrapping my arms around her waist, I kiss her neck, and she nearly spills the tea. "Stop!" She giggles.

"Just discussing how we're going to repay Tyler," I say.

"Oh, I've thought of something. When we have our first kid, if it's a boy…"

My eyes go wide at the mention of having a baby, and the moment she sees my reaction, she starts laughing.

"That'll work," Tyler says, adding to my mini heart attack. "Firstborn gets my namesake. Love it."

CHAPTER SEVENTEEN

MADDIE

IT'S BEEN eighteen days since Liam and I have had sex, and I'm moodier than ever.

Tyler's ridiculous *no-sex* rule is making me insane.

I might be going crazy because it's all I think about. I knew once I lost my virginity and really learned what I was missing, I'd be one of those sex-crazed women who'd want it all the time. And I wasn't wrong. Another reason I was determined for Liam to be my first and hopefully—*only*.

It wouldn't be so bad if he didn't look hot as sin all the damn time. Maybe if he'd pull back his witty comments and snarky charm, and I don't know, wear a freaking garbage bag over his perfect face, then I'd be immune. But the asshole likes to torture me—something he's probably enjoyed for the past four years—and wears cutoff T-shirts that show off his biceps and tattoos.

Then there's his *fuck me* smile he flaunts around that makes me squeeze my thighs together. Every time he looks at me that way, I have to stifle a moan that threatens to release.

Good lord, who have I become?

My sisters, that's who.

Those horny bitches teased me during my teenage years, and I was front and center of their white-hot relationships with their now husbands.

It's totally unfair.

"Are you alright?" Sophie asks as I grind my teeth and pout on the couch.

"I'm fine," I snap, then clear my throat. "Why?"

"Because you look like you're ready for a fight."

I growl at the word *fight* and narrow my eyes at her. "I'm done with finals, and I'm bored as hell. Liam's training every day, then works in the afternoons and is keeping me at arm's length. Last night in bed, he wedged a pillow between us so our bodies wouldn't touch! A FUCKING PILLOW!"

Sophie chuckles as she grabs the remote and sits down next to me. "Sounds like you need some trashy reality TV to get your mind off getting laid."

"There's nothing that powerful," I retort.

"Not even *Love After Lockup*?" she taunts, waving the controller in her hand.

I scowl, not giving in to temptation. Though it doesn't work. Five minutes into the show, and I'm hooked. Dammit.

After two episodes, Liam and Tyler walk in, dripping with sweat.

Lord have mercy. *Why?*

He always looks sexy after a workout, but since he's been training, his arms and chest are bulkier.

"Hey, baby." Liam peeks behind me and smacks a quick kiss to my cheek. "Whatcha girls doin'?"

I inhale sharply, his sweaty smell surrounding me, which I love. Knowing what he's doing, what he *has* to do, makes me sick. Feeling this way is selfish, but I miss him.

I miss *us*.

I miss the connection we fought for so hard, and now it

seems like we're breaking all over again. Liam was mine in secret and was ripped away before I could comprehend what was happening. Now everyone can know we're together and in love, but sometimes it doesn't feel that way.

Perhaps this is part of the relationship stuff I wasn't prepared for. I'm supporting him the best I can, though I hate what he has to do with a passion. I want to handcuff him to me and run away, take him from all this pain and drama he doesn't deserve. But even I know leaving wouldn't help anything. It'd only make it worse, just like before. He has to face this head-on, but I don't trust JJ or his word. What if this isn't the last of it, and he'll want something else after? If Liam wins him a lot of money, will he want him to keep fighting and winning? Will I always be what they use against him?

I can barely deal with what's going on as it is. JJ's nearly killed us with that car explosion, and I don't doubt he would go even further if Liam doesn't follow his orders.

But I hope this doesn't kill us and our relationship in the process.

"Watching TV, waiting for our men to come home and entertain us," Sophie teases.

"Feelin' like the fifth wheel over here, so off I go to take a shower," Tyler quips.

"Liam's not putting out, so trust me, you aren't wheelin' nothing."

"You poor girl…" Liam mocks. "You waited twenty-one years, I think you can wait a couple more weeks." He presses a kiss to my forehead, then walks to the kitchen.

"Perhaps Tyler can take your place until then?" I shout, knowing both of them are within yelling distance.

Liam stomps back into the living room, his eyes narrowed as he scowls at me.

"God, leave me out of this before Liam breaks my jaw." I look over my shoulder at Tyler who's shaking his head and chuckling. "Trust me, he would." Then he walks upstairs, and Liam stares at me.

"What?" I fake innocence. "I was *kidding*."

"Mm-hmm." Liam studies me. "Can you put on some clothes? You wearing that isn't helping."

I look down at my tank top and sweat shorts. "What's wrong with what I'm wearing?"

Sophie stands and groans. "Quit torturing the man." She takes my hand, then pulls me up. "Go put on a parka, so he's not tempted to break the rules."

Groaning, I stomp around the couch. "He used to love breaking the rules with me!" I shout, walking to my room.

Liam returned from Vegas four days ago with double black eyes, sore ribs, bloody knuckles, and a cut lip. He looked worse than when he came back from the mob boss's guards kicking his ass. I nearly cried when I saw him, but he reassured me he was fine, though I knew he wasn't. He iced his entire body for two days straight before Tyler made him get back into the gym. Apparently, this Dice guy didn't take it easy on him and taught him how dirty they fight in the underground world, which meant teaching him how to defend himself if he ended up on the ground and couldn't get up. He even had a shoe imprint on his back.

Just the thought of what he went through made me want to puke. If something happens to Liam, and we don't get one last opportunity to be intimate, I'll always regret not showing him how much I love him. I can show him in other ways, but hardly touching each other or being close feels like the opposite. I hate the distance.

Instead of changing like Sophie demanded, I strip off my tank top so I'm left in my sports bra. Then I take off my shorts and replace them with my spandex leggings. After I fix my hair and put it up into a high ponytail, I grab my yoga mat and go back into the living room.

"What are you doing?" Sophie asks as I roll out my mat.

"My daily yoga routine," I tell her casually, getting myself into a sitting position.

She snorts. "I haven't seen you do your *routine* in days."

"I need to catch up," I say, but I know she's not buying it.

"This isn't gonna be good…" I hear her mutter before she walks upstairs.

I move into an upward-facing dog and hold it while my back arches and legs stretch. After a moment, I switch into downward-facing dog and exhale.

"What the fuck are you doing?"

Turning my head, I grin when I see a pissed-off Liam.

"You've seen me do this a hundred times," I say innocently. "Should we do another yoga bet? See if I can beat your ass this time?"

"I asked you to put some more clothes on," he says firmly with a plate in one hand and a sandwich in the other.

"And I asked you to get naked and fuck me last night, so it looks like neither of us is getting what we want."

Liam nearly chokes on his food and smacks his chest before it goes down his throat. "Jesus, woman."

I release my hold and go into a warrior position. "Don't watch me if I'm such a temptation then," I quip.

"You could make this easy and stop trying to get me to break," he states, keeping his eyes glued to mine. "Wearing that and doing yoga in front of me is just cruel."

I hold back a smirk. "You didn't seem to mind it when you kept me in the friend-zone all those years."

"That was different, and you damn well know it."

"Hmm…agree to disagree." I shrug.

"So what, this is payback for all the years I wouldn't bang you?"

"No, just the first time." I adjust my sports bra, lowering it down my chest. "The time you nearly ripped my dress in two and then screamed at me to…and I quote…'get the fuck out.'"

"You're not seriously still pissed I wouldn't have sex with a minor, are you?" He sets his plate down and walks toward me.

"I was like, five months away from turning eighteen!" I argue.

"Oh yeah, I'm sure that's an acceptable excuse for the judge after they handcuff my ass for touching you," he retorts, standing in front of me now.

Instead of allowing his closeness to affect me, I move into dolphin pose so he can get a full view of my ass.

Liam's palm flattens on my lower back, and I inhale sharply at his touch. "Baby, if I had fucked you that night, there's no way I would've been able to resist you when we were reunited. I would've hurt you because I wasn't in the right headspace for something serious. We both had some growing up to do."

Then he slides his hand down my ass crack until it's between my legs.

"Your sisters would've found out what I did, and the guys would've killed me." With his middle finger, he rubs my pussy outside my leggings. My eyes slam shut as I soak in his touch. "Then you and I would've had no chance at a future." Then he rubs the pad of his finger against my clit, causing a groan to escape from my mouth. "So, trust me when I say waiting was the smart decision."

"Mmm…" I stretch out farther, giving him better access to my pussy.

"Which is why waiting another couple of weeks is also the smart decision..." He circles my clit, my thighs burning as I struggle to hold myself up while my body aches for more of Liam's touches. I feel the buildup as he adds more pressure, and my knees shake. Before I can beg for more, Liam removes his hand, then slaps my ass. "Two more weeks, baby. We got this."

Is he fucking kidding me right now?

My arms give out, and I drop to the mat, turning to scowl at him. "Seriously? That was mean!"

"Sorry, but you left me no choice." He shrugs with a shit-eating smirk as he sits on the arm of the couch. "You wanted to play with fire, sweetheart. Showing off your sexy nipple rings, wearing tight as fuck pants that show off your curves, and eating whipped cream off your fingers last night."

I stand, roll my mat, and stuff it under my arm. "The whipped cream was a happy accident when it fell off my spoon, but the other two, I have no idea what you're talking about."

Liam's head falls back as he bellows out laughter. "Mads, please. I've been watching this dance of yours for three years, remember? I know all your tells. Your flirty innuendos. And the not-so-subtle way you eye fuck me."

I growl. Damn him.

"Baby, come here." He waves me over, but I look at him cautiously.

"Why? You want to *almost* finish what you started?"

He chuckles and shakes his head. "Quit being stubborn and get your ass over here."

I walk over and stand between his legs, dropping the mat. Liam wraps his arms around me, pulling me closer until there's no space left. Cupping my face, his thumb brushes my bottom lip.

"Remember when you were ready to jump my bones and lose your V-card, but I made you wait?"

I groan. "Yes."

"And a couple of weeks later, we took the time to get to know each other and really explore our feelings. Wasn't making love that first time so much more special because we didn't rush?"

Shrugging, I answer, "I guess so."

"You *guess* so?" He lifts a brow, and I break out into a laugh.

"Yes, of course. It was very special." I wrap my arms around his shoulders. "But during those two weeks, we were still being intimate with each other, just not *all the way* intimate."

"And after the fight when we're able to forget about JJ and the O'Learys, won't waiting feel *way* more special?"

I lower my eyes. The emotions I've bottled up inside threaten to release, but I try holding them back.

"Mads?" He tips my chin up toward him. "What is it?"

"Nothing," I whisper.

"I know this isn't nothing," he says, wiping a tear that slipped out. "Tell me."

I swallow hard, feeling silly for getting emotional. "What if…" I start, then lick my lips. "What if there is no 'after the fight' because you don't survive," I finally croak out. "We abstain from sex and have no last time."

"Is that what this is? You're worried something's going to happen to me, and we'll have missed out?" he asks, wrapping a piece of loose hair behind my ear.

"Well of course, I'm worried!" I toss out my arms. "If you die, we wasted every last opportunity to spend together."

"Maddie…" he says slowly, grabbing my face. "I'm not going to die."

"You can't know that. I looked up videos on underground fighting, and it's really fucking ugly."

"Dammit, why'd you do that?"

I lean back slightly. "Because I wanted to know what my boyfriend was getting into. I have a right to know just how dangerous this is and how to prepare myself for the worst."

"You're right. It is ugly, but that's why I'm training so hard, baby."

"That doesn't guarantee the other guy won't have just as much training or hell, more. There's no way to know how this is going to turn out and—"

"Maddie, stop," he demands, then cups my cheeks. "I promise you, okay? I promise I'm coming back to you in one piece. There's nothing in this goddamn world that will keep me from you. Got that? We fought way too hard to be with each other. I'm not letting anything come between us now."

Tears hang at the corner of my eyes and slowly fall down my cheeks. I know he can't promise me that, but I hang onto every single word because it's all that'll get me through this until it's over.

I nod, unable to speak through my emotions, and Liam hugs me to his chest.

"I love you," he says softly.

"Always?"

His lips tilt up against my skin.

"Always."

Now that I'm on Christmas vacation, my days are starting to run together, and when I wake up to another morning of Liam already gone, it takes me a minute to realize it's Friday. One more day until our family Christmas party here with my sisters and their husbands. And of course, Tyler as well.

Too bad there isn't a fourth Corrigan sister because Tyler could easily blend in with our family. The guys all love him, and he's good with Lennon's kids. He's tall, dark, and handsome. *Literally.* There is nothing not to like about him.

"Get up, Madilocks!" He pounds loudly on my door. "Soph's trying to call you. Answer your phone!"

Okay, except for *that.*

After Liam left for Vegas and Tyler was put on "Maddie duty," he gave me a nickname after Goldilocks just to fuck with me. He thinks it's the funniest thing in the world since it annoys me. Then Sophie chimed in and said it was perfect since I moved into the house last and took over her bed.

"You're an asshole, Beanstalk!" I shout, whipping off my covers and marching to the door. "What?"

Tyler steps back and blinks. His eyes glance down once before snapping back to mine. "Uh, Sophie texted me to wake you up because she's trying to call you."

"Okay. I'll call her. Anything else?"

Tyler focuses on the ceiling and shakes his head. "Nope."

I furrow my brows, wondering why he's acting so weird. Looking down, I realize I'm only in my sports bra and shorts. "Oh, now you're shy?" I chuckle. "You walked in on me getting out of the bathtub naked, remember?"

He squeezes his eyes shut. "That was an accident."

"Mm-hmm," I tease. "Relax, I'll get dressed."

"Good, because Liam is getting really strong, and I don't want him kicking my ass for seeing you like this."

"What? Did he say something?" I jab my finger in his ribs so he'll look at me.

"Jesus." He yelps, stepping back. "I'm leaving now. Get dressed and call your sister."

I roll my eyes. "Yeah, yeah. Tell your possessive best friend that I'll walk around naked if I want."

"I wouldn't recommend that." He peels open one eye and squints. "The last time I made a joke about you, he had me by the throat against the wall. Remember?"

Guilt creeps up at the memory of how worked up Liam got while waiting for Victoria to file divorce papers.

"Is he getting that bad?" I ask. By the time I see him every day, he's already spent hours at the gym, then after he cleans up, he'll go track a fugitive until the evening. If I didn't know better, I'd say he was purposely avoiding me, but I understand he's trying to juggle a lot at the moment.

Tyler nods. "He's getting anxious not knowing who he's fighting yet, and JJ keeps texting him reminders about how important this fight is."

I groan. God, I hate that ugly ass piece of shit.

"Okay, fine," I surrender. "Getting dressed now."

Tyler walks away, and I check my phone, seeing eight text messages from Sophie. She has a full day of rehearsals before she's off for the holiday and asked me to run to the grocery store for some last-minute items she needs for tomorrow's feast.

Maddie: I'll grab everything, stop worrying.

Sophie: Thank you! Love you!

Maddie: Next time, don't send Beanstalk to wake me up, though!

Sophie: I had no choice, sleepyhead!

I snicker and set my phone down so I can get ready for the day. Once I'm dressed and presentable, I head to my car and crank it, but it doesn't turn over.

What the fuck?

I try it again and nothing. Well, great.

Grabbing my stuff, I walk back into the house and look for Tyler.

"Hey," I say when I see him in the kitchen. "My car won't start for some reason. Any chance I can take your truck to the store to get groceries for Soph?"

He looks at me, concerned. "It won't start at all?"

I shake my head. "Just makes a weird noise, then dies. I have no idea." Shrugging, I pout. "I can take an Uber if it's an issue."

"No, of course not. But I'm a little worried after what happened to the G-Wagon. You should let me look at it."

I smirk and cross my arms. "You know how to work on cars?"

"Don't look so surprised." He chuckles, then grabs his keys. "C'mon, I'll take you so I can buy some tools and oil. When's the last time it's had an oil change?"

I follow him to the front door. "Uhh…"

"Oh, Madilocks. I'm about to teach you some life skills today."

Groaning, I walk out to his truck. "That sounds like zero fun actually."

An hour later, we're back at the house with everything on Sophie's list and everything from the auto aisle. Tyler talks to me about car shit and what could be wrong with it, and honestly, he'd be better off talking to me in a foreign language because I don't have a clue what any of it means.

As I unload the bags, he changes and returns in old-looking jeans and a ripped T-shirt. "Come out when you're done. I want you to watch."

I give him a look that says I'd rather be anywhere else.

"Stop being a baby."

"I'm not! I just don't want to tinker around in an engine."

Tyler laughs hard. "You don't *tinker* in an engine, Mads."

I roll my eyes. "Whatever…can't you just fix it, and I'll give you a big hug in thanks?" I flash him a sweet smile.

"Nice try." He grabs the extra bags of parts he bought. "Meet me out in there in five, I mean it."

I grunt loudly. "Fine. I have to change *again* because I'm not getting my nice clothes dirty."

"Don't really care what you wear as long as it covers your body."

He's gone before he can see my scowl, and I grab my phone to send Liam a text.

Maddie: Is there a reason you've put Tyler on dress-code duty? He won't even look me in the eyes!

Liam: Well, hi. What's the matter, sweetheart?

Maddie: Don't be cutesy. I know you scolded Tyler for looking at me when I'm not 'fully dressed.' Don't you think that's a bit...macho?

Liam: Hell no. I love Tyler like a brother and owe him big time, but he still has a working dick.

I nearly gag.

Maddie: So does Mason. You're not threatened by him?

Liam: You never notice how Mason leaves the room when you enter or turns away when you walk in?

Maddie: ARE YOU KIDDING ME???

Liam: Baby, relax. It goes both ways. I don't look at Sophie, and he doesn't look at you. It's bro code.

Maddie: Something is seriously wrong with you.

Liam: I don't want other guys looking at my girlfriend.

Maddie: Mason is like my BROTHER. Ew!

Liam: Good. Keep it that way.

Maddie: I know you're really stressed right now, but you can't be all alpha-possessive.

Liam: I'd be less stressed if my girlfriend would tell me how much she loves me instead of yelling at me.

Then the jerk sends a smiley face. Damn him.
Inhaling a sharp breath, I decide to let it slide. *For now.*

Maddie: You're damn lucky I love you.

Liam: Always?

Damn him again.

Maddie: Always.

After a half hour of sitting outside and watching Tyler do God knows what to my car, I'm bored.
"Can I go inside yet?" I whine.
"Is your car fixed?" he counters.
"No clue, you're the know-it-all."
I hear him laugh as he messes with shit under the car. "Can you at least hand me the pliers?"
Releasing a breath, I get up and look in his tool kit. "What's that?"
He chuckles.
"Stop laughing at me! If I told you to get me a leotard, would you know what that is?" I fire back, digging around.
"Red handle with two grippers at the top," he explains.
Yeah, that narrows it down. I grab two items that kind of sound like that. "Any of these?" I ask, lowering my body to where he is.
"Come closer," he says. I inch farther. "A little more." I go on my back and wiggle toward him.

245

"You're an ass. I know what you're doing," I say with a smile. "Now I'm dirty."

"Welcome to workin' on your car," he taunts, grabbing one of the tools out of my hand.

I watch as he messes with shit, and I'm intrigued. "How'd you learn about cars?"

"My grandfather," he says.

"The one married to the grandmother who taught you how to cook?" I ask.

"Yep. Mimi and Pops. They practically raised me and taught me everything my mother didn't."

"And your dad?"

He shrugs. "Left when my sister was a baby."

"Are you and Everleigh close?" I ask, remembering his sister's name from when he first told me.

Tyler shrugs again. "Kinda. We text, but I haven't been home in years."

"So you haven't seen your sister in years?"

"She's come to Vegas a couple of times, but no, I don't see her as much as I'd like."

"You don't visit your grandparents?"

After he stays silent for a minute, I know he's not going to answer that question, so I ask him another one. "Any ex-girlfriends back home?"

"Nope."

"None? Wait. Ex-boyfriends?"

He turns and glares at me.

"What? I wouldn't judge. I don't care if you're gay, straight, upside down, or triangle. I'm just asking."

He snorts. "What the fuck is triangle?"

I roll my eyes. "I was just making a point."

"I didn't date in high school," he says. "Graduated and enlisted right away."

"So you were in the military!" I snap my fingers. He made a comment about boot camp in Montana, so I had a hunch he had been.

"Only for four years."

"Why?"

"Decided on a different path," is all he tells me. Trying to pry information out of Tyler is harder than when I was trying to crack Liam all those years.

"Why didn't you date in high school? I imagine you were popular. Probably the quarterback. Amiright?" I smirk and wait for any kind of expression from him.

Instead, he slides out from under the car, so I follow him, and he starts fidgeting under the hood. He wipes his hand on the rag, and I study his hard expression.

"There was a girl, wasn't there? I can tell."

"You've lost your mind."

"Hardly. I'm very good at reading this kind of shit. Ask Lennon. I knew she and Hunter were in love before she did."

He snorts. "How's that possible?"

"I'll tell you when you tell me a secret."

"I'm not that desperate to know. Plus, I'll just ask her myself."

I scoff. "That's cheating."

Tyler takes out a long metal stick, wipes it across the rag, then puts it back in its place. "Why do you want to know so badly? I'm not one of your girlfriends who wants to gossip about crushes and periods."

"Well, you did buy me tampons already, so we're halfway there." I shoot him a shit-eating smirk.

He groans, shaking his head. "If I tell you, will you leave me the hell alone about it?"

"Yes, promise!" I say overeagerly.

He sighs. "She wasn't my girlfriend, but her name is Gemma. She's my sister's best friend."

"Oh my God!" I squeal, my eyes widening in excitement.

"Shut it."

I hold back my laughter, but then fail and release it. "What else? Tell me more."

"Nope, that's all you get."

Sticking out my lower lip, I give him my best pouty face. "That shit might work on Liam, but it doesn't faze me."

I roll my eyes and cross my arms. "Rude."

Chuckling, he pushes off the car, then shuts the hood. "You need a new battery. I'll run and grab one."

"What, that's it? How do you know?"

"Because I checked it when you were unloading groceries, but you also needed your filters replaced and an oil change."

"Well, that's good, right? That means no one messed with it?"

"Nope, just normal age and slacking on car maintenance."

Whew.

I watch as Tyler packs up all his tools and supplies. "So… what's Gemma look like?"

"I haven't seen her in years."

"Not even on social media?"

He shakes his head.

"You weren't curious?"

"Curiosity killed the cat, Maddie."

"Oh come on! Is she single? Have any kids? Does she still live in Lawton Ridge?"

"No idea…on all three."

"Wow…you're weird."

He shrugs. "Guess so."

Tyler opened up a little more today and gave me some personal details of his life, but I'm determined to crack him in half before he goes back home. I don't know who hurt him or why he's so private, but I have a feeling there's a story behind it. And I want to hear it.

CHAPTER EIGHTEEN

LIAM

I'VE BEEN TRACKING this asshole for the past week between training, and the longer he takes me on this cat and mouse chase, the thinner my patience becomes. I have a lead to a house and watch it for hours, but I can't see him clearly enough inside to merit barging in without a warrant. I don't need one if I know without a doubt the fugitive's in a residence, but this sneaky bastard hops from one place to the next.

After another failed attempt, I decide to try again in a couple of days. Tomorrow's our Christmas party with everyone, and with the fight on our minds, it's been tense around the house. I'd like just one day when we can forget and have fun together.

"Hi, baby." I wrap my arms around Maddie as soon as I see her standing in the kitchen with Tyler. They're laughing, and I notice Tyler's face is covered in grease. "What's going on?"

I move around her and grab a beer from the fridge.

"Tyler taught me how to change the oil in my car," Maddie states, and Tyler snorts into his drink.

Narrowing my eyes at both of them, I watch them. "Oh, really? I find that unbelievable." I laugh when Maddie throws me a scowl.

"Excuse you, I could very well learn how to do that sort of stuff...*if* I wanted."

I smile as I take a sip. "And did you?"

"Well, technically...no. I watched and handed him tools."

Smirking, Tyler shakes his head when Maddie isn't looking. But damn she looks so proud. "Awesome, job, babe. Next, have him teach you how to change a tire."

"Uhh...that sounds out of the realm of things I can do, so how about you just always be available to come rescue me if I need it." She wraps her arms around my neck and smiles up at me. "What's the purpose of having a big, strong man if I can't have him changing tires for me?"

Chuckling, I nod. "It'd be my honor to always be around to rescue you." I flash her a wink, and Tyler groans.

"And that's my cue."

"Oh, c'mon, Beanstalk. I was just going to tell Liam all about our little chat today." She beams at him, but Tyler shakes his head, takes another sip, then leaves the kitchen.

"Why do you tease him?"

"I never had any brothers growing up," she explains. "This is my chance."

I laugh, bringing her lips to mine for a soft kiss.

"I got him to admit there's a girl back home," she tells me. "Eventually, I'll crack him and get the whole story."

"You're relentless."

"That's why you love me," she quips.

The following night, Hunter, Lennon, and the kids come over, and together, we put up the tree and decorate the house. Part of it feels foreign, a tradition I never got to have as a kid growing up, but it makes me appreciate it even more.

Sophie cranks Christmas music while Lennon sings and Maddie hangs lights and garland. We give Tyler the honors of putting the star on top since he's the tallest, and it's the first year with all of us together. Hell, it might be the last too.

Now that Mason and Sophie are married, I suspect they'll be looking for a house of their own soon. It's hard for me to think about the future, though I want one with Maddie more than anything. Until after the fight, we're living in limbo, but soon, my debt with the O'Learys will officially be paid off; at least I hope for good this time.

The girls made us watch a Christmas movie after we ate dinner. It was more fun than I thought it'd be, but they really know how to put together a feast. Then as we ate, Sophie suggested we all share a favorite holiday memory. We all died laughing as Sophie and Lennon shared memories from their childhood. Most revolved around making Maddie believe Santa walked around the house, leaving cookie crumbs on the floor. They even put reindeer poop tracks outside for her to find too. Being the youngest, she got the brunt of their pranks, which Maddie didn't find hilarious at all.

"You look really beautiful," I whisper in Maddie's ear as she sits on my lap. The sparkly red dress hugs her like a second skin.

"I wore it for you," she leans back and murmurs. "Even if you can't tear it off later."

Fuck if I don't wish I could.

"Trust me, I would in a heartbeat," I tell her.

I'm *dying* to touch her. To give in to our desires and make her my Christmas meal, but the pent-up tension and aggression is helping me in the ring during training, so I can't risk getting weak now. There are only ten days left until the fight, and I plan to make every day of training count.

After the movie, Sophie announces it's time to exchange gifts. We did a secret Santa with the girls and guys separate, and I got Hunter's name. Knowing he's an Aaron Rodgers fan, I managed to outbid a person online for a signed jersey and football. Then of course I got Maddie something, but it's nothing compared to what I really want to give her. I love her, but I also don't want to rush anything before we're truly ready, so I kept it simple.

"Dude, yes!" Hunter shouts when he opens his present. "This will get passed onto my son and his son and then his son's son…for generations, man." He's so happy, and I can't help but laugh.

"That's going on my mantel, isn't it?" Lennon deadpans, then shoots me a playful glare.

I throw my hands up and shrug. "You knew what you were getting into when you married him. Plus, it's better than the Playboy centerfold blowup poster I was going to buy."

Lennon points at me. "Better watch your back, Evans. This just gives me fuel to get you back next year."

"It's on." I shoot her a wink.

After everyone exchanges their gifts, Sophie makes her special peppermint hot cocoa with candy cane straws and marshmallows. Mason sneaks behind her and adds in vodka, and she scolds him for it.

The entire evening is surreal.

I've never had this experience before. My father tried his very best to give me what he could, but the warmth and laughter in the room are new to me.

"You want your gift tonight, or should I wait until Christmas Day?" I ask Maddie as we stand in the kitchen, getting hot chocolate refills.

"Hmm…" She smiles wide. "Now."

I laugh because I knew she'd say that. Reaching into my back pocket, I grab the thin pieces of paper and hand them to her. "Sorry they aren't wrapped…"

Her eyes light up as soon as she realizes what they are. "Oh my God!" she screams so loud, you'd think we were already at the concert. "Billie Eilish tickets! Are you kidding me?" She flings herself at me, wrapping her arms around my neck, and I catch her. "How did you get these? They sold out in like minutes!" She pulls back and searches my face.

I shrug as if it was no big deal to jump through hoops to get them. "I know people."

Maddie looks at them again. "The concert isn't until next summer." She arches a brow, tilting her head at me. "Does that mean you think we'll still be together then? Or is this like when a guy makes plans six months in advance so the chick will sleep with him now?"

"Fuck, you caught me." I grip her hips and pull her closer.

"I love it, thank you." Maddie kisses me softly, and I lean in, wanting more of her. "I hope you know what you just signed up for." She smirks, shaking her hips. "I have every song of hers memorized."

"I wouldn't expect anything less, honestly." I press my lips to her forehead. "I can't wait."

"Me too. We'll hopefully have a lot to celebrate by then."

Hell, I sure hope so.

"I feel bad now. All I got you was a personalized ornament." She frowns. "It…has our faces painted on it. With our names on the bottom. And the year." She slaps herself in the forehead. "I wanted to commemorate our first Christmas. It sounds super lame now that I'm saying it out loud."

Grabbing her wrist, I remove her hand and tilt her chin

up to look at me. "It sounds…amazing. Thoughtful. Very Maddie. And I already know it's going to be the best gift I've ever received."

On Christmas, I take Maddie to my aunt's house, where my dad and stepmom are temporarily living. I'm devastated about the fire that destroyed my childhood home and them losing everything. Luckily, they'll get an insurance check to help them start over and buy a new house or build one. My dad deserves to know the truth, but I can't tell him. That would be opening a can of worms about the O'Learys, and this is one of those "the less he knows, the better" situations. It was hard enough to explain to him that Victoria and I split and the babies weren't mine. He was so excited to become a grandpa, and having to witness the disappointment in his eyes nearly shattered me.

I think he was confused that I quickly jumped into a relationship with Maddie after, but he didn't voice a concern, so I assumed there was no issue with me "moving on" so fast. He knows I'll do whatever I want, but I'm grateful for his blessing either way. I want him to like Maddie and for us to be able to spend quality time together.

And if this is the last time I get with my dad, I want it to be special and memorable for him.

"Dad, I got you something," I tell him as we sit in the

living room with beers in our hands. Aunt Ruthie made hot apple cider, but then my uncle Matt came in carrying a six-pack.

"You didn't have to do that," he says, setting his beer down. We never exchange gifts, but I wanted to this time.

"I know, but I saw this, and it made me think of you," I explain, handing over the small package Maddie wrapped. It's also so he has one thing from me...just in case.

After giving me an incredulous look, he takes it. I drink my beer as he unwraps the paper, then smiles when he realizes what it is.

"This is a pretty nice lookin' watch, Liam." He takes it out and holds it under the light.

"Turn it around," Maddie tells him, beaming.

My dad does as she says, then squints to read the engravement.

"My hero," he reads aloud. My father's hardly an emotional person, but he chokes up. "Wow, Liam."

I stand and round the coffee table, then wrap my arms around him. "I mean it, old man. You stepped up and took care of me. I think about that every day. You're my hero, always."

My dad shifts and returns the hug, holding back tears in the process. "I love you, son."

"Love you too."

Aunt Ruthie serves everyone pie and turns on the fireplace.

"So, Maddie..." my stepmom begins. "You were Liam's roommate before you two started dating, right?"

Maddie nods and takes a large bite of her dessert, I suspect to avoid having to talk about our relationship since they think it's recent.

"How did things change from roommates to dating?" she asks. I know she's not being judgy, but it's uncomfortable.

"Well…" Maddie swallows her food, then smirks at me. "He finally came to his senses and saw what was right in front of him the whole time."

Alright, that's *mostly* true.

My dad chuckles, looking at his wife with pride. "Sounds like an Evans man."

I smile and shrug. "I thought she was too good for me."

"Oh, she is…" Aunt Ruthie teases. "Being in love is a good look on you, Liam."

Reaching over, I grab Maddie's hand and press a kiss on her knuckles. "It sure is."

We end up watching *A Christmas Story,* and as Maddie snuggles into me, I look around and soak in my surroundings. This has been one of the best days I've had in a long time, one spent with family and the love of my life, eating, drinking, celebrating.

If I don't come back, it's not only going to affect Maddie but also everyone who loves me.

And that feeling is enough to gut me.

The next day, I'm back to training and reality.

"Come on, Liam, keep your shoulders tight," Tyler

scolds. I swing at him and miss, then he swoops his foot underneath my legs, and I fall flat on my back.

Motherfucker.

"Get up," he demands, not giving me the chance to rest. "Your opponent gets you down, he's going to do whatever it takes to keep you there. You fall, you bounce right the fuck up. You got me?" Tyler sounds pissed, and I've been off my game all day, but yesterday really brought everything into perspective for me. Realizing how much this one fight might change my life is wearing me down.

"You should've just let me fake my death months ago when I asked you to," I chastise him.

"Or I could grab my gun and get the job done for real?" he mocks with a frustrating glare. "But then you know that means leaving me with Maddie, and we'll probably grieve together and get pretty close. Then I'll turn on my Southern charm, and well...I'll let you use your imagination for the rest."

"You fucking bastard," I hiss, jumping to my feet and storming toward him. He blocks every punch I attempt, smirking like an asshole.

"Whatcha gonna do about it when you're dead?" He moves his head to the side, and I miss his face. "You gonna give up and let me have your girl?"

"Over my fucking dead body, you motherfucker." I get a punch to his gut and another to his jaw.

"That all you got? If so, I'll have Maddie in my bed by Valentine's Day."

I fill with rage, wrap my arms around his waist, and push my head into his stomach, pushing him into the ropes and punching him in the ribs.

Tyler has his arms around my head, tightening his grip as I attempt to lift his body over my shoulders.

"She's gonna look so goddamn sweet underneath me," he continues in labored breaths. "Don't think I haven't noticed those perky nipple piercings."

Standing and meeting his eyes, I grit my teeth and drive my fist in his gut. Over and over until I grab his throat and squeeze.

"You're supposed to be my friend, you asshole." I seethe, pushing my thumbs into his windpipe. "Talking about my girl like that makes you the biggest douchebag in the world."

Tyler fights back, trying to loosen my grip, but the adrenaline pumping through my blood fuels my rage. I curse at him when he brings his knee up and drives it into my groin, making me drop to the ground.

He falls with me, sucking in air as he tries to catch his breath. I climb on top of him, throwing fists to his face, but he holds up his arms and blocks me. In one swift movement, he drives into my waist and flips me over, landing on my side. Tyler grabs my arm and pulls it behind my back as he pushes his knee into my ribs and other arm.

"Goddammit," I hiss when he yanks my arm harder.

"You fuckin' done?"

"Fuck you," I spit.

Tyler releases me, then stands as he chuckles. I look up at him as he shakes his head and crosses his arms over his chest. The asshole was purposely pissing me off. "You're ready."

CHAPTER NINETEEN

MADDIE

THE LAST FORTY-EIGHT hours I've been lost in my head about this damn fight. We've been counting down the days for weeks as Liam has trained and prepared, and now the day he leaves is here. Time flew by so quickly and honestly, I'm scared of what could possibly happen. Things never seem to go the way they're supposed to, and while Tyler has explained to me several times how ready Liam is, it doesn't make me feel any better about the situation. I understand the consequences, and it's much more than him just getting his ass kicked. He could be killed. Losing him isn't an option, but it could very well be my reality.

Tonight, I can't sleep. I've been tossing and turning, and eventually, I roll over and look at the time on my phone to see it's just past three. I've laid here with my eyes closed, counted to one thousand backward, but nothing is helping me get my mind off Liam leaving in the morning. We'll say our goodbyes, and he'll get on that plane and not return to me. Just thinking about it nearly brings me to tears, but I try to hold it in, something I've gotten really good at doing. Liam knows I'm upset regardless of how much I've tried to stay strong. Our future is literally in his opponent's hands, and the unknown of what could happen drives me insane.

Eventually, I drift off, but it seems like only an hour passes before I'm being woken up by Liam. He nuzzles into my neck, and I smile at the way his lips brush against my skin.

"Morning, baby," he whispers, and I turn to face him. "I have to get ready to leave in a couple of hours." His voice is strained and sad.

"Morning." It doesn't matter that my eyes are burning or that I'm exhausted, I decide to get up too because I want to spend every minute I can with him before he leaves. After I brush my teeth and pull up my hair into a messy bun, I go into the kitchen where Liam is standing shirtless, filling up a mug with coffee. I lean against the counter and watch him, memorizing the way he looks right now. Glancing over, he catches me gawking and smirks. All the training he's done the past few weeks has really done his body good.

And my vagina bad. Bad because all I want to do is jump him, and I've had to restrain.

After he takes a sip, he sets down the mug and walks over to me, then wraps his arms around my waist. I sink into his strong body, not wanting him to let me go, but our moment is interrupted when I hear a throat clearing behind us. Turning around, I shoot daggers at Sophie.

"Coffee." She points at the machine we're blocking like she's a caveman coming to claim hers. Sometimes mornings just aren't her thing.

I laugh, trying to ignore her. "I'm busy."

Liam kisses my forehead, then we pull apart. Sophie goes to the fridge and grabs the creamer, pouring it into her cup. She releases a sigh and smiles after she takes a sip. Moments later, Tyler and Mason enter the kitchen, chatting about the upcoming events. It's then I realize Liam's and my morning alone is short-lived. I don't know why the hell they're all up so early anyway. It's as if the smell of coffee brewing summoned them all.

Mason volunteers to cook breakfast, and I can't help but obsess over the fact that we only have mere hours left. Time is slipping between my fingers and there's nothing I can do about it. Feeling chilled, I decide to grab a hoodie from my room, and as I'm walking into the kitchen, I overhear Tyler talking to Liam.

"After the fight, you'll more than likely need to go to the hospital," he tells him.

Liam asks why, and Tyler continues to explain that he'll probably be messed up in some way and will need medical attention because he's not going to walk away unscathed. Tyler says he'll probably have broken ribs, black eyes, and be bruised. The visual my mind creates causes me to shiver with fear.

I sit next to Liam at the table, and the anxiety slowly takes over. It scares the shit out of me that something bad may happen, and he'll return injured. As if he notices, he places his hand on my thigh and tries to calm me. Mason finishes cooking and sets a plate stacked full of French toast in the middle of the table along with a jar of Nutella and bananas. Sophie grabs the syrup and plates while I grab the silverware, then we all sit.

As we eat, I try to push my worries away, but it's no use. My emotions are starting to bubble over. No one brings up the elephant in the room even though we all know what's coming. Tyler and Liam will leave for Vegas, and no one knows what's going to happen or when they'll return. The air is thick as we chat about randomness. Once our plates are clear, we thank Mason for cooking, and although I offer to help clean up, Sophie says she's got it. She gives me a small smile and tells me to go spend time with Liam instead.

Liam grabs my hand as we walk to the bedroom. After we're inside, he shuts the door, then slams his lips against mine, kissing away all my thoughts. He cups my face, bracing us, and pours all his emotions into me. I wrap my arms around his bare waist and hold him as close as I can.

"Liam," I whisper as a tear falls down my cheek. "I'm so scared."

He leans back, gently placing his finger under my chin and forcing me to look into his eyes. Searching my face, Liam shakes his head.

"I'm coming home to you, Maddie. I know you're thinking the worst, but things will be better after this, and we'll be able to finally live without fear. It'll all be over."

"But until you come back to me, fear is all I'll have," I admit, hating how weak I sound because I wanted to be strong for him.

The look of sadness on his face is evident as he rests his forehead against mine, sucking in a breath. "I'm so sorry to put you through this, baby. I wish things were different."

I let out a ragged breath, knowing the next forty-five minutes will pass by in a blink. "Just please be careful. *Please.*" I close my eyes as I beg him to stay safe.

"I will. Trust me, I'll do whatever it takes to win that fight and put this nightmare behind us."

We pull apart so Liam can finish getting ready. He grabs his duffel bag and double-checks what he packed, then adds extra clothes inside before changing. Sitting on the edge of the bed, I watch him. Once he's finally ready, Liam turns to me and smiles.

"I love you," he says, sitting next to me.

"I love you more, so much more."

He presses butterfly kisses along my jaw before meeting my mouth. Together, we're lost in the moment. I wish I could freeze time and keep him here with me forever. Unfortunately, it's not an option. Eventually, we break apart, and Liam stands.

"Should probably get going before Tyler yells at me." He's not happy about leaving either. I can see the turmoil brewing in his eyes.

"Yeah, you don't want to miss your flight." I walk with him to the living room where Sophie, Mason, and Tyler are sitting around drinking coffee. Liam announces he's ready to leave, and everyone stands, but Tyler runs upstairs. I plaster on a smile, but I'm dying on the inside as he wraps his arms around Sophie and gives her a big hug.

"Be careful, Liam. Kick some ass," Sophie tells him, then glances at me with a sad smile. If anyone in this room knows how much this is destroying me, it's her. I might be able to somewhat hide how I really feel from Liam, but with Sophie, I'm transparent. Mason gives him a side hug and tells him to call as soon as it's over. Tyler comes downstairs carrying a bag and says he's good to go.

"I'm going to be fine," Liam says, glancing around the room. "I'll be home in a few days."

He grabs his bag, and I follow him outside. Tyler gets in the truck as Liam wraps his arms around me. It's chilly, the cool breeze sweeping over my skin, and I shiver. Liam holds me, kisses me, and then leaves with an *I love you* and a reassuring smile. I watch his truck until the taillights are out of sight.

Yesterday, after Liam left, was horrible. I laid in bed and cried, sleeping for the better half of the day until Sophie forced me to eat dinner. Liam texted me when he landed and called me before he went to bed, but I didn't feel any better about him being there. Talking to him just reiterated how real the whole situation is. Somehow, I fell asleep without him lying next to me. My bed hasn't felt this empty in a long time.

I wake up the next morning, and I know my eyes are red and puffy. After I shower, I put on some jeans and a T-shirt, then grab a hoodie. While going through my morning routine, I realize that I need a new pack of my birth control pills. I got a three-month supply and put the extras in my nightstand.

As I dig through the drawer, I notice a white envelope with my name on it in Liam's writing. What the hell is this?

Ripping it open and unfolding the paper, I quickly realize it's a letter from him. Sitting down on the bed, I read it.

Dear Maddie,
It's after two in the morning, and I can't sleep. Knowing I'm leaving in just a few days keeps my mind wandering, and though I'm content to just hold you in my arms all night, I decided I needed to write you this letter.

I don't believe in coincidences, but I truly believe I met you for a reason. You've changed my life. Since the night we danced at that frat party, you've made an impact on me. Through all those times I fought it, I still felt there was a reason you and I were meant to be together. I hope you understand how deep my love for you is because I never want to be without you.

You're it for me, baby.

Though I'm not much of a praying man, I've been praying like hell we get through this. That I come back to you, and we can start our lives together forever. A year ago, I had no idea what my life would be like, and now I only picture you and me. Oh, how your love has changed me.

But the reality is, this fight is dangerous. The reality is, something bad could happen. I tried not to think of the what-ifs, but they've been hitting me harder and faster, and I can't ignore them. If something horrible does happen, I want you to know how deeply, insanely, madly in love with you I am. You need to know I wanted forever with you, and baby, if I don't come back, promise me you'll find happiness again.

I imagine you're rolling your eyes at me right now, but I mean it, Mads.

I'm going to fight like hell to hold you in my arms again, but if my time comes to an end, please keep living. Dance around the living room in your tiny leotards, practice downward dog in your too-tight leggings, and repeat your favorite movie lines when they come on the TV.

But never forget how much I love you.

So damn much, I still don't know what I did to be the lucky bastard that gets to kiss you every day.

I'll love you until the day I die, baby.

I love you always,
Liam

I'm sobbing by the time I finish reading his letter twice.

How could he leave me this? Was I meant to read it now?

If I say anything to him, it'll mess up his focus.

But it confirms what my heart is telling me what I need to do. It's New Year's Eve, and Liam is fighting for his life tonight, and as crazy as it sounds, I want to be there to support him. I need to be there. If what Tyler said is true, that he'll need medical attention afterward, I won't be able to wait here, not knowing if he's truly okay. My anxiety spikes just thinking about it all.

I pull out my laptop and search for plane tickets to Vegas. I don't give two shits about how much it costs. I just need to be there before dark. Five hundred dollars later, I have a flight booked that leaves at two o'clock. I pack a carry-on suitcase, then walk into the living room and set it by the door.

Mason is lying on the couch and peers up at me. "Where're you going?"

I turn and look at him. "Vegas."

He quickly sits up. "Maddie, what?"

"What?" I play dumb.

"*Why* are you going to Vegas?" he questions even though he already knows the answer.

"You're not going to Vegas," Sophie says as she steps off the bottom stair and walks toward me with creased brows.

I nod. "Yes, I am. I refuse to sit here while Liam is there.

I need to be at that fight tonight. I've already booked a flight."

"Mads, you can't do that," she tells me, but I know it's because she's worried.

"I can and will." I shrug. "If you're so concerned, come with me. Both of you. But I'm going with or without you. I have to do this, Soph. I know you understand."

Sophie looks over at Mason, and they have a silent conversation before she turns to me. "It's too dangerous."

"I don't care," I say firmly. "My flight leaves at two. I have a few hours before I have to go to the airport."

Mason goes to Sophie and looks at her. "Liam risked his life for you, and he's always been there for me over the years. I think Maddie's right. We need to be there."

"You've both lost it. He's participating in an underground fight. With mobsters! Fliers won't be passed around for that. Who's to say we'll even know where to go?" She makes really great points, but I'm two steps ahead of her.

"I've already figured it out. As soon as I'm there, I'll text Tyler and force him to give me the address," I say, pulling my hair into a high ponytail. All of a sudden, it feels hot in here. Mason laughs at my idea and shakes my head, but I ignore him. Tyler will tell me, right? I'll be persistent.

"Whatcha say, Soph?" Mason grabs her hand.

Her face softens, and she sucks in a deep breath, rolling her eyes. It's two to one. "Fine. There's no way I'm letting her go alone."

I laugh. "There's my protective big sister."

"I'll always be." Sophie wraps me in a hug. "I don't care how old you are."

"Guess we should start packing and searching for flights. Can you send me your reservation info so we can get on the same one?" Mason asks. I pull out my phone and forward my confirmation email.

"Did you already get a room in Vegas?" Sophie asks.

"Not yet. But I'll book something before we leave for the airport."

"Perfect."

The two of them go upstairs to get ready, and I plop down on the couch as a nervous excitement streams through me. I search for hotels and find one that looks nice and is affordable and make a reservation for two double beds, though we'll barely be there tonight.

After Mason and Sophie are ready, we decide to drive to the airport early since we'll probably run into holiday traffic. On the way over, we chat about random stuff, but my thoughts are in another place as I try to rehearse what I'm going to say to Tyler once we're there. I already know he's going to be pissed, but it's my right to be there.

Just as I expected, we're nearly bumper to bumper miles from the airport because of a stupid wreck. Traffic slows us down nearly an hour.

After we park and go through security, we have an hour to eat before boarding starts. I'm half-tempted to order a large margarita at the restaurant but decide against it, knowing I need to be in a good headspace when we land. Eventually, it's time for us to line up, and I'm anxious about the whole situation. After reading Liam's letter, I know this is the right thing to do, but I'm still nervous.

Sophie notices my fidgeting and places her hand on my shoulder and squeezes. "It's gonna be okay."

"I hope so," I tell her as we walk down the jetway, then find our seats on the plane. We take off, and I watch out the window as Sacramento drifts away, and the buildings below look like Lego pieces. Somehow, I fall asleep, and I'm being woken up when the wheels touch down on the runway. It hits me in full force that we're here, and all of this is really happening. There's no turning back now.

I've never been to Las Vegas before, and if I were here for any other reason, I'm sure I'd have an incredible time watching all the shows and walking down the Strip. We Uber to the hotel, and I can't seem to stop staring out the window. Everything looks like a large movie set with all the bright lights and tall buildings.

It takes no time before we're checked in and taking the elevator up to our room. Once we step in, I fall back on the bed and let out a loud sigh. Now comes the hard part, texting Tyler and demanding he give me the info I need.

Sophie and Mason sit on the edge of their bed and watch me as I sit up and pull my phone from my pocket. "Now or never," I say.

Maddie: I need to talk to you, but first of all, don't tell Liam I'm texting you right now.

His text bubbles immediately pop up.

Tyler: Alright. What's up?

Maddie: I'm in Vegas. Mason and Soph, too.

Tyler: What? Why?

Before I can respond, Tyler calls, and I pick up.

"Maddie, you cannot be here right now." He keeps his stern voice low.

"Well, we are. I want to go to the fight, Tyler. I need to be there. I can't sit around and wait, hoping he doesn't die. I need to know he's okay. I need to see it all go down." I'm talking a million miles per hour, my thoughts a jumbled mess.

"I'm sorry, but I'm not telling you where it is. I vowed to Liam to protect you, and that's what I'm doing. It's too dangerous, Maddie. You'll stick out like a sore thumb around the goddamn mob, and if Liam sees you, you'll be a distraction he doesn't need, and it could ruin his chances of beating this fucker. I can guarantee you that I'll keep you updated with what's going on. As soon as the fight is over, you'll be the first person I call. I promise."

I swallow hard, about to break down in tears. "Tyler…" I choke out. "Please. We're at the Westgate."

"Absolutely not. I'm not changing my mind, no amount of begging or crying will work. Stay at your hotel. You're safe there. Stay that way so then you can be there for him after the fight. We're leaving in about fifteen minutes, and the fight starts at the top of the hour. I'll keep my word, Mads. I'll let you know as soon as it's over."

Sophie and Mason continue to watch me, waiting anxiously.

"Okay," I say, defeated, and we end the call after he reminds me to stay put and out of trouble.

"What'd he say?" Mason asks.

"He won't tell me where the fight is." I blink away tears. "Says it's too dangerous, and I'll distract Liam if he sees me."

"Oh, thank God," Sophie blurts out, holding her hand on her chest over her heart.

I give her a pointed look.

She continues, "Tyler knows best. It *is* risky for us to be there around that crowd. At least this way, if something happens, we're not far from Liam. We'll be able to go see him right away." Sophie searches my face and smiles, and while I know she's right, I had an inkling of hope I could be there.

"I probably should've known he wasn't going to crack that easy." I close my eyes and take in a long, deep breath, then lay my head on my pillow. I'm so fucking scared about the outcome of this fight, and I hate that I have zero control over the situation.

"I honestly didn't think he'd tell you," Mason says. "So what are we going to do while we wait? We could walk around the hotel, go gamble a bit, keep our minds busy."

I look at them. "I'm too on edge to be around people right now. I might stab someone."

"Maybe we should get you a tranquilizer then," Sophie suggests with a laugh.

"That's not a bad idea," I tell her, somewhat serious because I'm anxious as hell and will be until I get a call from Tyler.

Sophie walks over to me and grabs my hand, pulling me up and forcing me to stand. "Come on, let's go get a drink and try to have some fun while we're here."

There's no getting out of it because Sophie isn't going to sit here and let me sulk. The fight could last ten minutes or it could last an hour; I have no idea. I feel as if I'm always counting down to something when it comes to Liam. First, it was my birthday, then the divorce, and now this, his ultimate fate.

As we head to the elevator, my phone vibrates in my pocket. I pull it out and smile when I see it's from Liam.

Liam: I love you, baby. I love you so much. I can't wait to come home and make love to you.

Maddie: I love you and miss you so much. Kick some ass and be careful, Hulk. I want you in one piece, alive.

Liam: I will, Mads. I promise.

We ride down to the bottom floor and go straight to the bar. One shot, that's all I'll need to calm my nerves. I send up a little prayer for Liam to be okay tonight, and that this will truly end all affairs with the O'Learys. Liam's my other half, and I'll never be the same if something bad happens to him. We've been through so much over the years, and now that we're together, I'm not sure I could survive without him.

I don't even want to think about it.

CHAPTER TWENTY

LIAM

THE FLIGHT to Vegas was uneventful. We were delayed for three hours due to mechanical issues, and as I sat there and waited, all I could think about was the look on Maddie's face when I left. By the time we landed, I'd asked myself a hundred times if I'd actually lost my mind because it feels like I have. I'm on edge and ready to get this all over with but have to wait nearly twenty-four hours before I can meet up with JJ. That's when I'll know where the fight is taking place. It's hush-hush so the cops aren't tipped off before the fight starts. The mob doesn't want any trace that an underground fight ring exists. Tyler has told me how much money is on the line, and if I win, JJ will walk away a very rich man. He'll make ten times as much as I lost, and we'll finally be even.

After we Uber to Tyler's house and grab his truck, we check into a hotel on the outskirts of town. Tyler takes a few phone calls outside of the room trying to figure out who my opponent is because it's still a mystery. There are details about the guy, but no name, which has him concerned, given the circumstances of this fight. At this point, I don't think it matters who it is, just that I beat the fuck out of him. I should be fighting to kill, but I'd rather not take someone's life if I can win by just knocking him out. After I get in the ring though, and realize it's my head or his, I'm sure my opinion will change. I'm already wound up so fucking tight that I can barely sit still.

Tyler's speaking with someone in the hallway, but I can't really make out what he's saying. The call ends, and he walks inside, looking me up and down as I stare blankly at the TV. "You need to carb up, hydrate, then get some rest."

"Any info?" I ask curiously.

"Not yet. I'm working on it, though. I just have a feeling that something more is going on." Tyler sits on the edge of the other bed.

"We're talking about the O'Learys. Of course there's more going on. Wouldn't surprise me in the least." I shrug, and Tyler gets up and walks toward the door. "C'mon, I'm starving."

Tyler drives us to a pizzeria and forces me to eat half of an extra-large thin crust. We're mostly silent as we sit together, neither of us knowing what to say. I load up on pizza and bread. Then on the way to the hotel, we stop, and he forces me to eat plenty of fruit and drink tons of water.

"Hydration is key so you don't get fatigued or muscle cramps," he explains as we haul everything up to our room. Although I'm full as fuck, I do what he says, because winning tomorrow is the only option I'm considering. If Tyler told me to balance on my head for an hour, then do forty jumping jacks in order to be a better fighter, I'd do it.

"I have to meet with JJ around five," I remind Tyler before I go into the bathroom to take a shower.

"I know," he tells me, and it seems he has something more to say but doesn't.

The next day, I can't get Maddie off my mind. I miss her so much and am worried about how she's taking this. I imagine she's a mess, and it drives me crazy we're in this situation. I eat, then rest most of the morning. But all I want to do is call and talk to her, but Tyler has told me it's best to wait so I don't get distracted. But not talking to her is distracting. Emotions are high and being in a different place mentally isn't good for the ring. Considering I had a dream about her last night when I told her goodbye forever, I've been knocked off my axis. However, I'm trying to allow it to fuel me to get through this.

Shortly before five o'clock, Tyler and I head over to JJ's penthouse, where he's dressed in a tuxedo and wearing a shit-eating grin. We're checked for weapons before we're allowed to fully enter the room. His cocky attitude is still intact, and I'm two seconds from clocking him right between the eyes when he looks at me. The two guys standing in the corner of the room packing guns stop me, though.

"You ready to make me a rich fucking man?" JJ asks.

Tyler stands to the side with his arms crossed, observing it all, but the disdain he has for JJ is written all over his face.

"Just give me the goddamn address," I demand, my patience waning.

JJ crosses the room and goes to a wet bar, then pours

himself a drink. My heart rate increases, and I can feel my pulse throbbing in my neck. With every passing second, I'm becoming more feral, angrier, and more agitated. After he sips his scotch on the rocks, he grabs a slip of paper and a pen from the counter and scribbles. He walks toward me and folds it in half before handing it over.

"Losing isn't an option if you don't wanna die," he warns, and I snatch it from his grasp and walk toward the door. Tyler follows me.

"I fucking hate that guy," I seethe as we step onto the elevator and go to the bottom floor.

"Me too. I'm sure there's a club we can join. He'll eventually cross the wrong person," Tyler suggests with a shrug. "Guys like that usually get what's coming to them."

"We can only hope." We step out and go to the truck. Once inside, Tyler programs in the address. Tyler starts the engine, and instead of putting it in drive, he turns and looks at me.

"If you're gonna back out, now is the time."

I tilt my head at Tyler. "They'll never let me be free if I do that." I'll always be on the run, and that's no life for Maddie."

"You're right, but just giving you the option," he says, shrugging.

"This is my only option," I tell him assertively.

During the drive, I text Maddie, wanting her to know how much I love her. Losing means losing her forever, and that thought will be what drives me forward tonight. So much rides on me being able to walk away from all of this. After twenty minutes, we turn into an area with rows of metal buildings. It looks like it's a bunch of old storage warehouses in an industrial area. Tyler parks as close as he can but is still a distance away.

"Every single person who walks through the door is

being searched, so no guns get inside. We should probably try to enter another way so no one sees you beforehand." He unbuckles, pulls his cell phone from his pocket, and checks it, then tucks it inside.

"They're just going to let us walk in, no problem?" I ask, confused.

He grins, grabbing the duffel bag he packed with extra towels, tape, and water. "Everyone knows who you are, Liam. They're expecting you."

A chill runs down the length of my spine, and I swallow. "I guess they are."

We get out of the truck and walk the distance. On the other side, there's an entrance that's being guarded by a dude who looks like he could crush bones with his bare hands. I'm a big guy, but compared to him, I'm small. After a rough pat down, we're allowed inside, which is nothing more than a long, low-lit hallway with doors on either side. Tyler leads us forward, and I can't help but randomly turn around and check behind us. It's creepy as fuck being in this building that smells like engine oil and dirt.

Voices travel down the hallway, and soon, the noise from the crowd becomes more audible. We continue forward until the hallway opens to a large arena. The lighting is still shit, and puffs of smoke from cigarettes linger in the air. I see the ring that's protected by crowd-control barricades to ensure no one gets in the ring who isn't supposed to. Folding chairs surround it, while most of the room stands, giving the onlookers the perfect view to watch someone die.

Tyler scans the crowd and lifts his hand in a wave. A minute later, a guy with blond hair and green eyes comes over to us. This must be who Tyler has been getting intel from. He looks Irish like he's related to the O'Learys.

"Lance," Tyler says, giving him a hard pat on the back.

The guy shakes my hand, then looks back and forth between us.

"What have you found out?" Tyler asks.

"Not much. I've heard rumors," he informs.

My face contorts. "About what?"

"Who you'll be fighting," Lance confirms.

"Why?" I shake my head. "Does it matter?"

Lance shrugs. "I guess it doesn't since you're prepared to fight anyway. But apparently, a nickname was used, so those who were betting would know who your opponent was."

"When will we know for sure if it's him?" Tyler asks, and I suspect he has an idea who I'll be up against, but I don't give a fuck. It doesn't matter because I'm already committed.

"Right before the fight starts, we'll know. I gotta go, though. Good luck," Lance says, then walks away.

I can tell Tyler is annoyed by this fact, but I'm not at all shocked.

"Do you want me to tell you what I know?" he asks.

"No," I tell him, not wanting anything to mess with my current mentality. When it comes to the O'Learys, they can't be trusted anyway. They do what benefits them, lying and manipulating people, treating them like puppets. But my patience is steadily waning. I check the time and notice we have a little over thirty minutes before this party gets started. Tyler leads me to an empty room and unzips his duffel bag, then pulls out tape and water, forcing me to drink.

"Bare-knuckle boxing. Gotta love it." I grunt, and the sarcasm isn't lost on him.

"Street fighting at its finest." He takes my hands and securely wraps my knuckles and wrists. While he's doing so, he coaches me. "Don't take your eyes off him. Be swift on your feet. Look for the opportunity of weakness. Every person will let down their guard at some point, and that's when you pounce. You're ready for this."

"I am ready. I have so much fucking pent-up aggression I might knock the guy out with the first punch."

Tyler chuckles. "Good. Do that, and the fight will be over."

The noise from the main room hushes, and I hear someone give a ten-minute warning. I swallow hard, then take my time stretching and warming up, giving Tyler a few good practice hooks.

"Ready?" he finally asks, handing me my mouth guard. I give him a single nod. The blood rushes through my body, and I can almost hear my pulse in my ears. Looking around the room, I see hundreds of pairs of eyes on me as I step into the ring and take off my shirt. I look over my shoulder at Tyler as the crowd bursts into a roar of applause. He gives me a thumbs-up as my confidence continues to climb. I keep my body moving, not wanting my muscles to go cold as the guy over the loudspeaker continues.

"And his opponent…Mickey DeFranco."

I drop my hands to my side as the room goes eerily quiet. "DeFranco?" I mouth to Tyler, who's shaking his head as his jaw twitches. Victoria's lover. The father to her children. What in the actual fuck? What has JJ done? I wonder if this is what Tyler found out and wanted to tell me.

The guy comes into the ring, glaring at me like he wants blood, and I'm sure he does. This isn't just a random fight, no, DeFranco wants me dead just as much as JJ does. This was a setup.

Fuck. Me.

Though the rules are given, I can't seem to focus on anything other than the bastard who's standing a few feet away, glaring at me. Mickey is my height with dark brown hair and eyes as black as night. His muscles look as if they'll break right through his skin, and I have a feeling he's not going to be following any of the rules that are read to us. He doesn't even have his hands taped, but I'm sure he's been fighting on the streets since he was a kid.

Moments later, a woman comes out in a bikini holding a sign that says "Round 1." I shove my mouth guard in and inhale a deep breath. This is it. Everything I've trained for over the past month. I need to stay focused, pay attention, and do everything Tyler and Dice taught me.

A loud bell rings, and Mickey clumsily rushes toward me. Quickly, I step to the side and swing my fist into his jaw with all of my strength. He grunts, as if I'd woken him up, and relentlessly throws punches at me. Although I block him at first, my arms waver, and one connects with my nose, and I stumble before grounding my feet. Blood drips down my chest, which is the wake-up call I need. Anger courses through my veins, and it's as if he flicked on a switch, and I see red at this motherfucker.

I focus on the techniques I've learned, doing my best to block and hit while staying on my feet. Mickey's good, even when he looks high and drunk as fuck, but that only means he won't feel any pain and will keep going. He gets a good punch in my ribs, but I throw a better one to his face, making him step back, blinking furiously. We're both sharp and strong, defending and tossing out hits until the bell rings after each round.

His vendetta won't give him the strength to end me. Not tonight.

Each time I feel pain, I become more animalistic and violent. There's no playing nice. Mickey DeFranco and JJ want me dead, but I'm walking out of here alive. My face is sore and bloody as hell, but I push through the pain and focus on taking him down indefinitely. The crowd is loud, cheering and shouting with every blow we make. It's annoying, but I don't let it distract me. I manage to get him on the ground, and as my knee goes into his stomach, I picture Maddie in my mind, which helps me put more power behind each strike. Somehow, he gets me off him long enough to gain his composure.

Each round is three minutes, but they feel like an eternity. My body is buzzing as we start the fourth round—a bonus since no winner has been determined yet—but I'm ready for this to be over. It's more than obvious that Mickey's getting tired as I stare him down. His mouth and nose are busted, and I can see his jaw's swelling as well. He spits out blood, then growls before rushing me.

I know if I can connect with his jaw one last time, I'll knock him out and this'll all be over. With all the strength in my legs, I swing with every inch of power I have, successfully connecting with his face. Mickey stumbles, then falls to the ground. The room erupts in cheers as I look toward them, lifting my fists in the air. The ref makes the call, announcing that I'm the winner. I'm covered in blood, my body is sore as fuck, but all that matters is that I'm not the one on the ground. Most guys in these underground fights would keep going, making sure the guy is as close to death as possible, but I'm not looking to do that. I hear Tyler's voice calling my name, and when I look at him, he's pointing at something behind me. The room is too loud, and I can't make out what he's saying. The next moment, I feel white-hot pain rip through my body.

It happens so fast. I glance down and see Mickey twisting a knife into my thigh, and I lose my balance, the paralyzing ache bringing me to my knees. Tyler rushes toward me, keeping me upright and from face planting the ground. He's talking, but I can't make out what he's saying. I hear gunshots ring through the room, and everyone scatters. I look down at my leg and the blood pooling around me. It's on my hands. It's on my shorts. Tyler takes off his shirt and rips it in half before wrapping it tightly above my wound. He struggles to get me up and out of the ring.

"That won't stop the bleeding for long. You need to go to the hospital," he says as he nearly drags me down the long hallway. He holds onto me, keeping my arm wrapped around his neck as his arm tightly holds onto my waist. Every few seconds, I lose consciousness, too light-headed to focus as the pain blinds me.

"Tyler," I say, but I don't know if any words come out. I can't see. I can only hear loud noises, people screaming, and then nothing.

CHAPTER TWENTY-ONE

MADDIE

WE SIT around playing penny slots until my eyes nearly blur over. I can't stop checking the clock. It's been over an hour since the fight started, and I'm beginning to panic, though I keep it to myself so I don't freak Mason and Sophie out. Shouldn't they have been done fighting by now? I'm two seconds from dialing Tyler's number when he calls me.

"Maddie," he says my name, but it sounds strained. There are loud noises and people screaming in the background, and I feel as if I'm suffocating. What the hell is happening?

"I'm taking him to Vegas General Hospital," he tells me. "Meet me there."

"Is everything okay?" I ask frantically. Tyler says nothing, and it speaks louder than his words ever could. "Tyler?" I choke out.

"There was an incident, but I'm taking Liam to the hospital now." It sounds as if he's out of breath when I hear a door slam shut.

"What?" My voice comes out as a whisper. "What kind of an incident?"

"Meet me there. I gotta go," he forces out, then hangs up.

I stand, but Mason and Sophie are already moving in on me, holding me from falling down because it feels as if I can't carry my own weight. "Vegas General Hospital. That's where they're heading."

"I'll get an Uber," Sophie says, pulling out her phone.

"Everything okay?" Mason asks, tightly holding me.

"Maddie?" I hear Sophie's voice and know she's standing close by me, but I'm too in shock to speak. Everything seems to be moving in slow motion, but the time is ticking so fast. *There was an incident.* Tyler's words play on repeat in my mind.

"Something happened at the fight. Tyler sounded worried." My thoughts are as stilted as my words.

They guide me out of the hotel, and once our driver arrives, we get in the car. Vegas passes by in a blur as we get onto the highway. The tears begin to fall, and I try to catch my breath, but I don't feel as if I can breathe. Sophie grabs my hand and speaks soft, encouraging words.

"He could just have a concussion or something."

"Liam's had plenty of concussions playing football, Mads. I'm sure Tyler is taking precautions," Mason adds.

I shake my head, disagreeing. "I've never heard Tyler sound the way he did. *Ever.* And we've been through some shit together."

It doesn't take long before we're turning into the parking lot of the hospital. Before we come to a complete stop, I'm unbuckling and nearly jumping out. I run as fast as I can to the emergency room entrance as Sophie and Mason rush behind me. As soon as I get through the sliding glass doors, I see a distraught Tyler standing in the waiting area.

"Where is he?" I ask, searching around. My eyes widen as I notice Tyler's shirtless with blood on his chest and hands. I'm becoming more hysterical with every passing second.

"They're prepping him for surgery to stop his bleeding," Tyler says, looking around me at Sophie and Mason. I turn to see how pale their faces are.

"Surgery?" I gasp. I know damn well you don't need surgery for a concussion.

"What happened?" Sophie asks, eyeing the blood too.

Sick people are all around coughing and sneezing, so Tyler takes us over to a secluded area. We sit facing him as he leans in, keeping his voice low.

"Liam was fighting really well, blocking hits and making punches, then in the last round, he took Mickey down. As soon as it happened, Liam was declared the winner, and everyone cheered. Then I saw Mickey pull out a knife, and everything went into complete chaos." Tyler pauses as if he's replaying every action in his head like a movie. "JJ orchestrated this fight between Liam and Mickey DeFranco, Victoria's *real* baby daddy, knowing one of them wouldn't walk away unscathed. Once we found out who Liam's opponent was, it was too late to do anything about it or train him differently. I tried to get intel during the past couple of weeks, but no one could tell me anything. By the time it was revealed, too much money was already on the line, and once you step into the ring, there's no stepping out when so many people are watching. Not unless you win."

I cover my mouth with my hands. This doesn't seem real. It can't be. Even I know weapons weren't allowed there. It jeopardizes not only the fight but also the people who bid.

"DeFranco had it out for Liam because of how everything went down with Victoria, and he wanted blood. And he most definitely didn't want to lose. He pulled a rusted knife from his waistband and stabbed Liam in the thigh, twisting it until I rushed in and grabbed Liam. I wrapped my shirt around his thigh to make a tourniquet to stop the bleeding. All of a sudden, there were gunshots, then mass hysteria broke out, but all I was worried about was getting Liam out of there I told him to hold pressure on his leg when we got in the truck, but he was in and out of consciousness the entire drive over here."

I can't believe what I'm hearing. It sounds made up. Glancing over at Mason, I notice his eyes are wide, and his jaw is clenched. Considering Liam has been his best friend for years, I can't imagine what he's thinking. They're like brothers.

"As soon as we pulled in, they rushed him inside and had a team of doctors working on him," Tyler continues. "They were checking his vitals and prepping him for surgery. That's all I know as of right now."

"Oh my God," I say between sobs. "How could this happen? I—" I bend over and cover my face, releasing the tears I can't keep inside. Everything Tyler just told us sounds like a complete nightmare.

"Mads, he's strong, and he's gonna get through this," Tyler states confidently. "This is the best hospital in the city, and I got him here right away. His risk for infection will be low, and there's no reason he shouldn't have a full recovery."

I'm sure that's supposed to make me feel better, but it doesn't. I'm a nervous wreck and can't sit any longer, so I stand, but Tyler quickly grabs my hand before I can walk away. He pulls me into the side of his chest and wraps his arm tightly around me. My emotions are going haywire, and I feel like I'm going to have a panic attack at any second. It's obvious by the number of tears streaming down my face that I'm not okay. The smell of the hospital is making me sick, and I think I might throw up if I don't get some fresh air.

"You alright?" Sophie asks as I pull away from Tyler.

"I feel sick," I admit. "I need some fresh air."

Sophie walks outside with me, and I sit on an empty bench close to the door as I suck in ragged breaths.

She places her hand on my shoulder and rubs down my back, trying to comfort me, but it's no use. "I'm sure he's going to be fine. Liam's one of the strongest people we know. He's not going to give up without a fight."

Fighting is what got him here.

I nod, tucking my bottom lip into my mouth. "But what if he's not?"

I'm not sure what kind of reaction I expect, but she doesn't give me one. Instead, Sophie looks out at the cars passing in front of the hospital as the cool breeze brushes against our skin.

"You know, there was a point in my life when I didn't think I'd make it." She keeps her focus on the busy street. All I can do is watch her.

"But I did, and I'm alive, and I think I went through all that because of moments like this, so I can be here for you during one of your darkest times. Whatever happens, I'll always be here for you, no matter what."

I wrap my arms around her, and she pulls me into a tight embrace. That's when I completely lose it, and the dam breaks.

"Liam's a tough guy. He risked his life to save me, and I know how much he truly loves you, Maddie. If there's any motivation for him to live, it's gonna be for you."

There are no words that come to mind as I cry on her shoulder. I think about how much Sophie has been through, and then my mind goes to Liam. If anything, she's proof I can survive this. The same strength that runs through her veins is in mine too.

"Thank you," I tell her, my voice cracking with every

word. Before I can say anything else, Mason steps outside, letting us know that Liam's going into surgery.

Nearly three hours pass as we wait inside, and it feels like an eternity. Mason gets me a bottle of water, but every sip I take, it seems like it's going to come right back up. I've cried off and on, my thoughts growing darker with every second that ticks by. Sophie stays close to me, not leaving my side. I'm so happy they came with me. I'd be completely losing it if she wasn't here.

Eventually, a nurse comes and tells us Liam is out of surgery and did really well.

"One person can be with him in recovery," the nurse explains.

"Maddie, you should probably go in," Tyler tells me. "He'll prefer to wake up to your face over mine." He flashes me a playful wink.

My heart races at getting to see Liam, but I don't know what I'm walking into or what I should expect. I stand and the nurse scans me in, and I follow behind. Double doors lead us down a hallway, and all I can hear are machines beeping from the different rooms we pass. It all feels like a blur when she opens the door and steps aside, letting me enter, and that's when I see Liam for the first time.

I gasp when I see his swollen face and broken body. I go toward him, not able to see how bad his leg is because he's tucked under a stark white sheet. I grab his hand and hold it, not wanting to cry any longer, but not able to help it either. He's alive, and that's all that matters right now.

"Liam," I say softly.

"Maddie?" he croaks, squinting his eyes.

"I'm here, baby. I'm here," I whisper, leaning over and gently touching his face.

"I think I'm dreaming…" he murmurs, opening his eyes a

little wider.

I shake my head. "No. I'm really here."

He looks at me as if I'm a figment of his imagination before he drifts off to sleep. I pull the uncomfortable looking chair up beside the bed so I can stay close to him. Scratches and bruises cover his arms, both of his eyes are swollen, and his lips are busted. He looks like he's been to hell and back. Tyler said Liam won and then was stabbed, which makes me wonder what condition Mickey is in at this moment. I can only hope he's suffering in pain and gets what's coming to him for doing this to Liam.

Eventually, a nurse comes in and lets me know they're about to transfer him to a room on the fifth floor. Once he's situated, we'll be able to continue our visit. It takes all the strength I have to leave his side, and I promise Liam I'll see him in a minute, even if he can't hear me.

"His vitals are doing great so far. We'll observe him for a couple of days to make sure his stats stay within the normal range, and that there are no signs of infection," the nurse tells me as she walks me out, and I'm actually comforted by her words.

"Thank you," I tell her. When I walk into the waiting room, everyone is eager for an update, though I don't feel as if I have much to report.

"He's tired, but there were no issues during surgery. They're moving him to a room soon, and then we should be able to go up and see him."

"That's great news," Tyler says, and I can almost see relief pour over Mason and Sophie. It takes about an hour before the nurse lets us know Liam was transferred to a room. We thank her and immediately go to the elevator. Sophie grabs my hand as we walk down the long hallway.

"He's banged up," I tell her before we walk in, giving her

a warning about the way he looks.

She nods, and we all enter. My heart races when I see he's actually awake, sitting up, and sipping through a straw.

His eyes go wide when he sees us all, and I rush toward him.

"Maddie, baby," he says through a painful smile. As I touch his shoulder, he winces. All I want to do is plant kisses over his broken face, but I know it's not a good idea. Instead, happiness floods me, and the waterworks turn on. I'm a blubbering mess, but I'm so fucking thankful. Confusion is written all over his expression as he makes eye contact with Sophie and Mason, but he pulls me close to him, not letting me go.

"I thought I imagined you were here," he says, gripping my hand as I sit on the edge of his bed. I'm careful not to move too much as I stare at him.

"I had to be here for you, baby. I was so scared of losing you. It was just…" I choke up. "Too much for me to be so far away." I swallow down my emotions and wipe more tears away. Liam places his hand on my thigh and squeezes.

"I promised you, Mads. I'll never break my promises to you," he tells me. "I love you too damn much."

I hold back the urge to wrap my arms around him and suck in a deep breath. "I love you. God, I love you."

Tyler speaks up, interrupting the moment. "Do you remember what happened?"

Liam stares at Tyler for a long while before nodding. "I just remember that asshole stabbed me after I won and then hearing gunshots. That's it. Everything after that is a blur."

"I'm still trying to figure out what happened, honestly. It was mass chaos and panic. I was worried," Tyler admits.

Liam chuckles at his admission. "If I would've died, I'd just haunt you the rest of your life."

"Not funny," Tyler snaps just as his phone rings. He looks down at it, then steps out of the room as Sophie and Mason walk to the other side of Liam's bed.

"I'm so happy you're okay," Sophie tells him as Mason stands with his arm around her.

"Yeah, we were worried fucking sick," he says. "If it weren't for Maddie, we wouldn't even be here right now."

Liam glances at me, and I shrug. "Yes, why are you guys here?" he asks. "Not that I'm not happy you are *now*, but I told you to stay away from this place because it wasn't safe for you."

"And you thought she'd listen?" Mason snorts.

"I found your letter," I admit. "Which I'm really mad at you for writing." I wipe a tear off my cheek, smiling at him because I'm not really upset about it, but still, it was hard to read.

"Oh, you found that, did you?" He smirks, squeezing my hand.

"What letter?" Sophie asks.

"Basically, an 'in case I die' letter," I deadpan.

"Would you rather I didn't, and then I really did die?" he counters.

"I wasn't going to allow that on my watch," Tyler interjects, entering the room. "Though I couldn't have predicted the shitstorm that happened tonight. Thank God he didn't stab you somewhere else or hit a main artery." His words send a shiver down my spine at the *what-ifs*. Tyler's right, Mickey could've killed him.

"I'm glad you did write it," I tell Liam. "I love you with all my heart. And if something worse had happened, I would've never forgiven myself for not being here with you."

"I know," he says softly. "And I love you too."

I lean over and gently kiss his cut lips.

"See, this is why I worry about you so much," he tells me. "You're stubborn. I should've known you'd find your way here, especially since I told you to stay home."

Sophie giggles, and Mason smiles.

"I'm not denying that one bit. I know I am," I admit with a smirk. "Have to give you a run for your money, though. Keep you on your toes, Hulk."

Liam shakes his head as Tyler rounds his bed, coming closer. If I didn't know any better, I'd say he saw a ghost by how pale he looks.

"What is it?" Liam asks, searching his face.

"JJ's dead," he says.

With wide eyes, Liam stares at Tyler. "What? Is that why I heard gunshots?"

Tyler nods. "Yep. It was Victoria," he says. "She found out what JJ had orchestrated between you and her baby daddy. She was pissed and wanted him to—"

Tyler doesn't even finish, but he doesn't have to for us to know what he was going to say. Victoria wanted him to *pay*. We're all in shock, and I have no words. Liam shakes his head and closes his eyes. "I didn't want any of this to happen."

"It's not your fault," I offer. "None of this is your fault."

"I can't help but feel somewhat responsible. Victoria killed her own brother. How could she do something like that?" he asks, confused like the rest of us.

Tyler sucks in a deep breath and exhales. "Love sometimes makes you do stupid things. Victoria wasn't exactly stable; look what she put you through. But I guess that means it's over now, Liam. You're finally free."

Liam frowns, shrugging. "But at what cost?" He looks down at his bandaged leg and bruised knuckles. "At what cost?"

293

CHAPTER TWENTY-TWO

LIAM

IT'S BEEN two weeks since the fight, and I'm recovering as expected. I was released from the hospital with a pair of crutches but stopped using them yesterday with hopes to find my normal again. Plus, I hated using the damn things.

There have been good and bad days since the fight, and I'm still moving slow, but at least the pain is becoming more bearable. One doctor told me that if I'd been stabbed one inch to the right, I would've died before I made it to the emergency room. It's something that still haunts me. I think about all that's happened over the past year, and my head is still spinning at the shit I went through. It all started with a poker game and ended with a murder.

I'm still in shock that JJ is dead. I hated the guy, but I didn't want him killed. Though I'm relieved that I can finally move on and not worry about any of the O'Learys.

I never thought Victoria was capable of killing her brother, but I should've known better. She made her own rules in life, and JJ pushed her to the limit by orchestrating one of the dirtiest fights in mob history, hoping I'd kill Mickey DeFranco for him or that he'd end up injured trying to kill me. The rumor is he found out his sister's babies were DeFranco bastards and lost his mind trying to get his ultimate revenge. He wanted DeFranco dead without causing a bigger war between the families so he planned the fight. I'd been blackmailed into doing his dirty work for everyone to witness and walked right into his trap. If I died, no one would've cared because I was just an O'Leary pawn. If I'd won, JJ's problems were solved, and his enemy was taken care of. Ultimately, he took a risk, but there's no way he could've envisioned Victoria ending it or rather *him*. She was always a vindictive bitch, though. Even I knew not to cross her at times.

Apparently, she was so enraged that JJ had set up a fight with Mickey that she loaded a gun, drove to the warehouse, and found him. Tyler told me the last thing she said to her brother before killing him was, "You gave me no choice." After the shots were fired, mass hysteria broke out, and everyone scattered. Victoria won't go down for murder. Considering she's Daddy's little mafia princess, I'm sure she made up some erroneous lie and completely buried the truth with her brother. Manipulation is her middle name.

As I roll out of bed, I can't deny how happy I am to finally be free from it all. I wasn't sure if it'd really happen, even if I won the fight. There are days when slivers of doubt randomly creep in, and I still can't go out in public without looking over my shoulder, but I think it's going to take time. Dealing with the O'Learys has made me more aware of my surroundings, and I learned a valuable lesson. I won't be trusting anyone I don't already know anytime soon.

After Maddie left for class this morning, I crawled back under the covers. I've been tired lately, and the doctors have told me to rest so I can fully recover. The fatigue comes and goes, but I'm eager to start working again and doing everyday tasks. The wound was deep, but it's healing nicely.

Rubbing my hands over my face, I grab my phone from the side table and go to the kitchen where there's still a half a pot of coffee from this morning and pour a cup. It's cold, so I place it in the microwave and warm it up while I check my texts. A smile touches my lips when I see messages from Maddie.

Maddie: My last dance class was canceled today, so I'll be home early!

I check the time and see she sent the message an hour ago. Before I can even return her text, the front door opens and closes. I walk to the doorway and see her drop her backpack on the floor, then walk toward me with a smile. Moments later, her arms are wrapped around my neck, and her mouth is gliding across mine.

"I need you," she admits as I grab a handful of her ass. "I'm dying. It's been too long."

I smile against her eager lips and groan. "Weeks. *Too* damn long."

Before the fight, Tyler implemented a no-sex rule, and I begrudgingly followed it. Afterward, I was in the hospital for a few days, where Maddie refused to leave my side before being released. The last couple of weeks have seemed like a blur while being in recovery mode, but the pain meds had a lot to do with that. Maddie has been sweet while taking care of me and extremely patient with my mood swings, but right now, she's looking at me with lust in her eyes. There's no way I can make her wait any longer.

Taking her hand, I guide her down the hallway into the bedroom. No words are exchanged, just pure emotion swirls between us. Our bodies say everything our mouths don't as I move my fingers to the hem of her sweater and peel it off. Gently, I lay her across the bed, where she smiles and giggles as I unbutton and unzip her jeans. Maddie wiggles out of them until she's in nothing more than her bra and panties. I take a minute to study every inch of her beauty, taking her all in, memorizing each and every curve. I've missed her so goddamn much, my restraint from holding in was dangling by a thread.

"You're so damn beautiful," I whisper, carefully removing her panties as she slips off her bra. Crawling onto the bed, I lay beside her, capturing one nipple ring in my mouth as I cup the other. She writhes beneath me, and our lips crash together. I feather kisses down her body until my face is tucked between her legs. Letting out a cute squeal, Maddie completely gives herself to me with her eyes closed, enjoying every second as I widen her thighs and dive in. I devour her pussy, taking my time and teasing her clit just enough to push her to the edge without spilling over.

Her breaths become more desperate and ragged, and when her back arches, I know she's close.

"Come on my tongue, baby. I wanna taste you." I slip my hands under her ass as she grinds against my face, the stubble from my beard scratching against her thighs. Soon, I'm tasting her sweetness as she unravels, moaning my name between pants. "Goddamn, woman. I've missed that."

"Holy shit," she pants out, her body limp as she looks at me with hooded eyes. "That was...intense."

I chuckle as I stand and remove my clothes. I've never needed Maddie more than I do right now.

"I feel like a reborn virgin," Maddie chuckles as I hover above her, teasing her entrance with my cock. Adjusting herself, she opens wide, giving me permission as I guide myself inside her. My cock is slick with her arousal. Our eyes remain locked as we move in rhythm together, my emotions bubbling over. We've been through so much together, and I love her so fucking much that nothing I do or say will ever feel like enough to properly explain it.

Digging her heels into my ass, Maddie encourages me to increase my pace as we both chase our releases. I love how frantic she gets, giving me access to suck on her neck. She's wild and untamed, the same Maddie I've fallen for long ago, and being intimate with her always feels like the first time.

"Liam," she hisses, scratching her nails down my shoulder blades before digging them into my arms. Pleasure mixes with pain as I slide my lips across hers, plunging my tongue inside as we make love.

"You're my everything, Maddie," I tell her, brushing her hair from her face.

"And you're mine." Her body tenses, and she bites down on her lower lip before adding, "Oh God. Keep. Going."

Her eyes roll back, and she comes so hard, my dick is nearly broken in half as she squeezes tight. I pound deeper and harder until I see stars, and my balls tighten.

"Fuck," I groan, rolling off her as I'm nearly catapulted to outer space. It's never felt like that before.

"Wow," she says as we both stare up at the ceiling, trying to catch our breaths. After Maddie lets out a satisfied sigh, we clean up, then crawl under the sheets and snuggle.

It's been a week since Maddie and I broke our no-sex rule, and we haven't been able to keep our hands off each other. Most days, we fuck more than we eat, but I have no complaints. After waiting so long, it feels like we're a couple of teenagers unable to get enough. She's just as insatiable as I am, which means we use every spare minute to get naked together.

The morning sunlight peeks through the curtains, and I roll over and wrap my arm around Maddie's body. She grinds her ass against me in response. "Morning, baby," I whisper in her ear, then flatten my tongue against her neck.

"I wanna skip school today," she whines, rolling over until our fronts are flesh together. "And stay in bed with you and sleep."

I nuzzle against her neck. "You know damn well we wouldn't be doing much sleeping." I chuckle, then add, "and it's my first day back to work."

"Boo, you whore!" She groans, causing me to laugh at her *Mean Girls* reference. Another movie she's made me watch.

Maddie pulls the blanket over her head just as her alarm buzzes. It's one of the most annoying sounds ever. She pops up, reaches over me, and turns it off, but before she can leave, I pull her to me and kiss her mouth. Morning breath and all. But I wouldn't have her any other way. I love that we can't get enough of each other. She smiles against my lips, and in a snap, she has my boxers down and like a cowgirl, rides me hard and fast. It doesn't take long before we're both breathing hard and finding our release, trying to stay as quiet as possible, though we're not very good at it. Something our roommates have become accustomed to now.

Quickies with Maddie are better than a breakfast buffet. Knowing she wants me as much as I want her has me wishing I could stay home from work today. I'm half-tempted to roll in the sheets with her all morning, but her second alarm goes off, bringing us back to reality.

She lets out a huff before standing and grabbing her phone for the second time. "I guess I'll go to class."

I stand and pull her into my arms, grinning at her pouty face. "Only four more months until graduation and summer," I remind her.

"It can't get here fast enough. Look how pale I am!" Maddie shows off her arms, and I grab her wrist and kiss it.

"You're starting to look like a vampire," I tease. "Do you feel like sucking…"

She playfully swats at me. "You're terrible."

"You created a monster," I counter.

"You were *already* a monster," she says with a laugh, walking to the closet and pulling out an oversized hoodie and jeans. I get dressed as well, actually excited to be on a job, searching for a fugitive and feeling normal again. It's been too long, and while I'm rusty, I'm sure once I'm in the swing of things again, working will be like second nature. Honestly, I've missed my life. I've missed how easygoing things were before I met the O'Learys and got caught up in a horrible situation. I'd much rather have the adrenaline rush from stakeouts than playing poker. That part of me is dead for good.

Maddie and I walk hand in hand into the kitchen where there's a box of a dozen donuts sitting on the counter with a note from Mason.

Sophie made me get you two lovebirds donuts. Apparently, I owe you one for breaking the shower. Don't ask. The plumber is coming later today.

Maddie snorts and shoves a donut in her face while she shakes her head. "Probably having rough sex again. Thankfully, I don't need to shower this morning. Geez," she says around a mouthful, snagging another one.

"You're probably right, but as long as donuts are involved, I kinda don't care." I shrug, snatching one and eating it in two large bites.

Maddie pulls a to-go cup from the cabinet and boils some water for tea. "You know what next week is, don't you?"

"Nope," I say, joking with her, but she takes me seriously. Her face falls as she grabs the milk from the fridge. "Seriously?"

"No idea." I take another donut, knowing I could probably finish the rest of them on my own.

"Liam!" Maddie sticks out her bottom lip, and I go to her, laughing at her pathetic lip tremble.

I plant quick kisses on her cheek until I find her mouth. "Babe, of course, I know what it is. Your birthday. Number twenty-two."

"You better have something awesome planned." She taps her pointer finger into my chest with a smirk.

"I thought I'd just dick you down all night," I joke.

Maddie rolls her eyes, but I don't miss the smirk painted on her face. "You were gonna do that anyway." She drops a tea bag in her cup to seep before glancing over her shoulder and biting her lip. That fucking taunts me, and if we both didn't have to leave in a few minutes, I'd be bending her over the kitchen island.

"Don't worry, it'll blow your panties right off. Guaranteed."

"Guess that means I better be wearing some?" She waggles her brows. This time, I really am two seconds from throwing her over my shoulder caveman-style and returning to her bed. She has that look in her eye, the one that says she wants me right now.

I glance at the clock on the stove and groan, knowing I can't. "Damn. There's never enough time in the day to spend with you."

Maddie steps toward me, closing the space between us, then wraps her arms around my neck, pulling my lips to hers. "We have forever, Liam."

Lifting her chin, I brush my lips against hers again and growl. "Forever isn't enough," I admit, knowing I'm greedy when it comes to her. "I want an *eternity*."

She flashes me a bright smile, and reluctantly, we break apart and finish getting ready, then go our separate ways.

For the next eight hours, I stake outside of an empty warehouse on the other side of town waiting for a guy to deliver stolen vehicles. He's been arrested and bailed out a handful of times but decided last month to skip his court date. All day, I wait and never run into the guy or really anyone. By the time I make it home, I'm frustrated, but this sometimes happens when the people I'm tracking know they have a warrant out for their arrest. As soon as I grab a beer and sit on the couch, Maddie comes bolting through the door. She's a golden ray of sunshine, and I immediately perk up when I see her.

With a plop, she kicks off her shoes, tuckers her legs

under her body and leans against me. "Missed you. How was work?"

"Sucked." I shrug. "Tomorrow will be better, though. How was school?"

"I should've stayed home and fucked you all day," she tells me, throwing her head back with a laugh. "Seriously, though. Nothing monumental about it. We've started preparing for our senior recital, and I'm not as in it as I thought I would be. Maybe after a few weeks when I actually have the choreography memorized."

Just as I'm about to respond, my phone vibrates in my pocket. It's an unknown number, but I answer it anyway.

"Liam." Tyler's distraught.

"Hey man, what's up?" The line is silent for a few seconds.

I'm about to ask why he's calling me from a different number when Tyler lets out a ragged breath. "I got arrested. I'm in jail and completely fucked."

My body goes into full alert, and Maddie notices my demeanor change. She stares at me, searching my face.

I put the call on speaker. "What did they arrest you on?"

Maddie's eyes widen in shock. "What happened?"

"Victoria set me up. Loaded the bed of my truck with pounds of drugs, guns with the serial numbers scratched off, and bricks of money. It looks like I was hauling this shit across the US. They booked me for possession with intent to distribute and sell."

"Fuck," I bark out loudly, running my fingers through my hair. "I thought this was over. She fucking promised she would stop and leave the people I love alone. She just unleashed the door to hell." I'm seething, already planning what I'm going to say to her when I track her down and choke her. I still have all those photos of her and Mickey, and even if she's not afraid of what her dad will do, I imagine the DeFranco family won't be as forgiving, especially after JJ's stunt.

"Did she know Tyler was your friend?" Maddie asks me. "Or just that he was the mole in getting me out?"

"She saw me at the fight with you, so she knows," Tyler says. "Wouldn't have taken her long to put everything together, especially with the people in her circle. Eric probably told her what I did too. She had more than one reason to get back at me," he explains.

"Goddammit," I hiss, balling my hands into fists. My heart races, and I'm seconds away from planning a full-on rage-revenge.

Tyler continues, "I shouldn't be as shocked as I am, but she went to the extreme, making sure I'll be fighting like hell to prove I didn't do it."

"When do you see the judge? I can get you bailed out once it's set. Are you in Vegas?" My legs shake anxiously, ready to go wherever he is, even if that means returning to a city I swore I'd never visit again.

"No, I'm in Sacramento. I was gonna surprise you and Maddie and was only fifteen minutes from your house."

"I'll figure out a way to get you bailed out at least until the court date," I tell him confidently. There's no way I'm letting him stay there.

Tyler blows out a frustrated breath. "It's gonna be high." His voice is nearly a whisper.

"I don't care," I tell him. "It's your first offense. You're a vet. You don't have a record. I'll call my lawyer friend, Serena, and see what she can do."

"Well, unless she's a miracle worker, I'm not holding my breath. The officer who put me in cuffs was a total dick. Before putting me in the back of his unmarked car, he whispered in my ear and said I should've never betrayed Victoria. Then he winked and pushed my ass inside."

"Who the fuck was the officer?" I ask, my adrenaline spiraling out of control.

"I'm pretty sure his tag said Officer Ferguson. Now I'm convinced she has everyone on her goddamn payroll."

I see red, barely able to contain my anger. "Blake. That motherfucking bastard." Then I glance over at Maddie. "Told you he was bad news."

Maddie tenses and shakes her head, frowning.

"Serena will know what to do. I'll have her come down and be your counsel. At least that way, you have someone on your side," I tell him, feeling helpless but wanting to save him the same way he saved Maddie and me.

"Even if I get out on bail or manage to somehow prove my innocence, she'll come after me again, Liam. I wouldn't doubt it if she planted shit at my house too. She's like a black widow and will seek her revenge one way or another. I have to play by her rules, and this is what she wants—to humiliate me and send my ass to prison. I'm convinced it's the only way out of this. It's the only way she'll leave everyone alone."

"I'm not letting you rot in there without a fight," I tell him.

"I appreciate that, man, but I'm afraid my destiny has been set." He sounds so damn defeated, and my guilt starts to weigh heavily on me.

"I'm sorry, Tyler. I'm so damn sorry." All I can do is apologize as the reality of it all sinks in.

"Don't apologize. I planned it, remember? I chose to go undercover, knowing the risks. It was worth it, Liam. I have no regrets and would do it again in a heartbeat."

"I love you, man," I tell him. "I'll get Serena down there as soon as I can, okay?"

"Thanks, I appreciate it." Without allowing me to say another word, Tyler ends the call, and I'm left standing there in shock. I turn to look at Maddie whose eyes are glassy with tears.

"I can't believe this," she says, wiping her cheeks.

"I don't care that she's about to pop out two babies, I'm tempted to fly my ass out there and give her a reminder of what I'm capable of," I mutter.

"What would that solve?" she counters, crossing her arms. "That'd give her another reason to come after us again."

"Maybe." I shrug. "Maybe not." Pulling out my phone, I scroll to Serena's number. "I'm gonna call Serena and beg her to help. Pay her triple if I have to."

Maddie gives me a sad smile. "I hope he'll be okay." She worries her bottom lip, and I wrap her in my arms.

"He's one of the strongest people I know. If anyone can make it through this, Tyler can."

CHAPTER TWENTY-THREE

MADDIE

SEVEN MONTHS LATER

"RIGHT CORNER POCKET," Liam announces, bending over and effortlessly sweeping the ball into the hole.

"Goddammit," Mason curses, slamming down his pool stick. Liam's killing him and only has the final eight ball left.

"Why you even try, bro?" Liam gloats, lifting his arms to show off his biceps. The guys have been playing pool for the past two hours, and Liam has killed Mason, Hunter, and Kilan each time. He's undefeated at this point.

"I'm grabbing a beer and finding my wife." Mason shakes his head and walks out of the game room.

"Do I get to play you next?" I ask sweetly from the other side, bending over just enough to show off my chest. My eggplant-colored dress leaves nothing to the imagination, which is exactly why I wore it for our last house party. Mason and Sophie moved out a few months ago, so it's been just the two of us, but we recently decided we needed a fresh start and found our own apartment.

"Not a chance in hell," Liam grumbles, stalking toward me. "You'll cheat."

"What?" I narrow my eyes as he snakes his arms around my waist. "How can anyone cheat at pool?" I ask innocently.

"You know exactly how." He leans down and tips my chin up toward him. "I keep having to give every guy in here dirty looks to stop them from looking at my girlfriend. I'm about to sucker punch Kilan in the face if he can't keep his eyes to himself."

I snort. "Kilan is harmless. Plus, you've known him for years, so I know you're just being extra macho." Kilan used to live across the street, but after he moved, they kept in touch. Since it's the final house party before we officially move out, it was only right to invite him for one last hurrah.

"Harmless or not, one more *glance* at your chest, and he's getting a fist to his nuts."

Wrapping my arms around his waist, I pull us closer. "Hmm...I like your possessive side. It *really* turns me on."

"Oh yeah?" He arches a brow. "How turned on are we talking here?"

"Like, you better get us to a room stat before I take you on this pool table. After all this time, why haven't we christened this damn thing?" I chuckle.

"Trust me, not comfortable," Hunter chimes as he walks in.

"Ew..." I mimic a gagging noise.

"Dude. You didn't even live here. What the fuck?" Liam scowls.

Hunter shrugs, then takes a swig of his beer. "I was a dumb college kid."

Smirking, I cross my arms. "Does Lennon know?"

"No..." He points at me with the bottle. "And don't you

tell my hormonal, pregnant wife either. I don't need to give her any more ammunition to knee me in her sleep."

"Huh," Liam says sarcastically. "Dick kicking in their sleep must be a Corrigan trait."

Laughing at both of their expressions, I shrug. "Well, Lennon's probably getting even after all the times you were an asshole. Maybe I *should* tell her…"

I still can't believe they're having another baby. After Aaron was born, they said they weren't necessarily careful but were also doubtful they could due to Hunter's medical concerns. Turns out, he's very able. Lennon's three months along now and moodier than she was with the last two pregnancies. Probably because she has two kids to take care of this time around.

"Keep your loud mouth shut, Maddie," he warns.

"Okay, on one condition…" I offer, turning to Liam quickly before looking at Hunter. "You keep guard while we give the room a proper goodbye."

Hunter chokes on his beer and shakes his head. "You two are worse than Mason and Sophie." Then he turns on his heels and shuts the door behind him.

"You're a bad, bad girl, Madelyn Corrigan," Liam taunts as I slowly unzip my dress in front of him.

"And you have about ten minutes to do very bad, bad things to me. So start strippin'," I order.

He waggles his brows and kicks off his shoes. "Yes, ma'am."

I giggle at our eagerness, and as soon as we're both naked, Liam wraps his hand around my neck and draws me into him, crashing our lips together frantically.

"God, Mads. Do you have any idea how much I love you? How crazy you make me?"

I wrap my fingers around his cock and stroke him. "If it's

half as much as I love you, then I'm guessing a lot," I say against his lips.

"Half? Do you not understand my feelings for you? Most of the time I hold back so I don't scare the shit out of you."

Tilting my head, I blink and look him in the eyes. "Don't. I want every single part of you. You were my first and only, so I want to experience everything with you."

"Maddie, baby. The feelings I have for you...they're so goddamn intense. I want you every second of every single day. And I don't mean just sexually. It's enough to just be near you. Close enough to touch you. Hold you in my arms, where you belong."

"Considering how our relationship started and everything we've been through, I wouldn't want us any other way. Desperate, intense, frantic. I like knowing you want me as much as I want you," I tell him honestly.

Liam startles me when he grabs my arms and bends me over the pool table, positioning himself between my thighs. I plant my palms down and arch my back, widening my legs for him. "I don't just want you, baby. I *need* you." He threads his fingers in my hair before grabbing a fistful and pulling until my head touches the felt of the table. "Physically, mentally, emotionally. Every fucking aspect of the word. I'd have no purpose without you in my life." Liam aligns our lips until our mouths are on each other's. I love every side of him —soft and gentle, sweet and caring—but I'm especially fond of his rough and passionate side.

He abruptly enters me, stroking himself against my pussy before he pulls out, then rams himself in again. I gasp at the intensity but want him to continue his sweet assault. Liam palms my throat, keeping my head close to him as he nips my bottom lip. Thrust after thrust, he brings me closer to the ledge, so damn close I'm about to cry out in misery if I don't come soon.

"Even though it's been months, I'm still torn up that I hurt you the way I did," Liam grits between his teeth as his free hand slides to my hip. "Every choice I made in Vegas led to me marrying that witch, betraying you, and you getting hurt in that car explosion. I fucking hate that I did that to you." He slides out slowly before thrusting back in. "The guilt eats me alive every day."

He mentions feeling guilty, and I know he's not just talking about me, or us, but Tyler too.

When Victoria set Tyler up after the fight in Vegas, Serena agreed to be his lawyer. Once the bail was set and the judge read his charges, Liam nearly lost his shit. With the number of drugs and guns they found, there was enough to put Tyler away for fifteen to twenty years. Even though it was his first offense, he crossed state lines, and the judge wasn't empathetic. Serena managed to get his bail lowered on account of him being former military and not having a criminal record. Liam made sure Tyler's bond was quickly paid, and he was released. While he awaited his next court date, Tyler wasn't allowed to leave California, so he stayed with us.

One morning I woke up and Liam was gone, leaving me with a note that he went to Vegas to handle Victoria. I was so goddamn pissed, but by the time he returned and told me what he did, I lunged into his arms in relief. He told Victoria his plans to tell the DeFrancos of their affair if she didn't fix this, and when she called his bluff, he drove to Mickey's and put a gun to his forehead. I'd never known Liam to be in such a full-on rage before, but he's loyal as hell to the people he loves. Once he told Mickey what evidence he had and what he'd do with it, he threatened Victoria into helping

Tyler or would leave her and the babies. Mickey cared more about his family finding out the truth than being with Victoria, but at least now Liam knows he has a secret weapon if Victoria ever tries anything again.

Unfortunately, it was too late to get Tyler out of his charges due to the physical evidence they found. She managed to pay off someone to reduce his sentence to eight years. Serena claims he'll probably get out in five years with good behavior, but anything could change between now and then. Though we're all devastated, it's better than the twenty he could've had.

Tyler started his sentence four months ago in April, and it's been an emotional whirlwind since.

I'd never seen Liam so distraught even after all the shit we'd been through. Watching his friend go to prison from events that Liam started has really hit him hard these past several months. I know he feels at fault, but Tyler chose to get involved. He knew the risks, and although neither of us could've predicted this would've happened, I wish he'd stop beating himself up over it. Proving Victoria's motive for setting him up would've been nearly impossible too. Tyler's not ready to confess all his sins and rat out the mafia, given the consequences he'd face for being a snitch. As disgusting as it is to think, he's actually safer in prison than in Vegas right now. So for that, I'm somewhat thankful. Hopefully, once he's out, all of this can be forgotten, and Victoria will leave us alone forever.

"I know, Liam," I say softly. "Use me, baby. Take out your frustrations on me. It's what I'm for."

Liam lets out a breath and slows his rhythm. "Not happening. I'll save that for kicking Mason's ass in the ring."

A giggle escapes from my throat, and Liam picks up his pace. "All I want to do to you is love you, so let me."

I suck in my lower lip and nod. His hand slips from my hip as he smacks my ass with a loud crack, pushing me forward. With a yelp, I catch myself and lower my body as Liam drives us closer to release. A few months ago, I told Liam I wanted us to sometimes be rougher during sex. Being that he's the only man I've slept with, I still want to try different positions and experiment. Though most of the time when he gets rough, he ends up slowing down and showing his sweet side. Even in Tahoe City, we experimented with the blindfold, but it turned romantic. He still thinks I'll break, but I'm ready to prove him wrong. I love it when we make love, but I also like changing things up too.

"Harder," I beg, lying on my cheek. "Don't be gentle."

"Maddie…" His tone is a warning, but I don't care.

"*Harder*," I press.

Liam grips both of my ass cheeks in his palms, parting them and pounding into me like I asked.

"Yes, like that," I say around a moan.

"Put your hands behind you, Mads," he orders. I quickly do as he says, and he reaches up, then wraps his fingers around my wrists, holding them there. "Fuck, baby. You look so damn sexy right now."

I smirk, looking over my shoulder. "Don't stop."

"Goddamn," he grunts. "So beautiful."

He keeps going, climbing us closer to the edge, and just when I'm about to unravel, he slides his palm up my back and yanks my hair so hard my pussy tightens, and I explode.

Liam follows me within seconds and then releases my hands before collapsing on top of me.

That was the best goodbye house party ever.

Dear Tyler AKA Beanstalk,

Your new cellmate, Archer, sounds like a douchebag, to be honest, but I guess I can't blame him. I'd probably be one too being locked up with you 24/7 :) Haha, kidding! I'm glad you have someone you can talk to and hopefully trust.

Liam and I just moved into our new apartment, and it feels strange not having to go to classes and dance practice this fall. I still can't believe I finally graduated three months ago! I'm like an adult now. How'd that happen? (Don't answer that!)

Oh, guess what? Sophie announced a couple weeks ago she and Mason are expecting! Which means I'm officially the only Corrigan sister NOT knocked up. I'm in no hurry, though. Being around them just means double the hormones and double the cravings.

I'll bring their sonogram pictures when we visit you next month, though I'm sure you don't care, but I don't want your wall to be bare. You'll be Uncle Tyler and love it.

Liam has been working a lot lately. Well, he always works a lot, but more than usual. I think he's nervous about money and making rent now that we're out on our own like a bunch of big kids. Though I told him not to stress because I'm getting more hours at the dance studio now that it's the middle of August. I'd like to save up and eventually open my own studio, but that's years down the road. Hell, I'm putting it out into the universe. By the time you get out, I'll have Maddie's Dance Studio, and you're going to come visit me, okay?

Even though you say you're never coming back here because of The Devil and the memories, you can make one exception for your favorite hostage. You did make me eat spicy sausage after all, so you owe me!

In all seriousness, I miss you and your ability to dodge my questions, though you did slip a few times. Like about Gemma ;) I expect you to go back to Alabama and get your woman. No exceptions! I know you're rolling your eyes at me right now, but I don't care. I have a sixth sense for these things.

> *Well, I'll let you go now. Love you, Ty.*
> *—Maddie*

I stuff the letter into an envelope and then seal it. Once I write out the prison's address I've memorized and put our return address sticker on it, I place it on the table to send out later. Tyler was sentenced to federal prison three hours away, so we visit him at least once a month. I wish he was closer so we could go every weekend, but between Liam's work schedule and getting settled into the apartment, it just isn't feasible to make the six-hour round trip. We only get thirty minutes of visitation with him, which sucks, but it's better than nothing.

"Baby, you ready?" Liam asks from the bathroom. I can hear him shoving shit into a bag. He totally surprised me when he told me this morning to pack some clothes and be ready by noon.

It's eleven fifty-five, and I haven't packed a thing yet.

"Almost!"

I scramble to the bedroom and see Liam's duffel bag is full and ready to go. He didn't tell me where he was taking me, so I have no idea what to bring. I unzip his bag that he's used for hundreds of work trips and notice it's starting to fall apart. I really should just buy him a new one and throw this away.

Pulling out his items, I see jeans and button-up shirts. Well, these aren't helpful. Liam always wears jeans and button-ups.

I wonder if he packed his swim trunks?

Maybe he's taking us to the beach.

When I don't find any, I look into the front pockets and then the deep side ones. My fingers brush against something hard, but also...soft? What the hell?

I pull it out and immediately gasp when I realize it's a velvet box.

Oh my God.

Is he...going to propose?

Blinking, I contemplate what to do as my throat goes dry. If I pretend I didn't see anything, I'll be totally obvious, and he'll think something's wrong with me. Acting coy isn't my strong suit.

I should put it back. *Yes, put it back, Maddie.*

"Mads, where's your—"

I spin around before he can finish his sentence, and his eyes immediately fly to my shaking fingers.

"Sorry! I wasn't trying to snoop, I just wanted to see what you packed so I knew what to bring and then I felt something weird, so I pulled it out, and oh my God, I'm sorry."

Liam chuckles at my ramblings. "It's fine. I'd rather surprise you with it later, but you can have it now."

ALWAYS YOURS

Wait, what? Why is he so calm and cool?

Why isn't he freaking out with me?

"Huh?"

Liam steps closer and grabs the box from my hand. "It was five years ago this month we first met, and I wanted to take you somewhere special, but then I saw these earrings and thought how beautiful they'd look on you. So I got them too."

What?

I swallow hard and blink again. "Wow, five years."

I hold my breath as he opens it and reveals gorgeous sparkling studs. "Blue, to match your stunning eyes."

Earrings?

"Earrings?" My voice comes out rough. As much as I'm freaking out, I really thought there was an engagement ring in there. Why isn't he proposing?

What is the man waiting for? Five more years to pass?

I force a smile so he can't sense my disappointment because they really are beautiful.

"Wow," I say a little too eager. "I love them."

Liam's face drops, and I know he sees it written all over my face. He steps closer until the space between us is gone and tosses the box on the bed. "Goddammit, Maddie." Cupping my face, he rests his forehead against mine, chuckling.

I'm very confused. My heart is pounding so hard, he can probably hear it over my harsh breathing.

"What?" I ask softly.

Then he retreats, grabs something from his back pocket, and gets down on one knee.

Oh my God.

What's he doing now?

"Didn't you learn from the last time you dug through my

317

things?" He smirks, holds out a different velvet box, and opens it, revealing a diamond ring. "I should've known you'd find the decoy box." Shaking his head, he reaches for my left hand and rubs the pad of his thumb over my knuckles. "I should make you wait since you snooped, but now I can't." Then he winks.

A gasp releases from my throat as I cover my mouth with my hand.

"Madelyn Grace Corrigan, my beautiful girlfriend, the love of my entire existence…" He leans in and kisses my knuckles. "You mean more to me than I could ever express, and I hope by now you know how much I love you. Before you, I wasn't really living, and it wasn't until you became mine that I had a real purpose. You gave me that. To look forward to every day just to wake up to your beautiful smile. To hear your contagious laugh. To kiss your soft skin. I can't think of how life can truly get any better than you agreeing to marry me. So baby, will you take morning showers with me and let me kiss you to sleep every night for the rest of our lives? Marry me, please."

"I don't even know what to say…" I wipe tears that escaped from the most heartfelt thing I've ever heard. "Except yes!"

Liam immediately swoops me up, and I wrap my legs around his waist as I hold tightly around his neck. He lays me on the bed and covers my mouth with his. "This was supposed to be so much more romantic, just so you know." His lips trail down my jawline. "Think roses, champagne, and being under the stars." He moves down my neck. "But I knew you'd have a bad attitude for the next twenty-four hours if you thought I brought you up there to give you a pair of earrings."

I laugh because he's right. I would've been in a sour mood.

"Smart man," I tell him, grabbing his face and planting my lips on his. "I can't believe you just proposed!"

"I can't believe it took me six months to find the courage."

"Six months!"

"I had to ask your dad," he says, leaning back. "So I flew out there."

"What?" I squeal, sitting up on my elbows. "You flew out to Utah and asked my dad for his permission?"

I'm shocked.

Not that Liam would do the right thing, but that I had no idea. He does travel for work a lot, so it was probably easy to deceive me.

"Yep. Had a nice little chat." Then he coughs. "Intimidating chat if I ever hurt you."

Laughing, I wrap my arms around him and bring him closer. "I can't believe how sneaky you were."

"But apparently not sneaky enough." Liam playfully rolls his eyes.

"That's right. Remember that if you ever try hiding a secret from me again," I tease.

"Next time, I'm blindfolding your ass and handcuffing you so you can't see, touch, or snoop."

"That sounds rather hot...We should practice that just in case."

"Fuck, baby." He palms my breast and squeezes. "I don't want us to be late, and we have the next two days all to ourselves, so let's go and enjoy being newly engaged."

My eyes widen at the word. "Engaged. Wow. That sounds...so grown." I laugh and think about the letter I just wrote Tyler. "Dammit, now I need to write Tyler another letter."

Liam presses a kiss to my nose. "Don't worry, he already knows."

"What?" I screech, and Liam stands, pulling me up with him. "So I don't even get to surprise him?"

"Don't worry, I told him to act plenty surprised."

I roll my eyes. "Please tell me my sisters don't know. Can I at least tell them?"

"You really think I called up Sophie and Lennon and said, 'Hey girls, I'm proposing to Maddie this weekend, but do me a favor and don't tell her, okay?'" He arches a brow, and I chuckle. "I know neither of them can't keep a secret to save their damn lives."

"That's true. They pretend they can, but they'd be dying to text me all weekend, waiting to hear the news."

"Exactly."

"I kinda want to mess with them…" I pause, placing a finger on my lips. "Tell them we got hitched on a whim or something."

"You're evil." He shakes his head, then grabs my hand. "Let's go before you conjure up more ideas."

"You're no fun," I tease.

"Don't worry…we'll be having *plenty* of fun this weekend."

EPILOGUE

LIAM

FIVE YEARS LATER

"MRS. EVANS?"

"Yes, Callie?" Maddie responds gently.

"Can you tie my shoe for me?" Callie flutters her eyelashes.

"Oh, uh…sure." Maddie attempts to kneel and struggles the whole way down. The little girl puts her foot on Maddie's knee, and once she's done tying, the little girl says thanks and runs off.

I'm positioned where she can't see me and softly chuckle as I watch my wife try to stand. After a moment, she gives up.

"There's a special place in hell for a man who laughs at their pregnant wife instead of helping her!"

Shit. She heard me.

"Would you like some help, baby?" I walk over and hold out my hand.

Maddie narrows her eyes and scowls. "No, I thought I'd stay down here for a while and enjoy the view."

Fuck, she's feisty when she's hormonal.

"C'mon, let's get you some tacos." I take her hand and help her up.

"Tacos? You act like I'm a hangry baby-oven crazy person."

I cup her cheeks and press a kiss to her lips. "I'd never think that."

Maddie walks toward her office, and I follow. At seven months pregnant with our second child, I'd wish she'd take it easy so she doesn't end up in preterm labor like she did with our first son, Tyler. Luckily, they were able to stop her contractions, but she spent the final six weeks of her pregnancy in a hospital bed. She's already considered high risk, but until her doctor demands it or she's forced, she won't slow down.

She grabs her purse, then shuts off her computer. "Okay, fine. Feed me tacos."

I smirk, knowing I was right.

"Wipe that shit-eating grin off your face right now, Mr. Evans."

Almost five years after we said *I Do,* and I still love hearing her call me that because I love being her husband. We got married on New Year's Eve the year I proposed, and it's been the best five years of my fucking life. We found out she was expecting two years later, and instead of getting back on birth control after Tyler was born, we decided not to take precautions. Just a little over a year later, we found out baby number two was on his way.

"We'll eat on the road," I tell her.

Once we found out Maddie was pregnant again, we started house hunting and bought something bigger that was closer to Maddie's dance studio. She opened it right before we found out she was pregnant again and has been going nonstop to keep it running. Considering she's been chasing after a toddler at the same time, I'm proud as hell with everything she's accomplished in such a short amount of time.

Every class of hers has a waiting list. She's hired three other dance instructors to help teach classes.

The most important thing is she's happy as hell doing what she loves. She gets to dance, teach choreography, and be around kids. I didn't even groan when she told me she hired Joel to fill in for when she goes on maternity leave.

I'm still a bounty hunter, but I stick to the local area, so I'm home every evening. Only once in a while will I take jobs out of state, but I'd rather spend time with my perfect little family.

I drive us home, and once we're inside the house, Tyler comes running into my arms. Catching him, I throw him up in the air before hugging him to my chest. He'll be two next month, which I can hardly believe.

"Hey, buddy. Were you good for Auntie Sophie?"

"He sure was!" Sophie singsongs, waddling over from the kitchen as she holds her daughter's hand. Layla turned four a few months ago and is the spitting image of her mom with dark brown hair and eyes. I like to give Mason shit and ask how he contributed, which usually ends in a punch to my ribs. "I got him all dressed and ready to go for your guys. Then he decided the dog's slobbery water dish was a bath, so after I found he dumped it all over himself, he had a *real* bath and got re-dressed."

Maddie chuckles, taking him from me. "You're a little stinker, aren't you? Just like your father."

I press a hand to my chest. "I was an angel. Just ask my dad."

Maddie snorts. "I did. He didn't tell me the same story."

Scoffing, I steal my kid back and walk into the kitchen for a bottle of water. Maddie shouldn't be carrying him anyway, but like always, she never listens.

"Thank you again for watching him today," Maddie says, and when I got back to them, I see Sophie's hand on Maddie's stomach.

"He's kicking," Sophie says, smiling at me.

Maddie then presses a hand on Sophie's big bump. "C'mon, baby girl. Kick for Auntie Maddie."

"She only kicks for her favorite uncle," I taunt.

With furrowed brows, Maddie turns and drops her hands. "You touch my sister…a lot?"

I roll my eyes. "I'm not stepping into that trap."

Sophie chuckles. "Wait, she's moving now." She brings her hands to her stomach, and Maddie's follows.

"Told ya," I singsong. "The kid loves my voice."

"The *kid* thinks you're Mason. Don't flatter yourself," Sophie says with a smirk.

"How crazy that you're going to have two girls, and I'm going to have two boys," Maddie says.

"Unless you try for a girl next?" Sophie says. "Keep going until you get a little ballerina!"

"Trust me, if it were up to Liam, he'd keep me barefoot and pregnant constantly. Then I'd still probably end up with all boys anyway."

"Don't get me horny now," I tease, waggling my brows.

Sophie glares at me for my word choice in front of Layla. I shrug.

"I'm content with having my nieces in ballet classes," Maddie says, but sometimes I wonder. Does she wish we could have a girl of our own for her to share her biggest passion with? I'd be happy to try for a girl the rest of my life, but I'm pretty sure she's already overwhelmed, and baby number two isn't even here yet.

"We'll see," I chime in, smirking. "I might be able to do some convincing…"

Sophie rolls her eyes with a gag, and Maddie shakes her head.

Maddie holds out her hand toward me as she looks at Sophie. "You see how I've gotten pregnant twice in three years."

I waggle my brows again and grin.

Grabbing Maddie's face, I press a kiss to her sassy mouth. "Change clothes so we can go."

"Alright." She kisses me back.

"Make sure to tell Tyler we all said hi and we'll see him Saturday at the cookout," Sophie says before she grabs her purse and Layla, then heads toward the door.

Twenty minutes later, we're finally on the road for a three-hour trip to pick up Tyler.

Today's finally the day.

MADDIE

As we pull into the prison parking lot, anxious butterflies swarm my stomach as I think about this being the last time we'll ever have to come here. *Finally.*

For the past five years, we've visited Tyler almost every month. During my last pregnancy, we weren't able to for about four months due to me being high risk, but then we came and brought the baby for him to officially meet. I'll never forget when we told Tyler we really did name the baby after him.

It was the first time I'd seen Tyler tear up with happiness.

Baby Tyler will grow up knowing what the man he's

named after did for us. How he risked his own life to save mine and brought Liam and me back together. I'll never forget his sacrifice and naming our first son after him felt right and perfect.

"I don't know why I'm so nervous," I say, my legs shaking as we wait for him to come through the gates.

Liam comforts me by putting his hand on my knee. "Settle down, Mads. It's not good for the baby."

I roll my eyes. He worries too much.

But I love him for it anyway.

Looking in the back seat, I smile as I watch Tyler sleep. He'll finally get more than thirty minutes to spend time with his Uncle Ty, and since he'll be living with us for a while, I hope they create a special bond.

"There he is," Liam says, and I snap my head around.

"Oh my God. He's wearing street clothes!" My emotions start to bubble over, and I can't wait any longer. I throw open the truck door and carefully hop out.

"Mads!" Liam groans, but he knows me well enough to know I won't listen to him anyway.

"Tyler!" I shout and walk as fast as I can toward him. As he approaches me, he opens his arms wide, and the dam breaks. I finally get to hug him after five years. Tears blur my vision as I wrap my arms around him, and he embraces me in a hug. "Oh my God, I can't believe you're out!"

Liam joins and pulls him in for a side hug. "Dude. You look buff as fuck."

Tyler chuckles. "Gotta make sure I'm prepared for the real world now, ya know?"

I wipe my face, and Tyler smiles at me. "You look huge."

Laughing through my emotions, I playfully push his chest. "Shut up. I know. And I have two more months still."

Tyler cringes. "Yikes. Good thing I'm only staying for a few weeks."

My face drops. "What? That's it? Why?"

We walk to the truck, and Liam helps me get into the back so Tyler can sit shotgun.

"You know I didn't even want to go to Sacramento," he says after we all buckle up. "I found a job back home. I need a fresh start. There's nothing here for me."

"Ugh," I say offended. "Me! And Liam and baby Tyler."

"And you all have your own lives to live. You won't mind me invading your space for a little bit, but after a while, you'll want to have your privacy again, so it's just best if I try to go back into civilian life the best I can."

Liam starts the truck and drives us out of the parking lot. "Babe, he's made his decision," he tells me when he knows I want to keep arguing.

I slump my shoulders. "Fine, but I'm using these next three weeks to change your mind."

"You will after you realize my cooking game is weak," Tyler teases.

Three weeks pass way too fucking fast. Tyler promised to visit, but I have a feeling he won't be anytime soon, which makes me sad because I was hoping he'd be here for Tobias's birth. But I do get why he needs to start over fresh. His grandma still lives in Lawton Ridge, Alabama, and I'm pretty sure his high school crush, Gemma, does too. Though he stopped talking about her in our letters, I have a feeling he'll be talking about her again soon.

"Why. Is. It. So. Hot!" I shout, ripping off my shirt. "Liam! We need to move!"

He pops his head out of the bathroom with a toothbrush between his lips. "Huh?"

"It's too hot here! We need to live somewhere colder!" It's the middle of August, and I'm dying of heatstroke.

Liam flashes an amused grin with a cocked eyebrow. "Oh yeah? Where would you like to go, baby?"

I pull off my shorts and chuck them across the room. "I hear Antarctica is nice this time of year!"

Liam snorts and toothpaste spews from his mouth. "Hold on," he mumbles before dipping back into the bathroom. He returns moments later and smiles. "You're hot because your blood pressure is spiked. What did the doctor tell you about *relaxing*?"

Groaning, I roll my eyes and release a slow breath. "That if I don't take it easy, I risk going into labor too early."

"Exactly," he says. "Now get that cute little ass of yours into bed, and I'll push some pillows under your legs."

Walking, I quickly spin around and poke a finger at him. "This is all your fault!"

Liam's lips twitch. "I know, and I'm *very* sorry. The next time you jump me in the shower, I'll put on a condom."

I know he's only saying that to amuse me, but it works for now. I'm hot and miserable, and these next four weeks are going to drag by until I can coerce this child out of me.

FIVE WEEKS LATER

"Tobias Liam Evans, you're late." I rub my nose against his small, soft one. "But I'll forgive you since you're so cute."

Liam takes him from my arms so our oldest can hold him for the first time. He's so excited that I can hardly contain myself. It's the picture-perfect moment, and my heart squeezes by how blessed we are. A houseful of boys and me. Ironic, considering I grew up with sisters, but I love it.

"I can't get over how adorable he is," Lennon says, leaning over and watching the boys.

"Of course he is. He's mine after all," Liam chimes in.

Hunter and Lennon's kids, Alison, Aaron, and their youngest, Aubrey —who's a little older than Sophie's daughter—take turns holding Tobias. Then Sophie and Mason visit, and Layla gets her turn.

"You're next..." I taunt Sophie, rubbing a hand over her large bump. She looks like she could pop any day now.

"I'm hoping the air in this room puts me into labor," she quips, fanning her hand around her face. "The air in hospitals is always special and pumped with good oxygen."

I snort at her dramatics.

"That baby's gonna come out when she's good and ready," Mason tells her.

Liam sets Tyler on his lap, and they sit on the edge of my bed. He leans over, then steals a kiss, making me smile wide. The moment I held Tobias for the first time, I fell in love all over again. I hadn't realized I could love someone as much as I already loved Tyler and Liam. But I do.

Then Liam, being his natural sweet self, told me how proud of me he was and *thanked* me for giving him another son. I know he wasn't always sure he even wanted a family, but with me, he wants everything.

I want to give him everything he deserves and more.

Not only is he an amazing husband and partner, but an

incredible father. When his dad found out we were expecting Tyler, he nearly popped a blood vessel he was so ecstatic.

"Did you two pick a name yet?" I ask Sophie.

"Yep. Layla picked it out." She beams.

"Aww…wanna tell me, Layla?" I turn and look at her, smiling as she holds Tobias. Mason sits next to her, making sure she holds him carefully.

She's shy, like Sophie, but she smiles proudly. "Lily. After my favorite flower!"

"Oh my gosh…" My eyes widen. "I love that!"

"We do too," Sophie says, rubbing her belly. "Hopefully, they grow up and are as close as the three of us are."

Lennon comes over and hugs Sophie, then grabs my hand. "They will be."

"All of our kids will be as long as the three of us are together," I say, squeezing her hand.

Sophie smiles. "Always."

Hours later, it's finally quiet when it's just Tobias and me. I told Liam to take Tyler home so he can sleep in his own bed and to come back in the morning.

"Should we FaceTime your uncle Tyler?" I ask him quietly. "I think he'd really like to meet you."

I hit the button on my phone and beam when I see his face. "Hi," I whisper. "There's someone new here."

Tyler smiles. "Really? Let me see!"

I turn the camera around so he can see him. He's sleeping peacefully on my chest.

"He's beautiful, Mads."

I turn the camera back. "Thank you. I wish you were still here." I pout, sticking out my lower lip.

Tyler chuckles, then we're interrupted by a feminine voice in the background. "Hey, Ty—" The dark-haired beauty behind him stops in her tracks. "Oh, sorry, didn't realize you were on the phone."

"It's fine. I'll be off in a minute," he tells her.

Once she leaves, Tyler turns toward me.

I raise both my brows. "Excuse me, who is that?"

He rolls his eyes. "It's not what you think. Her dad is my new boss."

I lower my voice. "Gemma?"

Tyler nods once.

"Oh. Em. Gee," I whisper. I managed to pry *some* info out of him over the years but just the basics. Gemma was his sister Everleigh's best friend growing up, and now he's working for her dad. He had a secret crush on her, but he's "too old," and after he joined the Army and moved away, he tried to forget about how he felt but has never been able to—well, that's what I got out of his not-so-easy to read between the lines. But I'm pretty good at putting things together. Now I'm guessing he'll play that 'I'm not good enough for her card' because of his past and record. I'll be changing his mindset if I can help it. "The plot thickens."

He groans, brushing a hand through his hair. "There's no plot. We're...*friends*."

I snort and nod. "Yeah, I remember when Liam said that for years, too. Good luck with that." I smirk.

331

"For someone who just gave birth, you're awfully energized."

"Don't change the subject," I tease. "So when are you gonna ask her out?"

"Jesus." He blows out a breath. "I gotta go, Mads."

"You liar! You're just trying to get rid of me."

Tyler smirks. "I'd never."

"I want details, you hear me? Text me all the juiciness."

He scrunches his nose. "I think you've confused me for one of your gossipy girlfriends again."

I narrow my eyes, trying to persuade him anyway. "Liam and I won't be able to have sex for six weeks. I need your dating life to hold me over."

"Maddie, I didn't enjoy *hearing* you guys in the next room for three weeks, so I most definitely don't enjoy hearing you talk about it."

"Geez, you're so dramatic."

"If you want a girl to gossip with, I'll give you my sister's number."

"Really?" I perk up. "Good. She'll tell me all the details of your love life."

"Shit. I really shot myself in the foot by saying that. Never mind. My sister doesn't have a phone."

"I gave birth today, but *I* wasn't born today. So nice try."

"Quit hassling the man," Liam's voice comes from the door, and I nearly jump in shock.

"What are you doing here? Where's Tyler?" I panic, but Liam comes over and presses a kiss to my forehead.

"Relax. My dad is sleeping over. I didn't want you two to be alone."

"Aww…" Tyler singsongs. "You two are disgustingly adorable."

"Dude." Liam looks at the phone. "How are things down in the South?"

"Fuckin' hot, that's what." He groans. "Especially in the garage."

"Hey, no bad language around the baby!" The moment the words come out of my mouth, I laugh to myself. There were so many times Lennon scolded me for the same thing when I'd slip around Alison and Aaron.

"How are the new jobs going?" Liam asks. Tyler put his car knowledge to good use and is a mechanic in his old hometown. He also works part-time at a gym, doing what he does best and trains people how to box.

"Not bad. Keeps my mind occupied, which I like, and off other things."

"Like Gemma…" I whisper with a grin.

"No, like the mafia princess who put me in prison," he retorts sternly.

"Tyler, you better not be thinking what I think you are," Liam states firmly.

He just shrugs. "I really do have to go, though."

"We love you!" I tell him. "Please call me soon. You know I'll be bored on maternity leave!"

"I will, Mads. Don't worry."

We say our goodbyes, then hang up.

"You don't really think he'll go after Victoria, do you?" I ask Liam, worried at Tyler's words.

"Fuck, I hope not. Though I can't say I'd blame him. He has five years' worth of pent-up anger to use on her."

I lean back on the bed and sigh. "And here I was hoping things would go back to normal with him out."

"It's not your problem to worry about, baby." He bends and presses his lips to mine. "Tyler's a big boy. Let's just hope he makes the right decision and leaves it be. I'm forever grateful he saved our lives, but I really don't want to have to repay him the favor and save *his*."

Liam settles into the bed next to me, and we both sit and stare in awe at our beautiful baby boy. Could life be any more perfect?

"So, you still wanna try for a girl?" he asks.

I grin. Somehow, I knew he was going to ask that. "Get ready. I'm going to jump your bones in six weeks when we're allowed to have sex again."

Liam shakes his head, smirking. He tilts my chin up and presses the sweetest kiss against my lips. "Good. I already threw out all the condoms."

Rolling my eyes, I chuckle. "Guess that means we'll keep trying until then?"

"No matter how long it takes."

"Or how many?" I counter.

"Nope. Even if that means we end up with a football team."

I lean over and press my lips to his. "Be careful what you wish for, Mr. Evans."

"Already got what I wished for the day I got you, Mrs. Evans." He smiles, brushing his thumb along my chin. "I love you."

"Always?"

"Fucking *always*."

Hunter & Lennon and their three children, Alison, Aaron, and Aubrey,

Mason & Sophie and their two daughters, Layla and Lily,

and Liam & Maddie and their four boys, Tyler, Tobias, Tristan, Talon, and their miracle daughter, Tiernan

...all lived happily ever.

Stay tuned for Tyler & Gemma's story in *Keeping You Away*!

ABOUT THE AUTHOR

Brooke Cumberland and Lyra Parish are a duo of romance authors who teamed up under the *USA Today* pseudonym, Kennedy Fox. They share a love of Hallmark movies & overpriced coffee. When they aren't bonding over romantic comedies, they like to brainstorm new book ideas. One day, they decided to collaborate under a pseudonym and have some fun creating new characters that'll make you blush and your heart melt. If you enjoy romance stories with sexy, tattooed alpha males and smart, quirky, independent women, then a Kennedy Fox book is for you! They're looking forward to bringing you many more stories to fall in love with!

CONNECT WITH US

Find us on our website:
www.kennedyfoxbooks.com

Subscribe to our newsletter:
www.kennedyfoxbooks.com/newsletter

facebook.com/kennedyfoxbooks

twitter.com/kennedyfoxbooks

instagram.com/kennedyfoxbooks

amazon.com/author/kennedyfoxbooks

goodreads.com/kennedyfox

bookbub.com/authors/kennedy-fox

BOOKS BY KENNEDY FOX

TRAVIS & VIOLA DUET
Checkmate: This is War
Checkmate: This is Love
Duet 1 Boxed Set

DREW & COURTNEY DUET
Checkmate: This is Reckless
Checkmate: This is Effortless
Duet 2 Boxed Set

LOGAN & KAYLA DUET
Checkmate: This is Dangerous
Checkmate: This is Beautiful
Duet 3 Boxed Set

BISHOP BROTHERS SERIES
Taming Him
Needing Him
Chasing Him
Keeping Him

Made in the USA
Monee, IL
06 December 2020

51200801R00204